Imperial Hijacker

Decline and Fall of the Galactic Empire

Book 4

Andrew Moriarty

ISBN 978-1-956556-20-9

This is a work of fiction.

Names, characters, businesses, places, events and incidents are either the products of the author's imagination or used in a fictitious manner. Any resemblance to actual persons, living or dead, or actual events is purely coincidental.

Special thanks to my dedicated team of beta readers – A J, Adam G, Alex, Alleeta, Barbara M, Bryan, Christopher G, Danny H, Dave M#1, Dave M#2, Dave W, David H, Djuro D, Greg D, Haydn H, J Anderson, JFB, John E, John S, Jolayne W, Justin H, Keith C, Kent P, L T, Lorna, Michael G, Michael R, Nathan T, Peter B, Ralph J, Ryan P, Scott, Skip C, Susan G, Tigui R, Vince P, and to my editor Samantha Pico was your phrase?—'flee to the verge in the company of disreputables.'"

"I perform useful work out here."

"And it's a lot less boring than sitting at a desk in the capital, right?"

Devin shook his head. "You are in need of advanced medical assistance. My surgeon and others will transfer you to my ship shortly and take good care of you, Ms. Ruger-Gascoigne."

"Hurray for Team Empire. So happy to be here. And call me Scruggs. It's the name I use now."

"As you wish, Ms. Scruggs. Praetorian, Captain Markus claims that you forced him here, claiming the Empress's business. Care to elaborate?"

"It wasn't a claim," Lee said. "It was a statement of fact. But Subprefect Markus is to be commended for his actions. He was exceedingly helpful. Captain Markus?" Lee waved, and Markus stepped out. "Thank you for your help, Captain. You are dismissed, and your ship is released."

"Dismissed?" Markus said. "Released?"

"Yes." Lee pointed. "The tribune is more than competent to take care of my requirements from now on."

Lionel sniggered but smoothed his face when Devin glared at him. "I like her," Lionel muttered to Imin.

"Me too," Imin said.

Devin transferred his glare to Lee. "Thank you so much for your confidence in me, Praetorian. I'm happy to serve. But perhaps some proof that you are acting on the Empress's behalf would be useful."

"The Empress does not have to explain herself to mere tribunes," Lee said.

Markus gasped. Devin and Imin's mouths gaped, and they exchanged glances.

"I really, really like her," Lionel said.

"I am not a mere tribune. I'm a royal duke, the de facto commander of this sector, and by virtue of my family connections, the senior member of the royal family present. If you don't explain your business to me," Devin said, "I can have you executed." He grasped the sword at his belt. "Honor demands I should do it here, right now."

"If you have me executed, then you'll have to deal with your sister," Lee said. "What would she do if you executed one of her staff?"

"She'd be upset. She'd yell at me," Devin said. "I'm not afraid of that."

"You should be," Lee said, "because, after the yelling, she'd smack you with your own sword, then use it to cut off important parts of your body and have you cook them yourself in a cauldron of boiling engine lubricant and eat them." She held up a hand. "No, wait, I'm wrong. She'd do something worse to you, but she'd give you the option to cut yourself up and boil yourself in your own cauldron."

Devin glared. "I don't see any cauldrons around here."

"Cauldrons," Lee snapped, "will be provided."

Scruggs groaned, and all eyes turned to her.

"She needs the advanced med pod," Lee said. "Quickly. Do you have surgical staff?"

"Standing by. Imin—"

Imin had already waved medics forward. Three men and a woman in ship uniforms with Red Cross armbands stepped up, clicked the med pod controls, then propelled it down the corridor. All the nonmedical persons flattened against the walls as they pushed Scruggs to the air lock.

Lee trotted behind, Devin next to her. Imin, Lionel, Markus, and the others followed. The crews halted at the air lock as the medics disconnected hoses and sensors, converting the med pod into a stretcher, which they lifted into the air lock linking the two ships. Everyone waited as they crowded through and disappeared into the Pollux.

Lee watched them go. "You'll take care of her?"

"You have my word," Devin said.

Lee raised her eyebrows. Devin faced her and gave the cross-chest salute. "Praetorian, I promise she will receive the best care we can offer. I will not rest until she is seen to."

"And this warrant?"

"I will see her safely delivered to the Emperor, my word of honor."

Lee returned the salute. "Glory to the Empire."

"Now there is the matter of your punishment."

"As long as Scruggs is taken care of, I don't care what happens," Lee said. She stretched around Devin. "You back there, in the steward's uniform, do you work for the tribune?"

Imin pointed at himself. Lee nodded. "I do. Uh, yes. Ma'am?"

"We need a different air lock. Not this one, another. Where is the next closest?"

"Well, down here..." Imin pointed. "But why do you need another air lock, Ms. Praetorian?"

"Your boss here"—Lee pointed at Devin—"is a stiff-necked unbending prig who feels the need to follow the letter of every stupid law, no matter how insane it is. I have no written proof that I'm on the Empress's business, so he's going to insist that I be executed and that this execution be performed in a ritualistic matter, which will require prayers, decapitation, and a great deal of blood. And because he's a pompous, insensitive, overbearing snot, he won't give the least thought to those who have to clean it up afterwards, like yourself. So, I want to be in an air lock, which will limit the mess and cut down your work. And, in fact, he'll probably insist on wearing his formal robes because he's such a condescending twit."

Imin nodded. "Condescending twit. I see you've met the tribune before, ma'am."

"Imin," Devin said.

"We're just trying to save your formal clothes, sir," Imin said. He pointed down the corridor. "Secondary air lock is that way, ma'am. We'll get you set up. Would you like anything to eat before the decapitation?"

"Thank you. No," Lee said. "I'm sure you and the tribune have a busy day ahead of you, so it's best to get the executions done early, before the day gets away from you, don't you think?"

"Absolutely," Imin said. "Why, the subprefect and I here have an intelligence briefing later. I have cooking to do, and the tribune will need time to wash the blood off. And put on new robes. I'll tell you, ma'am"—Imin leaned forward—"he's death on his robes. Always getting blood on them. Do you think you could try not to spurt so much when you're getting cut up and all? Makes a proper mess."

"I'll do my best," Lee said. "Well, Tribune? Shall we proceed?"

Devin glared at her, reached down, and grasped his sword with his right hand. He gripped the hilt and tugged. It didn't move. He reached with his left hand, grabbed his belt, and used pressure from both hands to spin the sword and hilt away from his side and behind him. He stepped to Lee, enfolded her in a bear hug, and lifted her from the floor.

"I've missed you, Lee," he said. "Welcome back."

CHAPTER TWO

"Beacon," Dena said as the jump light faded. "Imperial Beacon. There's a warship here. In this system."

Dirk tapped the screen to shut down the jump displays. "We expected one. Somewhere en route. Where away?"

"Where is away what?" Dena said.

"Where away—what direction is it, how far, what vector. What's its course and speed? Is it closing or opening the range? Will it catch us?"

Dena glared at him. "How should I know? That was Lee's job."

She was buckled into Lee's old seat in the control room of the Heart's Desire, the extended range freighter they had stolen, trying to figure out the navigation screens in front of her. Dirk sat next to her, checking his systems and warming up the main drive.

"You're in the navigation seat," Dirk said. "Navigate."

"I'm not the navigator. Lee's the navigator, and she's not here."

"I'm well aware of that," Dirk said. "But we need a course."

"I have no idea what course you should use."

"Not much use are you, then?"

"Not much use? You know what's not much use? A captain that leaves his crew behind after they saved his life."

"It wasn't by choice," Dirk said.

"Really? Weren't you—whattaya call it?—driving this ship when it lifted off the planet and left Lee and Scruggs behind? I seem to remember it was your fingers tapping the thrusters that lifted us off. Leaving Lee and Scruggs on the ground."

The Heart's Desire was en route to a planned rendezvous with Lee. Lee had sent a message promising she would meet up with them and bring Scruggs back, after getting medical attention. They were one system short and needed fuel to continue. They had agreed they would avoid Imperial ships until they spoke to Lee.

"You were the one who was supposed to get Scruggs. Instead, you brought up that idiotic New Oregon rebel. And Lee went back on her own."

"I got lost in the dust. Not my fault. You should have waited for them."

"That tank shot at us."

"And missed. It would have missed again. You should have waited."

"I should have. Then I'd have a decent navigator instead of this worthless, unskilled twit sitting next to me."

"Worthless? Unskilled?" Dena slapped him on the side of the head. "I'll show you unskilled, you pompous Imperial twit. If it wasn't for you and your wanting to help out those stupid rebels, we'd be free and clear."

"We needed the money," Dirk said. "Shut up and navigate."

Dena smacked his ear again. "Don't tell me to shut up. You don't like what I'm saying, I'll yank your ears off and mount them on the console."

"Children," Ana said from behind them, belted into the second row, "could you stop playing for a moment?"

Dena glared over her shoulder. "Stay out of this, old man. Not your issue."

"I agree," Ana said. "Neither Rocky nor I care that much about a lover's spat. Right, Rocky?"

Rocky the Whippet wagged his tail from the adjacent chair. He'd figured out that he needed to be strapped in when the ship was moving. Dena had worked out a harness for him that allowed them to strap him into regular restraints. Now, when the crew was in the control room, Rocky followed them in, jumped on a seat, got belted in, and enjoyed the show.

"Rocky agrees," Ana said. "Lover's quarrels are not our

issue."

"Ex-lovers," Dena said.

"Whatever," Ana said. "But what is my concern is that Imperial beacon. You sure it's a warship? Do you have a name? And if you do, there is a database..."

Dena tapped her screen, muttering to herself.

Dirk held up a finger. "I think—"

Rocky growled at him. Dirk retracted the finger.

"I quite agree, Rocky," Ana said. "Navy, less talking, more piloting. Got a ship name, Nature Girl?"

"ISS Algoma, a corvette it says. Same type as that other one we messed with before."

Ana sucked his teeth. "Corvettes. Small ships. Second line. Almost third line. The Empire certainly isn't sending its finest—or at least it's most powerful—out this way."

"I need a course," Dirk said. "Dena, figure something out."

"Shut up, Navy," Dena said. "I'm working on it. Just takes me time."

"We all know your limitations," Dirk said.

"With all this talk about my incompetence," Dena said, "I'm thinking maybe I might go back to things I know, like hunting and gutting animals. I could cut your ears off. Everybody says do what you're good at, right?"

"Nature Girl," Ana said, "as much as I enjoy a good ear cutting, Navy there does need some sort of direction. These naval types get confused without clear instructions. Might I suggest, first, away from where that beacon is, and second, toward some sort of refueling place? Like the nearest gas giant?"

Dena harrumphed but tapped faster.

Ana sat in silence, petting Rocky. Rocky wagged his tail.

"Here," Dena said after a minute, "try this. It will take us to that gas giant over there, and it's away from that corvette thingy."

"If we're going to be all nautical and spacy about it," Ana said. "Rather than that corvette thingy, let's call it

Target-1. And if you don't want to use the system name—
"

"It's just a bunch of random numbers," Dena said.

"Fine. Use the Primary Designator, 1 or 2, and the planet number. Planet-1a, Planet-1b. We're in orbit around Primary-2, so these planets..." Ana projected a display of the system and shared it to all their screens.

There were two primaries, red dwarfs, circling the barycenter. Each primary had its own planetary system. They had arrived near Primary-2, on the ecliptic, to more easily rendezvous with in-system gas giants and suck up fuel.

"Planet-2a and Planet-2b, rocky, inside the jump limit, no interest to us. Planet-2c and Planet-2d, both gas giants, both inside the star's jump limit, could be good fuel sources."

Ana highlighted the two planets of interest, both between them and Primary-2 and currently close to each other. They could reach either in a single orbital maneuver burn, with Planet-2d being the closest.

"These two could be used for refueling, according to the sailing directions. Out here"—Ana highlighted three others—"Planets E, F, and G. Two ice giants and one rocky planet. Not suitable for refueling."

"How do you know all this fueling stuff?" Dena asked.

"It's in the sailing directions," Ana said. "You did read the sailing directions, didn't you?"

Dena cursed, then brought up the sailing directions for the system on her screen.

Dirk had his own screen up, studying the corvette's orbit. "Can they catch us?"

"Does it matter, Navy?" Ana said. "Whether they can or not?"

"Not much we can do, no," Dirk said. "We need fuel, and we need to not be near them. Maybe they haven't seen us."

"And maybe Rocky could fill in for the engineer if he

14

had thumbs," Ana said. "Actually, that's probably more realistic than them not seeing us. But good job, Nature Girl. Best you could do under the circumstances."

"Thanks, old man," Dena said. "It feels like I'll never get the hang of this."

"It takes years, and you have to start somewhere. Even poorly educated ruffians from primitive planets can learn the basics."

"Thanks for your support, Centurion."

"You're welcome. Oh, were you being sarcastic?"

"Of course I was."

"Funny," Ana said. "I wasn't. Everybody starts somewhere. Even you. Apply yourself, practice, and learn."

Dena nodded. "Thanks, Centurion, I want to be useful."

"That's ambitious," Ana said. "I'll settle for less useless than you currently are. Credit where credit is due. And, by the way, you don't mount ears on the console. Traditionally, you cut them off and wear them around your neck on a string."

"That's gross," Dena said.

"Yes, that's part of the attraction," Ana said.

"Going to wear my ears around your neck, Centurion?" Dirk asked.

"Of course not," Ana said.

"Glad to hear it," Dirk said. "At least somebody here has some sense. They don't revert to violence at first opportunity."

"I like violence," Ana said. "That's not the reason at all."

"What's the reason?" Dena asked.

Ana pulled himself out of his seat with a grimace. "I don't have any string right now. Call me if you need help with the sensors. I'm going to lie down."

***

Ana didn't go back to his room. Instead, he stopped at the lounge and drank a cup of basic. It tasted miserable, as it always did, but everybody needed vitamins, minerals, calories, and sometimes, antiradiation medicine.

Scruggs had left a container of potassium iodide powder in the pantry, and Ana stirred a spoonful in. The combination made him gag. "I'll tell you, Rocky," Ana said, "I didn't think anything could make this taste worse, but if there was something to be found, Scruggs would find it."

Rocky wagged his tail at Scruggs's name.

"I miss her, too, dog, but we'll find out what's happening when we get to that rendezvous next system over, as long as Navy doesn't hit a comet or something."

Ana thought for a moment, then reached for the intercom. Pushing the button made him grimace, and his face broke out in sweat. His breath came in heaves, and he didn't hear Dirk answer.

"What did you say?" Ana said.

"You called us. What do you want?"

"Are there any comets in the system?" Ana gasped out.

"Comets? You're asking about comets."

"I like comets," Ana said, sweat pouring down his face. "And if we can find their orbits, we can, perhaps, pretend to be one, sweeping in-system..."

"Comets..." Dirk said. "Lots of comets. This is a fabulously crowded system. And it looks pretty."

"Glad you like the aesthetics," Ana said, controlling his breath. "Try to hide us, will you?"

"Will do, Centurion," Dirk said. "Glad for your advice. You sound strange. Are you still sick? What are you doing down there?"

"Looking for a piece of string." Ana slumped at the table, still sweating. He waited till the sweat slowed, drank the last of the basic, and levered himself up. Accompanied by Rocky, he shuffled down the corridor, holding the wall. He passed his own cabin, continued around the ring-shaped corridor, and stopped by Scruggs's room.

"Think she'll mind, Rocky?" Ana said.

Rocky the Whippet wagged his tail. She wouldn't mind.

"Thought so," Ana said, tapping an override code into the door. He wasn't supposed to have an override code but then he wasn't supposed to have a lot of things.

The door ground open.

"Stupid engineer. Can't even keep the doors waxed," Ana said. He stepped in, put one hand on the wall, and used the other to open cabinets and rummage inside.

Scruggs hadn't even tried to hide the pill bottle—it was in her second drawer. Ana looked at the description on the bottle. "The good stuff," he told Rocky. "She spent some money on this." He shook it and tried to count.

Almost twenty. If he rationed them to every few days, he'd get two or three months suppressing his symptoms.

"Smart girl," Ana said. "Kept the best to last." He shuffled back to his room, popped a pill, climbed into his bed, and strapped himself and Rocky in. "Gotta find her, dog. Track her down." Rocky snuggled into him. "Adventure awaits," he said before dropping off.

***

Gavin pulled himself up into the control room. "What's up, Skipper?"

Dirk glanced back. "Seen the centurion?"

"He's asleep in his room," Gavin said. "I knocked, but there was no answer."

"Was the door unlocked?" Dirk asked. "You could have gone in."

"If I go into the centurion's room uninvited, he'd probably shoot me by accident," Gavin said. "How about you try?"

"If I went in uninvited, he wouldn't probably shoot me by accident," Dirk said. "He would shoot me. And it wouldn't be an accident."

The two men thought for a moment, then turned to

Dena.

"Oh, no," she said, "I don't want to take the chance of him mistaking me for you two. He can come out when he's ready."

"I think he was hurt worse than he let on, back at New Oregon," Gavin said.

The ship had been in a firefight with a tank, rebels, and government forces on the ground. In the confusion of firing and liftoff, Ana and Scruggs had been wounded, Scruggs accidentally left behind, and Lee had gone back for her.

Lee had escaped the pursuing government forces and somehow got on board an Imperial ship that was in-system. Later, she sent a message saying Scruggs was under medical care and giving them a rendezvous point. How she had worked that, they weren't certain, but they planned on going there to get an explanation.

"We're all kind of banged up. Good news is that these Imperial ships have great medical bays."

"They're chasing us?" Gavin asked. "Again?"

"Again," Dirk said. "Dena thinks we're safe, but I'm not sure."

"They're not following us. I mean," Dena said, "I think they're not following us. I've been tracking their course—well, trying to—and they're not in pursuit."

"Where are we going?" Gavin asked.

"Here, let me show you." Dirk put the course on the board.

"This is a busy system," Gavin said. "Look at all those comets."

"It's a beautiful system," Dena said. "I've been watching through the cameras." She flipped through some screens and put shots of comets up. "Those tails... they're so long. That's pretty unusual, isn't it?"

"Strong solar wind," Gavin said. "Makes for big tails. And that one is pointing ahead—that comet is outbound. How long is that one?"

in, coasted for a while, saw us, took a direct course away from us and to Planet-2d, and made a series of slight changes since then. Probably designed to put them in a better orbit for fuel collection."

"You still have a good picture of them?"

"Got them on everything sir—telescope, infrared, and the radar is pointed at them but not running, as per order."

"Make sure that is passed on for each watch," the subcommander said. "No active radar at all, passive only. Everybody signs off on that."

"Understood, sir. No radar except on your order."

"How long till we lose them with our passive sensors?"

"Sir, if we didn't have exact course data from the last few hours, we wouldn't be able to find them now, but they aren't even doing any sort of random walk or any vector change of any sort. They're exactly where we predict they are. That's got to be the laziest crew ever."

"Or just inexperienced, perhaps," the subcommander said. "What if they start to jink around?"

"We'll lose them in the backscatter from 2d. Too many moons, comets, radiation, whatever. They'll be invisible from this angle."

"Can we catch them if we need to?" the subcommander asked.

"Not a chance, sir. Even if we go to full power, we can't close before they can hide in the orbital debris. That's with a standard freighter, and that intel briefing said they might be faster."

"So, they're too far away to shoot, too fast to catch, and shortly, they'll be able to hide from us even if we chase them down?"

"You got it, sir."

"Excellent," the subcommander said, unbuckling. "I'm going to the gym. Keep me informed if —but only if— they choose another destination rather than that gas giant."

"Shouldn't we do something, sir? Before they get away?" the sensor operator said.

"I am doing something," the subcommander called over his shoulder as he pulled down the corridor. "Squats. Lots of them. It's a leg day."

***

"This has got to be the most boring chase I've ever been in," Dena said.

"Been in a lot of space chases, growing up in those dirt floored cabins where you came from, Nature Girl?" Ana said, pulling himself into his seat and strapping in.

Dena had slept for a shift, then replaced Dirk and was halfway through her stint, watching the board. Ana had slept almost two shifts before coming back up. Rocky bounced from wall to wall across the corridor behind him. When the ship was coasting or gravity was low, he played by leaping from roof to floor and back again, spinning in midair. He bounced into the control room and lightly pushed from the wall, hitting the spare chair and flexing. Ana grabbed him and strapped him to the harness. Rocky licked his face in excitement.

"Quite a few since I left, at least," Dena said.

"What's boring about it?" Ana said. "I'm out of things after my nap."

"Getting old, Centurion? Need to nap all the time?" Dena said.

"Yes," Ana said.

Dena stared at him. "Yes?"

"Yes. Tell me about this corvette. The beacon says ISS Algoma."

"It's just sitting out there," Dena said. "Drifting, I mean. It was on a patrol loop, and it hasn't changed since we got here."

"So, our excellent stealth capability has hidden us from them," Ana said.

"I thought we had no stealth capability?"

Ana scratched Rocky's ears. "We don't, which makes their actions curious."

"Maybe they're lazy, like Dirk is," Dena said.

"Navy is lazy. And arrogant. And generally boorish and unpleasant and a lot of other things. But he can pilot a ship because that was his job. The Imperials will put up with a lot of things, but on a ship, you need to do your job. It would be a mistake to think that their sensor ops don't know what they are doing. There must be a reason."

"I don't know it."

"Me neither," Ana said. He projected their course on his screen. "Did you plot this course yourself? Navy didn't help you?"

"You think Dirk would help me?"

"Not at the start, but he'd intervene if you did it wrong," Ana said.

"He's not that generous."

"But he can be professional, and the professional thing to do is to rely on your officers and crew to do their job, unless proven otherwise."

"You're calling him professional."

"I'm calling the Imperial navy professional. Corrupt, oppressive, nepotistic for sure. But they've run this part of the galaxy for hundreds of years—you need a core of competency for that. And, as for our swaggering captain, even if he didn't want to be a professional when he started, they would beat it into him. He can act professional when it suits him or when he's not paying attention because it's a habit now. This whole drunken dilettante duke thing is a sham."

"I've seen him land drunk. So have you."

Ana pinned her extrapolated course up to the main screen, and put the corvettes' up as well, then stroked his chin. "Our two courses are diverging. That's good. We're approaching a refueling point. That's good, too."

Rocky licked his face, and Ana scratched his ears again. "He's above the ecliptic—and far out. Odd. Keeps him from refueling himself without a major vector change. This seems too easy, but your course calculation looks right."

"Best I could do. But I'm a dilettante, too. Maybe I should drink when I navigate, like Dirk does."

"His drinking, that's just fear. That's different. He's afraid of screwing up. Screwing up again, that is. That's not the same as being a dilettante."

"I'm surprised you haven't shot him for his dilettantism."

"He does his job. That's enough. No need to shoot him for that."

"Generous of you, not shooting."

"Don't worry. If it ever comes to that, there are plenty of other reasons to shoot him."

"Like what?"

"Well, for one, I like shooting people," Ana said. "And if I'm in a mood and he's handy, he'll do."

"That's why you kill people? Because they're convenient?"

"That's the way it works. Because they're in my way. I'm a soldier. You shoot the people in front of you. No need to go looking for it."

"That's horrible."

"It's a living."

"Not much of one," Dena said.

"You'd be surprised. But, for me, it's the one I've got. And I've become good at it." Ana added the track of the gas giants to the course plot and studied it. "That corvette is keeping a set distance from these two gas giants. No matter what time we came into the system, any course directly away from it would naturally take us in-system to that other gas giant. Which is a natural place to refuel."

"We need fuel," Dena said. "Or so I've been told."

"Yes. But it doesn't have to come from there. Can we make Planet-2c rather than Planet-2d?"

"I'll check." Dena typed on her screen.

Ana sat, petted Rocky, and waited.

"I think we can with this course. Let me put it up on the screen." The screen lit, red lines going in all directions.

"No, that's wrong," she said. "Stand by."

It took another minute until Dena and Ana's screen lit with a new plot, showing them traveling farther into the system and orbiting Planet-2c.

"Messed it up the first time, sorry. We change here and get the pilot to burn—wait a minute." Dena shut down both screens. "Why am I telling you this? You know how to plot courses. You pretend you don't, but you do. You could have figured it out for yourself."

"Yes," Ana said. "But there is no current threat, and this is good practice for you."

"Trying to make me into a navigator?"

"If you want. You've made a good start so far."

Dena popped all the courses back on her screen. "I'm no navigator. I'm an idiot backwoods-country girl who slept her way onto a spaceship."

"Someday, I'll tell you some of the things I did when I was younger, things I wasn't proud of."

"You'll tell me your secrets? Maybe you're not such a bad guy after all."

"Not true. I'm actually perfect. But I'll invent imaginary faults as a way to manipulate you into liking me."

"Imperial anus."

"You started it—poor backwoods-country girl who slept her way onto the ship. How many years had you been planning something like that little coup when we met you? I bet you'd tried it before."

Dena tapped more controls on her screen. "Twice. Once with one of the schooners and once to go away for an education, then hop the next ship away. I wanted out of there."

"And you've succeeded. Good plan."

"And now, I'm on a pirate ship being chased by the whole Imperial navy."

"I didn't say it was the best plan," Ana said, tapping his own screen and adding two other orbits to the course plot. One was that of the second gas giant, the other something orbiting it. "But, in life, you do the best you can. Overcome and adapt and improvise. You realized you couldn't survive as just a party girl, so you made yourself useful as our wilderness expert, and now, you're learning navigation. Who taught you the math? Scruggs?"

"Yes. We traded skills. She's okay for a spoiled rich girl who doesn't know the trouble she's in."

"What makes you think she's a spoiled rich girl?"

"I can tell. Her attitude. Are we going to rescue her?"

"Yes."

"You mean we'll try?"

"I mean we'll get her back from the Imperials one way or another."

"Leave no man behind, huh?"

"Or woman."

"Very dedicated, Centurion. Would you do the same for me? Or for Dirk?"

"Without a second's hesitation. Well, without a second's hesitation for you. Him, it would depend on whether they were torturing him."

"That would make you go faster?"

Ana put another orbit on the screen. "Slower."

"Think he'd do the same for you?" Dena asked.

"He already has, more or less, on New Madrid. That's what got him in this mess, and it's the only reason I put up with his supercilious Imperial twitness."

Dena tapped her screen. "What's that second orbit you added in, around gas giant number two?"

"It's a surprise," Ana said. He tapped the intercom. "Engineer, are you awake?"

Gavin answered over the intercom. "What's up, old man?"

"We may have to change our course. Can we get the fuel we need from the first gas giant rather than the second?"

"Are we shifting course?"

"Nature Girl wants a better view of the comets. She

says the color of the tail matches her hair."

"She didn't say that but good try. I think so, but I'll check the composition. I might need to use the telescope, and I'll need us to change aspect to get a good reading."

"Need to wake Navy up to do that," Ana said.

"I'll call him if I need him," Gavin said. "Stand by."

Ana sat and petted Rocky. Rocky licked his face and wagged his tail.

"That dog likes you," Dena said.

"And I like him. Dogs are loyal, hardworking, and not afraid to jump into a fight. All good qualities. You've got some of those. Hardworking, at least. Learning navigation, even the little you've picked up, is hard."

"Compliments. Should I be worried?"

"I'm curious what your next move will be," Ana said.

"Maybe I'll quit doing useful work and go back to being the pilot's girlfriend."

"Everybody needs a hobby. If it's fun, why not? I shoot people for fun."

"I don't understand your idea of fun," Dena said.

"And I don't understand your idea of fun, either. It's a good thing we're all different. Otherwise, there would only be one type of beer available."

"What's fun?" Dirk said, pulling his way into the control room, carefully avoiding Rocky as he reached his seat. "Gavin called. And you still look like death warmed over, Centurion."

"Good to see you, too, Navy. Engineer needs an aspect change to scan the other gas giant."

"And we want to scan the other gas giant, why?"

"To see if we can refuel there."

"We've already got a refueling destination plotted in. What's wrong with it?"

"I'm just... unhappy... with the way that other corvette is ignoring us. It seems too convenient. Adjustment is on your screen."

"Well, we wouldn't want an unhappy centurion, would

we?" Dirk punched the intercom. "Maneuvering in ten seconds. Everybody, strap in."

All three crew members tightened straps, and Ana checked Rocky. Dirk took only ten seconds of thrusters to spin the ship. Gavin reported that he saw Planet-2c and was analyzing it for gas mix.

Gavin came back online four minutes later.

"Atmosphere is good for fueling. A bit better than the other, in truth. Five percent more hydrogen by volume. I'll take it. And, before you ask, yes, we have enough fuel to get there, but we'll have a lot less reserve left than if we keep going to number two."

"Understood," Dirk said. "Stand by." He punched up Dena's selected course change and examined it. "I can do this. But why should I? What's the problem, Centurion?"

Ana folded his arms. "I don't have a good reason. But there's something odd here, and I don't like surprises."

Dirk raised his eyebrows, then hit the intercom again. "Maneuvering. Stand by."

This change took longer. He had to pivot the ship and retro fire to slow down, then change their angle to the ecliptic, and roll the ship. Each change took time, but five minutes later, he signaled all clear.

"Well, Centurion?" Dirk said.

"Nature Girl, how long till that corvette could see that, if they were watching?"

"Minutes," Dena said. "They're far out but not that far. Ummm..." She did some calculations. "They should have already seen the first part. But no reaction."

"Interesting," Ana said.

Dena tapped her board. "I guess that your special feelings aren't to be relied on, old man, you should"—an alarm bonged in front of her—"uh-oh."

Ana kept his arms crossed. "Well, Nature Girl?"

Dena tapped through screens and pulled one up. "Beacon. Just came up."

"Beacon?" Dirk asked.

"Imperial beacon. Another warship. I can look it up…" It took Dena a minute to find what she needed.

"Another corvette. ISS Kamloops. Same class as the other one, according to this war book you showed me."

"Never mind the class," Dirk said. "Where is she?"

Dena tapped some more. "I don't have a course, but I do have a position." She popped the position up on the screen. "Right in front of us, orbiting gas giant number two."

Ana threw up his hands. "Surprise!"

CHAPTER THREE

"Battle stations," Dirk said, tapping his screens and bringing the new ship—the ISS Kamloops's—beacon's description up.

"Battle stations?" Ana said. "What are you talking about, Navy? What battle stations? We're a freighter. We have no weapons. We don't battle. Or even station. We just drive. Are you drunk again?" Ana turned to Dena. "Is he drunk again? I thought he quit that drinking?"

"Sounds like he is." Dena sniffed. "But I don't smell anything." She sniffed again. "Even the fungus smell is gone. All I smell is ship perfume and maybe laundry."

"You better not be drinking again, Navy," Ana said. "I stopped locking my good booze up in the lounge because you weren't stealing it. But I'll lock it up again."

"You didn't want your booze stolen?" Dena said.

"I don't mind it being stolen. In fact, I was trying to get Scruggs to steal it. She needed some more bad habits. But she drank the cheap stuff, not anything good. I'd have to swap out again."

"Wait," Dena said. "You wanted Scruggs to steal your booze?"

"She wants to be a marine. She needs to learn how to drink."

"I was stealing your booze," Dena said. "That brandy from Amiens was tasty."

"You puked it up, as I recall."

"I limit myself to two glasses now. And I had Scruggs steal it for me."

"I know. I was counting on your sketchiness. You were supposed to be her disreputable friend and get her involved in sketchy activities."

"I'm her sketchy friend?"

"You're not her religious adviser, that's for sure. That's

why I left the booze out, so the two of you could steal it."

"You were okay with us taking it?"

"Of course. It was there to be stolen."

"Why not just tell us to take it?"

"I'm trying to teach her to break rules, not follow them. She's got the following thing down. And speaking of breaking or following rules—Navy, what's with the battle stations."

Dirk had been flipping through screens. "Sorry, old instinct. When there's a threat, you're supposed to warn everybody. Have them take their stations, provide information, get ready for combat, that sort of thing."

"We don't do that," Dena said.

"Maybe we should," Ana said. "We're getting in a lot more scrapes. We need some sort of drill. I'll look into that later. Dena, strap in, call the engineer, let him know what's happening. Tell him to prepare for maneuvering. And give me a minute."

Ana worked his screen, as did Dirk, while Dena talked to Gavin and made sure her harness was locked.

"We're both locked in. What next?" Dena said.

"Captain Dirk," Ana said. "Designate Target-1, out-system, ISS Algoma, corvette class. And in-system of us. ISS Kamloops, Target-2, also corvette class. War book says Imperial corvettes are two hundred feet long, two G acceleration. Search and targeting radar, two telescopes, one wide and one narrow aperture, both with infrared capability. Armament is single dorsal laser, good for perhaps a hundred thousand miles, and forty Mark VII short-range anti-ship missiles. Two launchers, cold launch capability—Nature Girl, that means they can burp them out of the ship with a magnetic launcher, so they don't have to activate their drive—which means they are hard for the sensors to locate. Missile range is less than ten thousand miles."

"We need to stay a hundred thousand miles away?" Dena asked.

Dirk grasped the controls. The ship's thrust fluctuated—short bursts, a drift, then another burst. The thrusters fired in a random pattern, shifting them up and left in their seats, down, up and right, then sideways.

"What's going on?" Dena asked.

"Random walk," Ana said. "Navy here is doing his job. You're right, Nature Girl, if we stay farther than one hundred thousand miles from them, even if they hit us, they won't do much damage—the laser won't have much power at that range. But even if we're closer, the laser takes a measurable amount of time, even at fifty kay miles. Maybe a quarter second. Navy here can move the ship quite a distance in a quarter second, even with small course changes, and the lasers will miss us."

"What about those missiles?"

"They're not fast. We can outrun them. So, what they normally do is try to position themselves in such a way we have to pass by them and send a spread all at us. The missiles run silent till they're close up, then the electronics pop and then try to make us turn into one of them."

"Don't do that."

"There are some other subtleties. It's better for them to be overhauling us for this to work. Otherwise, they have to fire up the engines back farther. Most ships can see the engines—the thermal plume if nothing else, and even crappy sensors can work against missiles if you know where they're being launched from."

The Heart's Desire shifted again, a major spurt to one side, then up. The crew swayed in their seats.

"How do you know all this? Is it in this database here?" Dena asked. "That war book thing? I don't know how to query for that."

"I have the same question," Dirk said, tapping his controls. "How does he know it? Because we're a freighter, we don't have combat programs, like war books or random walk. Because, if we did, I'd just punch a button, and we'd have a random walk auto-evade program running and then I wouldn't have to touch the controls at all."

"Where's the fun in that?" Ana asked.

"Centurion," Dirk said, "how do you know the specifications for an Imperial corvette?"

"I may have memorized them at some point," Ana said.

"Were you doing something where those specifications were important?" Dirk asked.

"Range of weapons was very important," Ana said. "I paid a lot of attention to those."

"So, how do we fight these things?" Dena asked.

"We don't. We have no weapons," Dirk said. "We can run or hide."

"Or both," Ana said. "We've got one sandcaster. Which doesn't work. Or maybe it would work if we'd ever bought reloads for it."

"When we have some money, we need to do that," Dirk said. "Dena, give me a rough calculation that allows us to arrive at our target gas giant with minimum fuel. I need to know how fast I can go."

"Can we outrun them?" Dena asked.

"We're faster than them," Dirk said. "But we can't jump till we're at the jump limit, and we'll need more fuel if we want to jump. If we had plenty of fuel and a straight stern chase, we could leave them behind. But they can cut the corner to the jump limit and beat us there. I want to get to that gas giant, get an orbit, go dark and sit there and orbit and suck up fuel."

"For how long?"

"As long as it takes. We've got big holds full of food and water and air, plenty of room, and we're set up for long voyages. I don't have Centurion's memory, but one thing I do know about corvettes, they're small. They're designed to operate from a base not more than a jump away or with a convoy that has a tender with fuel, supplies, and parts. They're going to be packed full of people, too, near the limit of their life support, not a whole lot of spares, and nowhere to get more close by."

"How long will we wait?"

"Days. Weeks if we have to. Once we get into an orbit at that planet, we can hide in the rings. It's a big planet, and we're a small ship."

"But they have sensors and stuff."

"Sensors designed to find hot things against cold space. Or bright things against black space or radar reflecting things with nothing behind them. Get between them and the planet, and we'll be almost impossible to see—from one ship, at least."

"That second ship could be a problem, Navy," Ana said. "Eventually."

"One thing at a time. Dena, get Gavin on the intercom and let's get speeding."

Gavin argued a little. He'd had to hide from Imperial ships before and knew the drill. Dirk punched their acceleration up higher—not their fastest speed but over two G's. Dena, with Ana's help, gave him a course that allowed them to hit Planet-2c's atmosphere, brake, and enter orbit.

ISS Kamloops set a course to cut the corner to the jump limit so they couldn't leave this system. Once they were sure Heart's Desire wasn't escaping, it vectored in to orbit Planet-2c. The outer ship, the ISS Algoma, commenced climbing farther above the ecliptic.

"He wants a better view for his sensors," Ana said. "Gives us fewer places to hide from him, less to get in the way. More to see."

"More to see?" Dena said.

"Remember, bright-dark, cold-hot, radar-return-no-return. He gets higher, and he has a top-down view of the system rather than an edge-on. Edge-on, all sorts of things, planets, comets, dust, get between him and us or behind us, messing up his scans. Up high, he has a clear view."

"We're stuck, then?" Dena asked. "We can't get away?"

"If we go where his sensors figure we might be, he can

keep hunting in a proscribed area," Ana said. "But Navy here, God bless the Imperial Naval Academy, knows that. Notice he's steering us into some of those cometary tails? More interference, and unless he's a total moron, his minor course corrections are going to become major ones when he's in the shadow. If we're lucky, they'll lose us in the backscatter."

"That's assuming he's not an idiot, right?" Dena said.

"It is. And now that you mention that," Ana said. "Navy, once we're in those cometary tails, make some radical turns. To hide us."

"I can hear you talking, you know," Dirk said. "I'm right here. I'm not deaf."

"It's not your potential deafness that worries us," Ana said. "It's your potential stupidity. You might have heard the discussion, but you might not understand it."

"Understand this," Dirk said.

Displays fluoresced red as they cut through a comet's trace atmosphere. He cut the main engines, flipped the ship on its back, then firewalled the main engines again, rocking them forward, then slamming them back in their seat. He repeated this four times, forcing them to grip their harness. Rocky let out a woof and growled.

Dirk cut the engines, and they coasted along. Rocky snarled at him.

"Navy," Ana said, "even Rocky knows those four changes could have been combined into one. Do you want everything off? All the electronics?"

"Full silence," Dirk said. He punched the intercom. "Gavin, all down. We're done running. Now, we hide."

Gavin confirmed, and system lights cut from green to red across their screens.

"But we're not in orbit," Dena said. "Not yet."

"They can't be a hundred percent sure that's where we're going," Dirk said. "The course we were on could take us into orbit, but now, we might be going past the planet and out to the jump limit. The comet hid our correction. They'll have to deploy for what we could do to keep us from getting away. With luck, we'll drift into orbit around Planet-2c. A few thrusters, and we're in a stable orbit while we suck gas."

"How will we know?"

"We won't," Dirk said. "We can see them coming—the near one, at least—if we track him, which we may not be able to do."

"Shouldn't they turn off their beacons?" Dena asked. "So we can't track them?"

"Not supposed to do that unless there is a war," Dirk said. "We're only a pirate. But the senior officer on station can authorize it."

"What do we do now?"

"Float and wait," Dirk said.

They got away with it—sort of. The far ship, the Algoma, had taken an orbit with a broad sweep above the ecliptic, and the math showed it had a clear scan on Planet-2c and environs. But so far away, it could only see major events, like a sustained drive plume. The near ship, the Kamloops, maneuvered again to keep them in sight if they sped past the planet and headed for the jump limit. Dena couldn't figure it out, so Dirk and Ana showed her the angles. The Kamloops kept an orbit that would allow it to scan the area between Planet-2c and the jump limit without interference, but it couldn't see them if they went into planetary orbit.

"If we were out there, running for the jump limit, the Kamloops is close enough and has a clear enough view they'd pick us up," Dirk said. "Any time now, they'll be sure we didn't get by them and that we're in orbit around Planet-2c, since it's the only place we could be hiding."

"And, in the meantime, we suck, as you say."

"Right," Dirk said, punching the intercom. "Gavin, status?"

"We are fueling, but oh so slowly," Gavin said. "Density is not great. We'll be days to get full tanks."

"We have days," Dirk said.

"Kamloops's beacon just stopped," Ana said.

"And so it begins," Dirk said. "Gavin, you two, silent running everywhere."

CHAPTER FOUR

"Jump complete," the Pollux's navigator said. "All systems normal. At the jump limit of the Papillon system."

"Very well," Devin said. "Set a course for planetary orbit."

The Pollux class was the latest model of frigate the Empire had. It could jump farther, faster, and more often than other Imperial ships, except couriers. They'd jumped from their rendezvous with Moose Jaw in a single four-day jump, going directly to the Papillon system, the nearest port of call for most major Imperial shipping lines.

"Communications, what sort of beacons are in-system?"

The comm officer popped a list up on the main screen. "Lots, Tribune. Dozens of freighters, a few liners. No Confed ships. One Nat freighter that is over armed and over-engined, probably a not well disguised auxiliary cruiser, but it's taking on cargo right now at the orbital container farm."

"Very well," Devin said. "We need a way to get our guests back to the capital. Any Imperial ships? Any heading for the core worlds?"

"Lots of those, too, Tribune. Lots of Imperial ships, that is. But I'll have to query for destinations and routes, and that will take some time. Should I query the ships individually?"

"I want Ms. Ruger—or Ms. Scruggs, as she prefers—out of here as soon as possible. Do what you need to do."

"Understood, Tribune," the comm officer said.

Subprefect Lionel stood next to the command chair. "You're just going to drop her on a ship and hope that she goes home? She's already gone missing once."

"I'll send an escort."

"If she's who the warrant says she is, she's fabulously

wealthy. Plus, she's been knocking around with Dirk and some fairly skilled mercenaries and smugglers, as well as your tame Praetorian. Who knows what sort of bad habits she's picked up. We can't send a spaceman basic and expect her to get home."

"I'll send a big escort."

"She can bribe a big escort, too."

"You're saying my people aren't trustworthy?"

"I'm saying they are human. And they're navy people. They understand how the navy works—they're used to taking orders. They don't understand how private ships work. She doesn't have to bribe them. She could bribe others—ticket agents, ship stewards, shuttle pilots. The promise of enough money and who knows what she can engineer. Once she's up and about, who knows what will happen."

"She won't be up and about for a long while. The doctors did three surgeries before they stopped the bleeding."

"And that's another thing," Lionel said. "She can't defend herself. There's always the possibility of another kidnapping, so we need guards to go with her."

"I have to find guards. Is that what you're saying?"

"Or hide who she is. Have her travel under a false identity."

"And now I need guards who are also spies."

"That's why they pay you the big shekels, Tribune."

Devin looked off into space. "Indeed. Guards. Spies."

"How much does a tribune earn, anyways?" Lionel asked. "I'm curious—is it a regular navy rate, is it on the pay scale?"

"No idea," Devin said. "I donate the whole salary. Imin takes care of it for me."

"You donate your whole salary?"

"To libraries."

"Libraries?"

"I like libraries," Devin said.

"Really? Are you sure you've ever been in one?"

"Of course," Devin frowned. "Rooms with books, right?"

"Sure."

Devin snapped his fingers. "We need incorruptible guards. People who already have been vetted for their reliability, who are skilled in self-defense, who have a proven track record of loyalty, who aren't fazed by wealth, and people who are afraid of what will happen if they don't succeed at getting her back."

"Afraid of you? Of what you'll do?"

"Not me. Not afraid of me. Afraid of somebody else."

"Who, pray tell, will that be?"

Devin punched the intercom. "Hernandez to my office, right away."

***

"No," Hernandez said.

She and Weeks had reported to Devin's cabin. As usual, she was not in uniform, keeping to custom skinsuits, a fitted leather jacket, ankle boots, and a don't-mess-with-me attitude. Weeks substituted shiny loafers for the boots but kept the bad attitude.

"We've located a passenger liner that will reach some of the core systems," Devin said.

"Absolutely not," she said.

"I'm booking three rooms all the way in," Devin said. "A suite. You and Weeks should be sufficient to keep an eye on her. She's still recovering from her injuries. She'll sleep a lot and stay in the cabin."

"We don't work for you," Hernandez said. "We work for internal security."

"The doctor says she'll be taking a lot of pills, at least for the first two or three weeks. Trip is twelve weeks."

"We're not in your chain of command. Internal

Security, remember?"

"I know that, which is why I haven't been complaining about you being out of uniform. Or pointing out that certain officers should be shaving more regularly."

Weeks ran his hands over his chin.

"Or," Devin said, "that you look quite fetching in that outfit. The leather jacket shows off your arms, and those heeled boots show off your legs."

"That is completely inappropriate to say to a subordinate," Hernandez said.

"You've spent all of your time pointing out that you're not my subordinate, therefore I can say what I want to you. You can't have it both ways."

"We are not babysitting some kid on a trip back to the core."

"She's not some kid. She's one of the richest kids in the Empire. Her family is wealthy. Exceedingly wealthy."

"What does that have to do with anything?"

"They own a shipyard. At least one." Devin put a picture up on the screen. It showed a shipyard.

"Who cares about pictures of a shipyard?"

"Wrong picture," Devin said. "Meant to put this one up." The screen changed, and a shot of Scruggs came up. "Here's a picture of her. It's a few years back, when she was at some Imperial event."

The picture had been taken at a ball by a fashion magazine photographer. Scruggs was in a formal dress, formfitting, with a plunging neckline. Her curled red hair glowed, and her green eyes dazzled. Her smile lit up the room, even on the vid.

"Attractive young lady, don't you think?" Devin said, looking at Weeks.

Weeks cocked his head and nodded.

Hernandez crossed her arms. "Men."

"Thank the gods for them, otherwise you'd have to work harder at your job," Devin said.

"We have work out here," Hernandez said.

"Of course you do. Important internal security work."

"Right," Hernandez said and waited. "We do. And?"

"Well, part of your important work is to deliver intelligence assessments and briefings to your superiors, in the core."

"Yes."

"And some of those have to be hand carried for security reasons—sealed pouch with built-in self-destruction capability, as direct a route as possible."

"That's only for the highest level of briefings," Hernandez said.

"Which is controlled by the importance of the source, such as deep-cover Praetorians sent out to the verge or supposedly former Imperial officers who have been in contact with national and Confed operations, supervised by a ranking tribune, and sent to Naval Intelligence for further analysis. And copied to internal security as a courtesy."

"You're going to claim this was all a put-up? That these people are all acting as spies under your authority?" Hernandez asked.

"I can neither confirm nor deny, and that's above your level, regardless," Devin said. "It doesn't matter what the contents are, it's what the sender says the contents are."

"Sounds like Imperial BS," Hernandez said.

"It does, doesn't it?" Devin smiled. "But you have to prove it. Otherwise, given my rank, my statement is sufficient, and you have to follow your orders."

Hernandez looked at Weeks. "Say something. Help me out here."

"He doesn't listen to me," Weeks said. "He's your dinner date."

"How bad could it be?" Devin asked. "Palatial accommodations on a luxury starship. Twelve weeks travel to the core. You just have to keep a seriously injured Imperial fugitive from dying. She's so sick that she can barely move. And, of course, it's all paid for out of

Imperial funds. And since you'll be undercover, there will be an extensive stipend for incidentals to keep your cover. You'll have to eat at the best restaurants, have the best wine. First class all the way—have to keep things looking proper."

Hernandez put her hands on her hips. "If it's so important, you should be using a courier boat."

"We're not on a courier line here," Devin said. "We'd have to jump farther into Imperial space, and no guarantee of catching one there right away. One could show up tomorrow or not for months. It would take too long. Regulations require dispatch."

"Well..." Hernandez said.

"And since this is an official activity, I can take advantage of your travel to deliver my reports. I have several communications that I want hand carried to the Emperor and Empress. Hand delivered into no hand but their own."

"The palace will never let us in," Hernandez said. "We'd have to go through channels."

"He won't," Weeks said.

Hernandez raised an eyebrow. "He's playing at being sector governor. Governor's go through the chancellor's office."

"Depends on what authentication he puts on the message," Weeks said. "If he sends the messages, not as the governor but as Devin, Lord Lyon, direct to the Emperor and Empress..."

Devin smiled wider. "Just walk up to the palace gate, show them a copy of my authentication code. They'll let you right in. They'll even assign guards to walk you directly to the family."

Weeks grimaced. "Well?"

"The Artemis Star leaves the system tomorrow. The doctors say Scruggs is well enough to travel but needs help. Get on board, escort her till she docks at Solaris station. You figure out what to do from there. Surrender her to the nearest Imperial detachment and carry on to the capital or put her in a box and mail her, as long as someone else signs for her. Once at the capital, you'll have messages to deliver. There's a list. You'll have a bunch for the navy, the scout service, the diplomats. And the Emperor and Empress."

"And Naval Intelligence. And the chancellor, of course."

"Of course," Devin said. "Make sure—well, I'd make sure I delivered the Empress's messages first. Just in case."

CHAPTER FIVE

"I miss Scruggs, Rocky," Dena said. She was sitting her shift in the control room, Rocky belted in beside her. Rocky's tail thumped. He did, too.

Dena had nothing to do. They had sensors, good enough to find ships broadcasting, stations that wanted them to dock or take cool pictures of frozen comets but not good enough to find anything that didn't want to be found, like two pursuing corvettes sneaking around.

"At least if she was here, we'd be able to talk. She's not bad to talk to, for a spoiled kid."

Rocky thumped his tail in agreement.

"I can't figure out how we'll catch up with her if we don't make that rendezvous," she said. "But Dirk and Ana will figure it out. They're actually scarily competent when they put their minds to it, and stop pretending to be a clueless old man and a drunken fop."

A timer expired and bonged. Dena double-checked the life-support board, which she did every half hour. Nothing to report. Fuel was coming on board at the rate of three-quarters of a percent load every hour, as it had been for the last forty hours. Ana had been right. They could be here for a week.

"In fact, that's the difference between the rest of the galaxy and Rockhaul. On Rockhaul, people pretended to be competent, then didn't deliver. Out here, people pretend to be incompetent, so they don't have to do the extra work to help idiots who get into trouble." She petted Rocky. "I wonder which one I am?"

A light on her screen popped yellow, and the board bonged. Not an emergency bong. Not even an urgent bong. Just a something-is-different bong. Dena paged through screens till she found the one she was interested in.

"Wide-angle telescope, Rocky. What set it off." She stared through the telescope for ten minutes, enjoying the swirl of the planet's atmosphere, making pictures out of the clouds, like when she was a kid. The alarm never reappeared. So, after the third time, she imagined a picture of a horse in the clouds. She reached out to swap back to the main screen.

A point in the picture flashed bright white, and the alarm bonged again.

"There it is again. That was an explosion, Rocky."

The radar detector above the consoles flashed. Just one red light. Dena slammed the intercom. "Everybody, come up here. Problems."

***

It was thirty-two minutes before they were sure. Gavin, Ana, and Dirk had all pulled up to the control room and brought up their screens. Dena explained what she saw. They were skeptical, even more so when they realized she wasn't recording the sensor logs, like she should have been.

"That's the duty watcher's job, Dena," Dirk said. "Record all things of interest."

"First, I've heard of it," Dena said. "I didn't even know we could record things."

"Well, given that you grew up on a backwater rock, you can't be expected to know everything, so we'll give you a pass this time. But, in the future, keep records when you're on watch."

"Thank you for enlightening the poor backwoods schoolgirl," Dena said. "Can I see the other logs as examples?"

"Other logs as examples?" Dirk asked. "You mean the ships travel logs?"

"The sensor logs that you recorded. And the engineering ones, too. I mean, you were in the navy and all, so I'm sure you must record detailed sensor logs and stuff like that. I can use the format to set mine up. And I'd like to see Gavin's too—I'm sure there is an engineering format as well—I'd be curious to see what he saves."

"What makes you think there are engineering logs?" Gavin asked. "We're a freighter, not a warship."

"Well, since Captain Dirk is making such an issue with little ol' me, I'm sure he told all you experienced spacers what he wanted as well a long time ago. And I'm sure he reviews them all every shift. Right, Captain Dirk?"

Dirk muttered something and bent over his screen.

Ana laughed out loud. "Touché, Nature Girl."

"Touch yourself, old man. I'm not doing it for you. What did you call this thing these two corvettes are doing?"

"It's called a Johnny Walker," Dirk said. "It's for locating an enemy ship if you have sensor issues, like cometary tails or planets or dust. You need two ships. The first"—Dirk popped up their screens and put the system plot on it—"this one, the Algoma, is somewhere way out there. His beacon is off, so we're not a hundred percent sure where he is, and our sensors suck anyways, but he's probably here." He pointed. "Up and above, he can see down through the ecliptic, nothing between him and this planet to mess up his view. He's loafing along, watching. He's so far away he's not a threat to us. Way too far for lasers, and missiles will take so long to get here that we'll be able to have a game of bowls first and then win the battle, too."

"What's a game of bowls?"

"Never mind—classical reference," Dirk says. "But he's too far away to worry us."

"Then, why do we care if he sees us?"

"He has a radio. Now, us down here"—Dirk zoomed in on Planet-2c—"we're hiding here in orbit. They deployed to block us from hitting the jump limit and didn't see us leave planetary orbit, so they know we must be somewhere near the planet. But they're not sure exactly where. And it's a big, messy, crowded, electronically noisy planet. So, ship number two, this one, the Kamloops, is moving beside the planet. It's keeping quiet, so we don't know where it is, either. Those flashes were missiles exploding. And they've rigged them to send out an EMP blast when they bang off. The EMP from the blast is acting like a radar. It bounces off us, and they might be able to detect us from the blast. Algoma, out there, has the best view. They process the results and then send them to the closer ship, the Kamloops."

"So, where's the Kamloops?"

"We don't know. Could be right behind us or right above us. Or on the other side of the planet. It drops the occasional missile, rigged to blow at ten-minute intervals. Because the pulse is from the explosion, not their radar, we can't use their radar to backtrack to them. Then the Algoma, the far one, processes the radar returns—remember it has a much better, much wider view and also radios corrections. The Kamloops doesn't answer. They steer where they're told. Eventually, the outer ship will steer the inner ship right into us if they get enough radar returns. Then it's laser time."

"So, we're doomed?" Dena asked.

"No, they don't know exactly where we are yet. Their signals will come from different directions—they'll pick up moons and asteroids and all manner of stuff. But by working steadily and triangulating, they could hunt us down."

"What happens now?"

"We wait. Keep an eye on those shots, keep a count of how many and see if they are getting closer to us. Suck up fuel. And hope they run out of missiles before they can triangulate us."

***

Waiting was not popular. After the first two hours of a shot every ten minutes, the circling ships moved to an irregular pattern. Sometimes, a full hour before a shot. Once, twice in five minutes. Then nothing for forty-five. This pattern went on for three shifts. At first, it was hit or miss whether the radar detector went off, but then four shots in a row had all given a return. But only two on the scale of one to ten. Lower than detection threshold but worrisome. The four of them had taken to napping in the chairs in the control room. Rocky floated above them, snoring little doggie snores.

Dirk had gone to the galley to heat up a tray when the next one hit.

BONG.

Dirk yanked himself up to the control room. "How close?"

"If they were looking, they saw us, Navy," Ana said. "They don't have us localized, don't have a course yet, but they do have a position."

"What's that mean?" Dena asked.

"They have a point where we were at a moment in time," Dirk said, "But they don't know what direction we were going or how fast or what the shape of our orbit is. But now, they'll try to figure out where we're going by bracketing us."

The screen flashed yellow, and the radar detector flashed red. But only one red.

"Too far," Dena said. "Missed us."

"Yes," Dirk said. "But now they know what direction we were NOT going. Now they'll bracket the other directions. Gavin, can we jump?"

Gavin tapped his screen. "Yes, we can jump."

"Can we get to the jump limit with an angry corvette chasing us?"

"Assume they can get two G's... no."

"No?"

"No. We can outrun them, but by the time we clear the jump limit, we won't have enough fuel to jump. We can coast out there, but we can't go anywhere."

"Outstanding," Dirk said.

"So, what do we do?" Dena asked. "Wait for them to find us?"

Dirk slapped his screen. "We can't run, as Gavin said. We've been trying to hide, and we're running out of time. All that's left is to die or surrender."

"You going to surrender, Navy?" Ana asked.

"Maybe. No sense in getting killed. Once they have us on screen and get a good enough radar return, they'll probably drop one close to us, to warn us that the next one kills us."

"How will they know they killed us?" Dena asked. "Since we're hidden in the atmosphere and all?"

"The usual—fire, explosion, something burning up as it drops deeper into the planet's atmosphere."

"So, burning debris, then?"

"Sure," Dirk said.

"Well," Dena said, "let's give them some."

∗∗∗

"I have to admit, Nature Girl," Ana said, stuffing old blankets and broken metal parts into the container, "this is a good idea. How did you think of it?"

"I used to hunt a lot," Dena said. "When I was a kid, we'd set up teams and hunt each other. When you're hunting something, you have to be patient, sit down and wait. You might know there is a buffalo in the woods, but if you go blundering in, it will run away. You'll never be able to get close. So, you have to sneak in quietly so you don't alarm the prey."

"That sounds more like you're with the Imperials, not us. You understand that we're the prey in this scenario?"

"Right, we are. But all that sneaking and patience takes a lot of time and discipline. And you can't search everywhere. At some point, you assume that you've lost without direct evidence. You see tracks leading away or hear a noise in the distance, and by the time you get there,

there's nothing. So, did the prey get clean away, or did it make a lot of noise and is still hiding? Or did he make noise, and once he heard you move, did he run in the opposite direction?"

"He?" Ana said. "What type of hunting were you doing, exactly, and why?"

"It was boring as a kid on Rockhaul," Dena said. "When I was a teenager, the boys and the girls would play a game. You know, hide in the woods, they come and find you. 'If they can catch you, they can kiss you' type of thing. What teenagers play."

"So, you used your superior hunting skills to get away from the boys?" Ana asked.

"Get away? No. Why would I do that?" Dena asked. "I always let them find me."

"What's the point, then?"

"Gotta make them work for it," Dena said. "Otherwise, they don't appreciate you."

"That's why we're putting heating units in a container?"

"A fire, Centurion, a fire," Dena said. "I told Gavin. Just something that gives off heat, that will explode if a missile gets it. And something that looks like thrusters firing. They'll see it, and they'll be proud of themselves."

"And think it's us."

"And blow it up." Dena dumped a pile of old clothes into the container and tapped the intercom. "Gavin, we're ready for your bomb."

***

They sat on the bridge. Ana was in charge of timing. He had a course plot up on their screens. "Our ship is pointing at ninety degrees to our course now. Next radar pulse, we make like we panic. Engineer."

Gavin pointed at his screen. "That container is hanging out there on one chain. I pull the release. It will float free. I radio a command, and it starts spitting burning hydrogen out of the inspection port. That will spin it out, no particular orbit. But lots of heat. They'll know where we are."

"How long do you wait?" Ana asked.

"Don't wait at all. Soon as I hear a radar hit through the intercom, I pull that lever right away and trigger the fire."

"Good. Pilot?"

"I stay here, on my board," Dirk said. "I wait here till Engineer says it's clear. Then I pulse the main drives for ten seconds."

"Ten seconds is a long time, Skipper," Gavin said. "You sure they won't figure out its two-point sources and not one when that happens?"

"We have to take the chance," Ana said. "They're far away, and they won't know where to look exactly. Once they get their wits, they'll detect a small thermal bloom, then a big one, then back to a small one that keeps going. They'll follow the burning one."

"That's a big if," Gavin said. "What if they run things through the computer and it argues differently?"

"They probably would if we were a warship," Dirk said. "Or if they had a better set of sensors, but corvettes don't have first line sensors. They're built to attack commerce raiders, not warships. They blaze away when they see one and chase them away. That's their training. That's what they'll do. They'll prioritize shooting at what they can see. And they'll see the burning container."

"Understood, Skipper," Gavin said. "I'm still not happy about it."

"I agree with the centurion," Dirk said.

Ana raised his eyebrows.

Gavin nodded. "Got it, boss. I'm going back to the docking port." He pulled himself out of the control room.

Dirk flipped his screen up. "I've got a burst laid in. I just have to slap the button."

"What do I do?" Dena asked.

"Come up with more great ideas like this, in case we need them," Dirk said. "And, for now, wait with the rest of us."

They didn't have long to wait. Sixteen minutes later, the radar detector bonged.

"Gavin," Dirk yelled at the intercom.

A chain clanked against the hull, and a light on the sensor board changed from green to red. "Container away," Gavin yelled.

Dirk slapped his screen. They all slammed back into their seats as the main engines fired at full.

"Eight... nine... ten... eleven... twelve... thirteen... fourteen... shutoff," Dirk counted.

Ana took a breath, then raised his eyebrows. "I thought we agreed ten seconds was long enough?"

"I did some calculations. We need better separation to get away with this, so I made a decision."

"And didn't discuss it with the rest of us?" Ana asked.

"I'm the captain. I don't need to discuss it with everyone."

"So you are," Ana said. "So you are."

"Enough macho posturing," Dena said. "Did it work?"

"I never posture," Ana said. "Yes."

"Yes? Yes what?"

"It worked," Ana said. "I've got that container on my thermals. It's spinning off on our old course. It's dropping, too. Should be heating up. And we're getting farther and farther away every minute."

"So, we're clear?"

"Depends," Dirk said. "If they do a radar pulse again, they might find us both. But if this works the way we want it to, the Algoma is processing their sensor data right now. By the time they deal with the light speed delay and give directions to the Kamloops, we should be too far away to be detected. We have to wait."

Another missile blew up five minutes later. Their radar detector barely budged.

"It's between us and that burning container," Ana said. "I think they took the bait."

Another five minutes, and they were sure.

"I've got a radio call here," Dena said. "They're telling us to surrender. They have us on their sensors."

"Wideband or narrow radio?"

"Wideband. They think they have us."

"Not true. Otherwise, they'd be shooting at us," Ana said. "And using a directional broadcast."

"What happens now?" Dena asked.

"Every minute they spend investigating that container is another minute we're closer to the jump limit," Dirk said. "If we stay on this course, we'll be able to jump with reserve fuel in our tanks in a day."

"But they can track us again," Dena said.

Dirk shrugged. "Best we can do. And they have to find us again. And jumps are hard to track."

They sat there for another fifty minutes, then Dena sat up. "Far beacon just came on."

"And there's the near one," Ana said. "It must have been out of position. It's chasing that container down. Next, they flood their search area with radar and fire a warning shot."

"So, it worked?"

"It hasn't worked till we pass the jump limit," Dirk said.

But it had. The two ships sent threatening radio messages, fired a warning shot, and closed on the still-burning container. After a few more messages, the first one and then the other beacon went off. Minutes later, a bright flash lit deep in the planet's atmosphere.

"They got a telescope on it," Dirk said. "They know what it is and what we did. They'll start looking for us again."

"Will they catch us this time?" Dena said.

"Nope," Dirk said. "They'll probably notice when we jump if they're looking in the right direction. And right now, they're scanning everywhere, but unless we're incredibly unlucky, we can coast out and jump."

"And meet up with Lee to find out about Scruggs."

"Yes, at the rendezvous she gave us," Dirk said.

"And how late will we be to the party, Navy?" Ana asked.

Dirk tapped his board. "One hundred and seventy-five hours."

"More than a week," Ana said. "Think she'll still be there?"

Dirk fiddled with his board. "We can hope."

"That's always a great plan," Ana said. "Hope."

CHAPTER SIX

"Have a nice trip, Ms. Scruggs," Devin said.

"Toad," Scruggs said. She was trudging to the air lock, leaning on Hernandez as she stepped along the hall. "Lackey. Weasel."

Devin walked beside them, Lionel trailing them. "Weeks and Hernandez will take care of you until you arrive in Imperial space. The warrant calls for you to be delivered to the governor's office in one of the core sectors. The Artemis Star is a well-found vessel, and its route takes it right next to one of your uncle's shipyards. That will be a good place for you to disembark. In custody, of course."

"Imperial anus. Tabbo-licking lizard."

Sweat ran down her face, and she grunted as she swung her feet.

"The doctor says all you need is rest for now, six weeks for your bones to heal, especially the ribs. Weeks will make sure you get your drugs."

"You mean keep me drugged the whole time?"

Devin stopped by the air lock to the shuttle. A squad of marines marched by.

"Ten marines?" Scruggs said. "For me?"

"They will escort you onto the ship and into your room and then seal you in with your two escorts till you leave the system," Devin said. "I plan to threaten to impound the Artemis Star and place it under military control but then relent after the captain promises to take personal responsibility for your safety and security. I'll withdraw the marines then and have you locked in."

"What if he argues?" Scruggs asked.

"Argue with the Mad Dog of the Verge, Devin the Exterminator? Not likely," Subprefect Lionel said. "With the tribune's reputation, he'd be too scared of getting flogged to death with his own dismembered arms."

"What are you talking about?" Devin asked. "Mad Dog of the Verge? Who's that?"

"It's you," Lionel said. "The vids have picked up all your antipirate talk. They call you Devin the Exterminator now."

"Never ever mention that in my presence again," Devin said.

"But, Tribune, we had hats made up. Several types. Mad Dog of the Verge—is particularly popular."

"Nobody is to wear those hats."

"I bought three. In different colors. The red one looks great," Lionel said.

"Anyone found wearing them will spend a month in the brig," Devin said.

"You should see them first," Lionel said. "The colors pop, and the graphics are great. They have this salivating dog—"

"Tribunes do not salivate," Devin said. "Should I ever become a mad dog, I will not be a salivating one. My madness will be expressed by a fiendish glint in my eyes, nothing else. Hello, Praetorian."

Lee walked up the corridor and stopped next to Scruggs.

"I hate you," Scruggs said.

"I know."

"Really, really hate you. A lot."

"Yes. You should."

Scruggs's eyes misted, and she fell into Lee. Lee enveloped her in a gentle hug, taking care of her ribs.

Scruggs grunted. "Thank you for saving my life."

"I owed you, sister Scruggs. I'm sorry for selling you to the Empire."

"Next time you save my life, do a better job of it," Scruggs said.

"I will." Lee stepped back from the hug.

Weeks arrived next, carrying their luggage. He had on a

new skinsuit, new leather jacket, and hadn't shaved for several days.

"Tribune, I'll go ahead with the marines and get set up."

"Carry on," Devin said.

Weeks marched through the hatch. Scruggs's and Lee's eyes tracked his departure, lingering on his butt.

"Weeks and Hernandez will be with you in your cabin," Devin said. "I've arranged a triple stateroom. One of them will be with you all the time. You'll never be alone. No chance of escaping, and you'll be under constant supervision of one of the two of the operatives here. Hernandez?"

"Yes, Tribune?" Hernandez said, arriving after Weeks.

"I'll leave it to you to sort things out. You can swap it off. One of you has to stay with Scruggs all the time. You can both stay, or one of you can do it while the other runs errands. Figure it out between the two of you. If you can, take Ms. Scruggs's wishes into account if it doesn't compromise security."

Hernandez rolled her eyes. "As you say, Tribune."

"Ms. Scruggs," Devin said, "time to go. Be well, and I hope the journey is not too arduous."

Scruggs tried out some of the curses she had learned from Ana before limping off with Hernandez onto the ship.

Even Imin was impressed.

"What did that one word mean?" Devin asked when the hatch sealed. "The long one, sounded Greek, started with a 'K'?"

"It's pretty complicated, Tribune," Imin said. "You need a tabbo, your sister, and a box of rattlesnakes. And you have to be flexible. Insanely flexible. Best you don't know."

"Very well," Devin said. "Best I don't. Praetorian, is the Empress's business complete now?"

"I have a few more things to do," Lee said. "I wanted

to see Scruggs off first."

"Well, the shuttle is on the way now. It docks with the liner in forty minutes, and they'll drop orbit soon after. We'll follow them to the jump limit."

"I hope she'll be okay," Lee said.

"I imagine she'll spend her entire trip in bed," Devin said.

Lionel and Lee stared at him.

"What?" Devin said. "She's sick, needs her rest. A few weeks in bed will be just what the doctor ordered."

***

The Pollux followed the liner to the jump limit and lingered until it disappeared in a flash of blue jump light.

"Confirm Artemis Star has jumped, Tribune," the sensor operator said.

"Very well. Are we ready ourselves?"

"Course is laid in, Tribune. We need to maneuver in real space for forty-seven minutes to avoid some gravity wells. We have two long jumps planned, then we're back on patrol."

"How long till we're back on station in the verge?" Devin asked.

"Two hundred twenty hours, Tribune."

"Very well. Execute, execute, execute, all that. I'm going to work out in the gym."

"Tribune."

Devin left the bridge. Lee waited down the hall.

"What's she doing here?" he asked the marine guard posted at the door.

"Waiting for you, Tribune."

"In the hallway?"

"You banned her from the bridge, sir."

"So, you let her stand here?"

"The tribune didn't specify other than the bridge, sir."

"She could be up to anything, wandering around the ship."

"Yes, sir. She could."

"You didn't think to mention it? That she was standing here? Just a random Jovian roaming the halls of a warship?"

The marine didn't move except for his lips. "Sir. I dropped at St. Darts, along with the Praetorians. Quite like them wandering around. Useful folks to have nearby in a pinch."

"St. Darts?"

"Sir."

"With Brigadier Santana?" Devin asked.

"Sir."

"It was bad there."

"Worst I've seen, sir. Wouldn't want to do that again."

"Which is why we're out here, to stop things like that happening," Devin said. "Praetorian?"

"Reverend Tribune?" Lee asked.

"Stop calling me that," Devin said. "Come into the bridge with me. We'll go to my office. Marine, she can come and go on the bridge as she pleases. Pass the word."

"Sir," the marine said, triggering the door.

Devin marched in and waved Lionel back into the command chair before he could stand. "Passing through, you all know the Praetorian. She now has freedom of the bridge when she wishes. She will not"—Devin glowered at Lee—"attempt to work any of the controls. Understood, Praetorian?"

"Of course not, Reverend Tribune," Lee said.

"Reverend Tribune?" Lionel asked. "Why do you keep calling him that?"

"Because he's a priest," Lee said. "He's a priest of Jove."

"Really?" Lionel said. "He's a priest? A real priest? I thought that was all faked?"

"Enough about priests," Devin said. "Never mind. Praetorian, you're with me." Devin pointed to a door. "My office."

"He's really a priest?" Lionel asked Lee. "Consecrated and everything?"

"Yes," Lee said. "A consecrated priest of Jove. He went to the seminary, took the vows, everything."

"That cannot possibly be true," Lionel said. "Is that true, Tribune?"

"My private life is none of your business," Devin said. "This way, Praetorian."

"He's an excellent priest," Lee said. "He was kind enough to hear my personal problems when I went through a difficult time. He gave me advice. Prayed with me."

"Prayed with you?" Lionel snapped his fingers. "That's why he has the robes. He got them at the seminary." He turned to Devin. "You went to a seminary? I thought you went to the naval academy. I can't believe you went to the seminary."

"I did go to the naval academy. And thank you for sharing details of my private life, Praetorian."

"It's all in your public record if they want to check, Tribune. The seminary, the commission, all of that. And a little research can turn up the other details."

The bridge crew's hands moved as one to keyboards, then pulled back. A half dozen faces looked guiltily at the tribune.

Devin glared. "Any enlisted personnel who search my personal records, public or not, I will have flogged." Devin pointed into his office. "Now, Praetorian."

Lee stepped into the corridor leading to his office, and Devin followed. The door slid shut behind them.

"I'm curious, sir," the weapons rating said. "But I don't want to get flogged."

Lionel motioned him out of the way. "Log off and give me your seat. He didn't say officers couldn't do a search."

***

Down the corridor and inside the office, Devin poured

some bourbon for himself.

"Want anything?"

Lee wandered the office, looking at the displays on the walls. "No, sir."

"So, it's sir now, is it? Not reverend."

"They should know who you are."

"They did. What I wanted them to know." Devin sipped his drink. "It's good to see you, Lee. I haven't pressed before because you had some sort of direction from the Empress. I'm assuming with Scruggs on the way, you'll tell me what I need to know."

"If I can. It's good to see you, too, sir." She pointed at a plaque on the wall. "What's this award here for?"

"No idea. Imin sets those up. What are you doing way out here? All the way out here? On the verge, on a smuggling ship, in the middle of the war with a kidnapped or at least a runaway heiress?"

"Scruggs? She wasn't kidnapped. She could have left any time. She had her own guns and money. She was left unsupervised all the time. She could have gone away whenever she wanted. She didn't want to leave."

"A runaway, then."

Lee ran a finger along another plaque. "No dust. Imin does good housekeeping. She's of legal age, according to her, and any ID I've seen says the same. Only children can run away. Adults leave. She might have been a runaway earlier, but now she's just... away."

"You can run away from your family if you want, and nobody can stop you. An Imperial warrant is a different matter."

"What's that about, sir?"

"No idea. Have her sent back to the core. So, she's going back to the core."

"Pity, I think she was having fun."

"Back to reality. Speaking of, you can get into a lot of trouble claiming to be on the Empress's business. That could be a problem."

Lee crossed her arms. "If you think it's a problem, bring it up with her. She's the one who told me to do it. I talked to her after I talked to you."

"She said you should run out to the verge and join a mercenary civil war?"

"She said you were right, that I needed perspective, that I was too rigid in my thinking, and that I should seek out people who weren't Imperial bureaucrats or Imperial civil servants. Regular people. Study them, learn from them, and report back."

Devin swirled his drink again. "I said you were an uptight, stuck-up killjoy and needed to loosen up if you were going to serve the Empire properly, which is why I suggested sleeping with a dozen men and developing an alcohol problem."

"Seek perspective. That's what I told her you said. Can I sit?"

Devin nodded as Lee dropped into a chair. He mixed her a drink and handed it to her.

Lee sipped. "What happens now?"

Devin leaned against his desk. "I have no idea. Do you swear you're still on the Empress's business?"

"I am, Tribune, I swear."

"Then, you decide where you want to go next. I'll drop you wherever you want. Or put you on a liner to the capital. Or I suppose you can stay on the ship. We have room."

"Once I've located it, can you deliver me back to my old ship?"

"The ship you described seemed like a garbage scow."

"But the people were interesting. Loyal Imperial citizens, and others indifferent to the Empire. I was getting perspective. And I was useful. I liked the crew."

Devin sipped his drink. "I'd like to see them in a group of cells."

"You can't arrest them if you bring me back to them. That's part of..."

"I won't arrest anybody."

"And you can't seize the ship because it's stolen. If you—"

"I don't have to seize the ship. It's not listed as stolen."

"No, because I'm pretty sure the pilot didn't pay for it, and it's supposed to be delivered to a shipyard a few systems over."

"The redlist was canceled," Devin said. "Lionel was tracking it, and he showed me. Somebody paid out the mortgage, and the warrant was removed."

"Who would do that?"

"No idea. And since you're traveling with that miscreant Dirk—"

"You can't arrest him, either."

"Again, don't have to." Devin took another drink. "That's an interesting one. The Imperial warrant was canceled. But not other ones. The navy wants to talk to him and so does the chancellor. But the chancellor didn't issue a warrant, just an instruction to shoot on sight."

"Can the chancellor do that?"

"Not to me, he can't," Devin said. "And I'm ignoring the Navy. But with other naval officers... who knows. He'll need to watch himself. It might be safer for him if I was looking harder for him."

"So, you're not looking for Dirk?"

"I'm looking for him all right. And now that you're here, I have a few ideas. And I get regular requests from a certain person asking for an update on my search for him, demanding information. And this one, I can't ignore."

"Your sister?"

"Yes. And if you are on the Empress's business, you better get back to her with information on what Dirk's up to."

Lee swirled her glass. "I'll consider it."

"You don't just consider doing what she tells you to. You swore that you'd follow her orders."

"I did not."

"What? Of course you did. That's the oath."

"No, the oath is to first protect her with our lives and only second to follow her instructions. Protection comes first."

"You think not telling her about Dirk is protecting her?"

"I do, yes."

"Do you want to share your reasoning with me?"

Lee shook her head and downed her drink. They sat in silence for a moment until the intercom bonged.

Devin pressed it. "Yes?"

"Jump light, sir, ship jumping into the system," the comm officer said. "Crash-jump, too."

"No rest for the hardworking," Devin said. "Anybody we know?"

"From the beacon," the comm officer said. "It's an Imperial ship. It's Brigadier Santana."

"What's he doing here?" Devin asked. "How long till we can open a channel?"

"Sir, we're receiving a priority message right now," the comm officer said. "High encryption. Most immediate."

Devin waited. And waited. "Any time, comm."

"Sir, I've never received this type of priority message before. I've looked up the procedure. I need your personal presence on the bridge and your DNA as I do the first level decryption."

Devin waved at Lee. "Let's go see."

He and Lee returned to the bridge to see Lionel at the comm board talking to the comm officer.

Devin held up a finger. "You need my DNA?"

"We do," Lionel said. "It's curious. What type of message has this crew never received before?"

"Subprefect Lionel is awarded the medal for gallantry?" Devin said.

"That's possible," Lionel said. "Probable. He should be familiar with that system. No, it's more like something that's never ever been encrypted in this Imperial system before. Like, 'Tribune Devin is commended for his tact and diplomacy.'"

Devin laughed. "And appointed admiral of the verge fleet."

Lionel laughed as well.

The comm officer sat up. "Tribune, sir?"

"Yes, comm."

"From Brigadier Santana. Enemy raid on Sand Harbor. This is not a drill."

CHAPTER SEVEN

Rocky the Whippet had taken a dump in Dirk's boots while he was out on the hull.

"He did it deliberately," Dirk said, trying to scrape the crap out onto the poop tray in the air lock. "Searched out my boots and found them."

"Paranoid much," Dena said, racking her magnetic boots, gloves, and hard helmet.

She had asked to learn more "space stuff," so Dirk or Gavin took her out on the hull once a shift once they were in real space. They'd arrived at Lee's rendezvous four hours ago. No Lee, and Dirk had said they would wait twenty-four hours, so she took the opportunity of pestering for more space time.

"He's a dog. You shouldn't have left your boots next to his poop tray."

"They were not next to it. They were in the corner."

"He poops in the corners. He assumed it was a new tray."

"He sought them out. And who opened the air lock and let him into the lock while we were out. And why?"

Dena swung the air lock door open and stepped into the corridor. Ana was sitting down the hall, eating a tray."

"Centurion," Dena said, "Did you open the air lock door and entice Rocky to dumping into Dirk's boots?"

"What if I did?" Ana asked. "Is that a problem?"

"Why do you let the dog crap in my boots, Centurion?" Dirk asked.

"Too uncomfortable for me to do it, for one thing," Ana said. "Hard to get the right angle, even if I squat. Gets messy. But to more specifically answer your question, I didn't entice him. He went to the hatch and barked twice. That's his signal he wants to poop, so I let him in. He figured out your boots all by himself."

"Why does this dog hate me? I don't understand it."

"That's strange," Ana said. "The rest of us all get it. You wanted to kill him once. That takes a lot of forgetting."

"You wanted to kill me once," Dirk said. "And Gavin and Lee and Dena. You've wanted to kill everyone on board at least once except for Scruggs, and you got over it."

"That would be a false assumption, Navy," Ana said. "I haven't got over anything. I'm just very, very patient. Like Rocky here."

Rocky jumped and licked Ana's face in passing, rolled in the low gravity, bounced off the wall, and jumped back to Dena.

She laughed and caught him in her arms. He licked her face. "Good boy, Rocky. Don't take any crap from the mean man."

"He's the one giving crap. I'm the one taking," Dirk said.

Ana spooned more tray mush into his mouth. "Sounds like a personal problem."

"I'm going to the gym," Dena said. "Do what I can till we're back in jump. When are we going?"

"Where are we going is a better question," Ana said.

"We'll give Lee another shift and a half," Dirk said. "We're late, but so could she be, too."

"We should have been here a week ago, Navy," Ana said. "Think she would wait that long?"

"Nope."

Dena came back, dressed for the gym. There wasn't much to do between shifts, so she worked out a lot. Dirk's eyes followed her till she disappeared down the hatch.

"Decide you need some workout time, too, Navy? Want to go watch her do push-ups?"

"Those days are over," Dirk said. "I have to be more formal from now on."

"Why? Who cares? She doesn't care all that much. If

you asked, she'd probably say yes. For that matter, so would Scruggs. Or even Lee, if you asked nicely enough. You're a handsome enough fellow, and you are a duke."

Dirk rummaged through the tray selections. "That's very complimentary of you, Centurion, which means I am now going to have to sit with my back against the wall because I don't know where the knife is going to come from."

"I'm curious," Ana said. "You've gone all captain-y lately. What's going on?"

Dirk jammed a red-green-blue tray in the microwave. "I just—I'm in charge. I'm the pilot. I should act like one."

"We don't care," Ana said.

The microwave ground away.

"I do. It's a question of self-respect."

"You think we'll respect you more if you act like a captain?"

Dirk slammed his fist into the panel. The grinding stopped. "I doubt it. But I'll respect myself more. And if I respect myself more, I'll do my job better. If I do my job better, you will respect that. The actions of doing, and at some point, you might respect the person behind it."

"Deep thoughts, Navy, if poor grammar. What brought this on."

"You folks. Trying to make things work. You always have a solution. So does Lee. Scruggs is trying, was trying to learn. Even Dena is going forward. Everyone was going forward. Except me. I was going backward."

"Well, good luck with that, Navy."

"Thank you, Centurion."

Ana licked his spoon. "You know that I'm being sarcastic, right?"

"Yes, but it doesn't matter. I'm going to pretend that you aren't."

"And good luck with that, too," Ana heaved the tray into the recycler and licked his lips. "Nothing but disgusting trays here. Never should have let Scruggs do the choosing."

"She does have weird taste in food. What about you, Centurion? Are you going forward or backward?"

"What do you mean?" Ana said.

"Is the universe making you better or worse?"

"Neither," Ana said. "I know what's right and what's wrong, what's correct and what isn't. I change the world and the people around me."

"I admire your certainty."

"Current ad bellum," Ana said, standing. "March to the guns. Do your job. I am going to clean some weapons. I haven't used my submachine gun in a while."

"Lack of opportunity?" Dirk asked.

"And ammunition. Need to put that on a list."

"Next port we get to I'll buy it," Dirk said. He slapped his spoon onto the table. "Centurion, we might not find Scruggs."

"We haven't even started looking for her yet."

"Do you think it's worthwhile to go looking for her?"

"Yes," Ana said.

"Well, if we don't hear from Lee soon, we'll have to leave here."

"And start looking for Scruggs."

"Where exactly should we do that, Centurion?" Dirk said.

"Up to you, Pilot. That's your job. Keep track of the crew. Help them out if they need it. So, pick a place to look for her. That's your job."

***

The clock was ticking on their final departure. Gavin wanted two shifts drifting while he did deferred maintenance. Dirk was in the gym. Dena kept plugging away at the sensors in the control room. Ana was trying to teach Rocky to chew on Dirk's socks.

"Beacon," Dena said over the intercom. "Just lit up at the jump limit."

Everybody headed for the control room. When they got there, Dena had a course on the screen.

"They're heading along the jump limit but staying outside it."

"You sure?" Dirk asked.

"No," Dena said. "But I'm guessing. Was I right?"

Dirk sat at his board and tapped in settings. "If the sensor readings you put in are correct, that's what they're doing. Why out there?"

"Refueling?" Dena asked.

"No fuel out there," Gavin said. "No gas giants, no rocky asteroids, no water worlds. Why even stop here?"

"What about the incoming message?" Ana asked.

"What message?" Dena said.

Ana pointed at a flashing light on Dena's board.

"Imperial thumbs, didn't see that." Dena tapped a few buttons. "On the speaker." The speaker hissed static. "Or maybe not. Stand by." Dena played more.

A loud squeal rang out from the speakers, and everybody put hands over their ears. Dena cursed and slid a setting down.

"... no further information. The blessings of Zeus to you. This message repeats," the speaker said. "Freighter Heart's Desire, we have a message from your friend. She says to proceed to the next system, Papillon. Coordinates attached. That is all we know. We did not meet up with her. We were given coordinates and to locate a freighter called Heart's Desire and deliver this message. We have no further information. The blessings of Zeus to you. This message repeats."

Dena turned the volume down and looked at the others as it repeated.

"Well?" Dena asked.

"Could be a trap," Gavin said.

"A trap from who?" Ana said. "Who other than Lee knew this rendezvous? We didn't even know it till Lee told us."

71

"Could be the Imperials," Gavin said.

"If it was Imperials," Ana said, "They would have had one of those corvettes sitting here with hot lasers when we came in. They wouldn't have needed to hunt for us. Just sit here and blast us. I'd be more worried if it was one of those New Oregon people hunting us down."

"Still, we have to be cautious," Dirk said. "Dena, open a channel."

"Ummm... I forget... how do I..."

Dirk cursed and typed on his screen.

Gavin leaned over his shoulder. "Skipper, I don't like the sound of this."

"Was there video with the audio, Nature Girl?" Ana asked.

"You know I don't know how to check that, and you're going to show me how, aren't you?"

"Knowledge is power," Ana said.

"You like playing the superior type, don't you, old man?"

"Who's playing?" Ana asked. "Look here." He pointed to his screen.

Gavin and Dirk were arguing whether to try a directional laser to send a message.

"Well, look at that," Dena said. "Dirk, I'm setting course for Papillon."

"What?" Dirk said. "Wait, we need to figure this out."

"Nothing to figure out, Navy," Ana said. "It's not a trap. As soon as Nature Girl here has a course, let's drop and get to Papillon."

"And how do you know it's not a trap?" Gavin said. "Sounds like it to me."

"Only Lee knows we're here. Anybody else would have to hunt for us, and then there's this," Ana said, popping the video onto the main displays.

The screen showed the bridge of the ship sending the message. A middle-aged man dressed in a Free Trader's captain's uniform was speaking. He was neat, clean, and perhaps young for his rank. He was also, like the two officers flanking him, Jovian.

CHAPTER EIGHT

"Close Santana, get us in voice range," Devin said.

Pollux had gone to general quarters and was racing for the far jump limit to close Brigadier Santana's ship.

"Understood, Tribune," the comm officer said. "It will be nine minutes till we get there—they are maneuvering to meet us. There is a situation report coming in, one-way transmission."

"Put it on the main screen. Let everyone see it."

"Sir, it's coded secret display only, and—"

"Never mind that. Put it up."

The main screen display changed. It showed sensor readings from Santana's ship, the Valhalla. The Valhalla was an assault carrier—lots of marines, assault shuttles, regular shuttles, land weapons, and some basic space weapons. It could stand off pirates and civilian ships but would be in trouble if a real warship took an interest in it.

The course plot showed a planetary system, with a station orbiting an inner sand-colored world and groups of ships maneuvering.

"Identify those ships," Devin said. "The ones in front."

"First two are Confed frigates, a little smaller than us, a thousand tons or so. Not sure of the exact class. The one behind it is a destroyer, and by the drive plume, it's one of the older City class, for sure."

"Three warships. A substantial fleet for the verge. What's in the back?"

"Merchant ships, sir, five of them, various models, and two auxiliary merchant cruisers."

"You sure they're merchant ships?" Devin asked.

Lionel broke in and tapped the screen. "Front units are pulling away at double the acceleration. They're heading right for the orbital base. The rear element is coasting in."

"Well, it's an incursion but hardly a war," Devin said.

"No reason for that many Confed warships to head into one of our systems, but that could be resolved diplomatically rather than with force."

The screen changed, and the time hack moved forward several hours. The Valhalla's output showed them to be drifting past the jump limit.

"They stayed to watch," Devin said. "Good for you, Santana."

"He could hardly do otherwise," Lionel said.

"He could have said he was threatened by one of the warships," Devin said, "and wanted to save his marines. Or at least argued that was the case, even if it's not true. We both know commanders who would run and do that."

"There are three groups now."

Warships were setting up for a high-speed pass of the base. The computer highlighted energized weapons on the screen. Auxiliary cruisers maneuvered between the two other groups. The trailing groups had slowed further.

"Santana's people have flagged the second unit as the assault, going to land and seize an air lock. Then the third unit is the garrison and supplies."

"What's at Sand Harbor?" Devin asked. "Where is it even in relation to us?"

"Three merchant jumps. I've been there," Lionel said. "Minor repair dock and a fueling facility. Small garrison, some communications. Courier boats call there. Not much commercial traffic. A small orbital container farm."

"Is the planet habitable?"

"Barely. It's small, about half Terran standard. Shallow, mold-covered seas. Breathable atmosphere but wet. Plants are mostly ferns. Small population. A couple thousand on the whole planet, maybe. Rains all the time. No real food options, they have greenhouses, no minerals to speak of. Except sand, thus Sand Harbor."

"Why is it even in the Empire?" Devin asked.

"We got it in a treaty fifty years ago, after the last war. It was on a list of exchanged territories. The Nat's got it from somebody else, some local grouping that disappeared during the war, and we inherited their claims. We put a base there to keep an eye on the Confeds."

"It's not strategic, then. No shipyard? No exports."

"Rubber, it exports natural rubber in bulk. There's no shipyard, no repair yard—no special facilities. It's a gas station and supermarket, where minor ships can refuel as they patrol the border. And it's small. I'm not even sure that the light cruiser we see there could dock at the station. No docking bays big enough for it."

"Who starts a galactic war over a useless station?" Devin asked.

"Gotta be a reason," Lionel said. "Doesn't have to be a good one."

"Brigadier Santana on screen, sir," the comm officer said. "Down to two second audio delay."

The bridge crew turned to the main screen, where Brigadier Santana's face appeared.

"Tribune. We have news," he said.

"So I see. We haven't watched all your sensor data yet. Give me the bottom line."

"A small Confed squadron dropped out of jump into the Sand Harbor system. They ignored communication attempts from the base. After destroying the two cutters defending the base, the lead element fired on the remaining fixed defenses, who replied. At least one of the Confed ships was critically damaged, and the other ships took hits, but all the remaining Imperial weapons and forces appeared destroyed. The Confeds launched shuttles at the base—not assault shuttles but regular shuttles from merchant ships—and by the time we left the third element of civilian class merchant ships, they were in the process of docking."

Lee had been standing quietly in the corner of the bridge. "Were you detected?"

"We think so, but they might have thought we were a freighter. They sent one of the frigates to chase us, not the destroyer. My officers tell me we might defeat a frigate and give the others a good fight, so if they knew who or what we were, they would have dispatched a stronger force. We jumped at that point and have been traveling continuously. We stopped twice for fuel but came directly here, as we figured this would be the most likely place to find Imperial forces or to get a message to the Empire."

"Why would they do this?" Devin asked.

"Tribune, we have no clue. We don't get along with the Confeds, but there has been nothing big happening recently, not that we know of. Nothing big enough to warrant this response."

"Brigadier, was your visit scheduled in advance? Could they have been targeting your marines and missed them?"

"No, we've been loafing around on exercises. Our visit was random and unscheduled. I've been amusing myself with staying close to the tribune as long as my orders allow."

"We'll have to talk about those someday," Devin said.

"Why now? Why here?" Lionel said. "It doesn't make sense. And why the non-naval ships? The Confeds have plenty of real assault carriers and military transports. Why not bring the troops in with them?"

"They don't have them in the verge."

"Do they think they can get away with this?"

Devin shook his head. "Surely, they don't expect me to sit idly by while they do this. I'm going to collect Imperial forces and push them out. I thought you said they know I'm here."

"After those vids, everybody knows that. The Mad Dog of the Verge."

The comm officer answered a bong on his board. "Sir, new beacon. A courier ship has entered the system. They're broadcasting a priority message for you. Personal and private."

"Close them as well. Brigadier?"

"We'll conform to your movements, Tribune."

"Very well. Helm. Execute. Execute. Execute."

***

Fifty minutes later, the Pollux, the Valhalla, and the courier ship, which had only the numeric designation MB-237, drifted near the jump limit.

The courier ship had asked for logistical support and fuel, and a fueling tanker was outbound from Papillon to deal with it.

Devin had received several messages and retired to his office to read them in privacy.

The surge of activity relating to the Confed incursion had dissipated. Lionel kept the bridge crew busy calculating least fuel, shortest time, and most direct courses to Sand Harbor. Plus, a plot of all Imperial ships in the vicinity and a discussion on how to reach the other Imperial forces in the sector.

"They're not many out here, Subprefect," the comm officer said. "Us, the Moose Jaw, four other corvettes—if we can contact them all—they're spread around the sector. The brigadier, a fleet replenishment tanker transiting to the adjacent sector, two couriers, including this one, and a survey vessel that may be lost."

"How can a survey vessel get lost? Did the Confeds get it?"

"Only if they got it six months ago, and in a system fifty light years coreward. It was surveying some empty systems. It's not reported missing or anything, just overdue from a long duration study of uninhabited systems." The officer frowned. "I'd be more worried about the fleet replenishment tanker. It's not reported missing, but it is overdue."

"Very well," Lionel said.

The bridge was crowded with extra personnel. All the weapons systems were manned, and everybody looked stressed.

"Secure from general quarters."

"Sir? The tribune—"

"Is not here right now, and I'm the executive officer."

"Understood, sir."

Red lights changed to yellow, and the crew got up from their chairs and stretched. Some headed for the galley or the heads.

The intercom flashed.

"Tribune?" Lionel said.

"You changed the alert level."

"Currently, I do not see any grave and imminent threats, Tribune. You may override me of course."

The tribune could be heard shuffling something over the microphone.

"I'm coming up."

A minute later, Devin arrived on the bridge.

Lionel vacated the command chair and raised his eyebrows. "Your orders, sir?"

"Put our three ships on the screen here," Devin said.

The comm officer obligingly put up a smaller display. The Pollux and the Valhalla drifted in concert. The MB-237 hung between and below them, waiting for its tanker.

Devin rested his chin on his hand for a moment, tapping his finger, then brought up a comm screen. Brigadier Santana appeared, giving direction to somebody offscreen.

He turned as his display bonged for attention. "Tribune?"

"Come to dinner please," Devin said. "Take a shuttle over here."

Santana looked offscreen, then back to Devin. "It's not dinnertime."

"Imin will cook something. We'll make it dinner."

"There's an armed invasion of the Empire, and you want me to visit for drinks and light conversation?"

"Yes."

"Is this an order?"

"Yes," Devin said. "You're ordered to come here, to

the Pollux. With a shuttle."

"I can take the ship's boat. Easier and faster."

"No. A full shuttle. One big enough for a company of marines."

"Why do I need space for a company of marines?"

"I have no idea," Devin said. "None. But you may disagree with me."

Lionel's eyes widened, and he muttered into his comm.

Devin muted his connection and yelled, "Lionel. No."

"Tribune, if there is—"

"No. No. Don't do it."

"You don't know what I'm doing."

"I have an idea. I don't need it."

"I—"

"No." Devin unmuted his comm and returned to the brigadier. "Brigadier, you are ordered to come to dinner. Yourself. Take a shuttle. That's an order, too."

"And bring marines? Is that an order."

"No," Devin said. "That's up to you. But I would like to ask a favor."

"You mean give an order?"

"No, a favor. You can refuse."

"Depends on the favor, Tribune."

"I'd like those two pilots from the message boat to come over as well."

"So, ask them."

"I don't want to ask them. I'm asking you. Could you stop by on the way and pick them up?"

"Without you asking them?"

"Yes."

"What if they don't want to come?"

"You could convince them—or not."

"Tribune, I—"

"Brigadier," Devin said, "I want you, your shuttle, and whoever or whatever else you think is important in my docking bay in fifteen minutes. Be there. Bring who you like. That's an order."

Devin cut the connection and tapped another. "Imin?"

"Sir?"

"Bring me my sword. And my formal robes. Quick as you can."

"Sir," Imin said.

Devin flipped the switch and waited.

"What's going on?" Lionel asked. "Did you get new orders?"

"I did," Devin said. "Some surprising ones. And some contradictory ones. I need more information before I go forward."

"Are you going to share them?"

"Not right away—"

"Shuttle outbound from Valhalla, sir," the comm officer said.

"Course?"

"They declared to us," the officer said. "But they're getting close to that message boat. Close enough to dock if they want."

"Very well."

Imin appeared at the back of the bridge with bundles.

"Tribune?"

Devin allowed Imin to buckle his sword on and drape him in his formal robes. "I'll try not to get these dirty like the others, Imin."

"No worry, sir, we can cope," Imin said.

Devin stood and flapped his robes. Imin had a holster on. "Imin, are you armed?"

"I am, sir."

"Whatever for?"

"Captain's steward can always be armed when in the presence of the captain, sir. It's in the regulations."

"I don't like it."

"Sir. Yes, sir. How's your sister, sir?"

"My sister?" Devin said.

"The Empress, sir. I know she sends you messages frequently."

"Messages from my sister are personal business, Imin."

"Indeed, sir. But I didn't get messages from my Clara, and she's always been sending them. Sends them every day. But none in the download this time."

"Perhaps she was busy. Or they were on another message boat."

"Could be, sir, but messages to the crew—the navy's happy to send duplicates, so I always get something. Always. Every boat. Not this time, though."

"Is that a fact."

"It is, sir. In fact, I had a quick chat with me mates, none of them got any family messages either. Not a single one. Suspicious, seems to me."

"Suspicious of what?"

"Bridge," Lionel said. All the officers on the bridge sat up. "Any of you who got a personal message transmitted from that boat, raise your hand."

Every bridge officer shook their heads.

Lionel stepped to his console and flipped channels. "Sergeant of marines?"

"Here, sir," a new voice answered.

"I want all of your men to the shuttle lock. Right now."

"We're already here, sir."

"Already, what are you—I mean good, but—"

"Unscheduled weapons readiness check, sir. Keeps the troops on their toes."

"Who suggested that?"

"The bosun, sir. He called me, said it was a good time for a drill. He spoke to Imin earlier."

"Indeed," Lionel said. "It is indeed." He cut the connection.

Devin fingered his sword hilt, and the whole bridge sat silent.

Nothing happened for fifteen seconds. Then the comm officer answered a bong on his board. "Valhalla shuttle inbound to our dock, sir. They say ETA five minutes. They, uh, while I was distracted, they docked at the message boat. Long enough to transfer passengers. If they were quick."

"Don't get distracted again," Lionel said.

"No, sir."

Everyone waited.

Finally, Devin cleared his throat. "Subprefect, will you join me at the dock to welcome our guests?"

"With pleasure, Tribune," Lionel said. He gestured to the bridge door. "Lead the way."

CHAPTER NINE

"You owe me new socks, Centurion," Dirk said. "Rocky ate two pairs."

"You're the captain. You bring it up with him. Take it out of his share of our smuggling profits."

"He's a dog. He doesn't get smuggling profits."

"Neither do we these days," Ana said. "Neither do we."

The Heart's Desire was in the run-up to emergence in the Papillon system. Dirk and Dena were in the front seats. Dena played at navigating, but neither Dirk nor Ana trusted her enough to let her courses go without checking things. Gavin was at his usual station in engineering. Rocky the Whippet was belted in next to Ana, licking his lips and looking pleased with himself.

"You showed him how to do it."

"When the student is ready, the master appears," Ana said. "I don't know how he stands the smell, though. Dena, we're waiting for that course on emergence."

"Same way that we handled the smell from Dirk before," Dena said. "Gagged a lot. And the course is coming. I want to double-check it."

"Double-checking is good," Ana said. "Just double-check faster." He sniffed. "What's that?"

Dena sniffed as well. "Ship perfume, in fact." She leaned over and sniffed Dirk. "Have you taken up bathing now, Pilot?"

"I always did bathe."

"You've obviously increased the frequency," Dena said. "Here's the course."

Dena had plotted the position of all the major planetary bodies of the Papillon system, its known trade routes, and their emergence point. She'd then overlain a course that would bring them in at standard G's to Papillon orbit and put the fuel consumption on it.

"That looks... good," Dirk said.

"Outstanding, Nature Girl. You are officially slightly less useless than milk-producing organs on a male cow."

"Slightly less useless?" Dena said. "That's all I get?"

"It's a graded system," Ana said. "Before, you were as useless as said organs. Now, you're slightly less useless. Baby steps."

"Thanks, old man."

"But you'll forgive us if we double-check everything on emergence."

"What if I'm not in a forgiving mood?"

"I'll try to live with the disappointment. Emergence clock is running."

Dirk looked at the timer counting down on his screen. "You know, Centurion, you spent a lot of time early in our voyage telling us how little you understand ship systems or engineering, but now, you seem to be pretty comfortable as a navigator."

"Navigating isn't all that hard, Pilot. You just need to know what programs to run. Same with piloting."

"Indeed." Dirk looked Ana in the eyes. "You don't happen to know how to pilot a ship or maybe have any engineering training, do you?"

Ana smiled. "Emergence in thirty seconds."

The blue jump light faded, and regular stars appeared on the monitors.

"How'd I do?" Dena asked.

"Let's see," Ana said. He highlighted points on her course plot one at a time. "Primary, check. Planets... check. All in proper place. Moons within parameters." Ana tapped his screen. "Your course holds up. But you missed a few things in the sailing directions."

"What?"

"Well, there's a smaller moon around Papillon you should have highlighted. It could mess up our orbit."

"Okay."

"There are comets inbound that should be on the plot. They won't affect our course, but you should show them. It's a good habit to have."

"I'll do better in the future, old man."

"Of course you will, of course you will."

"Good job, Dena," Dirk said. "Centurion, should we proceed on her course?"

"Not yet. There is one other thing that you missed."

"What's that," Dena said.

"Well, you got the planets and the moons and even the trade routes," Ana said. "But you missed one thing."

"What did I miss, Centurion?"

"This." Ana popped more things onto the screen. "Looks like an Imperial task force. Flagship is ISS Pollux, under the command of Navy's old buddy here, Devin the Lord Lyon. He has his guns unmasked and pointing at us." Dena's screen bonged. "That's probably him now, wanting to talk."

***

Tribune Devin and Subprefect Lionel stood facing the air lock, waiting. Two squads of armed marines lined the walls with drawn weapons. Lee had attached herself to the tribune's party and stood behind them.

"What's she doing here?" Lionel asked.

"Ask her," Devin said.

"What are you doing here?" Lionel asked Lee.

"Tribune gave me freedom of the ship. I'm making free. I want to hear about the war."

"Purported war," Devin said. "If it really happened."

"Why would it not have happened?"

The hatch light changed from green to red. The ship vibrated as the shuttle docked.

"Big shuttles on those marine assault ships," Lionel said.

"The biggest," Devin said.

The marines in the room clattered into position,

pointing weapons at the hatch in front of Devin. "Is that necessary, Sergeant?"

The sergeant snapped to attention. "Sir, yes, sir."

"I could order your men to relax."

"You could order that, sir, if you want."

Devin shook his head. "This day could turn out to be a disaster if we're not careful."

"For you?" Lionel asked.

"I don't care what happens to me. But it could be a disaster for the Empire." Devin's comm bonged. "Bridge, I'm busy."

"Sir," the comm officer said, "that freighter you asked us to watch for, the Heart's Desire, just came out of jump a hundred kilometers away."

"Oh, good," Devin said. "Dirk's here. Things can only get better."

Lee stepped next to Devin. "Dirk? What's he doing here?"

"He's following the instructions you gave him in your message," Devin said.

"I didn't send any message," Lee said. "I didn't give any instructions."

"I know," Devin said. "I did. Sent a dozen of them to every system within jump reach. Vague, confusing, but enough to convince him to come here. Great timing on his part. Bridge?"

"Sir?" the comm officer answered.

"Fire at that freighter. Warning shot, close as you like. Threaten death if he moves. Dire consequences. Keep him there."

"What dire consequences, sir?"

"I don't care. Do your best enraged Tribune impression. You know what I sound like."

"I need a—"

"Yes, yes. Execute." The light over the air lock changed from red to green. "We have visitors. I have to go."

Devin cut the channel and waited. Lee opened her

mouth, but Devin waved her off and shook his head.

The hatch swung open, and Brigadier Santana stepped out alone.

Santana saluted the full Imperial cross-chest salute and stood at ease, waiting.

Devin returned the salute and also waited.

The hatch screeched farther open and clanked against the stops. The air lock appeared empty.

Nothing happened for a full five seconds, then Brigadier Santana said, "Reporting as ordered, sir."

"Indeed," Devin said. He leaned sideways to peer into the lock. "Reporting alone?"

"The rest of you come out," Santana yelled over his shoulder.

Figures stirred in the hatchway.

All the marines in the compartment pointed or cocked weapons.

The first man out of the compartment stumbled. Seeing all the weapons pointed at him, he raised his hands. The woman behind him did the same.

"Don't shoot," he said. "We're unarmed."

Devin regarded the two figures for a moment, then waved the guns down. "You're the courier pilots?"

"Yes, sir. The brigadier said we were to report to you. He brought some marines and left them in charge of our ship and the messages."

"Put your hands down," Devin said. "Did you read your mail Brigadier?"

"No, sir," Santana said. "Decryption problem. All my mail was garbled and unreadable."

"Indeed," Devin said.

Santana smiled at the assembled marines. "Well, I'm here, Tribune, and I understand some talk was of dinner."

"Right, of course, Imin. Dinner for"—Devin counted on his fingers—"eight. Right away. Something good. No, something great."

"I'm back here, Tribune," Imin said from back by the

wall. He stood with the marines, carrying a rifle. "And great lunches don't come out of thin air. I'll need time for something great, but I can whip up something for everybody."

"Where did you get the rifle?" Lionel asked.

"Sergeant gave it to me."

"He did, did he? Sergeant, do you give rifles to everybody who asks?"

"Mr. Imin is not everybody, sir," the sergeant said.

"Imin, you sure you know how to use that?" Lionel asked

The assembled marines burst out laughing, and even Devin grinned.

"I say something funny, Tribune?"

"Yes, yes, you did," Devin said. "Imin, give the rifle back and get us some lunch. Myself, the subprefect, the brigadier, the bosun, the Praetorian, one of these pilots—who's senior?"

The woman in the back raised her hand. "Pilot Darkrey, Tribune."

"Pilot Darkrey." Devin sniffed. "You stink, Pilot."

"We're on a message boat, Tribune. Our supplies are rationed, and we came direct from the core without resupply. We had no water ration for bathing."

"Direct from the core? You didn't pass your messages along for further transit?" Lionel asked.

"No, sir. Direct from the core, flank speed, jump, refuel, jump, no diversions or retransmissions permitted. Whatever was loaded into the databanks at the capital, that's what you got."

"And no other copies?"

"Not that we know of, Subprefect. But we're just the messenger."

"And thus not worth shooting, as the saying goes," Devin said. "Imin, find these two pilots a room. A nice room. With its own fresher and water ration. Feed them well."

"Sergeant will take care of it, sir," Imin said. "He'll keep them there until you need them. Might I suggest giving them some other clothes and equipment. We can clean their clothes and other personal items while they wait."

The sergeant gestured to two marines.

"Personal items, Imin?"

"Like weapons and new communicators, sir."

"Communicators get dirty?"

"Filthy, sir."

"Mine doesn't."

"That's 'cause we polish it every night while you sleep, sir."

"Right, put them in the room."

The sergeant gestured again, and two of his troopers escorted the pilots out of the docking bay.

"Praetorian, how many on your old ship?"

Lee played with her comm. "Four of importance, Tribune."

"Lionel, send a shuttle for them."

Lionel waved four troopers over.

"Tribune, the crew of my old ship is somewhat..."

"Feral, savage, bloodthirsty?"

"I was going to say difficult, but perhaps dangerous is a better word."

Lionel waved the four marines back and gave them their rifles.

"Outstanding," Devin said. "Just a friendly lunch between friends."

***

It took another hour for officers, shuttles, guests, prisoners, weapons, chairs, tables, soups, and sandwiches to be organized to everyone's satisfaction.

Santana had called an aide over from the Valhalla.

Pollux's boarding party had demanded an emergency engineering rapid response team after they got a good look

CHAPTER TEN

"You're using too much water," Scruggs said to Weeks.

Weeks had stepped out of the suite's fresher unit, draping a towel around his waist and shaking his head.

"Really, baby girl?" Weeks said, running his fingers through his hair and rubbing his beard. "I'm taking a shower, not lolling in a bath."

"You should only shower on alternate days." Scruggs levered herself up from the chair and grimaced. "Helps cut down the strain on the water recycling on the ship."

The table area with four chairs was to the left of the main entrance to the suite. Scruggs leaned over and rested both hands on the polished wood table, contemplating the green knitted rug below. If she vomited, it would make a nice yellow contrast to the rest of the suite.

Everything was green—flowering plants on sideboards, green couches on the far side where Hernandez sat, green abstract jade sculptures on low polished wooden tables. The biggest sculptures had bronze panels on them with names like "Man and the stars" or "Courage and resilience." Hernandez called them "two goats copulating" and "bird poop drying in the sun."

"It does, baby girl?" Weeks said. He had stepped out of the fresher unit in the far corner. Even on a luxury starship, plumbing and water was expensive.

"Yes, that's why I only shower every other day." She picked up one of the sculptures. "I wonder if I could make this. And stop calling me baby girl."

"But I like showering every day."

"I'd like to shower every day, too," Scruggs said. "But we shouldn't. Saving water is prudent on a long journey."

"Good point. Tell you what, baby girl," Weeks said, "how about this—we shower together from now on? To save water, you know." He beamed at her.

Scruggs glared at him. "I'm not showering with you."

"Suit yourself." Weeks pointed. "Toss me that towel, will you? I need to dry my hair."

"And that's another thing," Scruggs slumped. She needed to use a hand to steady herself. "We use too many towels. That's wasteful, too.. Use the towels more than once."

"Another good point," Weeks agreed. "Keep those for next time, then."

"Towel consumption notwithstanding," Hernandez said, "one of us has to go out to pick up food, and it's your turn. You'll look stupid with wet hair."

"Yet another good point," Weeks said. "You're just full of great ideas, baby girl. I have a solution." He snapped the towel off from his waist, leaving himself nude, and used it to dry his hair.

Scruggs blushed.

Hernandez laughed. "Now you've made her blush."

"I am not blushing."

"Don't take it too hard, Ms. Ruger-Gascoigne. He does this to all the women. He can't help himself. He likes to embarrass people."

"I'm not embarrassed. I'm sad for him. And I always look away when people show their own shortcomings." Sweat beaded Scruggs's face, but she held herself up with the table.

Hernandez laughed. "Ms. Ruger-Gascoigne has spirit."

"Call me Scruggs, both of you. Everybody does."

"Okay, Ms. Scruggs, I will," Weeks said. "But I don't think I should be embarrassed."

"Not if it was really, really cold in here, no," Scruggs said. "But it's warm, so what's your excuse now?"

Hernandez laughed again. Weeks laughed, too, draped himself in the towel, and went away to dress.

Scruggs used both hands and dropped back into her chair. She took deep breaths till her breathing stabilized. "I think I'll take another pill."

"Don't take too many," Hernandez said. "Or at least don't complain when you're sleeping all the time."

"Hurts. I'm going to my room," Scruggs said, tossing her room key plate in her hand.

Hernandez stood. "And it's time for an inspection."

"No," Scruggs said. "Not again. I want my privacy."

"Can't give you that. Sorry," Hernandez said. "We let you turn off the security cameras. That's all we can do. Have to deliver you safely."

"And I'm unsafe in my own bedroom?"

"Can't be too careful."

"I'm still sick. I can barely move, and you have all my clothes out here under lock and key regardless."

Hernandez extended her hand. "Pass key, please."

"No," Scruggs said. She leaned on her door frame.

"I can take it off you if need be," Hernandez said. "And move you away from there."

Scruggs tossed the key up and down. "Pretty tough, beating up a little girl."

"We're the same size." Hernandez extended her hands. "Gimme."

"Okay, here." Scruggs tossed the key at Hernandez, who caught it one-handed. "What are you going to do when this is over? This whole transport thing."

"Not your concern, Ms. Scruggs. We're just delivery."

"What I'm going to do," Scruggs said. "I'm going to be talking to a lot of people. Rich and important people. People asking why I ran away, how I got back, things like that. I'm going to have to tell my story to all of them."

"Good for you. What's your point? We're just escorting you."

"I know that," Scruggs said. "And I can't fault you for keeping me in the room. Your boss, that tribune, and all the Imperial people will think it's a necessary precaution."

Hernandez brushed past her and put the key to Scruggs's door. The door slid open behind Scruggs, but Scruggs remained standing, blocking it.

"Going to let me by?" Hernandez asked. "Or do I have to take some action here?"

Scruggs didn't move. "In fact, they'll probably commend you for keeping me safe. Of course, they might have questions, like why you kept me from wearing decent clothes. Wearing my own clothes. And why you had to inspect my room, like I was a criminal. And I'll bet these important people will ask why you did it. And even if I'm in trouble, it's kind of insulting, to me, to my uncle, to my family. I'll make sure they know it, of course, and I know your names, so I'll ask them if they know you. Maybe they'll ask some questions, too."

Scruggs stood aside and gestured at her room. "Go ahead and search. Don't worry about me running off. I'll be right there with you, watching, so I can describe it later."

Hernandez stepped up to Scruggs and leaned into her space. "I'm just following orders. I don't want to be here."

"You think I want to be here?" Scruggs asked.

"We're guarding a high-value Imperial target from possible attack."

"What you're doing is abducting and restraining an Imperial citizen against her will. And that's what I'm going to tell the first police or Imperial unit I meet, unless things change."

"That's why we're not letting anybody talk to you, and that's why you have no comm." Hernandez leaned in closer. "Understand?"

Scruggs leaned in herself, enough that her nose brushed Hernandez's. "You have to let me go at some point, turn me over to a governor or whoever. And then I can tell whatever story I want."

"The tribune will protect us," Hernandez said.

"The tribune won't be here," Scruggs said. "But I will. And no matter what happens, I'm a lot younger than the tribune. When he's dead, I'll still be here. Waiting."

Scruggs and Hernandez glared at each other from ten

centimeters apart, then Hernandez leaned back. "I'm just doing my job."

"I know, but you don't have to be mean about it. I'm going nuts in here."

Hernandez sighed, then held out the key. "Let's make a deal. No room inspections."

Scruggs crossed her arms. "And what else?"

"You get out of the room. The suite. Once a day for... an hour. Walking the promenade."

"Three times a day. For an hour and a half each. Walking the promenade, shopping and dinner at the restaurants."

"Twice a day," Hernandez said. "Dinner, and an hour earlier, doing whatever you want."

"The gym?"

"You can barely move. You can't go to the gym."

"When I get better."

"Fine."

"And no room inspection or cameras."

"Okay." Hernandez held out the key.

Scruggs reached for the key.

Hernandez jerked it back. "What do I get in return?"

"No comms," Scruggs said. "I'll use the ship entertainment, but I won't demand comm access. And I won't try to get away while we're out walking. You can monitor me the whole time. Agreed?"

"Agreed," Hernandez said, handing her the key. "If you're good, we'll get along."

"We'll get along." Scruggs turned, went into her room, and used the key to lock the door. When it shut, she made a rude gesture with her hand. "If I'm good, oh, you'll see how good I am."

She fumbled a drawer next to the acceleration couch. She poured two pills into her hand, then hid them in her socks. She climbed down onto the ground beside her accel couch, wincing as her ribs strained under their bandages. "I'll be good. Pompous twit."

She started push-ups. The sooner she got healthy and in good shape, the sooner she could kick Hernandez's and Weeks's asses.

CHAPTER ELEVEN

"Imin, this soup is outstanding," Devin said.

"Watermelon gazpacho, sir, not soup."

"Excellent choice," Devin said, wiping his face. "Now that we're somewhat less angry with each other, we have a few things to discuss."

Imin cleared away the soup. Devin's statement about "treason" had captured everyone's imagination, but he had insisted on starting the meal before explaining.

"Time to talk of treason," Devin said. "Some introductions are in order. For those of you who don't know me, I am the Lord Lyon, Imperial Tribune, and Captain of ISS Pollux, the finest ship and crew in the fleet."

"Also known as," Lionel said, "the Mad Dog of the Verge, scourge of pirates. Thank you, Imin."

Imin served them all a green salad.

"And a member of the Imperial family," Dirk said. "Younger brother of the Empress, in fact. Do we get dressing with the salad?"

Imin handed out small containers of yellow paste.

"And many of you may have met Duke Friedel, captain of the..." Devin looked at Dirk.

"Heart's Desire." Dirk sniffed. "This is mustard. Tangy. Scruggs would be pleased."

"Also known as," Lionel said, "the butcher of New Madrid."

Dirk shrugged and spread his mustard. "True."

"And your ship's beacon says your freighter is from Pallas, and it's called Heavyweight Items."

Dirk turned to Gavin. "Engineer?"

"Sorry, Skipper. Forgot to turn it off."

Dirk turned back to Devin. "Tribune, there's no need for all this. I'm the one you want. Execute your warrant and arrest me. Nothing that's happened has any bearing on these people here. They're my crew. They've been following my instructions. They had nothing to do with stealing the ship. That was all me. Give everyone an excellent meal, then let them go, and I promise you no trouble. It's the honorable thing to do."

"You talk to me of honor?" Devin said. "You?"

Dirk forked some salad in his mouth, chewed, and swallowed. "It could be that I've learned a few things. About honor and duty and the like. Everyone, this salad is amazing, you have to eat it."

Dena picked up a forkful and sniffed, then put it in her mouth and chewed. Her eyes lit up, and she shoveled the salad into her mouth.

The marines were already munching.

Dirk took another bite and swallowed. "Imin, this is great. And good to see you again."

"You as well, Duke," Imin said.

"It's Dirk to you, Imin. You know that. Are you keeping the tribune out of trouble?"

"No chance of that, sir, but we all try hard."

"A full-time job, I would imagine." Dirk gestured at Lionel. "Imin, is he the one... ?"

"Pulled the tribune out of that fire, sir."

Dirk put down his fork and faced Lionel. "Subprefect. It's a pleasure to finally meet you. I've heard only amazing things about you."

"I can't say the same about you," Lionel said. "You and your group of desperadoes."

"About that," Ana broke in. "I'm confused as to why a big Imperial muckety-muck would lower himself to have dinner with a group of desperadoes. And, in fact, I'm curious as to why his security staff would allow us to get so close. What if we tried to assassinate him?"

"Is there more salad?" Dena said.

Every eye flicked to her. "Sorry, but this is the best salad I've had since I left Rockhaul. Could I have seconds?"

Imin produced a giant salad bowl and doled out second portions to everyone. "After this, a stew to follow."

"Centurion," Dirk said, munching, "Tribune Devin has many flaws. Cowardice isn't one of them. He leads from so far in the front I needed a telescope to find him when I served with him."

"Centurion what?" Devin said. "Who are you again? You look familiar."

"Senior Centurion Anastasios, sir," Ana said. "Pleased to meet you again. We spoke on the comm once, and why are we here? We have more important things to do. Like finding Scruggs. Where is she, freak?" Ana asked Lee.

"Ms. Scruggs is part of the problem—or of my problem, at least," Devin said. "And before you ask, she's as good as our medical team could make her. She was in no immediate danger. She was mobile, coherent, and healing. But it would take several weeks longer for the healing to finish. Since she seemed an energetic kind of young lady, I've dispatched her to the core sector with an appropriate escort to surrender her to the sector governor and, presumably, her family. Then she can do what she wants."

"I don't believe that was what she wanted to happen," Ana said.

"It was not. But I couldn't take her on board for medical work and then ignore the Imperial warrant. Besides, she'll be safer there than here, with the war."

"War?" Dirk, Ana, and Gavin said.

"What war?" Ana asked.

Santana spoke up. "Confederation naval units attacked Sand Harbor over two weeks ago. We watched it, recorded it, and came here to seek naval assistance and instructions."

"There's a war on, and you're sitting here eating boiled fish?" Ana said. "What type of marines are you?"

"Ones who would have been blown out of the sky

without naval escort," Santana said. "We would have been destroyed with no effect. If the tribune orders me back, I'll go, but I'd rather do something more useful." Santana took a spoonful of the stew. "This is amazing. These spices. Two other things." He gestured at Ana with his spoon. "I've eaten here before, so the war can wait till we finish a meal, and two, if you really are a senior centurion, I would expect you to call me Brigadier Santana."

"Sir," Ana said. "Brigadier, sir, you are correct. I forgot myself in the excitement."

Dena was making little mewling sounds of pleasure as she spooned the stew up.

"Devin, enough of this nonsense," Dirk said. "Arrest me, impound the ship if you need to. Let my people go and go off and fight your war."

"No arrest warrant for you," Devin said. "You're free and clear."

"What?" Dirk said. "Last time we spoke, there was an Imperial warrant, a naval warrant, and various other warrants, including some very pointed messages from your sister."

"Past tense," Devin said. "The warrant was canceled. By the Emperor himself. And the navy has instructions regarding you, but they all relate to your breaking out of incarcerations. But guess what came in the last message set but one? An Imperial pardon."

"A pardon?" Dirk said.

"A full pardon," Devin said.

"For what, exactly? I mean, we've been out for months. There may be some minor things that could cause problems."

"For all actions—let me see if I remember the verbiage—'for all actions and crimes occurring before the date of presentation.' So, Dirk Friedel, the Emperor in his wisdom and generosity, pardons you for all crimes committed as of this date. Congratulations, and don't forget to thank him for his generosity. God save the

Empire!"

"The Empire!" the table chorused.

"What about the ship?" Dirk asked. "I'm pardoned for stealing it, but it's still technically stolen property, so—"

"Not anymore," Devin said. "It's not on the redlist now. Not listed as stolen."

"How does that happen?" Dirk asked.

"Somebody bought it and canceled the red notice," Devin said. "I don't know who."

Dirk raised his eyebrows, then smiled. It widened as he scooped up the rest of his stew. "She did it."

"Who is she?" Dena asked.

"The Empress," Lee said. "She does that sort of thing. Very sentimental."

"You know the Empress, too?" Dena said. "I didn't know that."

"I work for her," Lee said. "I didn't realize that Dirk was her..."

"Ex-lover," Devin said. "Just as well. She got pretty snippy about the whole thing."

"You're the Empress's brother?" Dena asked Devin.

"We've established that, yes," Devin said.

"Is she prettier than me?" Dena asked.

Devin snorted. "Are you serious?"

"Of course."

"You can't possibly be as shallow a human being as that question indicates."

"Good to know that even tribunes don't know everything about some people," Ana said, standing. "Tribune, ladies, gentlemen, officers. If I understand correctly, you have no warrants for any of the crew of the Heart's Desire—or Heavyweight Items, for that matter. The ship isn't stolen, and you have no reason to hold us here. So, we'll bid you adieu, as they say, collect the Jovian there, and discuss how we're going to get Ms. Scruggs back. What is that wonderful smell?"

"Steak au poivre," Imin said. "The next course. With a

Bordeaux wine made from Old Earth vines."

Ana sat. "We'll bid you adieu after dinner, I meant to say. Does it come with potatoes?"

"New potatoes, yes," Imin said.

"Outstanding. Out of curiosity, Tribune, while we're waiting, what are you going to do about your war?"

"I'm going to show you some secret Imperial messages and ask you for your help."

"I love reading secret messages," Ana said. "They're so... secret. Ask away. But don't expect much help, though."

Devin gestured, and Lionel handed him a stack of papers. "A message boat normally carries hundreds of thousands of messages, sometimes millions, of differing levels of security."

"Do tell," Ana said.

"This one had six," Devin said. "Only six."

"That seems wasteful," Dirk said before stuffing a hunk of stew into his mouth.

"Suspicious is a better word. Of course, the pilots said they were loaded up at the capital and given special instructions and special software."

"Were they?" Dirk asked.

"Yes, they were. Now the messages. Some I got because I'm the sector commander. The senders forgot that the sector commander automatically gets copies of some messages. But first, the listing of all the messages on board. This is administrative and delivered to me as a matter of course. It showed only six messages total. Odd."

"Indeed," Dirk said.

"Second," Devin said. "One personal to me. It had an odd routing, and it seemed to have been a last-minute addition. It was a copy of the original directory that this message boat was to ship with. It said that the original message load had been over eight hundred thousand messages, but they were stripped out."

"Who sent that one?"

"No idea. That's the first two. The next two were about me, or for me. One was for all Imperial officers of Captain's rank or equivalent. Santana would have gotten a copy. But somebody blind-copied me the contents. The message was an arrest warrant signed by the chancellor."

The steaks arrived. Ana cut a slice and chewed. "This tastes incredible. How do you do this?"

"Butter," Imin said. "Best butter we can get."

"Outstanding," Ana said as the rest chewed. "My money is that it was for our friend the duke here, correcting an earlier mistake that left him free, but I'll ask the obvious question. Who was the arrest warrant for?"

"Me," Devin said. "Take me into custody and return me to the chancellor."

Everyone chewed in silence.

Ana swallowed and took a drink of the wine. "It washes the fat right out, so you could eat steak all day." He turned to Santana. "Brigadier, if we capture the tribune and deliver him to you, is there some sort of reward?"

The brigadier cut a chunk of steak and smeared it with sauce. "Unfortunately, we had a problem decoding our messages. Ours was garbled, so I have no official knowledge of this so-called warrant."

Ana pointed. "He just told you."

"Dinner conversation isn't enough to arrest a tribune," Santana said. "I'll wait till I have a more formal notification."

"Convenient," Ana said.

"Yes, thank the gods."

Dirk swallowed. "And the last two, Devin?"

"One to fuel the message boat up and return it post-haste, no stops, back to the capital after delivering the messages. And one other about your friend Ms. Ruger-Gascoigne. Scruggs."

The Heart's Desire crew sat up.

"About Scruggs?" Dirk asked. "What did it say?"

"This one is interesting. It's signed by the chancellor,

not the Emperor. The original instruction for Scruggs was simply a low level locate and inform but had been amended to locate, detain, and return to the core sector, care of the governor."

"Which you did," Dirk said.

"After the freak sold her to you," Ana said.

"If you are referring to the Jovian," Devin said, "selling her, as you call it, saved your friend's life and prevented her from being permanently crippled. Don't you think that's a good reason?"

Ana glared at Devin, then at Lee, then at the table. He drank his glass down. "More wine, please."

"In any event, given her condition, I was doing her no favors by keeping her here. I gave her an escort and sent her coreward. She'll be there in... twelve weeks approximately. She's traveling more or less incognito, so she'll be safe till she gets to the core."

"What do you mean safe?" Dirk said. "Is somebody going to hurt her?"

"The original warrant was administrative in nature. I doubt the Emperor ever saw it. It was issued as part of a group by one of his subordinates, who were convinced by somebody suitably important."

"Why did you say safe? Is she not safe?"

"The new warrant is signed by the chancellor, not the Emperor. But it's a full-fledged Imperial warrant, nonetheless."

"Devin," Dirk said, "what are you saying?"

"The new warrant is much broader and can be executed by any Imperial official with the ability. In fact, all Imperial officials are required to enforce it."

"We know this, Devin," Dirk said. "Are you saying every Imperial official has to arrest her if they see her?"

"No, it's not arrest. It's death. It's an Imperial death warrant."

CHAPTER TWELVE

"Would you like the rest of my caviar?" Scruggs asked Hernandez.

The two women were seated in the back of the Artemis Star's first-class restaurant. As befitted services in one of the swankiest and most luxurious of the Empire's passenger liners, the restaurant only sat twenty, and reservations were impossible to get. Unless, when the ship's first officer made his daily call to find how Tribune Devin's special guests were going, one of said guests causally asked which restaurant was the best place to eat for dinner. Then a reservation magically appeared.

"You don't want it?" Hernandez said.

"I've never been a fan," Scruggs said. She picked at her food. "You can have it all if you want."

"I don't know..."

"It's already paid for," Scruggs said. "It will go to waste if you don't. Here." She scraped the caviar onto Hernandez's plate. Her knife screeched. "Sorry, this china is scratchy."

The crowd in the restaurant had quieted at the squeal, and most of the diners covertly glanced at them from behind drinks.

"They're all looking at us," Hernandez said. "The whole restaurant is staring. Why?"

"They want to know who we are, who got the special table," Scruggs said.

"What special table? This is just another table. In the back. And we're lucky there's nobody at those other tables right now." She gestured at the two nearest tables, both empty. "That would be a security issue. At least we're alone and away from the door. And if this is how they decorate exclusive restaurants..." Hernandez waved at the decor.

The walls were a horrid dark green, the tables cloths a clashing light green. The carpet made you want to vomit, just to compare the green colors.

"You don't get it, do you?" Scruggs said. "This type of restaurant. The tables are booked months in advance. Some people book them a year ahead. They take a trip once a year, and they book the table for next year when they leave. They could fill all of these tables any time from a list of a hundred people waiting for them."

"Why didn't they?"

"Tribune scared them. I'll bet they've been holding these tables empty this whole trip so far, in case we wanted them."

Hernandez slurped up the last of the caviar. "But we've been on the ship for two weeks. Surely, they haven't kept them empty the whole time?"

Scruggs examined her plate. "This is foie gras. I'm not fond of that, either. Here." She shoved it to Hernandez.

"I can't believe you don't like it. It's exquisite."

"It's fine. But it's boring. The food is boring. The restaurant is boring. Even the glasses are boring." She held up a crystal goblet with AS etched on the side.

"How can you get bored of this?"

"Anything can be boring if it's not what you want," Scruggs said. "Eat up. The food shouldn't go to waste."

"Why'd you order it if you didn't want it?" Hernandez said. She ran a finger along her plate and licked the last of the pate, then did it again. "This is so good."

"It was complimentary. They brought it without me asking."

"This prix fixe thing, you said it's the best deal. Good combinations of food," Hernandez said. "How much does it cost?"

Scruggs named a sum.

Hernandez dropped her fork. "Emperor's kneecaps. We can't afford that."

"If you think we can't afford this," Scruggs said, "wait

till you see the bill for the rooms."

"I thought—well, that we'd pay for it and the tribune would reimburse us later."

"Unless your luggage is full of Imperial gold credits, I doubt you have enough money to rent our cabin for an hour."

Hernandez's eyes grew round. "What? How much."

"Don't worry, we'll never get a bill. Or if we do, tell them to send it to that tribune guy. He's got plenty of money."

"How do you know that?"

"I remember him now. I met him when I was much younger. My uncle was polite to him."

"So?"

"My uncle isn't polite to many people. And the tribune was polite back. So, they move in the same circles." Scruggs pushed her food and glass away.

"If the tribune is this wealthy, then your uncle—"

"Excuse me, ladies." Their waiter materialized next to them. "You're not eating miss. Is the food not to your liking."

"This is the finest meal I've ever had in my life," Hernandez said.

"Thank you, miss," the waiter said. Somehow, he made "thank you" sound like "of course it is." "But you, Ms. Ruger-Gascoigne, you don't like it."

"You know my name?" Scruggs asked.

"The purser makes a point of keeping up on such things," the waiter said. "He briefed the whole dining room crew. We're pleased and excited that you've decided to travel with us. But can we get you something else to eat? The chef would be happy to whip something up special for you."

"No, I don't think so," Scruggs said. "No, wait. Have you ever eaten food trays, the ones they have as rations on freighters?"

"The ones that come in the metal foil?"

"Yes, the ones you microwave."

"I've eaten them before, when the need arose."

"With the three compartments, the red, blue, and green ones."

"Yes."

Scruggs smiled. "Could I have one of those? Heated up. With maybe some vinegar on the side to flavor it?"

The waiter raised his eyebrows. "You're in the first-class restaurant of the Artemis Star, and you want us to get you crew ration trays with a side of vinegar?"

Scruggs grinned wider. "Could you?"

"I need to speak to the purser. Just a moment." The waiter hurried off.

Hernandez chewed through the rest of her dish. It was a souffle of lamb. "I don't know how you can not like this."

Scruggs shrugged. "I like what I like. Uh-oh."

"What?" Hernandez sat up straight. She flipped her knife and held it with a stabbing grip. "Problem?"

"That girl—woman, I guess—who came in the door, I know her. We went to the same school for a while."

"Is she going to be an issue?" Hernandez reversed the grip on her knife, then reached over and grabbed Scruggs's knife.

Both hands dropped under the table, holding the knives.

"No, but she's annoying."

"Miss Ruger-Gascoigne." A man in a charcoal-gray wool suit and an obsequious smile approached the table, their waiter dragging behind. "I'm the Purser. My name is Deeve. I've been speaking to Brendan here. He must have misunderstood. Or perhaps he's having a little joke." Deeve glared at Brendan. "An unfortunate little joke, if that's the case."

"It's nothing serious. I didn't have an appetite for your main meal. I was wondering, if it's not too much trouble, do you perhaps have a red-green-blue tray, a spacer's tray?

And some vinegar for flavor?"

"A spacer's tray?"

"Yes."

"From our kitchen?"

"Oh, sorry," Scruggs said. "It's probably too much trouble. Never mind. We have some ration bars back in the cabin. I can eat those."

Deeve's mouth gaped, then shut. Brendan was smirking behind him. "Ration bars? We, I mean, I, the chef..."

"No, I understand," Scruggs said. "Sorry for the trouble. But it would have been nice if I could have them."

Deeve shook like a dog who had rammed a tree chasing a ball and took control of himself. "But of course you shall have them. Right away. Please wait three minutes. Brendan, with me."

They rushed off to the kitchen.

Hernandez watched the front of the room. "Your friend is coming."

"Outstanding," Scruggs said.

A woman Scruggs's age accompanied by a much older man strode to the table. The woman was blond, thin, and dressed in the shortest black dress Hernandez had ever seen. The man wore a formal suit, wide stitched lapels, with a giant gold pinky ring.

"Sandy! Little Sandy. I knew it was you. What are you doing here? How is your uncle." The woman cocked her head and examined Scruggs's coveralls. "And what happened to your clothes? Did you lose all your luggage?"

Scruggs gritted her teeth. "Hello, Alex."

A furor arose in the kitchen, then a waiter raced out, scuttled across the floor, and held the main doors open. A team of two white-hatted sous-chefs and another waiter pushed an elaborate room service cart across the door and out the halls.

"I go by Alexandra now," Alexandra said. "More appropriate for my current level of sophistication, don't you know? When I graduated, Papa promised to let me go shopping. Mama and I have been all over, buying some new duds. Do you like this?" She did a twirl, and her little black dress flared out. "Looks good, don't you think?"

"Great, Alexandra, great for you. And congrats on your graduating. I'm sure everyone at the school was... excited that you moved on."

"I think so, I think so. Such nice little people there. But you would know that. You always got along with those lesser kinds."

"I got along with some types, that's for sure," Scruggs said.

The purser raced up to their tables, Brendan following. "Good evening, Miss Alexandra. Miss Ruger-Gascoigne, we'll have your meal up shortly. We had to send out to our stores for a few special ingredients. They'll be here momentarily."

"Thank you, sir," Scruggs said. "I usually drank a spacer's drink called basic with that. Do you think perhaps I could have some of that, too?"

The purser gulped, snapped his fingers at Brendan, and pointed to the door.

Brendan scuttled in pursuit of the room service cart. "I'm sending for it as we speak." He nodded at them and withdrew.

"Special meal?" Alexandra asked.

"Doctor's orders," Scruggs said. "I'm sick."

"How sad. But where are my manners? This is my friend Michel. Michel, this is my friend Sandy, from back in junior school, and her friend... ?"

"Call me Hernandez," Hernandez said.

Michel leaned into a short bow. "Ms. Ruger-Gascoigne, Ms. Hernandez, the pleasure is all mine." He bent over, picked up Scruggs's hand kissed it, then reached for Hernandez.

She flipped the knife up to point at his descending nose. He glowered at her.

"You've got that right," Hernandez said.

Alexandra grabbed Michel's arm. "Michel is the third Baron Deeprock."

"Good for Michel," Hernandez said.

"Or will be when the second Baron Deeprock dies, as I recall," Scruggs said. "Isn't your father still alive?"

"Yes, we're still graced with his presence," Michel said.

"The old goat's still hanging on by his greasy fingernails," Alexandra said. "But that can't last forever."

"Wouldn't your mother..." Scruggs said.

"Died two years ago," Alexandra said.

"I'm sorry, I remember now. But didn't your father remarry?"

"He has a new friend, yes," Alexandra said. "But she won't be staying with us. Michel will take care of it."

"A payment should suffice to see the ignorant slut off. Otherwise, there are other ways to persuade her to depart if she knows what's good for her." Michel scowled.

"Outstanding," Scruggs said.

"Any old who," Alexandra said. "I'm surprised that you're on a proper ship. You always spent all your vacations at that little repair shop your uncle worked at."

"You mean the Imperial naval construction shipyard he owned?"

"That's what I said. That little shop."

Scruggs pushed her empty plate to the right. "I had fun there."

"Of course you did, of course you did," Alexandra giggled. "You would. But what are you doing out here? On the verge. It's so boring, and if Michel and I hadn't been out here already, Michel had some business in the confederation—"

"Alexandra," Michel said. "That's a secret."

"Hush, Michel. Everyone deserves to make a living. Sandy, whatever are you doing out here? Your uncle didn't—well, he didn't kick you out, did he? That would be so unfortunate."

"Kick me out, no," Scruggs said. "No, he didn't. We're

traveling, that's all."

"But why? Are you in trouble?"

"Yes," Scruggs said. She glared at Alexandra. "I am. I got bored, hijacked a starship, joined a mercenary company, learned how to shoot rifles and kill people with hooks, then I helped steal a couple containers of weapons, smuggle guns onto planets, fought in a civil war, destroyed a library, stole more weapons, trained as a sniper, and helped fight our way off the world. Then I was captured by an Imperial warship. There's an Imperial warrant out for me, one hundred thousand credits, dead or alive. Hernandez here is a Naval Intelligence agent, and she's escorting me to the core, where I'll probably stand trial for treason. She said she'll shoot me if I try to escape." Scruggs cracked her hands. "Oh, and I learned how to play poker."

Alexandra and Michel stared at each other. Alexandra giggled. "You're funny. Go on. Why are you really here?"

Scruggs glared at her, then sighed. "My uncle fired me. He said I wasn't sophisticated enough. He paid for me to take this trip. Hernandez is a dancing and fashion coach. She's teaching me proper table manners."

Alexandra giggled again. "That's much more likely, isn't it, Michel?"

"Indeed, it is," Michel said. "I often wonder why young women feel the need to exaggerate their accomplishments so much."

"Must be the lack of proper masculine guidance," Hernandez said.

"I was telling Alexandra exactly that before," Michel said. "What's wrong with your hands? And why doesn't Sandy have a knife?"

Hernandez lifted her hands above the table. She circled both knives around her fingers, walking them in a row, then flipping them back up. "Oh, she wasn't using them right now, so I took them away from her."

Scruggs lifted her fork and pointed it at him. She

gripped it like she would a stabbing knife. "That's me, fork girl."

"Well, I'm sorry to hear about your firing," Alexandra said. She gave Hernandez a once-over and leaned in to Scruggs. "But if you're paying her for her fashion sense, I think you overpaid," she stage-whispered.

"It was a package deal," Scruggs whispered back. "She does our hair, too."

Alexandra raised her eyebrows. "Oh dear." She stood. "Well, Michel and I have to go. Perhaps we'll see you again before we disembark."

"Will you be on the ship long?" Hernandez asked.

"We're leaving at the next stop," Alexandra said. "Michel's father is sending his yacht for us. Some weird insurance thing. It couldn't take us all the way into confederation space, even to the Verge, not sure why."

"I see. That's a shame that you had to be here, on the ship."

Michel raised an eyebrow for a minute, then curved a dazzling smile at Scruggs. "Perhaps we can meet socially some evening before we disembark."

"Could you teach me poker?" Scruggs asked. "I have always wanted to learn."

Michel's smile seemed to reach behind his head and met in the back. "I think I could do that."

"That would be wonderful." Scruggs smiled. "I'll have to bring some money, of course. How much should I bring?"

"We could have a friendly game. You can tell me about this Imperial warrant."

"Outstanding."

The room service cart and crew sped back into the restaurant, sliding past the table.

The sweating purser approached the table. "Ms. Ruger-Gascoigne? Your meal and drinks will be ready momentarily."

"Thank you," Scruggs said. Deeve bowed and returned

to the kitchen.

"Well, ta-ta for now, little Sandy. Good seeing you. Come along, Michel."

Michel cocked his head at Scruggs. "I just got it. Ruger-Gascoigne? The Ruger-Gascoigne? The arms manufacturers."

"Sandy's uncle owns a shop, makes ship parts, like I told you, doesn't he, Sandy?"

Scruggs nodded. "Parts for ships, yes."

"But I thought the owner didn't have any daughters... you're the niece. Is he really your uncle?"

"I call him uncle," Scruggs said. "He doesn't object."

"I'm sure that Sandy isn't his real niece, Michel. Don't embarrass the poor girl. If she was really the niece of someone like that, he wouldn't send her all the way out here."

Hernandez laughed. "No. He probably wouldn't send her all the way out here."

"I won't be here for long," Scruggs said. "Aha, dinner."

A team of three waiters arrived, along with a fourth pushing a cart. The first positioned an inscribed china plate in front of her, laid down three silver spoons, and placed a crystal goblet to the right.

The next flipped the cart open and ladled the contents out onto the plate. First, she plopped three ladles of a white mush, then two of green mush, and finally, a single ladle of red mush onto the china. The third waiter carried a tray of four tiny crystal pitchers.

He arranged them in front of her. "Balsamic Vinegar, Red Wine Vinegar, Malt Vinegar, and Distilled White Vinegar."

You could hear the capitalization.

The fourth waiter filled her cup with an orange-colored liquid, then placed a stainless steel carafe on the table. "Miss's drinks, premixed." He added a tiny bowl filled with orange powder next to it. "Extra, for mixing to taste."

Scruggs clapped. "Oh, this is wonderful. Thank you so

much."

"What is all of this?" Alexandra asked.

A mutter ran through the restaurant. The other patrons leaned and stretched to discern what the commotion was.

"The chef calls it his basic meal," the purser said, loud enough for the whole restaurant to hear. "The ingredients are extremely difficult to locate. He only serves it to his most favorite customers. Bon appetite."

The wait staff withdrew.

Scruggs happily spooned up the mush, pausing only to smother each portion with one of the vinegars. "I missed this."

"Well, we won't bother you while you are eating," Michel said. "It's a pleasure to meet you."

"Thanks," Scruggs said.

Michel beamed his dazzling smile and extended his arm. The two flounced out the door, waving greetings. They paused at the door while Alexandra chatted with a couple. Michel glanced back at the table, his face inscrutable.

Scruggs continued to munch down the basic.

"Little ship repair shop?" Hernandez said.

Scruggs rolled her eyes, shoveling food in her mouth.

"Fashion consultant?"

This time, Scruggs shrugged.

"Kill a man with a metal hook?"

Scruggs swallowed the red mush, then took a big gulp of basic. "You use it like a knife—thrust at the belly. Don't get fancy, Centurion says."

"He's the one who taught you to kill people, this centurion?"

"Yes," Scruggs said. She turned the distilled white vinegar pot upside down, but it was empty. She looked up, but the waiters were already on the move. One reached for it. "One moment, miss."

Scruggs handed it to him, and he nearly ran back to the kitchen.

Hernandez crossed her two knives on her plate. "Killed a lot of people, then."

"Yes," Scruggs said.

Hernandez waited, but Scruggs didn't say anything more. Ten seconds later, the waiter returned with two jugs and put both in front of them.

Scruggs thanked him, drenched her plate, and continued eating.

"How many?" Hernandez asked.

"Not sure," Scruggs said.

"Not sure if you killed anyone?"

"Oh, I killed them," Scruggs said. "A half dozen at least, with the rifle. Maybe a dozen. Hard to tell. But they were good shots. No, my problem is the tank centurion and I blew up. We didn't know how many were inside."

"You blew up a tank?"

"Helped. Yes. Two of us. That counts."

Hernandez nodded. "I've never blown up a tank."

"I'll show you how when I'm better," Scruggs said. "I'm not up to it right now."

"Right," Hernandez said. "I'm looking forward to it."

"Do you have a tank with you?" Scruggs asked.

"I hide it in my luggage," Hernandez said.

"Michel was interested in who I was and where we were from."

"He was, wasn't he?"

"When they stopped at the door, he stood there. He was looking at me. A certain way."

Hernandez grinned. "Men do that. You should be used to it by now."

"Not that way." Scruggs slurped down more basic. "I know that way. No, he looked at me differently."

"How did he look at you?"

"Like money," Scruggs said. "Like he saw lots and lots of money."

CHAPTER THIRTEEN

Ana almost got his revolver pointed at the tribune. But Gavin grabbed him from the left, and Dena got both hands on the gun from the right. They struggled and flipped backward over the chairs. Dirk was only a second behind them, landing on Ana's legs, and reaching to help hold the revolver down.

"Keep him down," Dirk yelled. "Keep him down." He leaned into Ana's chest and lay on his hips, straddling him.

Ana rolled from side to side, trying to bring his gun hand up. Dena pushed down, got her knees on his arm, and gripped his hand. Dirk pinned him and grabbed Ana's fingers.

"Let me up." Ana's face flushed, and his breathing labored. He strained against his holders but could only jerk his arms up an inch.

"Drop your gun," Dena said.

"Not a chance," Ana said.

"Then, no chance of getting up," Dirk said. "We can do this all day."

"I can't," Dena said. "Can we shoot him or something?"

"We can't just shoot him," Dirk said.

"Why not?" Dena said. "He'd shoot us."

Ana twisted, then deflated and laughed. He laughed some more. "You're right, Nature Girl, I would. I'd have shot you already. Here." He opened his fingers. The revolver hung loose, and Dena pulled it away, then rolled back on her haunches. "Got it."

"Centurion?" Dirk asked, "are we done?"

"Will we go get the girl? Go get Scruggs."

"Right away," Dirk said. "Soon as we can."

"What about your friend, the tribune?" Ana asked.

"I said right away, Centurion."

"Fine," Ana said. "I'm good. I'll wait to hear the plan."

Dirk sat up. "Gavin, let him go."

"You sure, Skipper?"

Dirk nodded. Gavin released Ana's arms.

Ana sat up and massaged his arm. "Good body hold, Engineer. Where did you learn that?"

"You taught it to Scruggs," Gavin said. "I watched."

"So you did. So you did," Ana said. He rolled to the side and put one hand on a chair and the other on the table and hoisted himself up.

Dena retreated two feet and looked at Dirk. Dirk gestured with his finger. Dena reversed the tiny revolver and handed it back to Ana, butt first. Ana put it in a pocket on his coveralls.

The four of them turned back to the table. All four of the guards, Lionel, and the two marines had their weapons out and cocked.

They were all pointed at Lee.

Dirk's eyes tracked sideways. Lee's revolver was pointing across the table at Devin. "Lee, what's going on?"

"If you four are finished, we should go get Scruggs."

Dirk turned to Devin. "Tribune?"

Devin was chewing. "Of course. Go ahead. You can leave now. If you want."

Dirk flexed his fingers, then sat. "Give us the rest. There must be more to this story."

"There is no other rest," Devin said. "You're going to get the young lady. I'll give you the courses, supplies, weapons, and whatever is necessary. Money, I suppose. My honor is at stake here. I want you to get her before she gets to the core, and in trouble. Praetorian, why are you pointing that weapon at me?"

"To go help Scruggs."

"What gave you the impression that I wasn't going to help Scruggs? Or stop you from helping her? And for that matter, how will shooting me help?"

Lee bit her lip, rolled the revolver vertically between

her thumb and finger, and returned it to the holster hidden inside her outfit.

"Good. Finish your steaks, everyone. There is a dessert later," Devin said.

Lionel kept his pistol pointed at Lee. "May I have that weapon please, Praetorian?"

Lee shook her head.

"Lee," Dirk said, "give it to him. For now."

"Ana doesn't have to give up his."

"Ana didn't point it at Lionel's boss. He'll give it back."

"Yes, Pilot." Lee slid her revolver across the table.

"You're getting into this pilot-captain thing, Navy," Ana said. "I'd almost think that you were starting to take charge of things."

"Shut up, Centurion," Dirk said. "Devin. We have to help Scruggs."

"Of course. I never would have sent her in that way if I thought this was going to happen. But I find myself in something of a quandary," Devin said. "I promised the Praetorian that I would take care of Ms. Scruggs, as she calls herself. I even pledged my honor on it. So, that, I must do."

Devin chewed his last bite of steak, then drained his glass of wine. "Excellent choice, Imin. What's for dessert?"

"Apple cobbler, Tribune," Imin said. "If the rest of you would finish your meals?"

The remainder of the tables chewed their steaks. Imin provided Ana with another steak knife to replace the one that had gone missing during the altercation.

The Heart's Desire crew stared at each other, then Ana shrugged and cut the last pieces from his steak. The marines kept their weapons lying out on the table.

Devin pushed his empty plate aside. "Outstanding. I must rescue Ms. Scruggs. Honor demands it. On the other hand, this war requires a response as well. The Confeds cannot simply attack Imperial territory unmolested. Honor demands a response. The Pollux is the most modern frigate in our inventory right now, and it's also the closest to the frontier. Given what I understand about our weapons, we should be able to simply move out and destroy those forces that oppose us. Is that not so, Lionel?"

"By ourselves?" Lionel asked.

"That is my plan, yes."

"What about the station itself? How will we secure that?"

"We'll bring the marines," Devin said.

Santana and his aide both grinned.

"And we'll need to send a message to the other systems," Lionel said.

"Well, we'll send the message boat, of course," Devin said.

"The Pollux is one ship. If we encounter other systems, they may need a temporary guardian."

"Subprefect," Devin said, "you're going to suggest I collect all the forces in the sector?"

"The corvettes at least," Lionel said.

"One of them."

"Four."

"Two."

"Deal. Unless we can get four."

Dirk rapped the table. "I'm glad that is settled. Back to Scruggs?"

"Hang on," Gavin said. "You're just going to go charging out there and attack the nearest Confeds? Haven't you heard of planning or reconnaissance or gathering forces or... Help me out here, Skipper."

Dirk picked up a fork and spooned up the apple cobbler Imin had slid in front of him. "I missed your food so much, Imin. Those are good questions, Tribune. Why not wait?"

"First," Devin said, "the Empire has been attacked. We will respond. We must respond. There is no alternative. Second, I don't believe there will be any other Confed forces there because the Confed's don't have any other forces to spare out here. Using those civilian freighters is a giveaway. This was hastily organized by local authorities to take advantage of temporary circumstances. And third, we will do it that way because I am an Imperial tribune, and that is how I say we will do it. I do not need advice from jumped-up mechanics on how to conduct my business. Imin?" Devin held up his empty glass, and Imin waved one of his assistants to fill it.

"What circumstances?" Dirk asked.

Devin took a slug of wine. "Hmmmm?"

"What circumstances? You said take advantage of temporary circumstances. What temporary circumstances are the Confeds taking advantage of?"

"A shortage of naval units in the sector," Devin said. "Strike while the iron is hot, you know."

"Unless I miss my guess," Dirk said, "there's no shortage. Not in a relative sense. There're probably more naval units out here now than in years. I don't remember the Navy's latest model frigates being assigned to the Verge in the past. Nor do I remember assault carriers accompanying them. Did you relieve a ship when you came out here, Brigadier Santana?"

Santana supped his wine down. "We did not. I was given orders to conduct an extended training cruise and to be in the vicinity of the tribune while I did so."

"Isn't that interesting? Why would the tribune need a battalion of marines?"

"Originally, I was told that we would be needed to help arrest a Mr. Dirk Friedel, an Imperial Deserter. But it seems that rather than sending squads of marines to capture you, it's more efficient to invite you to dinner." Santana took a spoonful of the apple cobbler from his plate. "I have to say, that method has its attractions. I might be willing to go to jail for a long time for several meals like this one."

"There are more ships here now than there were last

year," Dirk said. "Because Devin is here. So, if I was a Confed intent on attacking the Empire and getting away with it before anybody could respond, I'd have done it long before now or wait till the Lord Lyon goes home to his estates, which is bound to happen eventually. What new circumstances are we talking about, then?"

"The arrest," Lionel said. "That's new."

"I thought there was no arrest?" Dena said. "No message."

"Officially, there isn't," Lionel said. "No such message has been received."

Dena nodded at Lionel. "Sub-whatchamacallit dude. I don't know anything about Imperial politics," she said. "But if you got a letter from the Emperor telling you to arrest your boss, wouldn't you do it?"

Lionel scooped some food from his plate. "The Emperor would never send such a letter."

"His wife wouldn't let him," Dirk said. "The Emperor's wife is Devin's sister."

Devin nodded.

"Okay..." Dena said. "But even if he was rebelling or something like that, what would happen if he decided to take over Papillon?"

"We'd tie him up in his cabin till he sobered up," Lionel said. "The Duchy of Lyon is ten, a hundred times the size of Papillon, if you include the adjacent systems. And a thousand times richer. Devin has no need of money. Nor of Papillon."

"Really?" Dena smiled at Devin. "Do you have a girlfriend, by chance, Lord Devin? Can I call you Devin?"

"I'd rather you didn't," Devin said. He turned to Lionel. "And I'd rather you didn't flap your mouth." Then he turned to Dirk. "And I'd rather you stopped asking questions and went out to rescue Ms. Ruger-Gascoigne."

"Who?" Ana said. "Who's Ruger-Gascoigne?"

"Your Ms. Scruggs," Devin said.

Ana's eyes widened, and he laughed. "Ruger-

Gascoigne. She's Ruger-Gascoigne. I'll be. Did you know she once borrowed ten credits from me to help buy lunch?"

"She probably didn't need it," Devin said.

"Who's Ruger-Gascoigne?" Dena asked.

Dirk shook his head. "I didn't see that coming. No wonder you sent her back with an escort."

"Who's Ruger-Gascoigne?" Dena asked again.

"I had to look the name up after," Lee said. "But it doesn't matter. She saved my life once, and we need to save hers."

"She saved your life?" Devin asked.

"Yes. One time, when I was swimming."

"You can swim?"

"No. That's why I needed to be saved."

"If you can't swim, why were you in the water?" Lionel asked.

"Never mind," Lee said. "It's complicated. But we need to get Scruggs back before she's killed."

"This makes no sense," Dirk said. "First, the Confeds attack the Empire at the worst time for them to do it. Second, the acting sector commander is supposed to be arrested, and third, the richest heiress in this part of the galaxy is sentenced to death. This doesn't make any sense."

"Richest heiress? Scruggs?" Dena said.

"You have the timing wrong, Lord Duke," Lionel said. "I think the order was—first, the heiress is sentenced to death, then the arrest warrant, then the attack."

"Why that order?" Dirk asked.

"Somebody needed money, a lot of money, so they started extorting it from businessmen, and anybody that wouldn't play ball had to go. Thus, Scruggs. Second, a popular commander needed to be recalled to the core to be dealt with before he could gain too much influence over naval or marine units and put a stop to that sort of thing. The best way to do that is to blame him for mismanagement of Imperial forces. Weakening the defenses in the verge, for example. Then all we need is an actual border incident that overwhelms local forces and embarrasses said commander. Thus, Sand Harbor. That's the order of operations."

"But who would do this?" Dirk asked. "Who had this type of access to codes and message boats, and who could do this? And it doesn't make sense. How did the Confeds know now was the time to strike."

"Somebody told them," Lionel said. "Somebody important. Somebody with access to codes. They knew—or thought they knew—that there would be some chaos and confusion in the military hierarchy here."

"Giving information about Imperial fleet depositions is treason," Dirk said.

"Absolutely," Devin said, signaling for his glass to be refilled. One of Imin's stewards obliged him. "I told you the topic of this lunch was treason." Devin swirled the liquid in the cup. "Just not mine."

CHAPTER FOURTEEN

"Eighteen, nineteen, twenty," Scruggs counted, collapsing in a pool of sweat.

She'd been able to do a hundred push-ups every time Centurion asked before, but after the "accident," as she called it, twenty was a stretch. A hard, long stretch. She'd worked up from five, but her body was complaining. And the med bay would shoot her full of drugs if she let it check her blood pressure right now. She rolled over on her back and lay there until she regained her breath. Then she stripped naked and pulled two towels over herself. She glanced at the mirror. Her hair was matted, and she looked like she had just woken up. Good.

She stepped out of the cabin and sauntered to the fresher. Weeks was sitting in the corner of the suite, reading something on his comm. He nodded at her and went back to his reading. Scruggs dragged her towels, exposing more leg. She made sure her towels were draped to show some skin but not too much. Dena had told her she should show legs, shoulders, or belly—but only one at a time.

She grit her teeth, then forced a grin. "Could we go to dinner, later, Mr. Weeks?"

Hernandez had gone to the gym, leaving Weeks in charge of their cabin. They'd been on the ship for thirteen days and called on five ports in short jumps.

At each port, they'd been met by an in-system shuttle rather than docking at an orbital port. The vessel had been waiting near the jump emergence point and had ensured they could swap passengers, then travel in and out of the system quickly. But they'd started a five-day jump that doglegged through a less populated part of the sector. This was to be their last port in the Verge. Next stop would in the Arcturus sector, and after that, they'd be in the core sector.

Scruggs had developed a plan. First, she would seduce Weeks. She also would learn how to properly cheat at poker. She figured she could do both at once if she was careful. The two long jumps with their regular routine would help.

"Are you asking me for a date?" Weeks said. His eyes tracked down her towel to her exposed legs. "I thought you and Hernandez had a thing going. All girls together and all that."

Scruggs blushed. "It just... it just seems unfair. The restaurant only has two seats, so you never get to eat there. Enjoy the food."

"But you don't," Weeks said, "enjoy the food, that is. You make them serve you those horrible food trays."

"They're not horrible. I like them," Scruggs said. "And they don't have to serve me anything. I'll eat their regular food if they made me. I just don't want to."

"Don't want to? Don't want to eat food specially cooked for you by a master chef at a five-star restaurant, but they make you. So cruel, these cruise liners. So cruel. But maybe—no, Hernandez will be mad at missing things. You can go with her later."

"She's going to be at the gym for at least two hours doing some sort of Marathon run thing. And I'm hungry now."

"Two hours won't kill you," Weeks said.

"The med bay says I should eat before taking my pills. And my prescription has changed. I take them earlier now."

That was a lie. She'd stopped taking the painkillers completely two weeks ago. It hurt, but she could stand it.

"Well..."

Scruggs arranged her towel to show more leg. "Please? I'm hungry. I need my pills, and Hernandez is great and all, but it would be nice to have somebody different to talk to for a change."

"Well..." Weeks said again.

"And they're serving duck tonight," Scruggs said.

"I like duck."

"You can have mine. I always give my meal to Hernandez."

Weeks nodded. "Okay. Are you going dressed like that?"

"Like what? Oh." Scruggs pulled on her towels. "No, I'm not going to wear these."

"Well, if you do decide to do that, you might want to fix the back."

"What's wrong with the back?" Scruggs checked and realized the second towel had become unwound. Her butt was visible and had been the whole time.

***

"Ms. Scruggs, welcome back this evening," her favorite waiter, Brendan, said.

"Hello, Brendan. This is Mr. Weeks. He'll be joining us tonight."

"Of course, your usual table is ready." Brendan led them to the back.

"Swanky," Weeks said. He was wearing black pants, a black-collared shirt, and black ship boots. He'd grown his beard and mustache out so his face was peppered with black hair. He'd be hard to find in the dark. "What are they eating over there? It seems popular."

A quarter of the tables had china plates with piles of red, green, and blue mush on them, accompanied by glasses of orange liquid.

"Ms. Scruggs was gracious enough to allow the chef to share her recipe with the other patrons," Brendan said. "They are eating his special basic meal plate."

"Basic meal plate?" Weeks peered at a plate on a nearby table as they sat. "But isn't that just a pile of—"

"We'll need the menus tonight, Brendan," Scruggs said. "Mr. Weeks will want to read what's available."

"Of course, of course," Brendan said, stepping away.

Weeks waited till he had left. "Are all those people eating cheap tray mush on expensive china?"

"Yes, with glasses of basic on the side."

"Do they know what it is?"

"All they know is that they're getting charged a fortune for it. It's in limited supply—not everyone who orders it can have it, and that the special VIP table with its own waitstaff gets it every meal."

"Trays taste horrible," Weeks said. "I've had to live on them for months before."

"I like them," Scruggs said.

"You're the only one in the entire galaxy, kiddo. And this is a big galaxy. You're telling me these pretentious fops like what they're eating?"

"Nope," Scruggs said. "Liking it has nothing to do with it. They need to act fashionable. And stop calling me kiddo."

Weeks raised his eyebrows. "They'll eat cheap trash to seem smart."

"Seeming is more important than being to some people," Scruggs said. "That's why I left home."

"Ran away?"

"Only children run away. Well, at the start, but later, I left."

"I heard you hijacked a starship."

"My uncle's people were tracking me down. I needed to get away from that station before they brought me back."

"Why didn't you say no?"

"They can be very persuasive."

"And you didn't stand up to them?"

Scruggs scooped more basic up. "You're on a starship heading to the core, 'babysitting some little girl,' as I heard you tell Hernandez. Why didn't you stand up to that?"

"That's different. This is our job."

"You joined the navy to be a babysitter?"

Weeks's duck arrived, and he dug into it. "Not really."

"Why did you? Join the navy, I mean?"

"I don't share personal secrets with..."

"With criminals? Thieves? Traitors? Children? Little girls? Which one of these am I?" Scruggs said. "I'll tell you. None of them. I'm trying to make my way, and somebody important wants to stop me for some reason. What have I done wrong, exactly?"

"Well"—Weeks chewed more—"none of those, I guess. But you must have done something."

"That's why you've kidnapped me—I must have done something? Great logic training in the navy."

"Nope. Hernandez and I checked this out. The tribune is the Emperor's proxy. He can legally order you detained, which he did. His orders to us were specific. Escort you using the 'minimum amount of coercion and restraint necessary' to the nearest directly appointed palace official."

"Palace official?"

"Somebody who personally works directly for the Emperor, not a cabinet position, not an independent department."

"I don't understand."

"The warrant wasn't issued by the navy or internal security or whoever. It was issued by the royal family. So, the tribune has to follow it, and we have to follow the tribune's orders. And we have to deliver you to a palace official. We can't dump you at a local police station somewhere."

"So, the whole Empire is out to get me?" Scruggs said.

"Technically, yes, according to Hernandez," Weeks said. "But the flip side is that, according to her, Imperial Palace warrants have to be presented to the senate to be valid, so all the Senators read them. That way, they can decide if the Emperor is exceeding his authority."

Scruggs slurped up more of her tray. "Thanks for your help."

"I'm doing my job. And there are worse ways to get

arrested. And it was my family."

"Your family what?"

"Everybody in my family joined the navy—or tried to. Except stupid cousin Carlos, who joined the marines. But we all join the Imperial forces—or try to—do our one tour and then get on with our lives."

"Why?"

"Habit," Weeks said. "Seemed like a good idea. All my cousins, me, we get out of school, join the military for a few years, then get on with our lives."

"And stick with military jobs?"

"Nope. My cousin's family, they run a real estate sales company. Him and his sisters were administrative officers. Afterward, they sell real estate. And my great uncle's kids are all in theater. Set design artists. They paint a lot."

"Military painters?"

"It happens. Camouflage. They had a fascinating discussion with me one night. They said that color-blind people make better sensor operators, since they see patterns differently. Interesting stuff. Why'd you run away? What were you looking for?"

Scruggs licked her spoon free of the white mush, then picked up the red. "Some people like to mix them together. I like them all kept separate. Keeps the tastes clear."

"They don't have any taste."

"They do. My mom was a professional dancer. She had some wild times when she was younger. Then she met my dad. He's a professor. He's boring. He's always been boring. He was a great dad. But he's always been boring. Growing up was boring. College town. Vacations when school was out. Mom sent me to classes. It was so... boring."

"Your life now isn't boring. It's kind of dangerous."

"It's been a lot dangerous," Scruggs said.

"Do you like it?"

"Not sure yet," Scruggs said. "People get hurt. And bad

things happen. I might get out of this later. I can always go back to being a professor's kid."

"Some people would be jealous of your resources."

"Not my fault," Scruggs said. "I didn't pick my parents. It just happened. I'm only trying to make my way."

"Lots of people would appreciate a boring life," Weeks said.

"Maybe I will, too, after I don't have one for a while," Scruggs said. "Only one way to find out."

The two chewed in silence.

Scruggs swallowed, stared at Weeks, and said, "You have pretty eyes."

Weeks burst out laughing. "Wow. You are so not good at this."

Scruggs blushed, glared at him, then laughed, too. "You do have pretty eyes."

"Other people, other women, have told me that. Good try, though."

Scruggs sighed. "Are you and Hernandez... ?"

Weeks shook his head. "Nope. She's like a sister to me. Besides, she likes older men. I think she fancied the tribune."

"Him? He's an old man. As old as my father."

"Maybe not that old," Weeks said. "And she's older than she looks. She's older than me. Good genes. And she likes decisiveness in her men. The tribune is decisive."

"Good luck to her," Scruggs said. "Meeting men is hard. Ones who don't want to meet your uncle through you, at least."

"It will get easier, for you at least."

"So, does that mean—"

"This is a job. I can't, won't get involved with you," Weeks said. "Not something I do."

"All right," Scruggs said.

And it was. Dena had coached her on this. The first step was to make them say no. Then be patient.

Weeks drank his wine. "Where does this rich uncle that

you and Hernandez talk about come in?"

"He's an engineer. He builds starships for the Empire. Lots of them. That was kind of fun. But only building them would be boring, too."

"She said you're rich."

"Apparently," Scruggs said, "he's rich. And he likes me, and I'm his closest relative, other than Mom and Dad. And they would be a disaster running a construction company. Even they know that. I've been away. I haven't been keeping up on things. But something happened. The crew of the ship knows who I am. Which means it was worthwhile for somebody important to keep track of me. That's disturbing."

"Because it means that they're interested in rich people?"

"Because they're interested in me, which means something has happened to my uncle that makes me important now."

CHAPTER FIFTEEN

"Fuel?" Dirk asked, tapping his comm.

"Check," Lee said. "Filled to the brim. Tribune was generous. I didn't know that Imperial ships were authorized to fuel civilian ships."

"There's probably some sort of rule about that, but he paid for it himself. Do you have a course yet?"

"Computing it now. It should be ready by the time you're done out there."

"I'll be up once we're settled back here. Out." He cut the intercom and examined the cargo hold.

Every food and spare storage locker was full, and extra crates were strapped to the deck. Gavin was using tie downs to hold them in place.

"Can this Tribune guy really buy fuel for other ships?" Gavin asked.

"I'm fairly certain he buys fuel for his own ship," Dirk said. "This design for a new frigate—the Pollux class, has been mooted for years. It was supposed to have great weapons, longer range, higher speed, a whole bunch of new stuff. But it's as big as old-school destroyers and costs twice as much to operate."

"What's that have to do with fuel?"

"It's not a surprise that Devin got this class of ship. The captain of an Imperial ship is usually a noble, and they pay for a whole bunch of extra things. The navy gives them a flat budget per man and per month, for food and consumables and suchlike. And allowances for distance traveled, jumps, and under power. But they ration how fast he can go and how often. I'll bet Devin has been buying his own fuel the whole time. And there's no way the navy paid for that dinner."

"He can afford to buy the fuel for a warship? An entire warship?"

"A fleet. A flotilla, anyway. I'll bet he's over-crewed to deal with all his purchases. His accounting section is probably super efficient."

"Warships have an accounting section?"

"Most important part of the ship," Dirk said. "You might survive a battle, but once fleet HQ accounting gets their hands into you, it's game over. They'll pester you till you're ready to walk out an air lock without a suit. Glad you could join us, Centurion."

Ana had appeared at the hatch. They were in zero G, so he floated in ahead of two marines from Pollux, pulling two large crates.

"Is the cargo loading finished?" Ana asked. "I tried to time it so that I wouldn't have to do any work. Thanks, marines." Ana shook the hands of the two marines who had towed the crates in, and they disappeared into the corridor. He pushed the one crate gently across the deck and strapped it in.

"It was finished, old man," Gavin said. "Till you brought more crates to tie down."

"Oh, I'm going to take care of this one myself," Ana said. He guided the second crate into one of the fenced off, secure areas. "In fact, I'm thinking of bringing these beauties into my quarters."

"Cargo goes in the cargo hold, Centurion," Dirk said. "That's why it's called the cargo hold. And they're too big regardless. Won't fit between your bunk and the wall. Did you supervise the weapons loading?"

"Of course, Navy. Half dozen boarding shotguns. Dozen revolvers. Shock sticks. And ammunition for everything."

"How much ammunition?"

"Hundred rounds for each, some extra spares. And they gave me ammo for my personal rifle and submachine gun."

"The marines treated you well," Dirk said.

"They did. They even gave me these beauties." Ana

popped the top of the crate he was strapping in and displayed a silver metal construct. It had a grip like a gun, an oversized magazine below, and an odd-looking barrel. Rather than a standard tube, a series of rings coiled around two parallel spikes. "Love the finish. It's almost sexy to hold." Ana ran his hand along the butt. "So smooth. Baby smooth." He rubbed the barrel along his cheek. "So soft. So deadly."

Dirk and Gavin exchanged glances. "Whatever it is," Gavin said, "I don't think it should be in your room alone with you."

"You afraid I'll shoot myself, punk?"

"Do something to yourself, at least." Dirk extended his hand. "Can I see that, Centurion?"

Ana pulled the gun back. "Are your hands clean?"

"Are my hands—what in the Emperor's name?" Dirk said.

Dena wandered back from the lounge, where she had been working. "All the food is stowed. We have a six-month supply packed away, at least, and other crates back here. And they gave us three more crates of basic than we need or can stow. Gavin put it somewhere in the back. Is that a new toy for you, Centurion?"

"Oh, yes," Ana said, caressing it and smiling.

Dena shielded her eyes with her hand. "No. More. Smiles. And that one is extra creepy. Stop that. That's a funny-looking gun. What is it?"

"It's an Imperial Gauss gun," Dirk said. "Am I right, Centurion?"

Ana nodded.

"What's a guess gun?" Dena asked.

"Gauss. Powerful magnets and a strong, long-lasting battery. It uses metal needles. The magnets accelerate the needles along a guide to the target."

"You're going to sting people to death?" Dena asked. "With actual pinpricks?"

"The needles go so fast," Dirk said, "that they go right

through skin and clothes and bone and most armor for that matter. Plus, when they hit something solid, they have so much kinetic energy they explode. With that one gun, the centurion can take on a squad of marines behind cover, shoot through the cover, and kill them."

"Pretty cool weapon. Why haven't I seen them before?"

"They're expensive, and they're restricted. Only senior marine officers have them. And they have some drawbacks."

"Such as?"

Ana put the Gauss gun back in its case. "The barrel is short, so accuracy is a problem. And the needles go so fast that they go through people, so if you shoot a person in the arm, or the leg, it hurts, and it might cause internal injuries. But sometimes, it leaves a pin hole all the way through, and the heat cauterizes the injury instantly, so people don't feel it. You can't shoot to wound. You have to kill people with your first shot or mow them in half with rapid fire."

"Sounds wonderful, mowing people in half. Great way to spend your time," Dena said. "Happy birthday. What's in the other box?"

"Ammunition," Ana said. "Ten thousand needles."

"Ten thousand? Ten thousand needles. What you need that for?"

"To shoot five thousand people," Ana said.

"Five thousand?"

"Sure. You always double tap," Ana said.

"Why not shoot three thousand three hundred and thirty-three in three rounds?" Gavin said.

"That's crazy talk." Ana closed the crate. "Three shots is wasteful. Waste not, want not."

Dena, Gavin, and Dirk traded looks.

"Are we finished in here, then?" Dirk asked.

"All set, Skipper," Gavin said. "Cargo is secured. Engineering is ready to go. And Devin's crew replaced a bunch of pumps, seals, and things on my list. For the first time in months, we're up to speed on regular maintenance."

"Food's all set," Dena said. "Trays for you boys for weeks. And those technical people that Devin sent fixed all the things in the galley that the engineer ignored for months."

"The microwave doesn't grind now?" Dirk asked.

"Nope."

"Outstanding," Ana said.

"They were supposed to upgrade the sensors," Gavin said.

"They said we didn't have the software," Dena said, "and we only use the sensors once a month, but we had to listen to that stupid microwave every day."

"You traded a working microwave for military class sensors?" Gavin said.

"They put something in, a better telescope. And our radar detector is better now. It can tell what type of ship has that radar pulse, and we can record something—sensor signatures, so we can tell which ship uses that combination of radar and infrared and such like."

"Everything helps," Dirk agreed. "Let's get going then. Centurion, can you stop playing with your guns?"

"Unfortunate choice of words," Gavin muttered.

"What?" Ana looked up. "Sorry, Navy, let's get going." He patted the crate top. "Five thousand people. I can't wait."

***

Dirk's radio farewells to the Pollux were terse. Pollux's bridge crew was occupied in some sort of complicated three-way shipping issue. Apparently, they had chartered a freighter but had neglected to hire the crew along with the freighter, and the watch officer was convincing them to stay on board till the contract could be finalized.

Dirk spoke instead to Imin.

"Thanks again for dinner, Chief."

"No problem, Lord Duke."

"It's Dirk to you. I don't suppose you'll give me any recipes?"

"Not before the heat death of the universe, no, Lord Duke."

"It's like that, huh? Not even if I did anything for you?"

"You're a criminal deserter who fled Imperial jurisdiction and committed crimes—'too numerous to mention,' according to the pardon document I saw."

"They're not that numerous," Dirk said. "I could list them easily."

"Okay, list them, then," Imin said. "Quickly."

"I mean—never mind. When does the fleet leave for Sand Harbor?"

"First, that's classified," Imin said. "And second, it will be when the tribune decides it's time to go, and third, that could be a long time."

"The tribune's not a man to dawdle," Dirk said.

"He's not. Which is fine if you have one ship going from prepared base to prepared base, but he needs a small fleet, the marines, scouts, all of that. He's never done it before, and he's over his head."

"I've never heard the tribune admit that."

"Doesn't mean it isn't so, Lord Duke. He spends most of the day yelling at his staff."

"Why is he yelling at the staff?"

"Duke," Imin said, "there're officers and ratings on this ship who can run the targeting software on every weapon we have and most weapons we don't have. There're engineers who know how to configure the settings for every type of jump, run every sensor, configure every computer in the fleet. If the tribune called for volunteers to get onto the hull and jump at that station with knives in their teeth and take it back from the Confeds, we wouldn't have enough skinsuits or knives to fit out all the volunteers. But line us all up and ask us how much fuel we need to collect to support the ships that support the ships that fuel the other ships, and we mostly stare at each other. Or ask us how many days' rations can be packed in a standard container and what it costs. We look at each other like concussed tabbos. None of us have ever done anything like this before, and every theory we've come up with crashes into the harsh reality of things we don't know."

"We want to help," Dirk said. "We owe the tribune."

"You can help by getting your friend. He sweats over the fact that he promised to look after her, and now, he can't. He's upset about letting your Praetorian down. You take care of that, and he'll be happy." Imin frowned. "But if you do come across a fleet logistics support ship, send it this way."

"I will," Dirk said. "Good luck, Imin."

"The Empire," Imin said, saluting.

Dirk returned the salute and checked Lee's course. "I didn't realize you knew the tribune that well," Dirk said to Lee.

"He was my priest for a while," Lee said.

"You didn't say anything before, when we talked," Dirk said.

"What was there to say?"

"Hey, that's my priest? And he's not a real priest. He's a naval officer."

"He trained when he was younger. His family sent him. He was consecrated but then not assigned."

"What happened?"

"His brother died..."

"Right. He had to go into the navy, then. But I thought his sister was the heir."

"She was. Is. But when she became Empress, she lost all that."

"Aha," Dirk said. "I'd forgotten that happens." Sitting Emperors or Empresses had to abdicate all other titles and rents. That way, all their money had to go through the senate.

"No private means for the crown," Lee said.

"Still, you should have told me," Dirk said.

"It didn't matter," Lee said. "And it would have made you suspicious of why I was with you."

"Why were you?" Dirk said.

"Lord Devin said I needed perspective. So, I went out to the universe. I was disappointed by the people I met, my fellow Praetorians. They're not as loyal—or, well, as good as they should have been. Not like you."

"Not like us?" Dirk said. "What do you mean?"

"You stole a ship, but it's not listed as stolen now. You were arrested and jailed, then escaped, but your warrant has been canceled. You're a free man. Why are you going to help Scruggs?"

"Why are you?"

"Because she helped me. I think of her as a sister. Because it's the right thing to do."

"I can't abandon her. She's crew."

"So, you're heading back into the middle of the Empire that arrested you, betrayed you, chased you, and made you into a criminal because it's the right thing to do? That's why we're rescuing Scruggs?"

"That's exactly why we're rescuing Scruggs," Ana said, sliding into the seats from behind. "Because it's the right thing to do. Navy here promised we'd go help her. Also, I'll kill you all if you don't help me."

"You do enjoy your threats, don't you, old man." Dena said, strapping into the seat next to Ana.

"Enjoy is too strong a word," Ana said. "Let's say they comfort me."

"Glad that we're comforting you, then," Dena said. "Dirk, are we going soon?"

"Yes, computer has to calculate our course to the jump point. Lots of junk in this system. Centurion, you do understand that, if you kill us, we can't help find Scruggs?"

"I know that, Navy," Ana said. "You're all safe for now."

"Thank the Empress, then," Dena said. "Otherwise, he'd be threatening to pull out our intestines and strangle us with them if we don't get going."

"Don't be silly, Nature Girl," Ana said. "I wouldn't say that."

"Because maybe you're starting to appreciate that we're on your side?" Dena asked.

"Of course not," Ana said. "It's because it's factually incorrect. It doesn't work. If you drag somebody's intestines out and try to strangle them with them, you can't get them tight enough. They're so slippery they kind of slide around the neck. Takes too long. The person dies of shock before you suffocate them."

The computer bonged.

"And it's not important how I know that. Oh, look. Course is set. Off we go." Ana smiled. "Adventure awaits."

CHAPTER SIXTEEN

"Can't I just say execute, execute, execute?" Devin asked. "Details bore me."

"You're the commander. You can do what you like," Lionel said.

They had returned to the bridge after seeing the various ships' crews off at the shuttle dock.

"But you don't think that's a good idea," Devin said.

"No. First, if you're going to be a task force commander, you need to act like one," Lionel said. "Ask for status reports on the ships under your command to start."

"Pollux is ready," Devin said. "Pollux is always ready, thanks to you and the crew. Let's go kill enemies of the Empire."

"I agree. Let's," Lionel said. He folded his hands.

Devin sat in the bridge chair and glared at him. His favorite scan technician was on duty, sitting in the navigator's chair. "Deguals?"

"Tribune?"

"I plan to single-handedly conquer the entire Confederation of States. You, me, and a few others will surge beyond the borders, defeat their navy, and occupy their capital world."

"Outstanding, Tribune. We're all with you. May I begin plotting the jumps to take us into battle?"

"I was hoping you would say that." Devin said. "Execute."

"One moment." Deguals fiddled with his board.

"Why are you at navigation, Deguals? You're normally at scan."

"The subprefect said I could cross-train, Tribune."

"He made you?"

"I volunteered, sir. If I have to be in the navy, I want to

learn as much as I can."

"So, you wanted to learn navigation?"

"No, sir. I wanted to make sure I'm always on your ship, no matter what I have to do. Course laid in, Tribune. Permission to drive to the jump limit to execute jump one of two hundred and forty-six?"

"Say again?" Devin said.

"Jump one of two hundred forty-six, Tribune. Your permission."

"How many jumps was that?"

"Two hundred forty-six, Tribune."

"We're two hundred forty-six jumps from the capital of the Confederation of States?"

"No, sir."

"Good, I was worried for a moment."

"It's actually two hundred forty-seven. I felt that they would surrender to us once we arrived at their adjacent military depot. After having defeated the entire combined fleets of the confederation between us and their capital, of course."

"I see," Devin said. "Out of curiosity, how were we going to do that?"

"I was hoping they would line up, sir. Then we could use our lasers—well, positron guns—to destroy more than one at once. It would have to be a tight line, though, and they'd need to be close together for it to work." Deguals nodded to Devin. "And it would take a long time. The confederation navy has a great many ships, sir."

Devin grunted, then turned to Lionel, who kept his arms crossed. "It's not nice to mock your commander, Subprefect."

"Who's mocking?" Lionel asked. "Give the order, and we're all going to go charging in. Stopping for the enemy to line up and be killed as necessary."

"We need to have a meeting, don't we?" Devin asked.

"Staff is on the way," Lionel said, "with the tribune's permission?"

"Emperor's hairy armpits," Devin said. "This was easier when I was younger."

"Most things are," Lionel muttered. "Most things are."

It took twenty minutes to get the necessary staff into the tribune's office.

Santana's ship linked in as well.

"Right, Tribune," Lionel said. "Commander's goal. Recapture Sand Harbor? Chastise the enemy? Minimize casualties?"

"In that order," Devin said. "Talk to me."

"What's our issues for recapturing Sand Harbor?" Lionel asked the assembled group.

Heads of every department were there, either in the office or on video links.

"Fuel," the engineering officer said. "We can't run out of fuel in an enemy controlled system. If we don't have enough fuel to jump out, we're dead if we encounter a superior force. Or even a motivated inferior one."

"So, we bring fuel with us," Devin said.

"We can do that, sir. Who will protect us while we refuel?"

Devin motioned at the planetary list on the screen. "We can go into the gas giant... No, we can't. They'll chase us, stop us from fueling. And we can't refuel in-system, because we can't maneuver while we are fueling."

Lionel put a map of the Sand Harbor system on the screen and highlighted it. "Nothing smaller than us and not many things bigger can come within the range of our beams and live. Problem is, if they don't come within the range, they can wait us out."

"We need fuel to get in and get out. I assume you have a solution?" Devin asked.

"Tankers," the engineering officer said, "or ships converted to tankers. We do some work on some local ships, we jump with them, arrive in a nearby system, jump to Sand Harbor with full tanks. We can maneuver all we want, fight all we want, and anybody who is damaged or overwhelmed can jump back to the tankers, refuel, and flee."

"Planning to fail?" Devin asked. "Seems a bit dishonorable."

"If the tribune would like to make a statement regarding the courage of his officers or the crew of his ships, then he should make a direct accusation," Lionel said. "One that could be answered by facts. Otherwise—"

"Otherwise, he should keep his mouth shut." Devin looked at the video displays, catching the eyes of each one. "I apologize, Subprefect. I'm frustrated. Not a man or women here who hasn't followed me, no matter what the odds. Continue with your briefing, please."

"Engineer?"

"Three merchant ships, Subprefect. Loaded to the brim with fuel. Extra containers with extra fuel bladders. We load them up, and they jump with us. We refuel from them as needed, stop one system short of Sand Harbor, take on the last of the fuel and jump in. They have to wait there. If worse comes to worse, when we jump back, they'll have enough fuel to pull us back from pursuit."

Lines of numbers appeared on the screen. Lionel and Devin stared at it.

"Subprefect," Devin said, "you know that I'm not actually a moron. I just play one for effect. But that's a lot of fuel. More than we need."

"More than we need," agreed Lionel. "But not more than our task force will need. Our freighters, tankers, whatever, they need fuel, too. And their escorts will need fuel."

"Of course we need to leave an escort with them," Devin said. "I get that, but still—"

"Second problem, Tribune, Subprefect," said the logistics officer, "will be consumables, spare parts, and so on."

Devin watched the discussion play out. This had obviously been prepared in advance, or they knew their jobs so well they knew when to interject. He listened to the engineering's, logistics', and weapons officers range over their requirements.

"Right," Devin said, after almost an hour. "If I understand all you properly, we need three tankers and three more general cargo ships that we requisition, take a week to reconfigure or load up, and we can have the whole thing set up in six weeks?"

"Correct," Lionel said. "We can go in four, with a smaller margin in fuel and consumables, and we'll be in trouble if we have a major defeat. We'll lose a few ships getting back. If we wait till six weeks, that's the most conservative. Nothing good happens after that."

"Santana?" Devin said.

The marines had said nothing during the last hour.

"The Valhalla will deploy to recapture the Imperial base as soon as the navy puts us in proximity to it," Santana said.

"You'd prefer sooner rather than later," Devin said.

"I'd prefer tomorrow, Tribune," Santana said, "or mid next shift. That will never happen, though. But we have to assume their defenses will improve given time."

"Improve by how much?"

Santana shrugged. "No way to tell. But the longer we wait, the higher the casualties will be."

"How many." Devin licked his lips. He'd never asked this question exactly this way. "How many more marines will die for every day we spend out here?"

Santana shrugged again. "No way to tell exactly, Tribune. More than zero. Less than a thousand."

"Why pick a thousand?"

"That's more than all the people under my command. No matter how badly you screw up, that's the worst you can do."

Devin folded his arms and sat silently, looked each person in the eyes, then at the video links. "Subprefect, what's our best mix of delay and action? How soon should we move?"

"Two weeks, Tribune," Lionel said. "Do as much of this as we can in two weeks, then jump with what we have. In a month, the battle of Sand Harbor starts."

"Longer isn't good?"

"Perhaps. I don't think so."

Devin polled his officers. They all wanted longer. They all said they'd have some things done in two weeks but much more would still be undone.

"Lieutenant Kent," Devin said to the engineering officer in charge of fueling. "Will the fleet be optimally fueled and ready in two weeks, given what you've heard?"

"No, sir," the lieutenant said. "It's possible, and even with bad luck, we'll be close enough to go, but it won't be optimal."

"What will you do if I order us to attack in two weeks?" Devin asked.

"Sir." The lieutenant gave a full formal salute. "Current ad bellum. The Empire."

"The Empire," Devin agreed, returning the salute. He punched the intercom. "Helm?"

"Sir?"

"Do you have a course for Sand Harbor?"

"Sir, I do. The subprefect has given me a plan for the task force."

"Execute it fourteen days from right now. Mark."

"In the computer, sir."

"Outstanding. Everyone, we sail for battle not later than fourteen days from now. Current ad bellum." He gave the formal cross-chest salute. "The Empire."

"The Empire," everyone answered.

***

It was, of course, not that simple.

"Captain Ramisa," Devin said, checking the captain's name on his screen. "I understand your concerns, but I do not share them."

His engineers had done sensor scans of all the freighters in the system and given him lists of the ones with the highest fuel capacity, as well as those most likely to have the needed supplies. One purpose-built tanker carried nothing but hydrogen and oxygen, but it wouldn't be enough by itself. It was orbiting the planet but wasn't answering calls. His communications officer was trying to chase it down. In the meantime, he was going through the list of other ships they would need.

Captain Ramisa was tall, dark, and belligerent—not the type of man you wanted to have yelling at you if you were trying to get something done.

"Which means they aren't your concerns, then," he said. "Because any fool with half a brain would realize what I'm saying is true."

"Nothing is going to happen to your ship," Devin said. "We need supplies hauled to nearby systems. Supplies which you already have on board."

"If nothing is going to happen to us, why do we need warships with us? No thankee, I'll stay here and do my regular route."

"Your ship is advertised up for charter. We want to charter it."

"I'm up for charter to carry container loads of custom drugs from one industrial planet to another, from a high port to a high port, drop a container at the container farm, and have a tug slot a different one in, and get paid that day. I'm not interested in taking myself away from my regular customers for three months. I've got commitments. If I break them, I'll get sued."

"We pay well," Devin said.

"Pay well once. I've got multiyear contracts with some of these factories. And they pay shipping invoices on delivery. I've worked for the navy before. You have to file paperwork and paperwork and wait for it to be queried, then amended, then sent to a different office. One bill took two years to be paid, and that was only for eighty percent of the promised charges. They excluded my fuel escalation clause as 'not negotiated properly.'"

"I promise you the navy will pay. If necessary, I will make good myself."

"You say that now. I call you up two years from now, and you'll be asking who am I again?"

Devin leaned into his video pickup. "Are you questioning my honor, sir?"

"Just your memory. And not to put too fine a point on it, Tribune," Ramisa said. "This is some sort of military operation, going some distance. Which means the Confeds. What happens if you get killed during it? Where's your guarantee then?"

"I serve the Empire," Devin said.

"And I pay for it, through taxes, on trade income, which I can't earn if I cut loose my regular customers to go off on some ill-advised jaunt across trackless space. My ship is not open for charter. Good day to you, Tribune." Captain Ramisa cut the connection.

Devin stared at the screen, then at Lionel, standing nearby. "Did he hang up on me? Hang up? On me? An Imperial tribune?"

"I don't think he thinks of it as hanging up on a tribune. I think he sees it as avoiding an annoying customer who isn't worth the trouble."

"This is why I didn't go into trade," Devin said.

"You didn't go into trade because you are fabulously wealthy already and had no need to earn a living while messing with the navy and, apparently, the priesthood," Lionel said.

"Have any of the captains responded positively?"

"One. A Captain Lesana, but she wanted to talk to you directly. She's the one with all the food and similar consumables. She'll sell us the whole shot. Even deliver it."

"Let's talk to her, then," Devin said.

It took only ten minutes before a thin woman in a blue

coverall with captain's stripes was on the screen.

"Tribune, a great pleasure to meet you."

"You're the only one, then," Devin said. "Everybody else hangs up on me."

"Who wouldn't want to meet the Mad Dog of the Verge?" she said. "Is it true that you spaced a shipload of pirates?"

"Not a whole shipload, exactly—"

"And you single-handedly executed some treasonous locals at Bishop's World?"

"I didn't—Captain, I want to buy your cargo, all of it. And have you ship it to a destination of our choice. I'll pay well."

Lesana straightened on the video. "Your subprefect said that. I gave him a complete inventory. Food trays. Cleaning equipment. Clothes, belts, shoes, undergarments. Spare parts—nothing military, the spare parts. Refrigeration units, toasters, wire, that sort of thing."

"We'll take it all, provided you deliver it in your ship. We can't tell you the destination, exactly, but—"

"The subprefect has our fuel capacity and range. He says we'll be away less than a month, and you'll provide refueling along the way and back."

"That's correct," Devin said. "You have no complaints?"

"None at all. The hire sounds straightforward. Our standard contracts will handle it. If the final destination for the goods is an austere environment, we're not equipped to unload the containers there. You'll handle that with your crew."

"Of course we can figure that out," Devin said. "It shouldn't be a problem."

Lesana nodded. "Have you ever undertaken deep-space ship-to-ship operations before, Tribune?"

"No, but how hard can it be?" Devin asked.

"Indeed. Well, in any case, the contract will stipulate that we're only onsite at the transfer point for seven days, and after that, we depart with any remaining goods."

"Of course," Devin said. "Seven days is more than enough time."

"Then, we have a deal," Lesana said. "Tribune, I heard you personally executed those traitors back on Bishop's World?"

"That's the duty of a tribune sitting as a judge," Devin said. "It was necessary. I take no pleasure in it."

"I understand you did it with a sword."

"I... yes. A sword is traditional."

"Cut their heads off. With one blow."

"We don't normally cut heads off. It's not that simple. Perhaps, perhaps we can change the subject."

"I would love to see that sword. Take a look at it. Run my hands over it."

"Umm." Devin waved to Lionel to interrupt him.

Lionel, off camera, shook his head and grinned.

"Perhaps you could come for dinner during this journey. Bring the sword with you."

"I regret that my duties won't allow me such leisure."

"That's a shame." Lesana licked her lips. "Perhaps I could come by for dinner myself sometime. You could show it to me. The sword, I mean."

Devin kept making cutting motions with his hand, but Lionel had stepped back, blocking the commo officers view, so Devin couldn't claim he wasn't obeying orders.

"I don't think that would be possible."

"Dinner would be marvelous," Lesana said. "You could wear your sword, and I have my captain's outfit, of course. Not like this one, my formal one. It's more—"

"Sorry, I have to go," Devin said. "Comm, cut transmission. Now."

The channel chopped at once.

"Why didn't you cut the channel instantly?" Devin asked.

"We always obey the tribune's properly formatted requests," Lionel said. "But sometimes, you can be confusing. Best to make your orders in a dignified manner."

"To the gods with my dignity."

"I believe that woman wanted to get her hands on your sword," Lionel said.

"Or something else. Under no circumstances is she allowed on this ship. Ever. Not now, not during the voyage, not in the future."

"Understood, Tribune." Lionel's console bonged, and he checked it. "She signed the agreement we sent over. She's already loaded up. We have to give her a departure date and a course."

"Good." Devin bit his lip. "Did you get that part about the cargo transfer? Ship-to-ship operations?"

"No. But it's too late now. As you said before, how hard can it be?"

A call down to engineering proved it could be very hard indeed. The engineer finally tracked down a chief petty officer, who'd been on a merchant run before.

"Air locks, Tribune. Cargo air locks, we don't have them," the PO said.

"We have plenty of air locks. Six, if I recall."

"For people, sir, but not for goods. The shuttles have their own locks, but they're designed to only mate to them. We've got cargo hatches, not air locks. And we can open the hatches to get into the hold, but that means we have to depressurize the whole hold. Some items can't stand that. And then there're the questions of how we get everything out of those containers and across to us."

"How do they do it on station?" Devin asked.

"Containers mate to a container lock, pop the doors open, and you're connected to the station, then deliver as needed. They have moving belts and electric carts. In deep-space special ships, with internal container locks, can break bulk inside their cargo bay. They have special locks that mate to our cargo hatches, so we don't need internal locks. She can't do that. How many containers, Tribune?"

"And if you tell them when I'm going..."

"I don't know when you're going, Miss," Brendan said. "I'll get your drinks now."

Hernandez frowned at Scruggs after Brendan left. "This is a stupid game. Stop encouraging these people."

"I'm not encouraging anybody," Scruggs said. "I haven't spoken to any of these people, nor have I given Brendan any information. People were going to ask about us, and by giving him the extra tip, I make sure we get the latest information on who's asking what."

"How do you know this?"

"Rich people spy on each other. The easiest way to do it is to bribe the staff. This way Brendan's on our side, and he won't let anything out we don't know."

"It must be strange being rich," Hernandez said.

"I wouldn't know," Scruggs said. "I heard all this second hand."

Brendan returned with their drinks.

"Anything else new, Brendan?" Scruggs asked.

"Ms. Watson continues to press her son to meet you, but he's chasing a team of female volleyball players traveling to the sector finals."

"Who on the team is he chasing?" Scruggs asked.

"My information is three of them. Together. At the same time."

"Ewwww," Scruggs and Hernandez said together.

"Yes, I'd suggest washing your hands after if you are ever introduced," Brendan said. "But one curious thing."

"What?" Scruggs said before drinking her basic down.

Brendan turned so his back was to the door. "Those two couples behind me, the ones to the right of the door, offered me a substantial bribe to point you out when you came in, and to answer questions—what time you came and so on."

Hernandez flicked her eyes at the group, then to Brendan. "Really? They're not even looking at us."

"They haven't looked at you since you came in,"

Brendan said. "I was watching. But earlier, they were interested in the two of you, and your other friend, how often he accompanies you, that sort of thing. And they bought their tables."

"What does that mean?" Hernandez said.

"They paid the regulars—Salis, and who else had it, tomorrow. Tom Tomkins? Either way, both groups contacted the management and said these others would be using their reservations this week. That usually happens only when good friends are on board or when money changes hands."

"Maybe they're friends with both families?" Scruggs said.

"The Tomkins and the Salis boarded at different times, in different planetary systems. They've never spoken to each other. Not in my presence, at least. They didn't act like they knew each other."

Scruggs scraped up some basic paste. "I guess they're just interested in new people. Where did they board from? We weren't scheduled to dock anywhere for two days."

"They didn't come from a dock," Brendan said. "They came from another ship with a shuttle that met us here. Another cruise liner."

"You can do that?" Hernandez asked. "Divert a cruise liner to meet with another one?"

"You can," Brendan said. "But it's expensive."

"I've never heard of that," Scruggs said. "That's a first for me."

"First for me, too," Brendan said. "We've never done it before. I've never even heard of it being done before."

"I guess that they're special," Scruggs said.

"Somebody's special," Hernandez said. "Might not be them."

***

"Weapons check," Hernandez told Weeks the next morning after Scruggs went into her room. "We should be armed when taking her out from now on."

"Why?" Weeks said. "What's happening?" He sounded querulous but also reached into a bag nearby and pulled his revolver out.

"The opposition is here. Two couples showed up yesterday—two young couples. Two fit-looking young couples. This morning, they ignored us."

Weeks flipped the cylinder out of his revolver and popped the shells into his hand. "You're upset because they didn't pay attention to you?"

"I'm upset that two young men went out of their way to not look at me, especially when I was on my way to the gym later, dressed like this." Hernandez gestured—she was wearing skintight leggings, exercise shoes, and a crop top, displaying lots of tanned skin.

"I'd jump you if we weren't working together," Weeks said. He rolled his sleeve up and flexed his bicep. "What do you think?"

"I can do better," Hernandez said.

Weeks laughed and reloaded his revolver, methodically inspecting the bullets before clicking them into the cylinder.

Hernandez finished checking her own revolver, then holstered it.

Weeks snapped on his own holster and fitted it under his armpit, then covered it with a jacket from the closet. He pointed at Hernandez's holster. "If the ship's staff sees you with a weapon displayed, they'll go insane. Especially if the other passengers see it."

She frowned down at her outfit. "Hard to hide something here. I'll need a purse or something."

He stepped into the fresher and returned with a towel he threw at her. "Hide it in that."

"Good idea. Keep an eye out while you take her on her rounds. What's today? Casino, cards, or promenade?"

"My least favorite," Weeks said. "Clothes shopping. Again."

"That girl has turned out to be a clothes horse. I wouldn't have expected it from the descriptions."

"She doesn't just buy them. She rents them or something like it. But she's always returning one thing or another and replacing them with something else."

"Hernandez," Weeks said, "why do we have to do this?"

"Because the tribune ordered us to and pulled major rank to override what Naval Intelligence told us and took over our tasking."

"No, why are we taking her in? And why is she going along? She's an adult. She could walk away from us. We don't need to hide her. We could announce that she's along?"

"She can walk away from us if she wants," Hernandez said. "But then she'd be transported by some sector governor or something in the hold of a cargo ship, not first class on a liner paid for by his greatness Devin, Lord Lyon. Why would she walk away from us? The door's open if she wants to escape. Besides, she's hurt worse than she lets on. She sleeps a lot, and those pills the doctor gave her are strong. I looked them up."

"She's a good kid," Weeks said. "I feel bad for her. She hit on me the other day. Asked me to dinner."

"That can't be the first young girl who asked you to dinner—young woman, I should say. She's old enough to know her own mind."

"As you say. She knows her own mind, so why is she putting up with this warrant thing?"

"An adventure? I don't know."

"My real question is, which are we doing right now? Keeping her from"—Weeks hooked his fingers into air quotes—"'escaping'? Or are we protecting her from kidnappers or assassins or something."

"Nobody's going to hurt anybody under my protection," Hernandez said.

"Who's protecting who, though?"

166

"What do you mean?"

"The crew knows who she is—if she wanted it the captain would divert to circle the nearest black hole or something like that. The tribune made sure he's following the warrant he saw, but he did it in such a way that she can't possibly complain. We're a nuisance to her, but we're also keeping her safe for now. If she needs it. I hope it didn't escape your notice, but she's spent the last long while with a mercenary company. She must have picked up some skills."

"Where is this coming from?" Hernandez asked.

"This group you noticed. It doesn't sound good."

"Could be nothing."

"Then why did you have us arm up again?"

"Because... because it might not be nothing."

"Should we ask for help? Next station, we could go to the local Imperial base, show the tribune's order, ask for a guard squad or a transport."

"That's an overreaction, but maybe. I'll think about it."

Weeks looked at his comm. "Two days to whatever the next place is called. Middle of nowhere, just a turn to catch the liners coming in from confederation border space. Then that long run and we're in Antares."

"We'll be in Antares in a week. We can decide then."

Scruggs's door opened, and she stepped out, one hand leaning on a cane, the other carrying a box of clothes.

"Guess what time it is? Clothes shopping time!"

CHAPTER EIGHTEEN

Devin grunted as his sword stuck in the shoulder of the target dummy. He yanked. The dummy swayed, but the sword stayed stuck. The wooden stand and base plate tilted but didn't topple. He screamed in frustration, grasped the hilt, and yanked back. The dummy dragged across the floor, but the sword didn't unstick.

His vision dimmed, and he swung the sword back and up. The dummy followed, flipped up, and arced over his head. He slammed it headfirst into the floor behind him, knocking splinters off. He grunted, changed his grip, swung it in a circle at waist-level, spun it twice, then slammed the base plate into the wall. The wooden stand shattered, and the base plate flew off, struck the wall, and bounced away. The top half split vertically, and his sword came free.

He spread his legs, swung the sword above his head like an ax, then slammed it into the wooden torso, cracking it in half. He did it again and again, crying out each time. The final try snapped the remaining torso into three pieces and jammed the sword in the debris. He grunted, yanked the sword free, and let it drop.

He panted in the stillness. The sweat dripped down his face, and he transferred the sword to his right hand and used his left to wipe his brow. It came back covered with sweat and small pieces of wood, which he wiped off on his training robe.

A whisper caught his attention, and he jerked his head. The gym was full when he started. Two officers in the corner were muttering to each other but turned pale and silent when he looked. He swung back to the door. A rating released the intercom button he had been holding down. Devin glared and gasped for air.

Thirty seconds of silence later, the door slid open, and

Subprefect Lionel stepped in. He took in the sweating tribune, the silence, and the white-faced spaceman first class by the intercom.

"Deguals?" Lionel said, looking over Devin's shoulder.

Devin hadn't even noticed the rating behind him.

"Sir?"

"You're late for the officer's meeting. You better hurry."

"What officers—yes, sir. Right away."

Lionel gestured with his thumb. "All of the rest of you, if you leave now, you can make it as well."

The officers rushed to the door. Only two ratings at the intercom didn't move. "You two," Lionel said, "report to the officer of the watch on the bridge. Now."

They didn't even answer, just scurried out.

Devin staggered to the bench at the wall and slumped into it. "What do you want, Subprefect?"

"I have a report on our latest merchant conversion, Tribune. The Ester Barnby."

"Stupid name for a ship," Devin said. He wiped his sword.

"I agree. You want the good news or the bad news?"

"I could use some good news. Give it to me first."

Lionel sat. "Nobody died."

Devin stopped wiping his sword. "That's the good news? Nobody died? What's the bad part?"

"It had a fuel leak."

"A hydrogen leak?"

"And oxygen."

"Both?" Devin set his sword down on the ground. "Why aren't they all dead?"

"It didn't explode. Yet."

"The Emperor's sweaty armpits."

"It's been leaking for some time, we've been told. Problems with the gaskets at the entry ports. When the master used to fuel up before, it would vent to the void."

"He vented surplus fuel? At a fuel dock?"

"It leaked every single time it was fueled up. He didn't mention it. Nobody noticed or cared or whatever."

"They could have been killed or blown up a station or their fuel crew or random passers-by."

"Yep," Lionel said. "And guess when we found this out?"

"During our preflight safety check?"

"After we'd added the second internal tank. Our crew put the second tank in, checked all the couplings and the transfer pumps. For the new addition. They assumed that the crew would have told them any problems with the existing fuel system. Once they fueled up, it started leaking, and by the time they figured out what was happening, hydrogen and oxygen mixed all over the place. Inside and outside."

"All right," Devin said. "They'll have to drain both tanks and get that fuel out of there, right?"

Lionel shook his head.

"Why not? How hard is it to drain the tanks?"

"Guess where the drains are and what shape they're in?"

"The drains leak, too?"

"Yep."

"Why aren't these people dead already?"

"Don't know. Explains why the owner was so willing to charter for cheap."

"I don't understand," Devin said. "What does this have to do with the charter price?"

"She figured that we'd put extra stress on everything this voyage and something would blow."

"Her crew would be dead."

"Yeah, but she wasn't on board. And she has insurance. It would pay off handsomely."

"Emperor's mustache. What type of people are we dealing with here?"

"Just people. In any event, the conversion is now behind schedule. Again."

"They'll have to drain—no, they can't do that. Is it just sitting there?"

Lionel walked to the shredded dummy. He examined the front. "You're slashing again. Aren't you supposed to stab, like with a baton?"

"Stabbing is better, yes. I forget sometimes."

"I liked my baton training," Lionel said. "Imin's excellent with a baton. Did you know that?"

"He's good with everything," Devin said. "Any weapon, at least. This ship, the Ester Barnby, what's happening now?"

"The chief in charge ordered everybody off, jettisoned it from the repair frame, then reboarded it and has been jury rigging a nitrogen wash. He's been blowing gaseous nitrogen everywhere. Flushing out the liquid oxygen and hydrogen and so on. If he can get all of it out, he can pressurize the tanks with nitrogen and check for a leak. Then flush the internal atmosphere several times."

"If he gets it wrong, he'll blow up the whole ship."

"And himself. And nitrogen's not cheap here, by the way. We're paying through the nose for it."

"I don't care," Devin said. "Set this chief up for a medal of some sort."

"He's breaking all sorts of regulations by doing this. He should be in jail. It's supposed to be done by a full fleet decom unit."

"Another thing we don't have." Devin stood and kicked bits of the dummy across the floor. "How long?"

"That ship?"

"The whole show."

"Three weeks. A month, maybe. Everything is going wrong."

"What if I said go now?" Devin asked.

"Tribune. I might have to disagree. Publicly."

Devin stopped kicking the splintered wood. "You'd say something? To the crew?"

Lionel nodded.

"You've never done that before."

"You've never asked the crew to commit mass suicide before."

"I'll go by myself if I have to," Devin said.

"No, you won't. I'll be right there with you. So will all the others. But, Devin, it's not fair. It's not the right decision. All these kids. And what will it accomplish? If it would make a difference, I'd say do it. But we can't win. We can't even get there safely. Yet."

Devin picked up the largest piece of the broken dummy. "Where does Imin get the spares for this?"

"He buys them by the dozens," Lionel said. "Are you going to order us to go without the transports?"

"No. No, I can't do that. But we need to do something."

"We are doing something. We're getting there. Just not yet."

"I want to attack. I've been feeling frustrated."

Lionel kicked the piles of broken wood. "You don't say. Do you think anybody noticed?"

"Enough back talk. But, yes, I've got to stop taking out my backtalk on defenseless sword dummies."

"If it works, keep doing it. It makes the crew and you feel better. Sometimes, it's nice to break things."

Devin swung his sword in a circle. "Indeed. Break things. Indeed." He swung it again. "Break things."

Lionel raised his eyebrows. "Tribune?"

Devin went to the intercom and punched it. "Bridge?"

"Bridge here, sir."

"Officers call in my quarters in ten minutes. Stations for departure."

"Sir," the voice said, "should I inform the other ships?"

"No," Devin said. "Just the Pollux."

"Sir, Navigation is asking for a course, or at least a destination."

"Tell them we're going on a raid. We're going out to break things."

Imperial Hijacker

CHAPTER NINETEEN

"What's this place called again?" Ana said. "Planet of continual dust storms?"

Bakar-1b, second planet in the Bakar system, centered on the main screen. Whorls of brown and white covered the middle latitudes. Black, brown, and blue streaks extended southward from the poles, obscured by brown blotches.

"They're sand storms," Dirk said. "According to Subprefect Lionel's notes, it's coarse sand, not dust. Those are lakes up north, and they're water. Dirty water but water."

"Not according to sailing directions," Dena said. "I've been looking up each planet like you suggested, and it says no fuel or water here. Lots of storms. Big ones. And lots of wind."

"The Pollux went through here last year," Dirk said. "They did a survey as a matter of course. Lionel said that there was liquid water, but you needed to get a break in the storms to land."

"And I'm sure we can trust our Imperial masters to send us the safest way," Ana said. "I saw some red marks on that course plot Lee got from Milord Devin. Rogue comets? Asteroid debris? Excessive solar flare activity?"

"We need to take some unusual shortcuts to catch up with Scruggs," Dirk said. "Or would you rather we didn't do that? Just let her fly away? Goodbye, Private?"

Ana compressed his lips but shut up.

"Anything live there?" Dena asked, petting Rocky.

The entire crew except Gavin was seated in the control room, watching their approach. Gavin was, as usual, online from engineering.

"Nothing, according to Lionel," Dirk said. "There was an Imperial fueling base there for several hundred years, but it got closed down sometime last century, and everybody was evacuated."

"Why was it closed?" Dena asked. "If there really is fuel."

"No longer needed. Better jump drives, better navigation and charts. And population moves. Colonies were founded farther out and given a choice, freighters—or military ships for that matter—want to jump from inhabited world to inhabited world. More supplies, more people, more commercial opportunities. Once a new trade route opens up, old places get less and less traffic. And after a certain point, they close up unless the military subsidizes them. Now, the main trade route swings out to the Confed border, loops and comes back, on the other side of this rift."

"So, we're going this way, why?" Dena asked.

"Shortcut to Antares," Lee said. "And a way to beat Scruggs." She put two courses up on the screen. "Red is us. Blue is Scruggs's liner."

Dena studied the display. The blue line hopped from planet to planet in a dogleg out to nearly the confederation border, then swung back on a parallel course running deeper into the Empire. The red line cut the corner but crossed empty space.

"They have... eight jumps, and we have three. We'll beat Scruggs's ship."

"Glad you can count, Nature Girl," Ana said. "Useful skill to have. And, yes, we should be ahead of her ship by then. Provided we don't dawdle. Navy, you going to get us on the ground so we can refuel anytime soon?"

"Patience, Centurion," Dirk said. "Nobody wants to rescue Scruggs more than I do, but we need to do a few orbits to get a feel for those storms."

"If we don't find Scruggs before they kill her," Ana said, "and if it's somehow my fault, are you planning on cutting off my arms and beating me to death with them?"

Dirk turned. "I wasn't planning on it, no."

Ana smiled. "Since that would be my reaction to you if we fail, I'd say that I, at least, want to rescue her more than you do."

Dirk's drop was hair-raising, but they were on the ground without incident less than an hour later. The main ramp came down, pushing up swirls of dust, and Dena and Gavin climbed down, coughing. Rocky ran past them, wagging his tail, and circled the ship, peeing on each landing leg.

"Does he have to pee on the ship every time?" Gavin asked.

"It's his way of showing appreciation," Dena said. She gulped once, covered her mouth, and swallowed. "Blegh. At least I didn't puke this time. What a dump."

Silver-gray bushes dotted the slope. Stunted dark green trees lined the stream nearby. Rocky padded to the nearest bush, sniffed twice, then cocked a leg and peed on it. Dust puffed up as he scrambled uphill to the next cluster of bushes.

"I'm sure that bush appreciates being peed on," Gavin said.

"It's all in how you take it," Ana said, striding down behind them. He slung his rifle over his shoulder and fiddled with his scanning binoculars. "I'm thinking of taking it up myself. If he doesn't feel up to it, I'll take care of pissing onto the trees myself. For appreciation's sake."

"Forget I asked," Gavin said. He walked out from the shade under the ship and shaded his eyes against the sun. "Hot. Very Hot. Are those trees poisonous?"

"Sailing directions doesn't mention any poisonous plants," Dena said. "But it did say nothing edible, and they all have thorns. Or needles."

"Any dangerous animals?"

"None noted, but survey incomplete, is what it said."

Gavin pointed at the stream nearby. "Let's drag the hose over that way. There's a path between the bushes."

"What's that down there?" Dena pointed into the

distance. "Those look like buildings."

"They are buildings, abandoned buildings," Ana said. "That's the old Imperial fueling base. Abandoned—and probably everything of value taken away years ago."

"And we didn't land there, why? Isn't that a big lake next to them?"

"A shallow lake," Dirk said, coming down the ramp with Lee. He coughed. "Lionel said their scans suggested that lake disappeared at certain times of the year, and he couldn't be certain if it would be there. But that base was positioned there because of the mountains." Dirk waved. "See all these highlands? They all drain down there, with creeks and streams, and it's only when you get close that they're big enough to have a flow. Half of the year, they got major water flow, and those big square things are storage tanks. They stored water in the winter for the summer dry season."

"And there is the question of salts," Gavin said. "We can handle salty water, but the less salty, the faster we can run it through the purifier and the faster we fuel. Even with less flow from the river, we'll fuel up faster."

"Geography," Ana said. "Exciting stuff. Sorry to miss all this, but I'm going to go up top and scan the area. I'll do it for four hours and then Scruggs can—I mean, I'll..." Ana swung his rifle down, clicked a round in, and stomped back up into the ship.

The others watched him go.

"I'm amazed how worried he is," Dena said. "I didn't think he had any human feelings at all."

"Me too," Lee said.

"Me three," Gavin said.

"You'll all be embarrassed someday when I remind you of that," Dirk said. "Commanders get attached to their troops."

"Did you?" Dena asked.

"Yes," Dirk said. "I did. And troops can get attached to this commander."

"The Tribune Devin seems pretty attachable," Gavin said. "You worked for him?"

"Best commander I ever had," Dirk said. "I learned lots from him."

"And he was your priest, Lee?" Gavin asked.

Lee shrugged.

"Think he can pull off this war thing with the Confeds, stop things before they get started?"

"If anybody can, he can," Dirk said. "He's brave, resourceful, and he's got guts. He'll go charging in." Dirk coughed as another cloud of sand swept through. "But he needs a good staff. He's not good with details."

Lee laughed.

"Regardless," Dirk said. "If we're going to beat that liner to Antares and get Scruggs, we need to get fueled up. Engineer, what do you need me to do?"

Gavin flipped open the access panel on the landing leg. "Just guide the hose here. Dena and I will drag the end to the stream over there, then she and I can start the suction up. We've done it before, so we know the drill. Lee, I've got engineering diagnostics running. Standard ones, but I need to know the acceptable parameters of the new installations that the tribune's people did. Can you monitor the board and call me right away if anything logs red?"

"I can." Lee nodded.

"Will this take long? Dena asked. "I want to do some hiking."

"Exercise is good," Lee said.

Dena sniffed "And the boys smell like feet."

"Not sure exactly," Gavin said. "But a couple shifts at least."

"Why does it take so long?" Dena tapped the hose. "This hose is huge. And before you ask, yes, I say that to all the guys. But we'll pump a lot of water with this."

Gavin shook his head. "Pumping isn't the problem. Cracking it is. We can pump faster than we can crack the H and O. Once we fill up the raw water tank, we're limited by how fast the fuel purifier—and the cracker—operates. The water has to be filtered, the gases sucked off. That's what takes the time, making the hydrogen, not pumping the water."

Lee disappeared into the ship. Rocky continued sniffing, squatted, then pooped on a green leafy plant. He raised another cloud of dust as he kicked dirt over it.

Dirk fed the hose out—a useless endeavor because it was on a roller—but it gave him something to do while Gavin and Dena dragged it to the creek. They dumped the end under the water and Dena covered it with rocks to hold it down. Gavin returned to the ship.

Gavin checked the gauges attached to the hose. "Will we get Scruggs back?"

"Yes," Dirk said.

"Long way to go for one girl," Gavin said.

"I'd do the same for you," Dirk said.

"No offense, Skipper, but I'm not sure I'd do the same for you."

"Doesn't matter," Dirk said. "It's not about you or her. It's about me. I look after my crew."

"You sound more and more like you're back in the navy," Gavin said.

"I do, don't I?" Dirk said. "I kind of like that."

Gavin confirmed the water was sucking up. Nothing unusual came out of the engineering report. Dust devils swept by—some large enough to obscure the terrain—and required goggles to work outside. Rocky sucked water out of the river and peed on everything he could find. After a desultory meal, they all napped. It was coming on night, ship time, but planetary day was almost eighty hours, so it would be sunny the whole time they were grounded.

Dirk awoke refreshed and climbed through the dorsal hatch. The sun was high, and the ship's hull had heated, so Ana was seated under an awning on top of a blanket. He had his vision-enhancing binoculars strapped to his head. Weapons were strewn beside him. His rifle was assembled, loaded, and ready to fire. He continued stripping a revolver as Dirk crawled up next to him.

Dirk watched as Ana pushed a cleaning rag down the barrel. Ana worked in silence. He polished the cylinder, snapped it in, spun the gun, and dry fired it through all six of the empty chambers.

"The dust gets in," Ana said. "Slows the action. I have to clean it a lot." He polished the barrel some more.

"Uh-huh," Dirk said.

"Nothing to report here, Navy," Ana said. "No movement at all within visual range. Plenty of rocks to hide in and keep us under observation, but I haven't seen anything move. No animals, nothing."

"Were you expecting anything, Centurion?"

"What do expectations have to do with it? Lots of people die because they see what they expect to see instead of what's there. Best to keep an open mind."

"Interesting. What do you expect to see when we get into Antares Sector, with Scruggs on that ship?"

"I expect we'll rescue her. I expect that we'll do what's necessary to bring her back safely."

"We might not be able to do that. They might have already killed her. Some local governor. Or they might have put her on a military transport before she got there. Or this war might be bigger than we thought, and the transport might be requisitioned. Or rerouted."

"We'll deal with that when we get there," Ana said. "Let's get fueled up and go see." He held up the gun.

Dirk's face reflected in the shiny barrel. "What if she doesn't want to come back with us?" he said. "Apparently, she's rich. That liner reeks of luxury. Maybe she likes it better."

"Maybe she does," Ana said. "I'll ask her. When we find her."

"This might not work out the way you want," Dirk said. "Devin gave me a lot of money, you know. And paperwork and canceled warrants. We could split the money up and go our separate ways. Rich. Well, rich enough."

Ana flipped the cylinder open and fed shells in one at a time. "That what you want to do, Navy?"

"It has its attractions," Dirk said. "I'm not a hunted man any more. None of us are. The ship isn't stolen. I could go back to the core. Or go out and join this war. It doesn't seem much of a war, but it's all we've got right now."

"A good war is hard to find," Ana agreed. He spun the loaded cylinder. "She stood right next to me, you know, while we were fighting that tank. Didn't even flinch. Helped me load."

"You ever blown up a tank before?" Dirk asked.

"Technically, it was a tracked self-propelled anti-tank gun, not a tank. But, yes, I have. Five of them. Six, including this one. Three in one day, a long time ago. That wasn't a good day. I'm assuming this was her first. Quite a watershed for her. You always remember your first, they say."

"I don't think that they meant destroyed tanks when they said that, but your point is valid. What's she doing out here acting as an untrained mercenary if she has all that money?"

"Why'd you join the navy? Why did Lee leave her Praetorian friends? What's Gavin lying about that we can't figure out? Why did Dena try to kill her sister?" Ana spun the cylinder again. "For that matter, why did I leave Pallas and join the army? These are the questions. But they don't matter. What matters is what we do now."

"We're going to go rescue Scruggs, one way or the other," Dirk said. "I've decided."

"The freak, Lee, wants to help Scruggs because Scruggs saved her, and she has some sort of weird Praetorian-sister connection. Dena and her have become good friends. Opposites attract and all that. For me, she's..."

"She's every soldier that you lost over the years. You

think this is your fault."

"Of course it's my fault. I didn't give her the training I should have. That's a failure on my part. If she'd had slightly more training, she could have got away from that problem."

"You're not seriously suggesting you should have taught her how to blow up tanks while she was on a starship?" Dirk said.

Ana grimaced. "It does sound stupid when I say it. But even stupider when you say it. Why are you going to go get her?"

"Because I'm in charge. I have to act like I'm in charge."

"You're an officer again?"

"I don't want to be," Dirk said. "But it's what I do. Or should do."

"Listen to the Imperial Duke," Ana said. "Next thing you know, you'll be charging off with your buddy, Tribune Devin, to attack the Confeds."

"After we get Scruggs. There'll be time."

The hatch clanged behind them, as Dena used it to lever herself up onto the hull.

"Time for what?" She walked over and flopped down under the awning.

All she had on was shorts, ankle hiking boots, a sports bra, and a breezy attitude.

"Time for somebody to take over my watch," Ana said. "Is it you?"

"Lee said she would, if she could do it from the control room," Dena said. "She said to tell you the new cameras are so good that she can see as well from there as up here. She'd much prefer to be in an air-conditioned ship."

"Thank the tribune next time you see him," Ana said. "It's his doing. I'm going to nap for a shift then. What are you doing up here?"

"I'm going to go for a hike. Either of you want to come?"

"Dressed like that?" Ana said.

"Too much?" Dena said. "Should I take it off? Would you like that, old man?"

"I've seen better," Ana said.

"I doubt it," Dena said.

"Someday, I'll explain," Ana said. "But not right now. Ask the pilot what he wants to see. I'm going to take a nap." Ana walked along the hull and climbed down through the hatch.

"Want to go skinny-dipping?" she asked Dirk.

"The stream is two feet deep. There's nowhere to dip."

"Lee and I checked it out. Those new cameras are amazing, and she got some overheads as we landed. There's a pool of sorts maybe four miles down the river. There's a trail. It follows that creek. Goes all the way from that old base up to the top of the hill here."

"A trail?" Dirk said. "I thought this place was deserted."

"An old trail. Nothing grows fast here."

"Every time I go anywhere on a planet, I freeze my butt off, or get chased by wild dogs, or dunked in sludge, or burned by acid."

"Don't worry, Mr. Big Pilot. Little Dena will look out for you."

"As long as you keep your top on."

"Why? Don't trust yourself."

"I've seen it before. I trust myself. I just don't have time for that right now. We've got enough problems without me getting involved with a member of the crew."

"So, I'm a member of the crew now? What about before?"

"Before we were friends. Now, we're kind of... colleagues?"

"Well, that makes it clear."

"Dena."

"Never mind. I get it. And I mostly wanted to get a tan, regardless. Come on down with me to that pool. We can walk the creek. Lee tested the water. We can drink it. We'll be sucking fuel for hours, and we've been cooped up on the ship. I'd go alone, but..."

"Going alone on anything is not a good idea. Fine, I'll go with you. It's, what, a couple hours hike? We'll do some swimming and then come back."

"If you're still bored, we can go look at that old base."

"What would we see there? And it could be dangerous."

"Just killing time. No buildings on this planet, no people, nothing. Just desert, dust, and ruins. What's there to be dangerous?"

"You never know."

"Come on, let's go see. You know what Scruggs would say."

"Adventure awaits."

They both chorused the reply.

CHAPTER TWENTY

"Coming out of jump in five minutes," Deguals said.

"Thank you, comm," Devin said. "Subprefect?"

"Course laid in," Lionel said, gesturing to the main screen.

The jump counter was running next to a display of the Kewa system's primary. Devin had conceived a ship raid into Confed Space on the supply lines to Sand Harbor. The Kewa system was chosen because it was within range and had military-use infrastructure but was unlikely to be heavily defended. He could show the Confeds the Empire would not take an attack lying down, that internal—well, near-border confederation systems were not immune to assault, and would collect valuable intelligence and operational data.

And he was frustrated and wanted to kill somebody.

Despite Devin's desire to travel alone, the Pollux had to jump twice in tandem with the single functioning tanker, refuel in deep space, then send the tanker back to Papillon. The refueling had not gone well, taking twice as long as expected and breaking the tankers main fueling port. Finishing up from the secondary port had proven problematic. The tanker had enough fuel to return to Papillon.

Pollux did not—not directly. They were two jumps from an Imperial planet with fueling capabilities, that they could reach ahead of any pursuit. Barely. But Pollux had extended jump capability not present on most Imperial ships and had never been seen on confederation warships, so they were secure from pursuit.

Hopefully.

"Broadcast ready?" Devin asked.

"As you requested, Tribune. Soon as we're clear of the jump limit, we're warning all the civilian traffic to stop."

"Do you have the—" Devin got a look at Lionel's face. "Never mind. I'm sure you've got everything ready." He punched a button on his console. "Engineering?"

"Here, Tribune," a voice said.

"Ready to spin up the... um... the..." Devin looked at Lionel. "The main drive, but not..."

"We're bringing up the GT drive as soon as we're out of jump, Tribune," the voice said. "The GT one is the fast drive but the one that chews fuel. We've been using the D drive up till now—the slower, more fuel efficient one. Is that what you meant?"

"Yes, that's it. Prepare to engage the GT drive on my command."

"On your command, Tribune? We can wait if you want, but we're tagged to the jump computer. As soon as it says we've cleared jump space, we were going to automatically engage it. But we can wait for your word if that's what you order."

Devin clicked his comm off, bit his lip, then flipped it on again. "Strike that last comment. Carry on with what's planned. Um... execute, execute, execute." He clicked the comm off. "Subprefect?"

"Tribune?"

"That was a remarkably stupid order, wasn't it?"

"As the tribune says, of course."

"Why in god's name do you follow me?"

"Morbid curiosity, Tribune. Only Jove himself knows what sort of trouble you'll get us into next. It's fascinating in a sort of horrific way. It's like watching a baby tabbo climb along an electrified wire over a vat of boiling lava, while being chased by snakes, surrounded by carnivorous pigeons, and being shot at by a squad of drunken marine sharpshooters. We know it's going to end horrifically, but we can't figure out which horrible thing will happen first."

"A baby tabbo?"

"Yes."

"Drunken marines?"

"Not just regular drunken marines, Tribune. Sharpshooter drunken marines."

"I see."

Lionel grinned at him. "You're also the most personally brave person I've ever met, completely devoted to the Empire, and you'd stab yourself in the eye before you let anybody mistreat your crew."

"Nobody mistreats my crew except me," Devin said. "Wait, that didn't come out right."

"Current ad bellum, Tribune," Lionel said. He gave the cross-chest salute.

Devin returned it.

"Emergence in sixty seconds," Deguals said. "Board is green."

Lionel and Devin sat silently while the counter ticked down.

Devin gestured Lionel to stand near him and whispered, "Is there anything for me to do here?"

"Nothing," Lionel whispered back. "Shut up and look stoic. The sensor and weapons people have it."

The blue jump light dimmed, then disappeared. The ship stuttered into zero G for five seconds. Then engineering confirmed the switchover, and the acceleration built up as the GT drive kicked in.

The Kewa system appeared on the plot—the primary star with its planetary system and the secondary star and its planetary system. They had come in exactly on the jump limit and were racing for Kewa-1e, a gas giant with an extensive moon system.

Deguals played with his screen. "Engineering confirms drive shift. Acceleration on profile. Stand by for sensor report." He tapped his board. "Sensors report four orbital fuel crackers in the planetary atmosphere, with two tankers shuttling fuel back to the main fueling depot on moon, Kewa-1e-17, four automated mining barges running back from the outer asteroid station. All matches the intelligence estimate."

The ship rocked.

"Missile one away," Deguals said. "Target first mining barge. We've located a satellite array at the gas giant and multiple comm arrays at the various Lagrange points."

The ship rocked with a double whammy.

"Missile two and three away," Deguals said. "Warship! Radar says... some sort of minesweeper class. No threat to us. No missiles. Single laser, limited sensors. Short ranged rockets to destroy mines as detected."

"They can still shoot at us if we get close," Lionel said.

"Will we get close? Close enough to shoot?" Devin asked.

"Not on its current vector, Tribune," Deguals said. The ship rocked again. "Missile four away."

"Anything else?"

"Sir, there appears to be a second mining facility. We're tracking four more mining ships. Can't locate the mine yet. Not sure what asteroid they're on."

"Never mind," Devin said. "Fire missiles when you have a solution on those barges. Take the barges out, and that stops the mining, wherever it is."

"Yes, sir," Deguals said. He and the navigation officer put their heads together and spoke in low tones.

"Missiles," Lionel said, "are expensive."

"You're my accountant now?"

Lionel shivered. "There's a job I'd hate. Telling you how you spent your money. That would give me a drinking problem."

"We don't want that."

"It wouldn't be so bad. I'd be able to charge it to your personal expenses."

"That would be dishonorable."

"Only if I hid it. My plan is to put it in plain sight—alcohol, case, expensive, for the relief of Subprefect's despair, caused by an uncaring Tribune's actions. Quantity ten."

"There're probably already entries in my accounting

journal like that. Which I would know, if I cared to read it, which I don't."

"Wrong phrase. Perhaps I should have said missiles are in limited supply."

"We have a full magazine."

"We had a full magazine. Now that you've shot some, it's not full anymore."

"Do we have enough?"

"For what? Every mining barge in the sector? No. To send the Confeds a message that we won't be messed with? Yes. For now."

"Did you find that fleet supply ship?"

"Nope."

"I'll hang that captain for being late."

"No, you won't."

"I won't? Yes, I will."

"No, Tribune, you won't."

"First, you tell me I can't blow up mining barges. Now, you tell me I can't hang people. I'm an Imperial Tribune, remember? Acting sector governor, brother—"

"You're the commander of a ship that doesn't have a single room with more than an eight-foot ceiling. Hard to hang somebody with that drop. You could try, I suppose, but you'll probably mess it up. Unless you want to suffocate them instead of breaking their neck."

"Deguals!"

"Sir?" Deguals stopped his conference with the navigation officer.

"I'm contemplating hanging the subprefect from the neck until dead. How long a rope do I need?"

"One moment, Tribune," Deguals said. He played with his comm.

Devin gestured to Lionel. "If not hanging, what should I do to that lost captain?"

"Nothing," Lionel said. "He's on a standard run, and he's got supplies to deliver all through the sector. He's supposed to drop things at different depots and so on and only reload warships under special circumstances. He's probably not lost, just got a different cargo mix and changed his delivery route to optimize fuel or some such thing. And you better hope it's a he, not a she."

"How can that possibly matter?"

"Women are smaller than men, normally. The lighter you are, the harder you are to hang. Need an even longer rope—"

"Sir," Deguals said, "I'll need the subprefect's weight."

"One hundred eighty pounds," Lionel said.

"Five feet of rope, sirs," Deguals said. "For the drop length, that is."

"Too far, then. Won't fit in any of our compartments, then. Shame." Devin shrugged. "Thank you, Deguals."

Deguals shook his head. "Not too far at all, Tribune. Engineering ceilings are double height, and so is the shuttle bay. We could use those. And for that matter, any corridor will do. We start in zero G, then punch up the acceleration. Strap him to a hatch cover, fire the main engines. We can get a twenty-foot snap."

Devin grinned at Lionel. Lionel fingered his neck. "Thank you, Deguals."

"Best crew ever," Devin said. "Outstanding. But, Deguals, how do you have knowledge in such things?"

"Well, sir," Deguals said, "since people call my commander the Mad Dog of the Verge and claim that you execute people at random, I thought this is the sort of thing I might get asked someday, you know? Some scared freighter captains or something, so I looked into it earlier to help scare them into compliance to the tribune's wishes."

The bridge grew quiet.

Lionel laughed. "Best crew ever! Outstanding job, Deguals."

"Thank you, sir. Can I finish my calculations?"

Devin waved his assent and glared. Lionel kept giggling.

"Stop laughing," Devin hissed.

"I can't help it. You can't even discipline him because you asked the question yourself."

"I'm sorry I asked. Is wasting missiles on these mining barges worth it?"

"We can't swing out there to get them with anything shorter ranged, not without extending our stay here longer than we wanted."

"We won't get the mine, though."

"No, but they'll have to evacuate the mining facility itself," Lionel said. "They get their supplies, food, and such like on those barges. We should be careful we don't doom all the outposts in the system to starvation."

"Then, leave one tanker," Devin suggested. "That way, they can go out and evacuate anybody who needs to evacuate to the main station."

"Do we blow the main station?" Lionel asked.

"It's not military, so no, but we can't leave it alo—"

"Tribune, we have a firing solution for the second group of mining barges," Deguals said.

"Execute," Devin said.

The ship rocked three times.

"Missile five, six, and seven away. We're holding eight till we get a better angle."

"Very well."

"Planetary orbit in six minutes, Tribune," Deguals said.

"Very well," Devin said again.

The bridge was silent. The Pollux raced in. Two minutes later, the minesweeper made a vector change, angling back to the planet, hoping to intercept the Pollux before it could get closer. A minute later, the final missile fired. Four minutes after that, the minesweeper's engine switched off and drifted.

"Sensors, why did they switch off?" Devin asked.

"Not sure, sir, no evidence of drive failure. They were maneuvering to try to return to planetary orbit, then stopped."

191

"Why?" Devin asked.

"They did the math," Lionel said. "They've got a read on our course. They can't beat us in, not under any acceleration they can handle. If we come in as planned, we'll shoot in between the station and the planet, clean out the fuel crackers, take out every satellite we can find, probably get a shot at the tankers, too, and get clean away before they can catch us. So, they're waiting to see what happens next, maybe try to head us off somewhere else."

"Can we get both tankers?" Devin asked.

"One is diving into the atmosphere, Tribune," Deguals said. "We might have a shot, but I don't think we'll be able to penetrate that far down. Um, we might not have to."

"Why not?"

"With the acceleration profile we're seeing, unless they have power in reserve, they'll be so deep in the gravity well they'll never get out."

The screens flashed static for a moment, then rebounded. "What was that?"

"Positron guns fired, Tribune. First satellite destroyed."

"Is everything supposed to flicker like that?" Devin asked.

"Engineering gave it a hundred and fifty percent power to increase the range. The manual says not to do that."

"Let's not do that again," Devin said. "Unless we need to. Do we need to?"

"Not at this time, Tribune."

The Pollux swept on. They passed between the moon and the planet, as was planned to get them the best shots at the infrastructure. Every satellite or communications platform in range was destroyed. There had been a swarm of small ships, shuttles, broomsticks, and other small craft aloft. They had all fled or grounded as the Pollux raced in. It didn't bother with the grounded ones. The positron guns zapped the fueling crackers. The missiles blew all the automated barges to bits. One tanker imploded in the atmosphere, and the other grounded next to the moon station.

"They've probably abandoned it there," Lionel said.

"Will we pass close enough to the station to take a shot at that tanker?" Devin asked.

"Not if we follow the plan," Lionel said. "We had prioritized getting commo gear with the positron guns, which kept us too far from the station."

"Deguals, can you bring us in close enough for a shot at that tanker, the one grounded by the station?"

"If you want, Tribune. We'll miss one or two of the satellites."

"Never mind, then," Devin said. "Where's that minesweeper?"

"Out of the picture, Tribune. It's too far away to catch us. One pass around the planet and we're out of here. They'll still be drifting. I anticipate they'll wait till we leave, then assist survivors."

"It's all about the geometry," Lionel said.

"A successful raid, Subprefect," Devin said. "You are to be congratulated."

"It's not over yet, Tribune," Lionel said. "I'll celebrate when we're back home."

"Fueling capacity destroyed. Fuel stocks blown up. Mining capacity destroyed. Sensors, communication, and other infrastructure wiped out, and they'll have to deal with getting these survivors fed. Why, I wouldn't be surprised if they have to evacuate the whole system."

"Still..." Lionel said.

"What could still go wrong?" Devin asked.

"Still..."

"Warship," Deguals yelled. "Warship on the moon. Lifting to meet us. Range in twenty seconds."

CHAPTER TWENTY-ONE

Weeks was suiting up for his daily gym run when the door alarm bonged. He and Hernandez traded looks. Weeks stepped back, out of sight of the door, and drew his weapon, cocking it.

Hernandez cocked hers as well, draped a towel over her hand, then faced the door controls. She pushed the intercom. "Yes?"

"Clothes delivery for Ms. Scruggs."

"Leave it in the hallway, please."

"Can't do that, ma'am. I can come back later if you want."

Hernandez tapped the video button. She recognized one of the shop assistants. "Come on in, then." She pointed at Weeks's revolver. He had hidden it behind his leg. She keyed the door open, and a clerk came in and dropped a box of clothes on the table. She had another under her arm. Hernandez stepped out, checked the hallway, and ducked back in. "Thank you."

"Ms. Scruggs needs to thumb for it, ma'am."

Hernandez rolled her eyes and went to rap on Scruggs's door. "Your party gear is here, kiddo."

The door slid open and a pajama-clad Scruggs emerged, rubbing her hair and bracing herself against the wall. "Oh, good. Thanks for delivering them."

"Yes, ma'am."

Scruggs thumbed the comm for the order, and the clerk held up the other box. "This is for your friend, Ms. Flaujae."

"Right," Scruggs said. "She loaned me her blouse, but I spilled a drink on it. Tell her I'm sorry, and I hope this makes up for it."

"Of course, ma'am," the clerk said, then left.

"I wish I had your clothes budget, kiddo," Hernandez

said, poking at the pile of blouses and dresses.

"If you practiced with that blackjack book I gave you," Scruggs said, "you might get it. And don't call me kiddo."

"You always lose at poker," Hernandez said. "I don't see why you think you're a genius at blackjack."

"I'm not. But you're better with stress than I am. I'll bet you'd be better bettor. Better bettor. That's funny."

"Let's go," Hernandez said. "I want to get back and go to the gym."

Scruggs changed into another outfit before leaving, one with bright red-and-yellow polka dots. The day before was blue-and-black stripes.

"Is that what you're going to wear?" Hernandez asked.

"It makes a statement," Scruggs said.

Hernandez opened the door and led her into the hallway. "And that statement is 'Pity me for my colorblindness.'"

"You're just jealous."

"It's no secret why you're still a virgin. The colors scare the men off."

Scruggs blushed and leaned on her cane. "I'm sorry I told you that."

"We all were once. Are we playing poker, today?"

"Yes. And I'm going to try out the ceramics class they're offering. Maybe make some pots or something."

"Sounds boring."

"I think it's interesting. And I can sit down doing it. I'll be playing poker. You don't have to stand there the whole time, watching me."

"I kind of do," Hernandez said.

"I'll front you the money to play poker with me."

"You know I can't do that. I need to have freedom of movement, and I can't do that with my back to the door. If you'd just change your seat..."

"It's my lucky seat, with my back to the door."

They arrived at the casino entrance. "You lose every time. How can it be lucky?"

"I can't lose forever, so if I keep there, my luck will eventually change."

"That makes no sense but whatever you say. I need to watch the casino."

The door swished open, and they entered the casino. The poker room was in the back, in the right corner, separated from the main room by a velvet rope. Between were various games of chance, roulette, baccarat, and a few tables of blackjack.

They were familiar with the usual crowd. Space travel is boring. The passengers were rich, so the same group spent most of their time in the casino.

The two couples who had arrived days earlier—the "fantastic four," as Weeks called them—were there every time Scruggs arrived at the casino. They also overlapped on dinner but never ever spoke to Hernandez, Weeks, or Scruggs. Only smiles in passing. But since the four had arrived on the ship, wherever Scruggs arrived, one or two—or all four—would show up and position themselves so that they could observe what was going on.

Weeks had them pegged as agents of some sort, waiting till one of others made the first move—some sort of honey trap, perhaps. Hernandez wasn't sure, but she had allowed Scruggs to buy her an extensive, stylish purse big enough to keep a handgun in.

"Let's watch the blackjack for a second," Scruggs said.

Hernandez had automatically tracked the tables. "Your handsome friends are there."

"I'm more interested in their playing," Scruggs said.

"Now you're a blackjack expert, too?"

"They're cheating. I can tell."

"No, you can't. Stop making stuff up."

"Didn't you read the book I gave you? The sections showing card counting and signals? They've got all the classic signs. They're signaling the others in and out of the game."

As Scruggs talked, one of the fantastic four—the

shortest woman—sauntered back from the bar and took a vacant chair. She put her chips down, was dealt in, and got a twenty-one right off the deal. Her table mates congratulated her.

"See? They signed her in when the deck was plus," Scruggs said.

"Plus? What does that mean?"

"Lots of high-value cards. He's the counter. She's the player. Once the count goes high enough, he signals her in, and she takes the big wins."

"What are you talking about?"

"It's in the book. Watch. She'll keep winning till he signals her out."

Hernandez shook her head and followed Scruggs to the velvet rope. She scanned the interior of the poker room. Scruggs's regular table dominated the front, and her lucky chair sat empty.

"You know they save that chair for you because you always lose?" Hernandez said.

Scruggs had recently doubled her daily wager and was now losing a steady two hundred credits a day.

"I'm learning," Scruggs said. "It's an investment."

Hernandez nodded at the bouncer holding the rope open for Scruggs.

Management had been clear. Nobody but players in the poker room. If she wanted to gawk, she had to do it from the main floor. The table was packed with Scruggs's regular opponents. For a poker room, it was relatively low stakes, and her companions were mostly middle-aged women without access to too much money. They welcomed Scruggs warmly—she was always polite, always friendly, and always lost.

Hernandez stepped to a spot at the rear bar. By sitting behind it in the corner, she faced the entrance and watched who came in. She'd convinced Scruggs to sit where the angled mirror showed her back. The bartender brought her usual sparkling water—at an exorbitant charge to their room account—and left her alone.

Hernandez's eyes scanned. Front door. Mirror with Scruggs's polka dot back, side bar, any of the fantastic four. Any other threats she perceived. Then back.

This would go on for the next two hours—or at least until Scruggs lost all her money. Hernandez didn't enjoy it, but it wasn't fair to never let the kid out of the room. She needed some sort of stimulation.

People at the door—old man with gray hair and blue suit. Scruggs's polka dot back. Fantastic four guy tapping his fingers. Fantastic four woman betting. Old man sits at front bar, talking to bartender. Polka dots. Fantastic four guys tapping one finger. Woman betting. Drink order. Polka dots. No fingers. Fantastic woman gets up. Another old man in a brown suit at door. Were those the only two colors? Blue and brown. Polka dots, leaning over the table for a bet. Fantastic four guy, hand still. Empty chair next to him. New deck, new shuffle. Brown suit. Polka dots. Losing hand, all cards displayed. Brown suit. Blue dress. Where—there—polka dots. Another player passing by. Another hand, another loss. Cards displayed. Brown-and-blue suit talking. Polka dots stand and lean over. Hands tapping. Empty seat. Brown suit. Polka dots. Tapping fingers, woman sitting and betting.

Huh.

Hernandez lost her flow for a minute and focused on the blackjack. Scruggs was right! He was cheating. The male player drummed a woman in when the cards were right. He kept playing and losing. And perhaps every ten minutes or so, one woman came back, won a few hands, then went out.

How did Scruggs know? Empress's vagina. She'd been distracted—polka dots, were they still there?

Yes. Polka dots. She stretched. The cane was still there, too.

Hernandez shook her chin. "Gotta keep focused."

"Pardon, ma'am," the bartender said.

"Nothing. Nothing. Talking to myself."

"Another water, ma'am?" the bartender asked.

"Yes. Make it a double."

***

Scruggs leaned against the wall and watched the gameplay without her. She'd been leaning there for ten minutes while it continued. That day, she'd bought three hundred credits in chips and lost half as fast as she could. When her friend Flaujae arrived, she claimed she was tired of sitting and asked Flaujae to play her hands and her chips while she rested.

Since Flaujae wasn't a much better player than Scruggs, her usual companions had agreed. Easy enough to win money off one as the other. And they'd all had a good laugh about wearing matching polka dot dresses. From the back, they were indistinguishable. The switch had been accomplished in seconds.

Her favorite waiter, Brendan, appeared from the back of the room and nodded at the staff entrance. Scruggs snuck over, careful to stay out of Hernandez's line of sight, and dragged a hand across the wall while using her cane like she still had trouble walking.

Brendan waited inside the door. "Ready for your tour, Ms. Scruggs?"

"Thank you for arranging this, Brendan. And thank you for taking time out to show me the ship."

"All the passengers get a tour if they ask nicely enough, Ms. Scruggs," Brendan said. "And Deeve, the purser, said it would be okay to take some time off. Engineering has assigned one of the junior engineers to take you around. My cousin Suus. She's pretty excited to meet you."

"You didn't tell her who I was, did you?" Scruggs asked. "I want to be incognito."

"She knew already. But she's a good sort. She'll keep quiet."

"I want to see the engines and the bridge and the hold

and the environmentals and the other decks and the other gyms—" Scruggs said.

"Whoa, miss. You won't have enough time to cover all of that. At least not today."

"Maybe we could do it again tomorrow," Scruggs said.

"Well, if your mother's friend out there finds out—"

"She won't. We won't tell her."

"No, we won't."

"Thanks again, Brendan," Scruggs said. She produced a chip and slotted it into his comm. "Let me give you something for your help."

"No problem, Ms. Scruggs." Brendan clicked the chip in. The amount clicked onto the screen. "Wow! I mean, thank you very much, miss. That's very generous."

"You've been very helpful, Brendan," Scruggs said. "You know what I'd really like to see? I'd like to see the shuttle bay. Can your cousin show me that?"

Brendan looked at the amount. "Let me get my coat. I'll go with you. Make sure she shows you whatever you need."

CHAPTER TWENTY-TWO

"Deserts kind of suck," Dena said. "It's all heat, dust and thorns. I thought there'd be cute camels and hot-eyed desert nomad guys."

"What's a camel?" Dirk asked.

"It's like a dog, only bigger and friendlier," Dena said.

She and Dirk were clambering down the riverbed. They'd left the Heart's Desire two hours ago, climbed into the stream bed, and climbed down the hill.

The old Imperial base was visible in the distance. It sat at the base of the dusty hill country. Snow-capped mountains lined the horizon in all directions, white at the tops, then dark green, light green, brown, then almost gray. The melting snow coursed down steep ravines out of the tree-studded rock faces but then meandered between green scrub fields as the water leached out.

The Heart's Desire sat below the tree line, where the pine forest gave way to pine bushes, which led to dry scrub land.

"At least it's easier walking down here," Dirk said. "Dry but not as steep and none of those rocks."

"And less of those stupid thorn bushes now. Right, Rocky?"

Gray-green barrels covered with long thorns lined the trails. Rocky the Whippet wagged his tail. He'd followed them down to the river, lapping up water as needed, chasing anything that moved, and peeing on everything. He'd snapped at buzzing insects, sniffed at crawling ones, and chased burrowing rodents that ran between clumps of trees—even caught one. After shaking it to death, he sniffed it, then sat and dismembered the corpse in big bites.

"I can't believe he ate that squirrel thing," Dirk said.

"Sight hounds," Dena said. "If something moves, he

chases. If he catches things, he eats them."

"He's more dangerous than he looks," Dirk said.

"That's true of everybody. Or of us, at least. This would be a good spot." Dena and Dirk had rounded the corner of the river.

A thirty-foot ridge of weathered red-and-black sandstone pushed the river west. Smooth patches spotted the face where entire boulders had cleaved off and smashed down, landing in giant piles at the base. The river slowed at the bend, creating a shallow beach on their side, deepening to a dark lake at the base of the far cliffs. A sand spit ran almost the full way to the cliff's base.

Dirk pointed. "We could wade in over there, under that cliff."

"Yep. Rocky, this way."

Dena and Dirk turned right and walked to the base of the spit, then followed it out across the flats. The river deepened as it came close to the far cliffs. Driftwood littered the spit at the far end, with a six-foot-deep pool meandering by. The cliff's base crumpled into the water twenty feet away, exposing cracks and caves on the weathered rock.

"Big caves over there," Dirk said. "Big enough for people." He flopped to the ground next to the water, took his shoes off, and dangled them into the water before digging up piles of sand with his toes.

"I like it better over here," Dena said. "Never know what's in a cave. Fetch, Rocky." She picked up a stick and threw it down the spit.

Rocky bounded after it.

Dena kept throwing it farther. Rocky enjoyed the game, grabbing his stick, racing back with it, and dropping it at her feet, then retreating back a pace and crouching until she threw it again.

"That dog loves his sticks," Dirk said. "Look how focused he is."

"Dogs and men," Dena said. "Easy to keep occupied

by having them chase after things."

"You don't have the highest opinion of either," Dirk said.

"They both have their uses," Dena said. "But you have to respect their limitations."

"Thanks," Dirk said. "I think."

Her next throw bounced the stick not far from Dirk's hand, and he reached for it. When Rocky ran up and growled at him, Dirk withdrew before Rocky retrieved the stick and returned it to Dena.

Dena threw the stick along the water as far as she could. She misjudged, and it flopped into the water ten feet out and floated.

Rocky ran up to the shore next to it and shuffled into the water. He didn't go far but edged out until his feet lost traction, then turned and paddled in, coming back till his feet touched ground. After a few more abortive tries, he shuffled back onshore and barked once.

"You want me to get it?"

Rocky barked again.

"You don't to swim there?"

Rocky barked a third time and whined.

"Fine," Dena said. "Fine. I'll get it for you." She untied her shoes and put her socks next to them. Then she dropped her comm and the small carry bag. "Want to help me get Rocky's stick, Pilot Dirk?"

"I don't swim so well," Dirk said. "I learned once, but I'm not good at it."

"Have to help him myself, then." Dena crossed her hands over her shoulders and flipped her top off, then slid her pants down over hips and to the ground.

Dirk laughed at her. "Afraid of getting your clothes wet?"

"Yep," Dena said. "I don't want to have to wash out those salts Gavin mentioned later." She bent over and tidied her clothes, then sauntered into the water. Pushing it away with her hands, she stopped at knee-level and stretched, then walked till it was deep enough to dive and swim.

Dirk watched her the whole time. He was fairly sure neither bending over to fuss with the clothes or stretching before she dove in were completely necessary, but he enjoyed the view all the same.

Dena swam to Rocky's stick, towed it back in, and waded into waist-deep water. She threw the stick back and forth for Rocky several times, making sure to stretch exorbitantly as she did. After a dozen tosses, she'd waded out deeper, and Rocky would swim out and drop it for her before swimming back.

"Why don't you come out here, Pilot?" Dena called. "Help me with a stick."

"Why are you still calling me Pilot?" Dirk asked.

"We can play 'you're the handsome pilot of the ship, and I'm the poor little stowaway girl who'll do anything to stay onboard, anything the pilot asks.'"

"That's exactly what you said to get on the ship originally," Dirk said. "Pretty much word for word. And I got the bad side of the deal."

"Huh," Dena said. She was deep enough now that she was swimming every other step. "Not in everything but mostly true."

"As I recall, you were lying to me at the time."

"Not completely. Not everything," Dena said. She paddled her arms. "Well, I did want to stay on the ship."

"What a romantic streak you have," Dirk said.

"Fine," Dena said. "The water's warm. The sun is shining. There's nobody here except Rocky. We don't need to be back at the ship for hours, and I'm naked and horny. Why not come into the water with me? That romantic enough for you? And before you ask, this won't be a regular thing in the future. That's over, but we're here, and I need a break."

Dirk nodded. "I could use a break, too." He undressed, piled his clothes and comm next to hers, and waded carefully into the water. "It is warm. How deep is it?"

"Not very," Dena said. She stuck her feet down and pushed her shoulders up out of the water. "I can stand here. If I can, so can you."

"Good," Dirk said, wading out to her. "Can I touch the bottom."

"You should be able to the whole way out," Dena said. "Just step slowly."

"Okay," Dirk said, pushing up. His torso came out of the water.

"Don't take big steps."

"Why not?"

"Because you're on a rock."

"So?" He stepped, dropped, and sank under the water. Bubbles floated up, and thrashing hands broke the surface.

Dena watched from her rock. "Limitations."

Dirk surfaced, and spat out water. "Salty. You could preserve meat with this water."

"I'll say. Don't drown. I'll have to bury your useless corpse down here, and I'm sure that would have messed up my nails."

"You don't care that I might have been killed?"

"Don't be such a big baby. You were in five feet of water. And you scared Rocky," Dena said. She pointed at the black whippet lolling on the sand four feet away.

He wagged his tail when she glanced at him.

"He doesn't look scared. He looks happy."

"If he knows that I'm safe, he's happy"

"Never mind," Dirk spat again. He sniffed. "The air, something, feels weird."

"Electric." Dena said. "Like before a storm."

Dirk's communicator bonged loud. "What now?" He returned to the shore and rummaged through the clothes pile and tapped his comm. "What?"

"Get back now," Ana said. "Right away."

"As much as I appreciate your decisive, take charge,

lets-go-army attitude, Centurion, I'd like to remind you I'm the pilot, and I should be treated with some respect. Also, I know we don't have enough fuel yet to make it worth lifting. And third, why are you on the comm? It's Lee's shift."

"You Imperial anus," Ana said. "Look west."

Dirk frowned and peered at the sky. "There's nothing there."

"Over there, Dirk," Dena said, pointing in the other direction. She had followed him onto the shore. "That's west. What's that?"

Dirk turned to look across down the valley at the mountains. The tops of the mountains were still crisp white and green, but the bottoms had muddied to a dark yellow.

"What is that, Centurion?"

"Dust storm, big one. Changed direction after we landed. Lee and Gavin are outside sealing up the hoses, so we can still suck up water while it blows through. Get moving up the trail. Get on board before it arrives."

"Centurion," Dena said, "we're two hours walk away. That storm will be here much sooner. We can't beat it."

"Which is why I was calling you for the last twenty minutes. It's only after we found the pilot's override code I was able to beep you. I had to break into your cabin to get it."

"You're a starship," Dena yelled. "Fly down here and pick us up."

"The winds are already bad here. Lee says we need an experienced pilot to deal with the micro-bursts, whatever those are. And unfortunately, the most experienced pilot we have is that supercilious twit next to you."

Dena looked at Dirk, who was sitting naked on the sand and looking uneasy "I forget that sometimes."

"We all do. Get on your way up here as soon as you can."

"Stand by," Dena said. She stood and watched the sky.

"We won't make it. We need shelter. We can hide in the water, maybe, crouch behind a rock. How strong are the winds?"

"She's a better pilot than she lets on. If she thinks the winds are too strong, then we won't be able to walk in them. Or stick our heads up."

"There." Dena pointed across their tiny river. "Those cliffs. We can get inside them and hide from the wind. If it's blowing from the west, it will swirl past the cliff, but we can shelter inside."

"That would work," Dirk said. He bit his lip. "Dena, I'm not the greatest swimmer—"

"I'll tow you over," Dena said. "Into the water. Now." She thrust her clothes at him. "You'll float on your back. I'll drag you across. Hold on to these."

Dirk collected his and Dena's clothes and their comm and waded into the water.

Rocky jumped up and barked—something exciting was happening!

"Lay on your back," Dena said.

"I love it when a woman says"—Dena slapped him in a sensitive spot—"ow."

"Shut up and float. Stay relaxed, and you'll stay on top of the water. Go."

Dirk lay back and shut up. The river was only twenty feet across. Dena waded and steered him with both hands first, then swam beside him to keep him moving along.

Dirk blinked water out of his eyes and controlled his breathing, but it was hard. The wind blew ripples in the water, and waves washed over his face. His muscles seized.

They were three-quarters of the way over when the sun darkened. Dirk turned and got a face full of blowing sand. He gasped, rolled, and was underwater. He flailed till he got his feet under him. He stood, but couldn't see more than a yard. "Dena?"

"This way, quick." She grabbed his wrist and they stumbled forward. The wind whipped harder, and all he could see was a brown haze. He tripped and fell under the water. Dena yanked him forward, then his knees struck sand.

He dropped to both knees and crab walked, then staggered to his feet. The wind was up, waves chopping across the water.

Rocky barked in the distance.

"You nearly broke my wrist."

"You tried to drown me, jackass. Wait, Rocky, I'm coming."

Dirk stomped out of the water, breathing hard and shaking water from his arms. He'd dropped the communicators and the clothes. Grit stung his back, and he had to squint when he turned back to the lake.

He cupped his hands around his eyes to peer through the blowing sand. Dena had swum to the other side, and a yipping Rocky ran into the water. She scooped him into her arms, rolled on her back, and kicked her way across the lake. Dirk turned to the side to protect his face and covered his eyes and nose with his hand. Grit in the air slashed at his lips.

Dena rolled over, put her feet under her, and catapulted a yelping Rocky out of the water. Dirk grabbed her free arm and pulled her up, and they both stumbled forward. A dark mouth of a cave punctured a light cliff in front of them. Dena slid right, grabbed Rocky by the scruff, and dragged him along with them into the cavern.

The sun disappeared, and they staggered into the rocky door. The storm struck behind them.

CHAPTER TWENTY-THREE

"What type of warship? Where?" Devin said.

The Pollux's screens flashed as they closed in on the moon, information streaming in.

"Big one," Deguals said. "Five times bigger than us, at least. Lifting at three G, counter rotating around the moon, right on the terminator. It's moving behind—gone now. Passed behind the horizon. New ETA, ninety-seven seconds."

"Three G, that's no barge," Lionel said.

"Five times as big as us? A cruiser?" Devin asked. "There's no cruiser here."

Deguals looked over his shoulder. "Bigger, sir, could be almost battle cruiser size, but we only got a glimpse. Confidence is poor."

"Get us out of here," Lionel said.

Deguals's fingers danced. "Preparing to evade."

"No."

The bridge held its collective breath.

Deguals turned back. "Tribune?"

"Hold your tabbos, I mean. Stand by," Devin said.

"We can't fight a battle cruiser, Tribune," Lionel said.

"There was nothing in the intelligence assessment mentioning a battle cruiser being here," Devin said.

"Intelligence isn't always right."

Devin drummed his fingers. "Everything else has matched."

"Who brings a battle cruiser to an out of the way outpost and leaves it here without escorts?" Lionel said. "It makes no sense."

They stared at each other.

"Nobody," Devin said.

"You're the biggest ship the Empire has sent out here in years," Lionel said. "And that's only because you don't

209

want to be in the core, and they can't give you anything smaller. Are there Devins in the confederation?"

"We can close and fight," Devin said. "Those positrons give us an advantage."

"Not and live. If we can break contact, we'll be faster. If we do it while they're behind the moon, they won't even get a shot. We might get clean away."

"Tribune, Subprefect," Deguals said, "I have an evasive course set in. Permission to execute?"

Lionel shook his head. "Something is not right."

"Tribune?" Deguals said. "I have a counter running. I need a course."

Devin grimaced. "You're right. We can't fight a battle cruiser."

"Then, let's hope it's not a battle cruiser," Lionel said.

Devin grinned, then looked at Lionel. "Your advice, Subprefect?"

Lionel grinned back. "Current ad bellum."

"Indeed," Devin said. "Helm, dive at that moon. Close as you dare, maximum gravity assist. I want us to pick up as much velocity as possible. Do it now."

Alarms bonged, and lights flashed.

"High acceleration. High acceleration."

Straps snapped shut and latches clicked close.

Devin pulled his own straps tight. "Weapons, target them with the positron guns. Give the range you need to the helm. Helm, soon as you get that range, correct and close to fire. Ignore their missiles. Fire everything as soon as you see it and keep firing as long as it's in range. Don't wait for orders. Just do it. You won't have much of a window."

Lionel snapped his harness closed. "Max acceleration in four seconds."

"Deguals?" Devin said.

"Tribune?"

"Buckle up. You're about to expand on your education."

The rest of the bridge crew locked themselves down. On the mark, the engines fired. Devin's body weight tripled, then quadrupled, then climbed higher. His arms sank into their padded rests. His breath came in gasps, and drool slid out of the sides of his mouth as his cheeks were pushed sideways.

"Wead in ferv," Lionel said, his voice distorted by the acceleration.

The ship pivoted to the right, and the weight increased. Devin's vision clouded, and dark walls edged in from either side. Stars punctuated his view.

The weight disappeared, and the ship rolled thirty degrees and yawed almost one eighty.

"What—"

Lights darkened, and systems flickered off. Not damage, all the power had been shunted to the guns. Humming rose and fell, rose and fell, the capacitors of the positron guns charging and discharging. They rolled slightly and rocked an S-motion. The weapons officer had rolled the ship to bring the most guns to bear and was now jinking enough to confuse enemy targeting systems.

"Multiple hits," Deguals screeched, his voice distorted by the former acceleration. "More hits. Still hitting. Passing out of range."

"Damage?"

"Nothing yet. They launched missiles, but they couldn't correct—"

The ship rocked.

"They couldn't all correct to catch us," Deguals said. "That last one was detonated at closest approach, but it wasn't anywhere near enough to cause problems. No damage."

"Damage to our target?" Lionel asked.

"Multiple hits, Subprefect. At least twelve, perhaps as many as twenty. The target is streaming atmo, and entire pieces blew off and are floating behind it. But it's still under command. We see acceleration and a power signature."

"How many missiles did it launch?"

"Sixteen, Subprefect. No beam or energy weapons. And we got a better read on its size. It's at least ten times bigger than us."

Devin tapped his fingers. "That's not a lot of missiles for that big a ship. And no beam weapons?"

"None fired at us, Tribune," Deguals said.

"Monitor," Lionel said, looking up from his screen.

"Monitor what? Monitor who?" Devin said.

"It's not a proper ship. It's a monitor. Big weapons platform, slow ship. Take a moderate sized asteroid. Hollow it out, put some engines on it. And missiles. Lots of missiles. Slow, but it's all rock. Bury the missiles and sensors and power plants under a couple dozen feet of rock. Launch the missiles out tubes and let them vector themselves once they're out. Light ships can hit it all day and not damage it. Meanwhile, the missiles keep coming. Not super powerful, but nothing short of a battleship can damage it. Almost impossible to take it out of the fight."

"But we did?"

"We got close enough to use our beam weapons. And those positron beams chewed it up. We took out most of its power plants and engines, it looks like."

"Well done, Weapons," Devin said.

"Thank you, sir."

Deguals broke in. "Tribune, we're heading out of the system at high speed. Orders, sir?"

"Any targets on our list left?"

"Minor ones, Tribune."

"Slow us down to chase that ship, then."

"Tribune," Lionel said. "No need. It's heavily damaged, and it's heading in the opposite direction. We can chase it, but it will take time. And it will have missile shots at us the whole time. Those monitors have big magazines. This is a raid. We've made our point. Let's get out of here before some other surprise shows up."

Devin nodded. "Helm, take us to the jump limit, then set a course out of here."

The bridge crew busied themselves with navigation tasks. The monitor continued heading in the opposite direction, decelerating oh so slowly.

Lionel calculated it would take several days to stop relative to the planets and a couple more to return. Enhancement of the imagery showed mountings for six engines, five of which they had destroyed by blowing big chunks off. At least one power plant had exploded as well—atmosphere steamed out of a new crater.

Lionel gave a presentation on it to the officers after-action meeting.

"It's the perfect defense ship," he said. "It's so big that you have to target specific parts of it. Ninety-five percent of what's visible is random rock. The rock is as good as armor. Any small ship can pump a hundred shots at it and still not hit anything vulnerable. Meanwhile, it's shooting back. It moves, so you can't use unguided munitions. Something big has to get in close and pound it."

"Why don't we build all ships like that?" somebody asked.

"It can't run away. No jump drive," Lionel said. "If a superior fleet shows up, it's doomed. We were the superior fleet. But only because we could get in close and use those positron beams before they could react."

"I'm liking those," Devin said.

"Can we stop calling them lasers now, Tribune?"

"I suppose," Devin said. "Well done, everyone. Now, back to the fleet. Mission one successful. Now, on to the other missions."

CHAPTER TWENTY-FOUR

"Where's my clothes?" Dena asked.

"I dropped them," Dirk said, "along with the comms and everything."

"They're floating down the river now, then," Dena said. "Jackass. Ouch." She stubbed her toe on a rock. "It's dark in here. Watch this pile of rocks."

Dirk sneezed. "And dusty." He stepped back from the entrance, shading his eyes.

They were in a tall, narrow cave, leading back from the beach. It was more of a high walled crack than a cave. At some point in the distant past, a sliver of cliff had cracked and tipped away, leaving a long narrow passage open at the top. Falling rocks, dirt, and plant debris had covered the gap, forming a rocky roof. The angle and the depth kept the inner part of the cave clear of sand, but eddies swirled at the mouth.

"We're safe from the wind here," Dena said. "Just hope it doesn't last too long."

"Big storms can last days, according to Centurion. He looked it up. But this one didn't seem that large on the plot when we were landing, if it's the one he showed me. He thought it would go north around the mountains, but instead, it blew through the passes. At least it should blow out in a few hours."

"Meanwhile, we're stuck here. Right, Rocky?" Dena petted Rocky.

He wagged his tail and continued sniffing the cave. For him, every new place was an exciting adventure.

"And now that my eyes have adjusted, it's not that dark," Dirk said. "So, it can't be that big a storm. We have to wait it out. Just the two of us. My plan is working."

"Your plan?"

"Well, my plan to get you naked and—"

"Your plan sucks. I was already naked, and my plan had us lolling on a sunny beach in the sun, rolling around in the sand. Your plan has us cowering in a damp cave in the dark, sitting on rocks."

Rocky growled.

"See? Even Rocky agrees. Ouch." A wave of sand swirled in as the wind changed course. "Let's go farther back and find somewhere else to sit."

They trooped back into the dark. The narrow entrance required them to walk single file. Now that their eyes adjusted, they could make out shapes—walls, the ground, rocks, even get a feel for how gritty or how smooth things were. No colors. The passage widened after thirty feet and they could walk side-by-side.

"The ground looks lighter over there," Dena said. "Let's try it. Yep. Sand." She lay on the ground. "It's dry and feels pretty soft. It's not as damp in here as I expected."

"Me neither," Dirk said. He sat next to Dena.

Rocky growled from the front of the cave.

"Why does that dog dislike me so much?" Dirk asked.

"Good breeding, probably," Dena said, sitting up. "Your plan still sucks. We can try mine."

"What's that?" Dirk asked.

"This," Dena said. She leaned over, kissed Dirk on the lips, and put her arms around him. He returned the kiss, and she hauled him back on top of her. They lay there, intertwined, then Rocky barked frantically from the entrance.

Dena rolled slightly so her head was free. "It's okay, Rocky. The bad man isn't hurting me."

"Not unless you ask," Dirk said.

"An offer a girl finds hard to refuse," Dena said. She slid her hands behind Dirk and pulled him closer, kissing all the while.

Rocky growled, yipped, then barked and barked and barked.

Dena rolled sideways. "Stop it, Rocky. Stop it. What is the problem?"

Rocky quieted, and the sand slipped along the rock outside.

He growled again, a low growl, and they heard the answering shake of the rattles.

Dena shoved Dirk off into the wall. She rolled onto, leaped up, and ran to the front of the cave. Rocky barked again, and she caught a glimpse of the hissing, slithering form beyond him.

Rocky dodged left, crouched, then leaped right. Dena skinned her knees on the rocks as she dropped to her knees. She snagged Rocky's tail and yanked him back as the snake struck. Rocky yelped as she pulled him back, then barked. She hauled him back with one arm, scrabbling back with the other.

"Rattlesnake," Dirk said.

"Thank you, captain obvious. Sorry, Rocky, I didn't want you to get hurt." Dena released him, and Rocky licked her face before growling at the snake.

The snake slithered back, coiled itself, and shook its rattle.

"Is it poisonous?" Dirk asked.

"I'm not an expert on the reptilian life of obscure planets," Dena said. "But do you think evolution would have given it a warning rattle if there wasn't a good reason to stay away?"

"What do we do?" Dirk asked.

"Wait it out. Hope it goes away."

"Can't we kill it?"

"Sure," Dena said. "You hold it still, and I'll beat on it with a pile of sand till we exfoliate it to death. Idiot Imperial Navy, we have no weapons."

"Idiot Imperial Navy?"

"Sorry, I've been spending too much time with Ana. Rubs off on you. But he's not wrong."

"So, I grab it. Then what?"

"No, you don't grab it. It will bite you before you can say 'useless pilot.'"

"Will it kill me?"

"It could, probably—possibly. Don't know. Depends on the type of snake, type of poison, how much venom you get, a whole bunch of things. Snake bites are rarely fatal. At least they weren't on Rockhaul, but we only had a couple of snakes. Their bites hurt a lot, but you never died."

Diffused light illuminated the cave.

"It's red-and-yellow patterned on the back," Dirk said. "Does that mean anything?"

"Brighter colors usually mean deadlier poison," Dena said, "Warns people to stay away. Of course, some harmless Old Earth snakes mimic deadly snakes to trick people into leaving them alone. It is red and black."

"I just said—"

"We can see colors now." Dena peered through the brightening gloom. "Storm's passing. Sun's coming out."

"Good, we can get out of here," Dirk said.

"First, we have to pass Mr. Bitey," Dena said.

"Can we run by or throw rocks at it or something?"

"Yes, genius, if we had rocks, we could throw them. Do you see any throwable rocks in this sand-covered cave?"

An outcrop was near the front, behind the snake. Several rocks had split off the wall—large rocks for sitting on, not rocks for throwing.

"Not really."

"We could run by it. It can't bite all of us at once, but one of us has to carry Rocky."

"You're more concerned about a whippet than us?"

"Than you, yes. And second, he's twenty pounds. We're ten times that size. A bite that would make us sick will kill him. It's safer if the snake bites us."

"You'd let the snake bite you before it bit him?"

"He'd do the same," Dena said. "But he doesn't

217

understand the consequences."

Dirk glared at the snake. It was sitting there, flicking its tongue and staring at them.

"Can we wait it out?"

"Sure. Unless there's another storm. Or more snakes."

"So, the best thing to do is wait."

"Right."

The snake hissed and slid slowly toward them.

"Mr. Bitey face has other ideas," Dirk said. "Get behind me. Now."

***

"No response from them on the comm, Engineer," Ana said. "But they didn't sound too worried when I talked to them earlier."

"Well, I'm not going outside in this," Gavin said. He and Ana were sitting in the control room, monitoring the cameras. "Lee did a good job on burying the hose at the bottom of that pool of water. We're not getting any increase in particulates. Salt density is up, but we're well within parameters."

"Which means what for a crusty old soldier? We're here for another week or another day?"

"We can lift with full tanks in another three shifts. We'll be all topped up then. Assuming we have a pilot."

"Too bad Lee can't pilot us everywhere," Ana said. "She's not as good as Navy, but she is steadier."

"You've forgiven her for being a freak?"

"I never cared that much about that. What she needs forgiving for is leaving Scruggs behind with the Imperials."

"Seems like she saved her life by bringing Scruggs on board."

"She did, which makes it harder for me to keep my unreasonable grudge in place," Ana said. "But I'm working hard at it, and I've always been a hard worker. But I may have been wrong about her."

"Centurion, are you happy helping this Imperial tribune

guy?"

Ana transferred some notations from his board to Gavin. By dint of necessity, the crew had developed a standard watch keeping set of controls and reports. After being shamed by Dena, they even had standard handover reports.

He tapped the food consumption and stock reconciliation report to Gavin's screen and looked at him. "No. I don't trust him."

"You trust me enough to tell me that?"

"I mistrust everything and everyone," Ana said. "And because of that, I control what I share with people. I don't think you trust this tribune, either. I'm not sure why, but it doesn't matter. Given a choice between rescuing Scruggs and saving the Empire, you'd make the right choice."

"You want me to save the Empire?"

"No, you idiot, rescue Scruggs. And I know you didn't mean it about the Empire. You're not fond of the Empire, not sure why. You'd let the Empire collapse for half a glass of basic."

"Quarter glass," Gavin said. "Or a used fork. You don't need to tell the others that."

"Navy and Lee are on team Empire too often sometimes. Dena's always on Team Dena, but she may also be on Team Scruggs. We're all on Team Scruggs. Once we've got our tanks full this time, we can catch that liner, correct?"

"If all our calculations are correct, we can beat it to the next station. What do we do, then, Centurion?"

"Take some guns, board that liner, and steal her back."

"What if she doesn't want to be stolen?"

"She tells us that, fine," Ana said.

"And what if the people with her don't want her to go with us?"

"I've always wanted a glorious last stand against overwhelming odds," Ana said. "I see no reason not to extend that privilege to any guards who stand in the way."

"That's not the most sophisticated plan, Centurion," Gavin said.

"I'm open to suggestions," Ana said. "Long as it ends with Scruggs free to do what she wants, I'm happy. You're on board with that, aren't you?"

"I am," Gavin said. "She deserves to make her own decisions, and honestly, she's stood up for me and you in the past."

"We're sounding all noble here," Ana said. "Might have to go puke in Pilot's shoes and blame it on Rocky."

"What's Dirk saying to all this?"

"He'll help us get Scruggs back," Ana said. "I'm sure of that. He feels he owes her. He's in the same boat as me, wants to get her away from her guards and hear what she has to say. If she stays with us, fine, if she goes, fine, but she started with us. He views her as some weird crew member that he got into trouble."

"That's the way you think," Gavin said.

"That's the way I think," Ana agreed.

"And afterwards? Once we've got her back?"

"Pilot and Navigator have shown some disturbing tendencies to go back to work for the Empire. They may feel they have to help this Devin guy out."

"I wish they don't," Gavin said.

"I wish they don't, either," Ana said. "But no way to know till we're standing there with Scruggs in hand saying, 'What next?' and seeing what they do."

"Which might take forever," Gavin said. "Hopefully, they get back soon."

"If I know those two lazies," Ana said, "they're together, naked, in a cave somewhere, rolling in the sand. Kids today."

***

"Back, back," Dena yelled.

"I have to jig to the side." Dirk pushed her with one hand and waved at Bitey Face.

"Don't play with him. Don't threaten him. Just relax, and he'll slide away."

The snake hissed and slid at them. Rocky barked and snarled in Dena's grip.

"Cut it out, Rocky. Not now," Dena said.

"Keep that stupid dog quiet," Dirk said.

"Get away from the snake. Back up," Dena yelled.

Dirk leaped left, waved, and faked right. The snake struck out and lay full length. Dirk snatched at it. He grabbed it in the middle with both hands—a foot behind the head and held it. "Go, go. Get out."

"That's the wrong place," Dena yelled. "Drop it, or he'll curve back."

Dirk danced around, holding the snake. "Run, run."

Dena snagged Rocky by his ruff, grabbed his butt, and heaved the whippet past the struggling pair and out the front of the cave, into the lightening air.

"Aaaargah," Dirk said. He dropped the snake and jumped back, clasping his left arm. "He bit me."

"Of course he bit you, idiot. He's a snake. That's what they do."

Dirk jumped back, and the snake hissed at him from the ground and struck again. It missed as Dirk danced back, holding his arm.

Dena rushed up and grabbed Dirk and pulled him back.

"You were supposed to get out," Dirk said.

"Rocky's safe. Now, it's our turn."

Rocky's bark echoed from outside. He shook his head and flapped his ears to clear the sand from him.

"How do we get by that?" Dirk said.

The snake had slithered back, rattling its coils.

"We'll have to make a run for it," Dena said.

"This hurts like an SOB," Dirk said. "I'm not up for running."

"Want to get bit again?" Dena asked.

"Nope. Say when."

"I'll count to—NO, ROCKY. NO."

Rocky charged back into the cave, barking. The snake heard and spun, hissing. Rocky charged up, bowed, and barked. The snake hissed and waved. Rocky danced left, the snake's head followed. Rocky danced right, and the snake's head followed again. Then Rocky jumped. The snake struck.

And missed.

Rocky leaped sideways at the final instant, and the snake streaked by, landing fully extended, in front of his snapping jaws. Rocky's head darted down, and his teeth crunched into the snake's spine inches behind the triangular head. He set his feet and shook, shook, shook the snake slinging its tail up in the air, across and down.

The snake's spine popped, and the whole length shivered. Rocky continued to shake it to death, growling, snapping his head back and forth until with another crack and the snake hung limp in his jaws.

He stepped back, gave it a final victory shake, then dropped the twitching corpse at Dena's feet, wagging his tail.

***

"We're topped off, you two," Gavin said over the comm. "Pull it out and stow it away. Fifteen minutes to shut down the pumps and change over the valves, and we can lift anytime."

Ana waded into the stream and lifted the last rock off the top of the hose. "If we have a pilot. Did you have to put so many rocks on top of this, Navigator?"

"I didn't see you volunteering to sit out here in the sandstorm and hold it in the water, Centurion," Lee said, hauling another rock.

"Good point. I withdraw my criticism. You put the right number of rocks on top. As evidenced by the fact that the hose didn't break free in the wind."

"I've been on ships all my life, Centurion. I know about

fueling."

"I said I withdraw my complaint, and—shades of dead Emperors. Look at that." He climbed out of the water and stared down the stream.

Lee's eyes widened, and she climbed out of the water and keyed her comm. "Gavin, we need you out here."

"Problem?"

"Just come out," Lee said. "You need to see this."

Ana and Lee exchanged glances and waited for Gavin.

Gavin came down the ramp and walked following the hose. "What's going on?"

Lee pointed downstream.

Dirk and Dena were stumbling up the river bed. Dirk's upper left arm and part of his shoulder was a mass of bruises. A sling made from knotted leaves draped his forearm. Scratches covered his chest and legs, some dried, some showing lines of blood.

Dena supported him. Her knees and legs were scraped raw, and weeping red crust oozed blood through the sand covering her whole body. Dirt and green stains covered her from feet to knees.

Red sunburns covered their shoulders, faces, and necks as they limped up. Dena helped Dirk stumble up the river to stand in front of the three gaping crewmembers.

The two were naked, without even shoes.

Dirk coughed, spat, and shook off Dena's arm. "Engineer. Status report?"

"Umm." Gavin looked at the other two, then back at Dirk. "Fueling complete. Tanks are topped up. Some housekeeping tasks, but we could lift in thirty minutes."

"Excellent work," Dirk said. "Centurion? What's the weather report?"

Ana laughed. "Weather? Clear for takeoff, Pilot. Storm blew itself through."

"Outstanding," Dirk said. "Navigator, we have a course plotted?"

"To the jump limit, Pilot," Lee said.

"Outstanding," Dirk said. "We lift in thirty minutes. I, um, I'll need a little time in the med pod before we do, though."

"Perhaps find some clothes, too, Pilot," Ana said.

"Of course, of course," Dirk said. He hobbled up to the ramp and vanished inside.

The three of them swiveled their eyes to Dena.

"What happened?" Lee asked.

"Old man," Dena said, "you still keep that Amiens Brandy in that cupboard in the lounge?"

"Yup," Ana said.

"I'm going to have a few shots and then sleep. I'll pay you later."

"On the house," Ana said. "My treat. Where's Rocky?"

Dena yelled. "Rocky, let's go."

A furry black form charged up from the river bed. His tail was wagging, and a long form dragged from his mouth. Rocky ran up in front of the group, dropped his burden, and rolled on his back in joy.

"What in the name of dead Emperors is that?" Gavin asked.

"Dead rattlesnake," Dena said. "Poisonous but not lethal."

"How do you know that?" Gavin asked.

"Dirk tested it for us. I'm having those drinks and going to bed. Let's go, Rocky."

Rocky snapped upright, wagged his tail, grabbed the snake and followed.

The three others looked at each other.

"Well," Ana said, "I always considered myself a sophisticated man, and I've got my pride. I take second place to nobody. But I have to say, after seeing this—the snake, the bruises, the blood, the bites, and the scratches, I wouldn't be able to keep up with that girl in bed. She's too much of a handful." He shrugged. "Maybe the pilot is the better man, after all."

CHAPTER TWENTY-FIVE

"Those are the ugliest statues I have ever seen," Hernandez said.

"Agree," Weeks said. "Kiddo, have you no taste at all?"

"I have plenty of taste. Thank you," Scruggs said. "Aren't they beauties?" She lined up the four statues delivered to their suite.

Called "The Four Corners of the Planet," they looked like squat candles—burnished aluminum bases with carved wooden cylinders slotted into them. Geometric patterns, each different, etched each cylindrical column. All had the theme of a squared base melting into a rounded blob, with a colored knob at the top.

"I made them myself," Scruggs said, arranging them on the dining room table. "In that class. Aren't they beautiful? And don't call me kiddo."

"They're something," Hernandez said. "Why four of them?"

"They're a set," Scruggs said. "The four corners of the earth. We can have one in each room maybe. The colors stand out."

"If dark blue can be said to stand out," Hernandez said, "which, since the rest of this room is those ugly greens, it does. But I'll pass on one in my rooms."

"Me too," Weeks said.

"You'll be sorry. They're hand carved by master wood carvers at the last planet we visited. They'll be worth a fortune on the secondary market in the core." She turned doe eyes on Weeks.

"Fine," Weeks said. "I'll hide them in my closet so nobody sees."

"And," Scruggs said, holding up another statue, "this one is unique. You can custom select the materials, and I had this one made up special. I call it 'Comet's passing.'"

"Thanks all the same, but still pass," Hernandez said.

Scruggs held it out to Weeks. "This is for you. I made it special. Please."

Weeks rolled his eyes. "Fine, I'll put it on the dresser."

Hernandez grinned. "Are you going to play poker with your lady friends today?"

"Of course," Scruggs said. "Let me change." She ducked inside her room.

After the door closed, Weeks faced Hernandez. "This is not good. Going to the same spot every day for weeks. We should vary our pattern."

"Vary how?" Hernandez said. "There's a limited number of places to go here. Restaurant. Casino. Shopping. And the gym, and she never goes to the gym."

"She should be better by now," Weeks said.

"Next stop, maybe we'll get a doctor to look at her."

"Tomorrow? That backwater planet with the waterfalls?"

Hernandez checked her gun and put it inside her oversized purse. "Not there. Next real stop, in the Antares Sector. A week from now."

"Yay, another week of watching her play cards— badly—and buy ugly knickknacks in the gift shop."

"You don't have to take your turn if you don't want it. But remember, no casino, no dinner."

The dinner reservations were only for two people, and the purser had insisted no other tables were open.

Hernandez and Weeks had struck a deal—one of them escorted Scruggs on that day's boring activities but got the sumptuous dinner. The other got the day off. Both spent their extra time in the gym working out and flirting with rich twits who invariably treated them like hired help.

Weeks had been spending some time with a bored trophy wife, and Hernandez was known to take drinks from a surprisingly well-off insurance executive. "Insurance is much more interesting than people think," he would say to her. "Accounting too."

"It would almost have to be," she had told him.

Both kept a close watch on the fabulous four, as they called the suspicious couples who looked like professional kidnappers.

Weeks cracked his knuckles. He would stay in the room while Hernandez and Scruggs went to dinner. The room was never unguarded at any time.

"I thought she was some sort of kill-em-all high-powered army girl. She seems more of a vapid shopping type. Those freighter reprobates were lying to us."

"Could be," Hernandez said. "But Devin believed her, and he's harder to fool than he looks."

"So, it's Devin now, is it?" Weeks said.

Hernandez stuck her tongue out at him. "If I want it to be. But you're right. She should be better by now, walking unaided, and an active woman like her would want to go to the gym and work out or something like that. She spends way too much time alone in her cabin."

Scruggs finished dressing. Her bright clashing colors were the talk of the ship, at least if you counted the first-class passengers as the ship, and used the word sneering instead of talking.

One memorable day, she wore puce and mauve at the same time. She checked herself in the mirror. She'd had so much in the ways of clothes purchased, delivered, returned, altered, refunded, and given away that Hernandez and Weeks had given up keeping track. Her custom "favorite" above-the-ankle boots had hidden sheaths for cut-down knives she had gotten mixed up in a shipment of earrings and jewelry. She paired them with a tooled leather belt matching her pants with a flap in the back that would conceal a handgun, provided she wore a loose shirt. Of which she had many.

She rolled her long sleeves back and checked the scrunchies she kept on her arms. When playing poker, she practiced fiddling with her hair, palming a card she needed for a later hand and hiding it up her sleeve.

Her poker loses had stabilized. She lost every day but only a little. Alone in her room, she spent at least two hours every day working out, sits-ups, push-ups, weight lifting—that's what the constant stream of statues were for. The ugliest pair, called "Nighttime Over the Rings," were perfect as free weights.

She'd snuck away a half dozen times in the past weeks by matching her clothes to one of the woman playing with her. She always did it when Hernandez was watching, and her coplayers assumed she was on an assignation with Weeks.

She didn't disabuse them of the notion. Her game time wanderings and nonstop bribery had made her a crew favorite, and she'd been able to tour the shuttle, learn the docking and undocking procedures, access protocols, and places to hide. The next time the shuttle dropped, she was sure she'd be able to sneak on board.

Once on dirtside, with even a short head start, she'd be able to either take passage off-planet or hide in the locality until the Artemis Star left. She'd crewed a freighter, worked as a mercenary, and had shot people.

She knew her way with weapons.

She was dangerous.

Finally.

Scruggs took two deep breaths, checked her hair, and sprayed a sprig of perfume on her face. "Today's the day." She entered the main cabin.

Hernandez checked out Scruggs's outfit as she arrived.

The girl had good fashion sense when she used it. Which should be more often. This outfit was skintight pants, low-heeled boots, and a loose blouse that showed a surprising amount of cleavage. A sexy outfit. A very sexy outfit.

"You look good, girl," Hernandez said. "Great outfit."

"Not bad, kiddo. Not bad," Weeks said.

Scruggs walked across to him, leaned in, ran her hand over his shoulder, and punched him lightly. "I'm not a kid, remember?" She gave a brilliant smile, then strode out of the room. As the door opened, she looked over her shoulder. "I've got a package arriving in a while—it's for you, Weeks."

Weeks blinked twice and followed her with his eyes. Hernandez grinned as she realized he was staring at Scruggs's butt, then remembered Scruggs was out in the corridor unsecured.

"Crap." She darted out. "Pick up your jaw from the floor, Romeo." She cleared the door and was relieved to see Scruggs stopped down the hall, leaning on her cane.

"Sorry about heading right out like that," Scruggs said. "I know it wasn't part of our deal, but this one time, I needed to make an exit that he'd remember."

"He remembered it, I'll say," Hernandez said. "I wasn't kidding. That is a great outfit. Why don't you dress like that normally?"

"One of the poker girls helped me. She said I was a bit too... bright with my other clothes."

"I've been saying that for days," Hernandez said, walking beside Scruggs but keeping her purse ready.

"Could be I'm a slow learner," Scruggs said. "But I do think I've finally got it. I hope I made an impression on Weeks."

"You made an impression on Weeks, that's for sure," Hernandez said.

"That was the idea," Scruggs said. "Listen, dinner will be short tonight. We'll be going back early."

"You're not doing that shuttle tour of the rings are you? We didn't talk about that—it's not part of our agreement."

The Artemis Star was pulling into an orbital stop that night. They had shuttle tours for tourists who wanted to see the planetary rings and a short hop to the surface for a ground level visit to some waterfalls, but Theta Vadoria wasn't much of a planet—mining, forestry, a small spaceport, and tourist attractions for passing liners.

"Not interested," Scruggs said. "I've seen rings before. And waterfalls. We're going to eat quickly and head back to the room early."

"That'll be boring," Hernandez said. "Sitting, staring at me in the suite all night. I don't play cards, remember. What's left, watching vids together and trying on each other's blouses?"

"It will involve clothes, yes," Scruggs said. "But not yours."

"Our deal was you can't leave the suite unescorted," Hernandez said.

"I won't be leaving the suite, and I won't be alone."

"You think. Ohhhhhh. He thinks you're a kid."

"I can change his mind about that."

"Do tell."

Scruggs stopped walking, leaned the cane against the wall, fluffed her hair, pulled her cleavage open, and leaned back on her heels the way Dena had taught her. "Want to bet against me?"

Hernandez pursed her lips. "Nope. Let's get dinner. And, Scruggs?"

"Yes?"

"Good luck."

CHAPTER TWENTY-SIX

"Do we have enough fuel capacity to do this?" Devin asked the assembled group of officers.

He'd convened all his planning team in his office on his return from the raid. They'd been working on the invasion while he was doing his raid.

"Not for all the ships, no," his engineering liaison said. "And we still have problems with cross-loading and deep-space refueling."

"What about other supplies?" Devin asked. "Food, parts, that sort of thing."

"We can't feed everybody," the logistics officer said. "Not with a margin of safety. We don't have all the parts we need for the freighters and the tankers—they are all civilian spec, but they need lots of fiddly items. Some can be loaded up here, not all. The corvettes can take civilian specs items as well, so we need to make sure they get their share. And the Valhalla is new enough it's got a full set of spares on board. But everything on Pollux is military-grade. We'll be close to the line. We'll need to take a whack of those spares to convert if needed. If we could find that replenishment freighter—"

"We can't," Lionel said. "I mean, we can't count on it. Tribune, we're assuming that we lose the battle at the far end and have to retreat without any opportunity to refuel or replenish there. If we capture the station, even partly intact, with any reasonable luck, we can put things back together there. Plus, we'll want to leave a few ships there as a garrison, anyway."

"If we don't win, we'll have to retreat," Devin said. "But we can take the force that's there now. If they don't reinforce," Devin said.

"I agree."

"What if they reinforce?" somebody asked. "What if

they've already reinforced?"

Devin raised his eyebrows.

"No way to tell, Tribune," Lionel said.

"Well, in any event, we'll take the brunt of it," Devin said. "We'll strip the Pollux if necessary to give the other ships what they need—"

Lionel stood and walked to the door of Devin's office. Devin blinked. "Subprefect?"

"Ladies and gentlemen, the tribune and I need the room. Excuse us all, please."

The room emptied rapidly, leaving a standing subprefect and a nonplussed tribune.

"Well?" Devin said.

"Regardless of what happens on this raid, two ships have to come back if it's a fiasco. One is the Valhalla, and the other is the Pollux. We can leave the corvettes behind if we have to, and all the merchant ships are expendable. But we can't lose our only major fleet element and our only marine strike force in this sector because we gave up our fuel and spares to a forty-year-old reserve unit."

"We are not a major fleet element," Devin said.

"In this fleet, we are the major fleet element."

"Pollux is a frigate. We're supposed to protect merchant ships and convoys."

"Show me a convoy, and we'll start protecting. There aren't any. This is a strike to recover occupied Imperial territory before it's reinforced. If that garrison has been reinforced by now, then we've already lost. We load those freighters as lightly as is necessary, jump to the adjacent system, suck all their fuel over to the warships, leave them there, and hope we can come back for them."

"If we lose?"

"Jump back, collect survivors, scuttle the ships, and carry on or let the Confeds know where they are and that they are ready to surrender. Any Confed force that can beat us will be able to deal with them."

Devin's voice rose. "I will not send others to do my

fighting for me."

"That's your actual job now. You're not a frigate captain anymore. You command a task force."

Devin got louder. "Four corvettes and a frigate isn't a task force."

"It is now."

Devin slammed his fist on the table. "I will not cower behind some civilian freighters. I am not a coward!" The door light lit. Devin slammed the lock button, and the outer office door slid open. Devin's eyes flicked, and his voice roared. "What?"

It was Imin. "Beg your pardon, sir. You're shouting. Is everything okay?"

"Shouting?"

"Can hear you outside, sir. Through this thick door. You're shouting louder than I had ever heard."

"I... I... the subprefect is giving me some unpleasant news."

"I'm sure you'll be able to cope with it, sir. That's why you're the tribune, after all."

"Indeed," Devin said. He sat. "Indeed. Thank you, Imin. That will be all."

"Sir," Imin said, stepping out and closing the door.

Lionel sat at the table, contemplating his fingers. Devin glared at him.

"Well?"

"They ran the numbers before you got back. The logistics people. They showed them to me before the meeting. The corvettes are the problem. They're the shortest-legged, slowest, and hardest to refuel and rearm. Other than the freighters, of course. They'll take twice as long to get there if we make them arrive full of fuel. But if we strip them all to the bare bones, they can jump into Sand Harbor with us."

"But they can't jump out without refueling," Devin said.

"Nope. Just us and Valhalla. We can bring a freighter

in. Same problem. The other freighters will have to wait and hope we capture the system. Otherwise, they're in trouble, too."

"I will ride with the corvettes, then."

"No, you won't. Communication suites and sensors aren't good enough. You have to be on the Pollux."

"If we're outgunned when we come out of jump, they won't make it out."

"Correct. It's the only way."

"You sound pretty certain on this. Are you sure your certainty isn't defined by the fact that you'll be on the only ship to get away?"

Lionel held up his hand, the one missing fingers. "What do you think?"

Devin slumped behind his desk. "I'm such an ass. I'm sorry I said that. Arrange a meeting. I'll tell them."

"I already did, sort of. Everybody knows."

"Except me."

"You didn't need to know. You told us what you wanted done, and it's our job to do it."

"I can stop this. I don't have to go charging in there. I could call to the core and demand reinforcements."

"You could. You didn't have to charge into that burning compartment, either. But you did. And there's that small matter of missing messages, arrest demands, that sort of thing. This is a problem, and it's better for the Empire if the man on the scene deals with it and deals with it soon. Right now, this is some border-baron type of thing. You go in and thrash the Confeds' local thug. We get our system back. They hang whoever started this fiasco, and we all make nice. You don't do that, they get used to having that system, bring up their battle fleet, we bring up our core reserves. Next thing you know, we have a real Imperial war going on. Isn't stopping that worth sacrificing a freighter and a corvette or two?"

Devin dropped his head in his hands. "I hate myself right now."

"I suggest whiskey," Lionel said. "Tribune, I've got a tabbo-ton of work to do right now—fueling, cross-loading, threatening freighter captains. I need to go."

"Carry on."

Lionel stood, braced, and gave the formal cross-chest salute. "Glory to the Empire."

"Glory." Devin slumped. "Glory."

Lionel was as good as his word. Two corvettes left in three days, two more corvettes three days after that, in company with two freighters each. The freighters carried food and extra fuel. Lionel and his staff had drained the purpose-built tanker fueling them all up and confiscated every shuttle in the fleet to dump as many supplies from all the other ships into the ones leaving. He'd loaded up all the food and consumables he could find.

Each group of four ships was to make a jump, suck fuel from one of the freighters, then split up. The emptied freighter would jump back. The remaining three ships jumped again, emptied the remaining freighter, and jumped once more to the deep-space rendezvous. At the rendezvous, the corvettes had enough fuel for one more jump—into the Sand Harbor system. The freighters coasted with enough power to keep life support running for a long time, but they were effectively stuck in the dark till they were refueled.

The stay-behind ships spent the next two weeks reloading what they had donated to the slower corvettes, refilling the tanker, and fixing anything broken in the rush to get the other ships out into the dark. Lionel spent a lot of time doing math, which he hated, so he got Imin and the Bosun to help him. Devin spent most of his time killing dummies with his sword.

"Tribune," Lionel said, stepping into the crowded exercise room. After Devin had recovered from his initial hissy fit, he'd ordered mandatory combat exercise again, and the varied schedules meant the whole crew had seen him slamming headless wooden corpses. "How goes the dismembering?"

"Outstanding," Devin said. "Ready to give me more bad news? Another delay? More fake container loads? A giant sale on home entertainment units?"

Lionel had insisted on unloading all the storage containers of supplies he had bought before loading. Three had been empty. One contained stolen video display units instead of food trays.

"That sale proved extremely popular," Lionel said. "I got a display unit for the officers' mess. Excellent quality. Santana snapped up a bunch for his marines. The rest went to a consortium of on-planet schools."

"I'm glad I could help contribute to the primary education system on Papillon," Devin said.

"Oh, not those type of schools. Dancing schools. They're using them to teach dance."

"We delayed an Imperial fleet for a day so that a bunch of dilettantes can learn to tango?"

"The tango is hard to learn. I tried it myself. It's difficult. You have to bend. And I'm glad you're finally calling it a fleet. We leave end of next shift."

"Great herds of raging tabbos." Devin sliced at his dummy. "Will this ever end? Schools. Empty containers. Stolen Imperial war material. Delays. Endless delays. Wait, what was that again?"

"You have to bend." Lionel leaned over. "To tango, the man has to dip the woman, so he bends over like this, but if your back is hurt—"

"Not your dance moves, you preposterous twit. The other part."

"I'm glad you're calling us a fleet finally?"

"When do we leave? When do we leave?"

"Loading will be complete soon. We leave no later than the end of next shift."

"And you didn't think of telling me?"

"I just did."

"You said we would be days—"

"That freighter captain, the crazy one. She helped us out. Volunteered to help, in fact. She's good. Her crew shaved days off our departure."

"Outstanding," Devin said.

Two over muscled crewmen swaggered into the gym, snagged towels, then marched to the weight rack. They double-stepped at the sight of the tribune. One spun his hat backward. The other took it off, and they slid to the weight rack. Devin glanced at them, then whipped his eyes at their head.

"Halt," he yelled.

The two crewmen braced to attention.

Devin stalked over and pointed at their ball caps. "What is that? What are you wearing?"

"Tribune," the first one said, "we're lifting, doing a few sets, regulations allow any sort of convenient headgear while at the gym, and—"

"Not the type of hat, the writing. What do those letters mean—up there—M-D-V? M-D-V Crew. What's that mean?"

Lionel arrived. "Multiple daily vegetables? Make dozen vacuums?"

"Vacuums need crews? I think not." Devin crossed his arms. "Well, spaceman? What does it mean?"

The spaceman swallowed, then braced even harder and smacked an Imperial salute on his sweaty chest. "Sir. Mad Dog of the Verge, sir. Crew. Proud to serve."

"Mad Dog of the Verge?"

"Sir."

"You mean me."

"Sir."

Devin extended his hand. "Give me that." The spaceman pulled it off and handed it to Devin. The tribune rolled it in his hand. "Subprefect?"

"Sir, there may have been a delay in extending your order regarding headgear—"

"Never mind that. You're confident with your

departure estimate? Your new departure estimate?"

"Very confident, sir."

Devin raised his voice. "Spaceman?"

"Sir?"

"We leave for Sand Harbor next shift to fight the Confeds there and recapture the base."

The room erupted in cheers. Devin let it go a minute and then waved them down. When they were quiet, he continued.

"Are you ready to go, spaceman?"

"Just say the word, sir."

"We have sufficient supplies to reach the enemy and hit him hard. If faced by superior forces, we do not have enough to retreat. Not all of us. It could be a one-way trip. Still want to come?"

"Glory to the Empire, sir!"

The room cheered again.

Devin waited for it to settle. "Subprefect, continue your preparations."

"Tribune."

"This hat is confiscated," Devin said. He glared at the spaceman. "Any objections?"

"No, sir."

"Good." Devin rolled the hat in his hands again, lifted it and set it on his head, then gave the Imperial salute. The room cheered again. Devin tightened his sword belt, then marched out of the gym. Lionel trailed. Once clear of the gym, Devin strode toward his room but pulled off the hat and examined it more closely. "You were right, Subprefect."

"About the loading? I told you we'd figure it out."

"Not that. This." Devin brandished the hat. "The colors. They do pop."

CHAPTER TWENTY-SEVEN

"Emergence in one minute," Lee said.

The Heart's Desire was coming out of jump. The fuel from Bakar-1b had lasted the two jumps. They had one more to go to cut Scruggs's course.

"Right," Dirk said from the command chair. "We're going to stay just long enough to load the new course, then jump again."

Dena giggled while she typed on her screen. "Very masterful, Dirk, that tone of voice. Makes me hot. I might need some privacy."

"We might want to get star sights and calculate a position first, Pilot, before we jump," Lee said. "To refine the course."

"That's what I meant, of course," Dirk said.

Gavin's voice came over the intercom.

"And run a quick check on the systems. Make sure we're ready to jump."

"Of course, of course," Dirk said. "That's what I meant as well."

"So, we're stargazing?" Ana asked. "And repair-wishing and, in Nature Girl's case, navel gazing."

"If you're using your navel, old man, you're doing it wrong," Dena said.

"How long?" Ana asked.

"Well, you need to unbuckle and go back to your room," Dena said. "And get in the mood—"

"If I wanted to be in a good mood, I'd shoot somebody," Ana said. "How long will we be in this system?"

"Depends on the sights we get," Lee said. "Not too long."

"As long as we get ahead of the Artemis Star, we can organize rescuing Scruggs."

"Pilot, what if it took some other route?" Lee asked from the navigator's seat next to Dirk.

"It won't. She'll be there."

"Dirk, what if she left before they came into this system?" Dena asked.

"Her guards won't let her leave," Dirk said. "She'll be there."

"Skipper," Gavin said, "what if she doesn't want to be rescued? What if she wants to go back to her family or the Empire or whatever?"

"She won't. She's had plenty of time to do that before, and she never did. She'll come with us."

The blue light of jump faded, and the screens flashed as they correlated data.

"Centurion?"

"What is it, Navy?"

"You're normally the most negative of this bunch of frazzled pessimists. Haven't you got some sort of defeatist question to ask?"

"Not loaded up. Should I make something up?"

"It will sort of balance things out."

"Let's see... I know she'll be there. I know the ship will be there. I know she'll want to come back with us, and if they're stopping her, I know we can rescue her by force. I'm not sure what else could happen."

WHAM.

The ship slammed sideways, and they all punched into their restraints. The lights went out, fans stopping, and only the screens on emergency power glowed.

"I suppose," Ana said in the darkness, "that I could ask what would happen if our ship was destroyed by rogue space debris, but that's normally pretty unlikely."

"Normally." Dirk tapped the intercom. "Gavin? Engineer? Gavin?" He switched to the "all ships" channel. "Anyone in engineering, please answer."

"Gavin's the only person in engineering, Navy. Who else did you think would answer? Rocky?"

"It's protocol. I've got no helm control here, Lee. Main drive is dead. Or at least the display. You have anything?"

"Nope. Thrusters are up, but main screen shows no data for me."

"What hit us?" Dena asked.

"Don't know," Lee said. "The sensors hadn't adjusted from the jump yet. A hunk of rock, probably."

"Why are all the lights out?" Dena asked. "What's broken?"

"Let's find out," Ana said, unbuckling. "Pilot, you and the navigator stay here. Nature Girl and I will go see if Gavin needs help."

"I think—"

WHAM.

The Heart's Desire shook again. The atmo alarm bonged, and emergency lights flashed red.

"Hull breach," Lee said. "We're losing air."

Ana recovered from being rocked sideways onto the wall, then reached back and slammed the hatch cover shut. "How bad?"

"Slow but steady. Pilot, we need to suit up."

Dirk was already pulling his helmet on. Lee followed.

Ana fumbled above his seat for his emergency plastic bag. "I've got my temp one. Everyone, suit up, and I'll grab my regular one."

"Ummm..." Dena said.

The three paused, and she grinned. "My helmet is in my quarters—" Her face flashed white, and she pulled at her straps. "Rocky! Rocky's there. We have to get Rocky."

Ana stuck out a hand. "We need to keep the cockpit aired up, or we won't be able to conn the ship."

"But Rocky. He saved our life. Dirk?"

"Ana's right. We need to get in touch with the engineer, and—"

"Ungrateful snot. Just like you to leave somebody who helps you to die." Dena blinked. "Wait, that's not—"

"Be quiet," Dirk said. "Just be quiet, a moment." He

took a deep breath. "Centurion?"

"Hold Ms. Dog Lover here while you fix the ship?" He pushed Dena back into her seat. "I'm sorry, Dena. He's a great dog. He's loyal and friendly, and he keeps trying to bite Navy here. God bless his furry little heart, but we need to keep the air in while they figure things out."

"If we don't go now," Dena said, "while there's still some air, then I won't get a helmet, and we'll all be stuck in here. Or you'll suffocate me next time you need to open the door."

"You should have remembered to bring a helmet—"

"I grew up in a forest, you metal-headed toad," Dena pushed at Ana's arm. "How the heck should I know that? Did any of you space geniuses ever think to tell me that? And before you say 'I should have known,' you all should have known how to stay alive without freezing on a planet or how to swim so you wouldn't drown or how to shoot things with a slingshot and not a gun, but you don't."

"You can't go." Ana held her back. "Pilot?"

"Lee, how long till full decompression?" Dirk asked.

"A few minutes. We're at three-quarters now."

"Fine. Everybody, lock helmets and go to internal air. Those of you with helmets, at least. Centurion, take Dena back to the air lock and shove her in there. We can pressurize and depressurize that separately. Dena, check the cabinet in the lock, find a skinsuit or an emergency pack or something. Get suited up. Centurion, once she's in there, hoof it back to her quarters, open up, get the dog, and run him back to the lock."

"There's an emergency bubble thing for him in Scruggs's room," Dena said. "An inflatable thing she made up for him."

"Get that and dump it in the air lock. Worse comes to worse, you and that rabid mongrel get vacuum burn as we dump the lock air down. Then the two of you are stuck there for the duration. Go."

"Navy," Ana said, "why not leave her here, and I'll—"

"Shut up, Centurion," Dirk said. "I'm the pilot. We're in space. I'm in charge. Air lock. Dog. Suit. Air lock. Got it?"

Ana laughed. "Outstanding. The duke rides again. Got it. Operation Dog Rescue commencing in ten seconds. Helmets locked everyone. Dena, you'll want to hold your breath—don't—you'll rupture your lungs. Keep breathing normally. Got it?"

Dena nodded. "Let's get Rocky."

Ana checked his emergency pack was inflated and covering his head, and he had air flowing and grasped the hatch. "Opening in three, two, one. Opening now."

Ana set his foot and used both hands. The hatch didn't budge. He snapped up a panel next to the hatch, reached in, and twisted two handles in opposite directions, then yanked a lever. The equalizer valve snapped open. Air hissed out from the bridge to the rest of the ship.

With the hatch opened at a touch, Ana climbed through, Dena on his heels. In the dark, Ana relied on the handholds. Hatch displays glowed in the distance, and an emergency light burned ahead in the lounge. Without acceleration, they floated down the corridor. Ana came to the air lock, flipped the hatch open, and Dena dove in. Ana slammed the hatch shut behind her and carried on down the passage. Lights flashed behind him as she aired it up. Next to the locker were the fueling lines. The lines dangled loose, the black of space showing through cracks behind them.

"Pilot, something hit us at the fueling port. Lines are snapped, and there's a leak. Where's the patches? I can get that one. Pilot?"

No answer.

Of course no answer, you idiot. Anastasios, your helmet has a radio, not your emergency bag.

Cursing the whole while, Ana pulled himself through the lounge, past the first deck of cabins, and down to the second. The ladder rungs set into the floor were easy to

243

find in the dark, and he counted hand pulls to his room. He yanked open the door, found his locker, and pawed for his regular helmet and pack. Grabbing that, he steered it out to the corridor and climbed back up. Dena's and Scruggs's rooms were on this level.

Rocky was strapped onto the bed, pushing against his restraints, whining in the thinning air. White eyes, pink tongue, and white froth gleamed in the near dark.

"Let's go, furry buddy," Ana said. He unstrapped Rocky from the bed, and the dog bounded off, yelping.

The higher pitch of the yelps in the low air pressure made Ana grit his teeth. Higher pitch meant less air. He pushed into the hallway, grabbed his floating helmet, floating pack, floating dog, and trundled up to the bridge.

Rocky bounced off the walls. His eyes were wide, and his mouth was continuing to froth. The reduced air pressure made him pant.

"At least I don't have to tell you not to hold your breath," Ana said. His ears popped, and a breeze tickled his hands.

"Rocky, my boy, one of those cracks just snapped open. We need to speed up here. Once we get you in that bag, you'll be fine."

Rocky climbed into Ana's arms, trying to get as close as possible. His yelps had changed to whimpers.

Ana pushed around the corridor and pulled at Scruggs's door.

Locked.

"Emperor's balls."

***

Gavin flipped the mechanical breaker over. The Heart's Desire had electrical and computer-controlled surge protectors, but sometimes, things got confused, and old style mechanical backups were necessary. Something had shorted out two of the main electrical lines, in such a way the computerized breakers hadn't tripped.

He wasn't a hundred percent sure, but he figured it was the rock that had banged a chunk of the hull in on the other side of the engineering section, bending one of the main power conduits and also breeching hull integrity.

Gavin never went more than a hand's breath away from his helmet and emergency equipment, so he now had a full helmet, gloves, and boots on as the atmo dropped to near zero.

The breaker didn't hold for even a second but popped again. Gavin skipped it and moved down the panel, watching the engineering board as he flipped through the other breakers. Three wouldn't reset.

Two of those were the main drive, and one was the landing ramp. Main drive, he'd look at later. First, the leaks.

Lights blazed after he reset the environmental circuit. Heat radiated from the heating pads, consoles restarting, and fans whirred silently in a near vacuum. Gavin tapped through his screens, cut the fans, and turned off the atmo dump. Next, he dug out a can of hard foam from a cabinet, crawled to the power lines, and sprayed the dent until the foam stopped whistling out the dented metal. It would take a few minutes to set, so he turned to the communications screen.

He tried his radio. "Skipper?"

No answer. He flipped through his console again, found the internal radio repeaters, brought them online, then tried again.

"Skipper?"

Nothing.

He routed all signals to the intercom.

"Skipper?"

"Engineer?" Dirk said. His voice echoed out of every radio on the ship. "Status?"

"We've got power, life support, and most other electrical systems. No main drive. The drive isn't damaged, just the power couplings. I fixed a leak back here, and I'm repressurizing."

"Was your hatch shut for emergence?"

"Of course."

"Then, there's another leak somewhere else," Dirk said. "We've got near vacuum behind us. Ana took Dena to the air lock—fool girl forgot her helmet. He's rescuing the dog as well."

"Rescuing the dog?"

"Not now. Are you suited? Can you go forward and check things out?"

"Can do," Gavin said. "I'm airing up engineering right now, but that will take a few minutes. I'll have to go out on the hull to fix this bump, though, but I've got foam holding it."

"How long for main drives?"

Gavin shook his head, even though Dirk couldn't see it. "Not soon. Ten minutes in the main cabins won't make any difference."

"Find out what's going on. Why can't I hear them on the radio?"

"I had to restart the repeaters, but they should have heard me."

"What about the repeaters in the air lock?"

"Don't know," Gavin said. "I'll find out."

"We can go help look. We've got helmets," Dirk said.

"You have boots and gloves, too, Skipper?"

"Not vacuum rated."

"Pressure is way down. Space burn will set in right away," Gavin said. "And I'd rather we not lose the air in the control room yet, just in case. I can handle it. Hang tight and let me look." Gavin exchanged a few more technical settings with Lee to have her monitor the drive systems from there.

Her boards were coming up, and the power shutdown had dropped the control systems, but readings were reappearing.

Engineering was separated from the rest of the ship by

an air lock, which also had a ventral hatch for dropping to the surface of a planet or bringing up supplies.

He stepped in, checked that all the hatches were sealed, pumped the air out, and opened the door to the rest of the ship. He grabbed a crash kit hanging from a nearby bulkhead, including patches and foam, and pulled forward. The hold was bright and empty, and starkly clear without air to bend light or make shadows.

Gavin proceeded past the ramp and the locked cabinets, then climbed into the second hab unit. Ana's door was open, as was Dena's.

Random items floated by. An empty food tray. A sock. Part of a revolver cleaning kit. The crew knew better than to leave items unsecured when the ship was moving— somebody must have ransacked a drawer with no thought for wreckage. His own room was sealed.

"Gavin? Anything?"

"Nobody on Hab Two level," Gavin said. "Where are they?"

"Try the air lock," Dirk said.

Gavin climbed up to Hab One. Lee's, Dirk's, and Scruggs's rooms. All closed. The doors weren't airtight, but they would give some protection. But even if he knocked on it, he wouldn't hear an answer, and he didn't want to drag anybody out if they had some sort of air cushion in there.

He climbed through the lounge. No debris there—even Dena had been drilled to never leave anything that could float away if they had to maneuver. Next up was the air lock. He pressed forward and saw the hole near the fuel lines.

"Imperial toenails. Skipper, fuel master valves got beat up."

"Risk of fire?"

"I always drain them before we lift. There's no air left back here and no hydrogen or oxygen leaks I can see. We'll have problems refueling, though. I'm going to foam that hole."

"How big is it?"

"Big enough that it's probably the one that drained us."

Gavin pulled over and examined the hole. Whatever had hit them hadn't penetrated. Probably hit, smashed into pieces, and bounced off. But where it had hit a whole section of steel was punched in, with cracks and jagged edges bent in. The steel hadn't so much bent as shattered.

Gavin unfolded a number four circle patch, slapped it over the center of the biggest of the cracks, and methodically sprayed the seams. Two other small cracks radiated past his seal, and he sprayed those as well, which would have to sit for a while.

"Lee, I've got it patched. Can you give me quarter pressure?"

"Stand by," Lee said. "Pumps are running."

That would take ten minutes to air up this much of the ship, even to one-quarter normal.

"Can you hold it at five minutes and check for leaks?"

"Will do."

Gavin continued up to the air lock. This was the hard part. Either they were okay in there or dead in a cabin. But the ship comes first.

Gavin examined the board next to the air lock. It all showed green, except for the intercom. The red light next to Radio manual shutdown was lit.

"Skipper, they turned off the radio in the air lock," Gavin said.

"Why in the Emperor's name would they do that?" Dirk asked.

"No idea," Gavin said. "There's pressure inside, but I can't see through the window."

"Fogged?"

"Iced. Frost."

"Somebody alive in there, at least."

"Yep. Should I pull the overrides?"

"Lee, are we airing up?" Dirk said.

"First test passed already," Lee said. "Quarter pressure in five minutes. Half in fifteen. Full in thirty."

"Hold it at half," Dirk said. "Check for leaks and then yank the lock."

"Got it, Skipper," Gavin said. "Um, I could go down and check in the cabins..."

"If they're still in the cabins, they died ten minutes ago, before you even got out of engineering. Stay there."

Gavin went back and ran his hands over the fuel system. The rock had punched the hull in and smashed the main transfer valve. It was a set of cross-connect valves joining the external hoses, the landing line hoses, the drains, the fuel transfer system, and pretty much every fueling system on the ship. He'd have a heck of a time fueling or sucking in water from a planet or processing water into H and O. He could rig a bypass line, but he didn't have tools sophisticated enough to fabricate a multi-input-output valve.

"Half pressure," Lee said, "There's still another leak, but it's small. We can adjust. Or crack more air."

"About that." Gavin banged on the air lock door. Somebody inside banged back. "We'll talk fuel-cracking later. They're in there. I'm opening up."

The hatch wouldn't open against the difference in air pressure. Unlike the bridge hatch interconnects, these were designed to be hard to open. He'd have to fetch tools, unscrew plugs, and retaining bolts. After fussing with levers and bolts for five minutes, he gave up. In ten minutes or less, the pressure difference would be low enough he could open.

He removed his helmet and gloves and racked them on his belt, then stared at the fuel lines, biting his lip. The new air was cold and dry, and he took relieved breaths as he waited. The air lock lights flashed green, showing pressure on both sides. He spun the wheel and pulled the hatch inward.

A furry black figure shot out of the lock and hit him in

the chest, knocking him back. He bounced back into the hull. Rocky tried to lick his face. Rocky's tongue slapped inches from him but didn't seem wet. Rocky wore an emergency air bag system, secured with tape at his collar.

"What the heck," Gavin said. "Dena?"

Dena appeared in the lock. "Here. Give me a hand. We need to get Centurion into the med unit."

Gavin stepped through the hatch. Ana lay on the ground, wheezing, air mask on his nose and mouth and his face, and all exposed skin burned a bright red.

CHAPTER TWENTY-EIGHT

Scruggs and Hernandez returned to their cabin after the usual sumptuous dinner. This time, the chef had served braised pork cutlets with real peas, scalloped potatoes, and the usual scandal as Scruggs refused the main course and had a basic tray instead.

"Those peas were exquisite," Hernandez said.

"I hate peas," Scruggs said, kicking her ship slippers off. "Always have. My mom made me eat them when I was a kid."

"If my mom could make peas like that, I'd have eaten nothing but peas my whole childhood."

"Help yourself. I'm sure, if we ask, we can have them every night we have left."

"You think so? I still can't understand why you eat that mold they serve you."

"It's not mold. It's seaweed, and I like it."

"Weird habits." Hernandez put her purse with the hidden gun on a table by the door.

Scruggs marched to their bar table. A box had been delivered while they were gone. She snapped it open and pulled out a bottle of expensive-looking wine, two crystal glasses, then walked to Weeks's door.

"Speaking of weird habits, you sure you want to do this, kiddo?"

"Stop calling me kiddo."

"You're pretty young."

"So were you once."

"You don't know what you're doing."

"Neither did you."

"But look how bad I turned out," Hernandez said.

Scruggs put the wine and glasses on the table and crossed her arms. "Imperial navy. Promoted a couple times at least. Some sort of special ops secret unit. First-name basis with an Imperial tribune. Missions throughout the Empire and on the Verge. Currently spending her time lounging on a luxury liner, eating expensive food for free. How horrrrriibblllle for you."

"It's not all like that."

"But some of it is. Would you rather be a second-rate dance instructor, teaching little kids, or an accountant checking up on deductions for fuel storage units."

"Well, no."

Scruggs opened her hands. "Me neither." She picked up the wine and glasses and approached Weeks's door.

"He might not let you in."

Scruggs cocked a hip, thrust her chest out, and gave a sexy smile. "You think he won't?"

"Okay, he will. But you're hurt. What about your leg?"

"I don't know exactly everything I'm going to be doing, but I don't think it involves my legs."

"But..."

"But good night, Hernandez."

Hernandez sighed. "Fine. Good night."

Scruggs waited. "Good night."

"Oh, right." Hernandez used her keycard to lock the outer door. Now only she or Weeks could open the corridor door. "Good hunting." She went to her own room and the door slid shut.

Scruggs waited till Hernandez's door clicked shut, then let out a breath. She wiped her mouth and fluffed her hair. She stepped in front of the mirror by the door, arranged her hair, tugged her shirt tighter, and smoothed her pants. "Adventure awaits. Right. Adventure." She closed her eyes, breathed deep twice, then stepped across the suite and banged on Weeks's door with her bottle.

It slid open, and a tousled Weeks stood there, in shorts and a tight undershirt. He looked scruffily adorable.

"What is it?"

Scruggs pushed the wine bottle into his chest and used it to shove him back.

"Hey, I, oh. Where did you get this?"

"Special favor from the captain. Take these." She shoved the glasses at him, and he fumbled to catch them, stepping backward.

"Open the wine and pour us each a glass." Scruggs stepped into the room and palmed the door shut behind her. "Wow. I thought you'd be neater."

The bed was on the left. On the right was a built-in dresser, built-in lockers, and a bar sink at the back. Dirty clothes, random comm pads, shoes, and crumpled socks sprawled over the room. It looked like a suitcase had exploded. Twice.

"I put things where I need to find them. What are you doing here?"

"It doesn't match your personality. The whole military buttoned-up thing."

"That's my game face. I'm different off duty. And this is my room. You should leave."

"Good, I look forward to seeing your off-duty face. And the rest of you. Oh! You do like my sculptures." Scruggs pointed at his dresser. "Comet's passing. I'm glad. I had you in mind when I made that one—I knew you'd appreciate it." She fondled the blue-green cylinder.

"Why are you here?"

"A sophisticated man like you, and you don't get why a woman comes alone to your quarters at night with a bottle of wine?"

"I'm working. You're my—"

"Prisoner?"

"No, we're just protecting you from..."

"Nobody. You're doing what the tribune told you to do. And in another week, we'll be at a fleet base, and you can drop me off, and you'll never see me again, right? You'll be on some other mission or something."

"We have to go to the core and deliver some messages for the tribune, but I guess, there is no—"

"Hush." Scruggs walked to the dresser and placed the

sculpture. "Less guessing, more pouring."

"We can't do this."

"I think we can. My leg is way better now, see." Scruggs did a few knee bends. "I think I'll be able to manage it. Don't need a cane anymore."

"You're just a kid," Weeks said.

Scruggs stepped back, flipped her shirt up over her shoulders, and tossed it on the floor. Then she unbuckled her pants and slid them down to the ground. Underneath, she wore only a bra and panties.

"Do I look like a kid to you?" Scruggs said.

Weeks swallowed and then grinned. "No. No, you do not."

"Because I'm not. Now, you can ask me to leave again, or you can pour the wine. Your choice. I'd prefer you pour the wine."

"Okay. Wine. We'll have some wine and talk."

"At first," Scruggs said. "First, we talk."

"Got it." Weeks turned to the bar and set the glasses down and fumbled in a drawer for a cork puller. "I'm surprised at you."

"Why's that?" Scruggs lifted the sculpture out of the holder. The top part was molded plastic, carved in geometric shapes, the bottom a cylinder. The cylindrical part wasn't attached to the base. Once it came loose, she hefted it like a club.

"I didn't think you were attracted to me. You were always so shy but then you gave me that statue—I wondered if you made it for me?"

Scruggs swung the statue at his head behind the ear. It was a sap, not a sculpture. Firm handle, padded hitting surface so she wouldn't kill anybody, heavily weighted to give it heft. It was much heavier than it looked. She had drilled out the center of the top and put slugs of lead in it, topping it with that ridiculous blue knob of soft plastic.

Her body rocked as the club smacked him behind the ear. He moaned, dropped the corkscrew, and stumbled back into Scruggs's arms. Scruggs caught him and rolled him onto the bed.

She pulled her clothes back on, shredded some sheets and T-shirts, and tied him up with them. "It's true," she told the groaning Weeks. "I had you in mind the whole time I was making that sculpture."

Hernandez heard a soft yelp through her closed door. She dropped her comm and listened. Seconds later, she heard thuds. She grinned and returned to her reading.

***

Scruggs closed the suite door behind her. She'd swiped Weeks's keycard, tiptoed back to her own room, changed into more suitable clothes, and grabbed the escape pack she'd collected with her purchases.

She'd bought so many useless clothes that Hernandez hadn't realized that one purse was a backpack in neutral gray. She had enough regular clothes, money, and general items to survive unnoticed on a planet. Scruggs wished she'd been able to get projectile weapons or explosives but had contented herself with stolen cutlery from the restaurant and the sculpture in her room, which was converted to a weighted cudgel after she removed a few screws.

Hernandez hadn't gotten up when she left, and Weeks would be out for a while. Now she had to hit the shuttle bay. A late departure to the surface met up with a sunrise water cruise. Seeing the sun rise from the top of the local volcano was the in thing. She didn't care for the volcanoes, except that the shuttle had to go to the starport on Theta Vadoria to get there. And there were other ships departing from Theta Vadoria in the next day.

"Young Ms. Scruggs," Deeve, the purser said, when she arrived at the shuttle lock. He was supervising the planetary excursions that night. "A pleasure to see your smiling face again. You're out walking again."

As usual, he was wearing a fine dark-gray wool suit, a

fake smile, and an avaricious expression.

"I am Deeve, I am," Scruggs said. "My legs are finally feeling better, and I want to get out and walk around."

"That's wonderful news, Ms. Scruggs. I'm so happy to hear it. All of the crew, especially myself, has been concerned for your welfare from day one. It gladdens my heart to see you better."

Deeve's grin reminded Scruggs of the look on an old boarding school bully, who would take all her cookies to "help her with her weight problems, you know."

She smiled and considered what sort of weapon would be best for removing the smug grin. "Is this the volcano tour?"

"It is, miss, it is. An extravaganza the like most have not seen. Not yourself, of course, as sophisticated a young lady as you are."

Scruggs pictured a double palm smack to each ear. That would drop Deeve like a sack of used red-green-blue trays. "I'd love to go. I've never seen a volcano."

"Unfortunately, it's all full, miss. I'm sorry, no more seats down."

"Don't worry about that, Deeve," Scruggs said. "Put me in with the crew."

"Um, well."

"I'll pay the same as a regular seat," Scruggs said.

Deeve looked around for a moment to see if anyone was watching. Scruggs's bribes were truly spectacular. "Well, if you think you won't be bored..."

"When have I ever been bored, Deeve?" Scruggs extended a payment chip.

Deeve pocketed the chip and ushered Scruggs into the crew cabin, ordering out the steward riding down for supplies. That provoked a reaction from the pilots.

"We have to pick up fresh fruit—" the pilot said.

She was a cheerful older type, with a creased uniform and a slight weight problem. The kind who hiked the mountains every weekend with three big dogs named Blue,

Shadow, and Shutter.

"Jimen was supposed to help load. We don't do loading," the copilot said.

He was thin, shuttle pilot uniform also creased, and probably had his old navy uniform in a closet somewhere. Which he claimed still fit him just fine—thank you very much.

Deeve closed his fist on the payment chip Scruggs had given him. "Given the circumstances, perhaps some flexibility—"

"I'll help. It will be fun to pretend to be crew." Scruggs gave her stupid rich girl smile.

The pilot opened her mouth, but the copilot elbowed her in the side. "We can't have passengers loading cargo, miss. If anyone sees, we'll be in serious trouble."

"Who has to know?" Scruggs pointed at the nearby steward. "Here, swap your jacket and hat with me. Anybody watching will just see the uniform."

The steward hesitated, so Scruggs produced another credit chip and rolled it along her fingers and flipped it up. He had his coat off before she could offer it.

The pilots growled at Deeve, who hissed back while Scruggs put on the coat and hat, and replaced the steward in the jump seat.

"On your head, be it, Deeve. Strap in well, miss," the copilot finally said. "We used to be Imperial drop pilots. Over a hundred drops each!"

"Nearly two hundred in total," the pilot said. "Strap in tight. This will get rough."

"Sounds exciting," Scruggs said. "Adventure awaits."

After undocking, the shuttle dropped to the planet. The pilots chattered over the intercom about how difficult and dangerous the landings were going to be and made sure the passengers in back were strapped in and had sickness bags. They did four complete orbits before landing and never went over two G's the whole time.

"What do you think, Ms. Scruggs?" the pilot asked

once they were on the ground. "Pretty scary, huh?"

"Not really," Scruggs said. "To be honest, I have a friend who normally lands me. He does it in a single orbit."

"Single orbit? That's pretty hard. Big G forces."

"They sure are. We get rocked a lot."

"How many G's do you pull?" the copilot asked.

"Don't know. The ship's meter maxes out at five G. Pretty high, I guess. Things break off sometimes. Landing struts. Hatch covers."

"That's a pretty hard landing for a shuttle."

"Oh, it's not in a shuttle," Scruggs said. "My cap-pilot friend, he used to be in the navy. He lands us in a starship sometimes."

"He lands a starship at five G's from one orbit?" the pilot said.

"Every time." She frowned. "Is that dangerous?"

***

Dirtside, the passengers streamed off and headed for their tour. The pilots were at a loss without the steward to deal with cargo, so Scruggs rounded up the local cargo traders, arranged to get the pallet of fresh fruit delivered, and argued successfully for two dock workers and a pallet lifter to help her load up. Her hat and jacket, plus her nondescript clothes, made her invisible to the privileged passengers chattering by as they left for the shuttle to the volcano tour.

The pilots walked up as she was helping load the last of the fruit boxes. "Your tour is leaving, Ms. Scruggs."

She smiled at the pilot. "I'm not going on the tour. I'm meeting a friend."

"A friend?"

"A male friend. Somebody I think best my family not learn of. Or his family. You won't tell them, will you?"

Both laughed.

"Good for you, miss. Don't let them push you around.

Just make sure you're back on the Artemis Star before she leaves."

"I know exactly when the last shuttle leaves. Don't you worry."

"Say, you're pretty handy with that cargo loading gear. Ever need a job as a cargo handler, I'll put in a good word."

"Thank you," Scruggs said. "A cargo handler taught me some tricks."

"Cargo handler taught you things. You have navy pilots flying you, and I hear you play a mean game of poker."

Scruggs blinked. "Who told you that?"

"Word gets out. Some of the crew figured you were running a grift on those nice old ladies, cheating so you would always lose."

"Oh," Scruggs said, "listen, about me coming here to meet my friend—"

"Don't you worry, miss," the copilot said. "You're always polite and generous to the staff, not like some I could mention. Go have your fun. We won't rat you out."

"Thanks."

"Hey!" the cargo trader yelled from across the bay. "Artemis Star—you've got incoming!"

"Nothing on our manifest," the pilot yelled back.

"Too bad for you. Two new guests with cargo. Arrivals just called. We're to hold you till they get here."

"Not unless the ship"—the pilot's comm bonged—"never mind. Hold for two passengers and cargo. We stay."

"How we going to load that?" the copilot asked.

Scruggs yelled across the bay. "What's the ETA?"

"Five minutes or less."

She turned to the pilots. "I can stay five more minutes. I'll help load the cargo. Least I can do after you helped me out."

"Thanks, miss." The pilot punched Scruggs's shoulder. "You know, you're all right."

They didn't even wait five minutes till an electric cart rolled up, and two passengers hurried off. They checked in with the pilot and climbed in back. She assured them they'd lift as soon as their cargo was loaded.

Scruggs watched them board. They looked familiar. She couldn't get a line on the faces, but their clothes struck a memory. The cut of the men's jackets and the women's slacks. Too boxy. She grabbed a crate of fruit and sauntered to the cargo lock so she could hear them talking.

"All three of them," the woman said. "Four of us should be enough to take care of them. We get the girl, drug her up, and take her off."

"Take her off?"

"Tell the crew she got sick again. Carry her off to the hospital. They won't suspect a thing. Just a friend helping a friend."

"What about the other two? They won't stand for that?"

"That's what air locks are for. Out they go. They're booked through to next stop. Who will notice if they don't come out till then?"

The male passenger stopped near the hatch and gave his hand to the woman—unnecessary, because the step was six inches but allowed him to appear gallant. And to get his hand on her ass.

Scruggs recognized the woman as she turned and smiled. Alexandra. The man was Michel.

"Oh no," Scruggs said.

"What?" the pilot asked. "Problems."

"No, just... they're Confeds," Scruggs said. "The new passengers. Confederation citizens. Those are Confed clothes."

The pilot tapped her comm. "Yep. How did you know?"

"Clothes," Scruggs said. She put on her most vapid grin. "I like clothes. Come on, let's get you loaded up and out of here, and I'll go meet my friend."

The electric cart backed up, and the driver flashed a receipt. "Sign here."

The pilot reached to thumb it, but Scruggs stopped him. "Wait. Those aren't standard mini containers. They're wrapped or something."

"Yeah, these guys, they wanted them covered."

"Well, take the covers off 'cause they won't fit with them on."

"You take 'em off."

"Not our problem." Scruggs crossed her arms. "We haven't signed for them. Standard cargo contract says delivery must be in shiploadable condition."

The two pilots exchanged grins as Scruggs bickered with the cargo master. They would never have known what to say, and they found the whole thing entertaining.

After the cart's comm had beeped twice, the driver gave in. "Fine, I'll get a knife and cut them off if you help push them on your shuttle."

"Works for me," Scruggs said.

The driver glared at the pilots, who pointed at Scruggs and mouthed, she's in charge and continued grinning. The driver stomped off, returned with a knife, and cut the cloth cover on the mini containers. Under the cloth was a standard plastic shock case. The descriptions and identifying marks were painted over. Scruggs had seen these sizes of mini containers before but couldn't remember where.

"These are way heavier than they look," the driver said.

Scruggs and he pushed the first case on the lifter to get it to the shuttle cargo bay and shoved in. The second was a longer rectangle, two number three mini containers in shape. Scruggs struggled to get it positioned properly to slide in. The pilots watched from near the control room hatch but didn't interfere.

"Let me," the driver said. "You're pretty good with that lifter, but you need more practice with the nonstandard sizes. You spin it like so..." He turned the box ninety degrees on the lifter. "Then you use this flip feature, then spin it back, and in, it goes."

Scruggs watched the new passenger's cargo box slide in. It belonged to the two Confed-like passengers who were boarding there. The box was much heavier than it looked and had been shielded and covered.

All the identifying marks on the box had been painted over with black paint, but the painter had missed the small endpiece of this one.

Scruggs watched the crate disappear into the dark and focused on the end writing. She recognized the writing from other containers, on other planets. She even recognized the designation written there: G-APF-SS-1003. Grenades, antipersonnel fragmentation, ship safe, model 1003. The centurion's favorite model—big, powerful, and a real "door smasher," he'd called them. Which made the long narrow case the exact size to be full of revolvers.

She'd just helped arm a Confed Hijack crew on the liner.

CHAPTER TWENTY-NINE

"Cleared to land, Heavyweight Items. Docking Bay 94," station control said.

Dirk reviewed his board. "Lee, all I see is red lights. Is anything green anywhere?"

"It's all fuel warnings, Pilot," Lee said. "Life support, power generation, they're fine."

"I don't have any reds," Dena said. "Am I looking in the right place?"

"You only get comm and sensor things on your board, Nature Girl," Ana said, rubbing his face. He had cream on over the vacuum burn blisters he had acquired when saving Rocky. "We didn't want to confuse you with anything complicated. Like turning an air lock radio off instead of turning it on."

"Anybody could make that mistake."

"Anybody who doesn't understand the difference between 'on' and 'off'—yes, they could. But in your case, we want to take special preparations."

"'Cause I'm a girl?"

"The navigator is a girl. Navigation is hard. And precise and requires excellent math skills. She can clearly handle complicated things. Therefore, being a girl is not an issue."

"You think it's particular to me. You think I'm too dumb to understand, then."

"Nature Girl, you're learning how to use the few inadequate sensors this floating wreck has, along with handling basic comm traffic using our underpowered, unrobust comm systems. Since one of my goals is to teach you this, I've limited how many subsystems you can display on your board at once to make it easier for you to concentrate on one thing at a time. It has nothing to do with you being stupid."

"Okay." Dena tabbed a screen. "Thanks, old man. I'm

glad you don't think I'm stupid."

"Never said that," Ana said. "You could be as dumb as a bag of rocks as far as I'm concerned. That has nothing to do with having to teach you something." Ana tapped his screens. "And given some of the things you've reported from the sensors, I may have been seriously unfair to bags of rocks."

"Bite me, old man," Dena said. "And you know what, put all those other screens up. I can figure them out myself."

"Suits me." Ana tapped his console several times, and Dena's display changed.

"Ha," Dena said, paging through the new screens. "This isn't that hard to figure out. Look here. Engineering. Power systems. This one is air recirculation. Galley systems. Waste disposal. Water to the sinks. And this one. Okay, I don't know this one. What's that flashing red box there?"

"That's the low-fuel alarm," Ana said. "Means the main drives are almost out of fuel."

"But we were packed full of fuel in all the tanks. And those spare tanks and the container bladders."

"Which we can't pump after that incident with Milord's rocks."

"Right, that smashed main valve. Can we get a new one here?"

"That's the engineer's department. Ask him."

"I will." Another light flashed red on Dena's screen. "I don't know that one, either."

"No fuel alarm. The thrusters will stop working in twenty seconds, as soon as the fuel in the lines drains."

"That's bad, right?"

"Not if we're docked at a station."

"Centurion, we're not docked." Dena looked forward. Dirk and Lee were frantically tapping screens. "Are we? Doesn't look like it."

"We're close," Ana said.

"How close?"

An alarm bonged in the control room.

"Close enough the collision alarm is ringing."

"Should I be worried, old man?"

Ana pulled his straps tight and nodded at Lee and Dirk. "Do you think worrying will have any effect on what's going to happen any second now?"

"Nope," Dena said. She pulled her own straps tight and managed to not sway as the Heart's Desire crunched into the docking bay.

***

"Given the lack of fuel, the difficult approach, and the damage to some of our systems, it wasn't a bad landing, after all," Dirk said. "I'm quite proud of myself."

The crew had crowded into the main air lock, waiting for the station to confirm lock so they could swing the outer hatch open and meet the repair technician Dirk had arranged.

"On the radio, they said your approach was like dancing with a drunken tabbo that was short a leg," Dena said. "That's good?"

"It's a term of art," Dirk said. "Ask Centurion. The marines say that any landing you can walk away from is a good landing."

"Is that what they say, Centurion?" Dena asked.

"Close. What we do say is that any landing we can walk away from after shooting the worthless pilot is a good landing." Ana fingered his revolver in its snap-down holster. "Should I make this a good landing, Navy?"

"Not now, Centurion," Dirk said. "Gavin, what do you see?"

Gavin was peering through the viewport in the lock. "Standard docking bay. One technician. Repair cart with boxes on it, one of them big enough to be a new master cross flow valve."

"Outstanding," Ana said. "Can you swap that valve out yourself?"

"Child's play if I have a new one," Gavin said. "Takes time, though, couple hours at least to do a proper job."

"We don't have hours," Ana said. "We wasted enough time coasting into this stupid station. We're, what, three shifts behind where we should be catching up to her? What if we grab it and run?" Ana asked.

"No fuel, old man," Gavin said. "No fuel, no running. Pilot needs fuel in the lines to fire the maneuvering jets."

"You said there's plenty of fuel in the tanks."

"Which I can't get to unless we replace the main feeder valve—"

"Can you jury-rig something? Enough to get us moving out to the jump limit and off to the next system? Then fix it while we're in jump or something?"

"You want me to bypass the fuel system and run live fuel across the engineering room in temporary conduits?"

"If what you said will work, then, yes."

"Do you know how dangerous that is?"

"Nope. And I don't care." Ana gritted his teeth. "Please. I'm asking a favor. For Scruggs."

"Centurion, we get along well enough now, but you're not in a position to be asking that sort of favor."

"I'd do the same for you, something equivalently dangerous, anyway."

Gavin shook his head. "No, you wouldn't."

"Okay, you're right, that was a lie. But Scruggs would, wouldn't she? Help you out without a second's hesitation. You, the pilot, any of you."

Gavin wiped condensation off the viewport. "Gotta check the dehumidifying system. Fine, I'll do it. But how does that change things?"

"Grab the parts, run your bypass, get us out of here."

"No way this guy will give us parts. Not after we crunched his docking bay."

"Only one of him?"

"Only see one."

Ana unsnapped his holster and drew his revolver. "Right. I'll pistol whip him, knock him out, tie him up, and find a locker or something to stuff him in. You get your bypass thing started. Dena, grab those parts off that cart and get them loaded as fast as you can. Soon as we've got fuel in the lines, Pilot will get us out of here. Everybody ready?"

"No," Dirk said. "We will not do this."

"Navy, we don't have time."

"No. No. And again, no. I'm the pilot. I'm in charge. We'll do this my way. We can get what we need without anybody getting hurt or in trouble."

"We don't—"

"Centurion, I'm not going to do it your way." Dirk crossed his arms. "We're not leaving unless I drive us out. I won't. We can do this in a civil manner and still leave here in time."

Ana pushed his revolver down and snapped it shut. "We better get there on time to help Scruggs."

"We will," Dirk said. "We're going to help her, I promise you. Gavin, open the hatch."

Gavin spun the hatch in. Dirk stepped through, followed by all the others.

The crew assembled in the docking bay. The technician sauntered from his cart to stand in front of them. He wore dirty coveralls, a crowded tool belt, and a smug grin that said somebody had screwed up. And, for once, it wasn't him.

"Boy, are you folks in trouble. I wouldn't want to be the pilot. That would be..." He looked at their feet, stretching to see Dena's as she came out. He pointed at Dirk. "That would be you, shiny shoes."

"Hello, my good man," Dirk said. "I'm Duke Durriken Friedel, the pilot of this ship. We need—"

"Operations called. You're in deep doo-doo, friend.

They're sending a team down to assess damage to the dock. They want to talk to you. You're supposed to report to ops right away."

"Thank you for that information," Dirk said. "But, really, time is of the essence here."

"Oh, we'll have lots of essence, loads of time. Did you know, if you have low fuel, you're supposed to declare an emergency and be towed in?"

"I did know that," Dirk said. "We didn't have time."

"Should have made time. You'll have plenty now. No work to be done till the crew checks out the lock damage. Never should have come in hot."

"I was trained by the Imperial navy. And, in the navy, we're allowed to use our discretion to make the most appropriate approach."

"This isn't the navy. Only discretion you have now is whether you pay for the damage right away or let them seize the ship."

"I don't think—"

"How long till this crew comes and checks out the lock damage so we can get started on the repairs?" Gavin asked.

"Half a shift," the tech said. "At least. Longer if you torque them off."

"We don't have shifts," Dirk said. "We need repairs right away, and we're willing to pay a premium."

"Doesn't work that way," the tech said.

"How did you know he was the pilot?" Dena pointed at Dirk. "We're all wearing the same outfits."

It was true. They all had coveralls on with a generic space patch on the breast.

"Shoes," the tech said. He gestured. "Magnetic boots over there, vacuum ready. He's your engineer for sure. The mean-looking guy here—those are military issue, black, also vacc safe, and clean and taken care of, but well worn, so he's security or something. You"—the tech looked at Dena's feet—"high heels, leather. Stylish, solid, versatile. Not vacc safe but practical. And sexy. I'll bet you can dance in those boots."

"Like your best, sexiest dreams," Dena said.

"You'll be here a while. Maybe you can come out dancing with me?"

"Will it get the ship repaired quicker?"

"Nope," the tech said.

"My good man—" Dirk said.

"Listen, shiny shoes," the tech said. "And incidentally, that's how I knew you were the pilot. Shiny shoes, belt, all neatly stitched up, and waxed to perfection. Exactly the kind of useless work that pilots do. Now, here's the deal. Your ship is not going to be repaired. Not this shift, not the next, and not for a while. So, you won't be needing these parts. Operations wants to talk to you. The only reason I'm still here is because they want the pilot, and I'm supposed to show you where to go. Other than that, the only thing I'm doing here is chatting with this sexy woman and taunting this stuck-up ex-navy type." He folded his arms. "So, what's it going to be, former naval person? Head to ops or chinwag some more?"

Dena whispered to Ana, "I kinda like this guy."

"Me too," Ana said.

"Well," Dirk said. "Well, give me a moment to speak to my crew, coordinate tasks, those type of things. Excuse me." Dirk draped his arms around Gavin and Dena, and led them to a corner. "Centurion? Lee? Join us."

Ana walked over and crossed his arms, waiting. Lee leaned in.

"New plan," Dirk said. "We can't afford the time this will take. Engineer, bypass that valve, get some fuel in the thruster lines. I don't care if you have to use a bucket. Navigator, have a course ready to go to get us out of here. Centurion, beat that guy up, restrain him, stuff him in a locker somewhere. Dena, help Centurion if he needs it, then grab all those boxes off that cart and load them on the ship. Soon as you two are back on and lock us out of the station and Engineer gives me some fuel to work with,

I'll take us out of here. Any questions?"

Ana uncrossed his arms. "Outstanding plan, Pilot. Wish I'd thought of it." He unsnapped his holster cover. "Today is looking up!"

CHAPTER THIRTY

"I want to buy some equipment, please," Scruggs said.

The greasy, ponytailed guy behind the counter didn't stop talking to his friend. "Not the dropper post. It might disconnect."

"Ya think?" his friend said.

Instead of a ponytail, he had a man-bun rolled up on his head, and his skin supplied the necessary grease quotient.

"For sure, it might disconnect. Lot of bikes are like that." He gestured at the rack of bikes on the far wall. "The cheapo-depo ones."

"Wouldn't want that to happen."

"Excuse me," Scruggs said, hopping from foot-to-foot. The shuttle would lift in a few minutes. "I need to buy some equipment."

"In a minute, babe," Ponytail said. He spoke to his friend. "Nobody wants a disconnected dropper post."

"Right on, bro."

Scruggs tapped the counter. "Could you—"

"In a minute, babe. We're chilling here."

"I'll get it myself." Scruggs scooted down the aisle.

The sports and camping equipment store only occupied about three standard containers of space at the down port, and the selection was limited, but it was the closest point to the shuttle where she might get anything like a weapon.

Bribes or not, she would be inspected when she got back on board, so she couldn't buy guns or knives. Centurion had told her there was no such thing as dangerous weapons, just dangerous people. She needed to be dangerous if she was going to help Weeks and Hernandez.

The first aisle was tents and sleeping bags. Nothing there for her. She hit the second aisle and grabbed anything in that she thought might be used as a weapon. Spare ax handles—without the cutting heads—could make small staves. Heavy cans of food—projectile weapons.

Pork and beans? She spared a moment to wonder what they tasted like. How did that work? Stuff the beans? A shovel. Metal water bottles, some rope to tie up people after she won. If she won. She ran back to the counter. What else did she need?

A locked display behind the counter. Stoves for camping. Gas stoves with built-in fuel bottles and attached strikers. Explosives, perhaps.

"This is what I want. Can you ring it up?" Scruggs said. "And give me three of those stoves."

"Bro," Man-Bun said, "if you do that, you'll get air in the oil."

"No way, brah? Really? That would be totally odious."

"Yeah, odoriferous us. Who wants that?"

Scruggs checked her comm. She had only minutes to get to the shuttle with her improvised weapons. She could ride in the front, avoid Alexandra and Michel, race back to her quarters, and warn Hernandez. And untie Weeks.

"Could you speed it up, please?" Scruggs said. "I really want to go camping today. Give me three of those stoves."

"Ya, ya, in a minute, babe," Ponytail said. He examined Scruggs's fashionable clothes, heeled boots, and manicured hair. She'd got it done that day before she went to see Weeks. "Look, why don't you chill for a moment, huh, girly? You don't need three stoves. Find some other cool camping gear. You'll need a tent and a sleeping bag, anyway, if you want to get out there. Find some sweet sleeping deals and get out under the stars and relax in nature. You could use some relaxation-o from the looks of it."

He gestured at Man-Bun. "And if you get the air in the oil, dude, you'll be rocketing down some sweet hill and pull the brakes, and who will you be then? Rock face, that's who."

Scruggs didn't need to buy anything. She was free of her escort, alone on a planet with regular connections to the rest of the Empire. She had some of the credit chips that Tribune had pushed on Weeks and Hernandez. Plenty of money. She hadn't been missed. The Artemis Star wasn't going to wait for her or change its schedule for only one girl. If she hid out for six hours, she'd be home free.

But what about Hernandez and Weeks? Alexandra had said they would be killed. But was that her fault? She hadn't asked to be nearly kidnapped and brought into the core. Nobody had asked her permission. Weeks and Hernandez were nothing but her jailers. Jailers in a dangerous profession. They might be killed any time in their regular line of work.

But they'd been friendly. Almost friends. They'd treated her as well as they could, given their orders. They had a job to do.

"Totally bogus if we let oil into the lines," Man-Bun said. "But still, those are sweet derailleur. Imagine going around a curve, you feel the slide, and you drop a gear, then—"

Scruggs thumped the counter. "I'm ready to pay for these, please. And I want my stoves."

But what would Centurion say? Leave them to be killed for her? It would be her fault if they got killed by the people trying to kidnap her. He wouldn't be upset about people being killed. He'd be upset because it was her fault and she didn't do anything about it.

Man-Bun frowned over her pile, then gestured his friend. "Check it out, dude. Babe here still doesn't have her tent. You need a tent, babe. T-E-N-T. Aisle one. Call us if you can't lift it." He laughed. "If you can't lift it."

Ponytail giggled. "Yeah, little girl like you probably can't lift a tent. Tell you what—pick one you like down there. I'll come help you with it." He gave her a once-over. "Probably the pink one, right, kiddo?"

It was the "kiddo" that did it, Scruggs decided later.

She drew herself to her full height and smiled at Ponytail. He smiled back. She grinned and crooked a finger at Man-Bun. He leaned in.

Scruggs slapped both his ears with open palms as hard as she could. He screamed and stumbled back from the counter, grasping his head.

"Whaa?" Ponytail said.

Scruggs set a boot against the counter, bent in, grabbed his hair, and heaved. She dragged him, kicking over the counter to crash onto the floor. He yelled, and she hit him with the ax handle, remembering to turn it flat at the last instant. "Hit with the flat to disable," the centurion had said. "Swing like an ax to break a bone."

Man-Bun stumbled around behind the counter, holding both ears. He bashed into a display of sunglasses, knocked it down, scattered overpriced eye wear, then tripped and fell to his knees. Snot ran from his nose. Scruggs snagged his shirt and towed him in front of the counter.

Ponytail whimpered on the floor. Scruggs pushed Man-Bun against the counter, then leaned down and hauled Ponytail upright. He slumped next to his friend.

"Whaaaa—"

"Shut up," Scruggs said. "I gave you the chance to be polite, but you didn't take it, and I don't have any time. Now, get me three of those stoves, right now. Charge all this up, and I'll get out of here. I have to go. Go camping."

"Three stoves? Why you want three stoves?" Man-Bun asked, dropping the hands covering his ears.

"I'm going camping. I need to go camping with some friends. We need stoves. Get them for me now, and I'll pay."

He hesitated. Scruggs frowned. Man-Bun scuttled around the counter and dug into a drawer for keys. It took three tries till he got the display cabinet open and pulled out three stoves and dumped them.

"Three stoves. You're supposed to sign—"

Scruggs spread her arms wide, palms inward. Ponytail

started blubbering, and Man-Bun froze. Scruggs reached into her pocket and pulled out a credit chip. "Charge it to those."

"You can just go—"

"No, I don't steal things," Scruggs said.

Man-Bun's hands shook as he scanned the goods in and reached for Scruggs's payment chip.

"Wait," Scruggs said.

The two men froze, eyes wide.

"I'm buying three stoves, right?"

Man-Bun nodded.

"I should get a discount," Scruggs said. "Does ten percent seem fair to you?"

CHAPTER THIRTY-ONE

"He wasn't dead." Ana swirled the basic in his cup. "He was still breathing."

"Looked dead to me." Dena swirled her own cup. "He was sure hard to carry. I finally get what 'dead weight' means."

The two of them were sitting in the lounge, drinking basic.

Heart's Desire had jumped for their meeting with the Artemis Star. Gavin had gotten enough fuel into the lines to get them away from the station. Dirk had edged them clear with thrusters, then endured two hours of increasingly dire threats from station authorities.

"That stupid tech is not dead," Ana said. "Unless he choked on his own self-importance. I know dead. I'm good at dead. He wasn't dead."

"How can you be sure?" Dena grimaced. "He was barely breathing when I left you. This basic tastes like anus. What did you put in it?"

"Anal-flavored powder," Ana said. "Courtesy, Scruggs. We're still working through that antiradiation mixture she and Lee concocted."

"It even smells like ass," Dena said.

"Which our guy didn't," Ana said. "Which is how you know he wasn't dead. Because, if he was, the bowels would have released, and the smell would have told you."

"He didn't smell like that, but how do I know that you didn't go back and kill him when I wasn't looking?"

"Are you saying I'd be embarrassed to kill a man with you watching?" Ana asked. "You think I'd be ashamed or something?"

Dena swallowed the last of the basic and grimaced. "That's disgusting. No, I guess that doesn't make sense. Hello, Pilot."

Dirk climbed down the ladder from the bridge—or, rather, climbed along as they had taken little thrust into the jump. "Good first shift, Centurion, and you, too... We need a position for you, too, Dena."

"Her favorite position is probably on her back," Ana said. "Not sure what the official designation is for that."

"Not true," Dena said. "I like to be up high, where I can keep an eye on things. And react if necessary."

"React?"

"With my slingshot," Dena said. "Hurt you with the rubber when I snap it."

"Why would you do that?" Ana asked.

"If you're not doing what I want, I need to encourage you."

"By potentially maiming your lovers?"

"They should have paid better attention." Dena poured a glass of basic for Dirk. "Besides, I enjoy it."

Ana swallowed the last of his own basic. "You're meaner than you look."

"That's how I got on this ship," Dena said. "Being mean to people who deserved it."

Dirk gasped, gagged, and held a hand over his mouth.

Dena smirked. "For example, I know Pilot here hasn't been taking all of Scruggs's patented basic mix when he should, so I gave him a triple dose. For his own good. Or maybe to be mean."

"You know, I like that in a woman," Ana said. "Meanness. Of course, you could be lying about the slingshot thing."

"And you could be lying about the killing thing," Dena said. "Lee—basic?"

Lee arrived at the lounge table and sat, watching Dirk writhe. "What's wrong with the pilot?"

"Guilty conscience for not giving Ana enough credit for his plan." Dena shoved a glass of basic at Lee. "Lee, the old man here thinks I would lie about tormenting my lovers, that I wouldn't hurt them because I wouldn't want to seem mean. What do you say to that?"

"Navigator," Ana said, "Nature Girl here says I wouldn't kill a man in front of her, because she thinks her watching me would make me feel guilty. What do you say to that?"

Lee drank her basic down in one long swallow. "It's like you haven't been on the same ship together for months. Centurion will kill anybody he thinks deserves it or for fun—or by accident if he wasn't paying attention. And I'm sure Dena would maim a lover who didn't satisfy her in bed. And neither of you would feel guilty for a moment. It's like saying Rocky would feel guilty about licking his testicles in public. It's what you do." She spun her glass. "This basic was a little spicy. What did you put in it?"

Gavin climbed up from engineering. "Morning, all."

"Speaking of testicles," Ana said.

"The ground crew has a question for you," Lee said.

"Ground crew?" Ana said.

"You do security and ground operations and dismounted activity," Lee said. "You're ground crew." She explained the discussion to Gavin. "What do you think? Would either of them be embarrassed."

"What's more likely," he said, "they'd do it together. Dena would sleep with him, find out what secrets he had, then beat him senseless with her slingshot. Then Centurion would kill him barehanded and throw the corpse out an air lock. They'd both steal his stuff."

"That is grotesquely unfair." Ana got up to put a tray in the microwave.

Dena waved at him to put one in for her.

"The killing?"

"No, I'd do that. But I wouldn't steal his stuff."

"What if he had some super cool custom guns?"

"Hmm." Ana frowned. "How many guns, exactly? What type?"

"I wouldn't do that either," Dena said. "Well, not all.

I'd sleep with him. And beat him up if I needed to get away. But I'm not a thief."

"But what if he had some jewelry. Or shoes. Woman's shoes. Really nice shoes."

Dena scrunched up her forehead. "Woman's shoes? Which designer?"

The microwave dinged.

Ana pulled out the two trays and dumped them on the table. "Fine. We're both horrible people. Complete degenerates. Thieves and murderers. Why do you ship with us, then?"

Dirk finally croaked out a breath. "My god, that basic is horrible. We ship with you because you're competent, and you wouldn't do those things to us."

"That's not a safe assumption to make, Navy," Ana said, peeling the cover off his tray.

"It wasn't before. It is now," Dirk said. "We're together on this. Otherwise, why are we flying halfway across the sector to rescue a woman who may not need rescuing? Because she's our friend, that's why."

Ana and Dena scowled at him, then at each other, then started spooning tray mush.

"I hope she's okay," Lee said. "I thought I did the right thing, putting her in with the Imperials. She needed the medical help at the time, but I'm not sure that this is going to work out the way we want."

"You're the Imperials," Dirk said. "A citizen, a Praetorian, and 'on the Empress's service' no less."

"Which never caused us problems before," Lee said.

"For that matter," Ana said, "Navy here is playing the duke card more and more often. Can't be much more of a citizen than being in the nobility. And you were pretty tight with that Tribune."

"Which also never caused us any problems," Dirk said. "You never complained when it helped you out before. And you were in an Imperial regiment before, so you're probably an Imperial citizen as well."

"I'm not an Imperial citizen," Dena said. "We weren't citizens on Rockhaul, and we didn't care much about it. But now that I think about it, that's three of you with Imperial citizenship, and probably Scruggs now that we know who she is. That leaves me out in the cold."

"Rockhaul was an Imperial planet," Dirk said. "Which makes you an Imperial subject, not a citizen."

"What's the difference?"

"In theory, you pay taxes, but you can't vote. Not that you probably did either on that backwoods planet," Ana said. "Unless you sent regular shipments of beaver hides or something to the sector governor."

"Nope. Well, I don't care about the Empire," Dena said. "But I will admit to a bit of affection for you folks. You helped me get away from that mud ball, and you're not actively trying to kill me or steal everything I own. Not right now."

"Nature Girl," Ana said, "are you saying you trust us?"

"Well, yeah," Dena said. "I do. We look out for each other. We're all trying to make sure that Scruggs is okay, and we won't rest till we do. We're kind of—well, a crew. We look after each other."

Dena and Ana swallowed spoonfuls of mush. Lee and Gavin drank basic. Dirk wiped spittle off his chin.

"Think about it," Dena said. "Lee, you nearly died helping Scruggs."

"She's like a sister to me, and I owe her a life," Lee said.

"Dirk, you wouldn't let anything happen to her."

"She's just a kid," Dirk said. "We need to help her."

"And you, Ana, you'd kill anyone who hurt her."

"If any of you hurt her, I will torture you to death," Ana said. He examined the mush on his spoon and put it down. "Slowly torture you to death."

"Gavin?"

"She's a good kid. She's helped me out. I owe her a few favors."

"But that's just Scruggs," Ana said. "Not all of us."

"Old man, if I or one of the others, even Navy here, got into trouble or was picked up by the authorities, you'd happily shoot up a jail to get him out and rescue him."

"That's the proper thing to do," Lee said. "Help your shipmates."

"I'm the pilot," Dirk said. "I'm responsible for all of you. That's my job."

"You got me off that mud ball," Dena said. "I'm here. I'm fed. I'm learning things. I met an Imperial tribune, and there is at least the chance of a big score. Why not help you out?" She pointed at Gavin. "Well?"

Gavin shrugged. "I got nothing better to do right now."

Dena pointed at Ana.

"No," he said.

"No? Honestly? No."

"No."

"After all everybody has done helping you train Scruggs, the firefights, the thefts, the vandalism, the bad food? Still no?"

He pushed his tray away and glared at them. "Fine. If nobody was around to see and gossip about it, and if I wasn't too busy and it didn't cost me much, and if there wasn't a movie on the vid I wanted to watch, I'd probably help you out."

All of them cheered and clapped.

"See, Ana," Dena said, "I guess we're a crew now."

"I guess we are a crew." He shook his head. "Dip me in hydrogen and shoot me out the thrusters."

CHAPTER THIRTY-TWO

Scruggs raced down the corridor. A call from the store's comm had the pilots waiting for her to return before lifting. They didn't seem upset. Either they liked her, or they expected another stupendous bribe. Or both.

The backpack straps cut into her shoulders. She hadn't been able to properly size it before paying and running out. Downport security would have held the shuttle if the camping store reported she had stolen goods—they had video in the shop—but she doubted the clerks would report her beating. They had video of that as well, but she was pretty sure Man-Bun and Ponytail didn't want their greasy faces shown having their asses kicked by a little girl.

She cleared a corner and banged into a man coming the other direction. The man fell backward, and she bounced into the far wall.

"Empress's hair clip, sorry," Scruggs said, climbing up. She leaned down to pull the man to his feet.

He was taller than her, nearly as skinny, with a bemused expression. He wore spacer magnetic boots, dirty coveralls, and a crowded tool belt.

"In a hurry somewhere, miss?"

"Late for my shuttle, sorry."

"I've been late for a few of those myself," he said. He took her hand and stood. "Best not get in trouble with the chief of the watch."

"Chief of the watch?"

"Sorry, navy term. You civvies call them pursers," he said. "Better slow down, though, our captain released the crew for shore leave, so there will be lots of us swarming the station."

"Navy?"

"Imperial navy. Greetings from the Imperial Auxiliary Logistics Ship Hydrogen Queen, the finest fleet support ship in the galaxy, just arrived."

The pilots hadn't minded waiting for Scruggs, and no extra bribe was even mentioned. She hopped into the crew compartment and strapped herself in as they prepped for launch.

The copilot examined her seatbelt. "You sure know your way around shuttles. I'll give you that, miss. Why the change of plan? Not going camping. Where's your friend?"

"He couldn't make it down. Problem with his... well... he's married. So, he can't get away."

"Married?" Both pilots laughed. "After all you paid for that camping gear."

"Yes, it's a shame. I'll convert it to something else."

"Like what?"

Scruggs dug through her bag. "I can use the stove as an improvised explosive, the shovel as a sword, and I'll use the ax handles to beat people senseless."

The pilots laughed again. "Great imagination. You're not like our regular passengers, that's for sure."

The pilot's comm buzzed, and the copilot checked the ID. "Your friends again."

"Not my friends," the pilot said. She tapped her comm. "Yes, ma'am, we got our cargo. Yes, ma'am. We'll be lifting shortly. Yes, ma'am. You can tell the purser if you like. I'm sure he'll be interested. Yes, ma'am. No, ma'am. Ma'am, I have to lift now, the sooner you let me go——" He twisted his head. "She hung up. Get ready to lift."

The two pilots went through the start-up sequence. As soon as they lifted, they went back to their conversation. "Yeah, I wish all the passengers were like you, miss. That was your Confed-dressed lady. She and her friend were complaining about the delay. They're going to complain to the purser."

"I'm sorry I got you in trouble."

"We're not. If we had to load that cargo ourself, we'd still be there. When the purser saw the new manifest, he was running around, panicking, that we would have to lift without getting it loaded. Now that we're back with passengers and cargo, he'll soothe them and give them a free haircut or something."

"That sounds good," Scruggs said. "I wonder if I know those passengers. They did seem a bit familiar."

"Let me put them on the screen," the pilot said.

The camera to the passenger compartment flared up. Alexandra and Michel showed on the screen, scowling and whispering to each other.

"I think I've met them before," Scruggs said.

"Pretty girl," the copilot said. "If she would smile more."

"Probably complaining about the lack of shopping opportunities."

"The big guy looks pretty mean."

Scruggs fiddled in her backpack till she found one of the stoves. "He does. I wouldn't want to meet him in a dark alley."

"Don't worry, miss," the copilot said. "We'll watch out for you."

"Thanks," Scruggs said. She fingered the stove controls and examined the warning label. Do not turn fuel to high—extreme flame. It took six turns of the knob, but she ratcheted the fuel line up high. She wanted to be ready for anything. "It's nice to be taken care of."

Arrival at the Artemis Star was uneventful. Scruggs lingered in the cabin, not wanting to see "the mean Confeds," as the pilot, copilot, and the purser dutifully accepted their tongue-lashing from the arrivals. Scruggs snuck out behind Alex's and Michel's back, keeping her cap low over her brows, and stepped to the exit of the bay. After she cleared the metal detector, the grinning guards barely gave her backpack's contents a glance. Alexandra's harangue was better entertainment.

"Back already, Ms. Scruggs?"

"Just needed to buy some things for my friends," Scruggs said.

"Camping gear. On a ship?"
"It's all in how you use it."

***

Hernandez continued to read her adventure novel. She was unimpressed with the female heroine's choice in romantic partners and found the whole book unrealistic. Too much fighting and not enough filing pay vouchers and filling out command-mandated surveys.

In her experience, the ratio of actual fighting to bureaucratic nonsense was one to one hundred. And if she had been forced to choose between dying alone or hooking up with the odious male lead, solitary death looked much more attractive.

A bottle smashed. She put her book down and listened. Even for somebody as young and energetic as Scruggs was, this seemed surprising.

She returned to reading, but the sculpture on her table distracted her. It moved. Not a random shaking, but a steady shake. Thump, thump, thump—like a door or a wall being kicked. After dropping the book and pulling on the shoes she wore with her dinner outfit, she slid her door open.

Their suite was empty and unchanged. The main display screen on the far wall next to the entrance door was dark. The sectional couch between her and the wall was empty. On her left, the sitting area chairs were still covered with clothes Scruggs had bought. To her right, the large dinner table and its attendant aluminum chairs gleamed with a metallic green shine. The carpeted walkway to the door between them glittered with emerald highlights. On the table, the four apple-shaped statues Scruggs had bought the week prior spilled out of their shipping box.

"I still say that girl has no taste," Hernandez said.

"Green rocks? Jove save us."

She stepped to the next door over, Scruggs's room, and put her ear to it. Silence.

But still, that faint vibration. A faint noise. She stepped to the far corner, where Weeks and Scruggs were expected to be occupied.

Thump, thump, thump.

Hernandez raised her hand to knock but stopped. She didn't want to ruin the moment. She sometimes felt like Scruggs's mom, but in this case, she better be the big sister.

"Hey in there, I can hear you. You're keeping me awake. Better try a different position."

The thumping increased in volume and pattered like a dog scampering up a hill. Thud-thud-thud-thuddy-thud-thuddy-thud.

That didn't sound right. Too fast. Even Weeks couldn't keep up that pattern too long.

The tempo changed. Rat-a-tat. Rat-a-tat-tat. Rat-a-tat. Rat-a-tat-tat.

"Weeks, Scruggs, you okay?"

Thud. Thud. Thud. Long pause. Thud. Short pause. Thud. Short pause. Thud. Then three rapid thuds.

"The Empress's shiny metal shoes," Hernandez said. "I'm coming in."

Even with her override card, she had to confirm three times before the door slid open.

Weeks sat, twisted on his back, tangled and tied up in some sheets, rolled sideways, kicking the wall above a broken wine bottle.

"What should we call that position?" Hernandez sliced the sheets. "Sideways jackass? Crazed dog licking itself?"

"She hit me from behind," Weeks said.

"We'll need a new title. Not the Kama Sutra. Maybe the 'Karma's gonna get you, Sutra,' something like that."

"She's a devious little witch, that's for sure."

"I thought you liked that in your girlfriends."

As his hands came free, Weeks rubbed his head. "She's not my girlfriend."

"You didn't—?"

"Didn't have time. Barely got into foreplay. She took off some of her clothes. I was pouring the wine. And I wasn't going to sleep with her."

"Because you told her to put her clothes back on?"

"No. I'm not an idiot."

Hernandez pulled his legs around and examined the knots. "Of course not. That's why you're tied up in your own room, on your own bed. I'll have to cut these as well."

"We can get more."

"I'll let you explain to the steward why all of your sheets are shredded. Should be an interesting call. What'd she hit you with?"

Weeks pointed at the sculpture. "Comet's passing."

Hernandez hefted the sculpture. "It's a sap! She must have made it up special so it would knock you out but not kill you."

After slicing the last of the sheets and shirts used to tie him up, Hernandez stooped and picked up the statue. "Good length, firm grip, heavy but padded on the end. Girl knows what she's doing. Maybe she really is some sort of super mercenary?"

"I hope so. Kind of embarrassing to be beaten up by a little kid."

"The golf ball-sized bump on your head says you can't call her that anymore."

Weeks rubbed himself. "Bump is right. What do we do now?"

"If she's run, we'll have to go look for her. She can't have gone far."

"Really? After spending weeks fabricating weapons under our noses and staging this elaborate ruse, you think she wouldn't have an equally elaborate escape plan?"

Hernandez cursed, then hunted for her purse. She used

her comm to buzz the temporary address they'd given Scruggs. A bong came from the pile of clothes at the far wall.

"And that's her comm," Weeks said. "She's in the wind. We need to check what shuttles left."

"Right. You call that female waiter you were friendly with and find out what you can. Make a story up."

"What will you do?"

"If you don't get anything, I'll wake up the captain and pull the tribune's rank on him. I'd rather not do that right now."

"Fine."

Hernandez juggled "Comet's passing" back and forth from hand to hand. The balance was perfect for snapping people down. She held it high. It felt good. She tried a practice swing. Smooth. She kept it there while she debated what to do.

Which was why she had it in her hand when the outer door swished open with no warning.

Which was why the entering kidnap crew saw her with a weapon.

Which was why they shot her right away.

CHAPTER THIRTY-THREE

"Five, six, should be up here. Go. Go. Go." Scruggs counted and ran up the crew stairs.

She'd been in the maintenance corridors before but always with an escort and always asking questions and listening, wide-eyed to the answers, like all sufficiently impressed young ladies out of their depth.

And since she hadn't been paying attention, she got lost. After nearly ending up in the engine room, she backtracked, found the correct stairs, and ran up. The stairs were labeled, but she didn't understand the system. 3-17-4-L, the door read. That should be her door.

Centurion would be upset that she hadn't remembered the door number. He'd be upset that she hadn't learned the ship's numbering system.

He'd be even more upset if she charged into a fight without a plan. Her initial thought was to get into the room and warn Hernandez before Alexandra showed up. But she'd delayed so long they might be there already. Inside. Or waiting in the hallway.

Scruggs stopped and bent to catch her breath, then dumped the contents of her backpack. Distance weapons, three cans of beans. Stuffed her front pockets with that. Melee weapons—ax handle. Jammed that through her belt on the left side for a cross draw. Final holdout weapons. The stoves. She stripped all the braces and pot holders off. She was left with a palm-sized gas cylinder with a combination striker-valve setting on top. She clicked the striker, and a fifteen-centimeter green flame burst out.

She clicked the stove off, put one in her right sock, the other two in her back pockets. She was ready. Wait, key card? Tuck it in her bra. She showed enough cleavage she could put a ration tray there. How did Dena cope with it? She always wore low-cut shirts. Now ready. She reached out for the door handle and held it.

Last time she ran into a fight with the centurion on New Oregon, she'd nearly gotten killed by a tank. That had hurt a lot. Then and during the rehab. The rehab was agony. "She was lucky to be alive," Lee had said. And the Imperial doctor on the Pollux who helped her said she should have been maimed. Permanently wounded. One of the splinters was near her eyes. Eyes were hard to regrow. Sometimes impossible. She didn't want to be blind.

She took her hand off the door. Was adventure worth it? Was the risk worth it? She could go back on the shuttle, leave Hernandez and Weeks alone. They were in the navy, after all. She wasn't. But Alexandra might kill them. But that was Alexandra, not her fault.

And those boxes. Those weren't just for attacking her. That was a lot of weapons—enough, with the six of them to seize the whole ship. But why would the Confeds want somebody to seize a whole ship? The Empire would surely react.

She shrugged at that. Too complicated, all this Imperial stuff. That's what she had run away from.

Save her friends, get out of here, and get on with her life.

She pulled the steward's cap down over her face. "Adventure awaits."

Her room was twenty meters from the door, hidden behind the curve of the ship. The carpet scuffed under her feet, her legs dragging. Scruggs sweated, and her vision darkened. Bloodred wool fibers in the carpet in geometric designs distracted her. How did they make that elaborate a weave?

"Stop it." She took a deep breath. "Focus."

She held the first can of beans in front of her and stalked down the hall. Her door appeared. One of the fabulous four lounged next to it. His usual crisply fitting suit was marred by a revolver shaped bulge in his front pocket.

He saw a young woman in a ship's uniform confidently striding down the hall, carrying some sort of package, probably for a spoiled first-class passenger. What he didn't see was a struggling, crippled girl with a cane, dressed in outlandishly bright clothes, which was who he was waiting for.

Scruggs fumbled with the can, nearly dropping it. She closed to within three meters. The man's eyes swept down to the can, then back up at her face, then at the can, then back. His expression changed. He knew who she was.

She threw the can at his face.

And missed, hitting his knee instead.

He screamed and folded up like the stock on the centurion's favorite gun. He grasped his knee and moaned, rolling on the ground.

Scruggs fumbled another can from her pocket and hit him in the side of the head as he rolled by. He dropped flat, mewling.

She pulled the key card out and slapped it on the panel next to the door. Nothing. She tried again. Still didn't work. Again. Her pulse pounded in her head. She had to help Hernandez and Weeks.

What was going—idiot.

She was slapping the room number plaque on the left side of the door, not the entry code lock on the right.

Centurion had talked about this—the stress, the confusion. She licked her lips, focused. Door, can, can, ax handle, run in and charge. Hit whoever she doesn't recognize.

Breathe in. Breathe out. Breathe in. Slap door entry.

The door slid open. Light from the room blazed out.

"Stadani, what do you—"

Another of the fabulous four showed in the door.

This time the thrown can hit him dead in the forehead, and he staggered backward, falling over the couch.

Scruggs pulled the last can from her pocket and stepped right. Alexandra was behind the table. She threw it at Alexandra's face. Alexandra ducked.

Scruggs pulled the ax stave free and charged into the door.

She cleared the door, the stave in front like a sword. Hernandez on the couch to her right, holding a bloodred towel to her left shoulder. A nearly naked Weeks stood with his hands on his head and a big bump on his head in the left corner of the room. Alexandra ducked behind the eating table.

She charged into the room. Where were the others? She spun right, but the sitting area was empty.

Feet kicked her ankles. She tripped and went down, dropping the handle.

Michel had been beside the door to her left. He pointed a gun at her face. "Well, look who's here."

Alexandra's head returned, her revolver pointed at Scruggs's head. "Little Scruggs. Girl, your timing sucks."

"What now?" Michel said.

"We shoot the others," Alexandra said. "Tie her up. Once we have the ship, we dump them and bring her in for the reward."

"Shoot them now?" Michel asked.

"Should we have dinner first, ask for fashion tips?"

Weeks dropped his arms, scooped a statue off the side table, and rammed Alexandra's arm. The arm cracked as it broke.

"Aaaaa," she screamed and dropped her revolver.

Michel fired at Weeks. BOOM. Scruggs's hearing stopped.

Weeks dropped below the table. Michel advanced to his right, firing.

Scruggs rolled sideways, kicked her legs out, and knocked a metal chair into Michel. He fell over it. Scruggs pulled the stove out, sparked the flame, and stuck it on his hand. Michel yelled, flailed, and dropped his gun. The stove banged into the corner and lit a pile of clothes on fire.

Hernandez pulled herself up with her right hand, stepped across the couch, and scooped up the revolver. Her mouth moved. Scruggs's ears didn't respond. The gunshot had blasted her hearing.

Hernandez's lips moved, and she waved her gun. Scruggs heard her voice like underwater. "Nobody move, or I'll shoot. Weeks, get Scruggs."

Weeks scooted past the table, ducked under the wavering revolver, and kneeled next to Scruggs. "You're back. Are you okay?"

"Yes." Scruggs sat up. "I tripped. He tripped me."

"What are you doing here?"

"They were going to take the ship, shoot both of you. Couldn't let that happen."

"You came back for us?"

"Couldn't let you get hurt."

Weeks pointed at the bump on his head.

Michel stood, cradling his arm.

"I said stay put." Hernandez pointed the revolver at him. "Hands up and back into the corner, Now. Now."

Michel held up his hands and backed away.

"Where's that witch who shot me?"

Scruggs sat up, holding Weeks's shoulder. "Back corner."

"Stand up, or I'll come back there and shoot you."

Alexandra climbed up from behind the table. Her eyes ran with tears, ruining her mascara. Her right arm hung loose, her left was behind her. She spat a metal ring from her mouth. It tinged on the wooden table.

"I don't think so." She slumped into the wall, shielding her left hand.

"Show me your hands slowly, or I'll—"

Alexandra whipped her hand up.

BANG. BANG.

Hernandez shot her twice in the chest, center of mass like she'd been taught.

Alexandra banged into the wall and stuck there. Her

left hand jerked up. They could read the legend on what she held.

Grenade, Anti-Personnel-Fragmentation-SS Model 1003, aka G-APF-SS-1003.

Scruggs and Weeks clutched each other and watched as the hand holding it shook.

Hernandez edged closer, keeping the gun pointed at Alexandra. "Weeks, take her out the door now before—"

Alexandra slid down the wall. Her hand opened, and the grenade dropped into the middle of the table and landed next to the open box of Scruggs's last purchased sculptures. It rolled once, bumped into Sunrise of the Comets, and came to a stop next to Green Apple Alone. Once at rest, the handle popped out.

"Frag you, Imperial turds," Alexandra gasped, sliding out of sight.

CHAPTER THIRTY-FOUR

"That's a big ship docked there," Dirk said. "Looks like a warship. Navigator, what is it?"

"Little busy, Pilot," Lee said. "Our intercept with the station is marginal, since we have fuel problems and all."

"I thought that was fixed."

"Engineer says no." Lee fussed with her screens.

They were at the jump limit of Theta Vadoria, having outpaced official sanction from their last stop for beating up station staff and stealing parts.

Dirk keyed the intercom. "Engineer." No response. "Engineer, come in, please."

Behind Dirk, Ana swiped his screen. "Sensor response any time now, Nature Girl."

"Working, old man," Dena said. "Give me a minute."

"If this was a combat situation, we might not have a minute."

"If this was a combat situation, we'd be dead because we're a freighter, not a warship, and we have no weapons. And we're so short of fuel it's better to make the right choice rather than go off half cocked."

Ana shrugged. "Grumpy today, aren't we?"

"What fuel situation?" Dirk slapped his board. "We beat up that clerk and stole his stuff so that we would fix our fuel situation."

"Technically, I beat the guy up, Navy," Ana said.

"And I'm the one who stole his stuff," Dena said. "And Gavin fixed the ship."

"What do you do again?" Ana asked.

"Fly the ship," Dirk said.

"So, fly the ship and stop asking stupid questions. That is a big ship." Ana zoomed the display in. "What's that giant metal rack thing on the front."

"Pushing hard points, catch cage. Reinforced bow for

shoving ships around. What's this about fuel?"

"Course laid in, Pilot," Lee said.

"Fine, I'll—wait. Half a G?"

The intercom lit.

"What's up, Skipper? I'm busy with the pumps here."

"Thank you for being busy with the pumps. Why are you busy with the pumps? Why are we short of fuel? Why are we going at half a G?"

"Save fuel till we get the processing plant shifted over."

"You said we had enough fuel before."

"Enough fuel to jump. We've jumped. Now, we need to make more fuel."

"But our tanks are full..."

"Full of water. Which we can crack to H and O for the fusion reactor, the main drive, and the thrusters. But I need to rewire that master valve to bring the fuel processor online."

"Replumb," Dena said.

"What?" Dirk said.

"They're pipes. You don't rewire pipes. You replumb them."

"Why"—Dirk banged his head on the board—"why are we replumbing pipes?"

"The short answer," Lee said, "is because we didn't steal enough of them. Engineer has that master valve set up, but the connectors were cracked. So, he can pump converted fuel to the main engines no problem or pump water into the tanks or pump water to the converter, and the converted fuel back to the main tanks, but we don't have enough couplings to do all three. Need four more number seven fuel line couplings."

Dena nodded. "Regular threads, not left-handed. I had to learn about that."

"When we switch from pumping fuel to the reactor or the drives to converting it, we have to shut some things off. Lee gave you a course that uses the fuel in the working tanks. That gives Gavin time to cross-fix everything."

Gavin laughed. "That's pretty much it. If that was all, I'm busy. Call me later."

The intercom light clicked off.

"Emperor's shoelaces," Dirk said. "Will we never get a break? Why didn't I know this?"

"Didn't your read the reports I collated?" Dena asked.

"What reports?"

"Dena has become our new cargo master," Lee said. "At least administratively speaking. She's got us all sending in our reports and logs like you told us to do, and she puts them together in a master readiness report?"

"Like I told you to do?" Dirk asked.

"Sure," Dena said, "You dirtbags—or spacebags, in your case—kept hassling me about how important the logs were, so I started asking for them whenever I was on shift. They were interesting reading. Then I started making a daily report combining everyone's numbers, and requesting others. Now we get a daily status report on the state of the ship."

"Three hundred twelve days of food trays," Ana said.

"Medical supplies are at eighty-six percent, and she gave me a shopping list to refill at the next port," Lee said.

"And she gave a list of cargo to go on the trading board next trading station we meet up with," Ana said. "Plus, I now know we have three hundred rounds per revolver and more for my rifle and SMG, including a case of rocket launchers we picked up somewhere and I had forgotten about."

"And a shortage of parts for the fuel system," Lee said, "resulting in only two hours of fuel in the tanks right now."

Dirk blinked. "I guess I should have read those emails."

"I guess you should have, Pilot," Dena said.

"Unless those minor details are beneath his lordships notice," Ana said.

"Don't worry," Dena said. "Centurion and I will go

shoplift some pipe fittings when we're on station."

"Can't we buy them?" Ana asked.

"That's no fun."

"I don't shoplift."

"It's easy. We find a male clerk. I flash my boobs at him, and while he's ogling, you grab what we need and walk out."

"That's ridiculous. I'm not doing that."

"Fine." Dena tapped Ana on the chest. "You flash your man-boobs, and I'll take what we need. Better idea?"

Ana grimaced. "Make sure you wear a tight shirt. I'll bring a bag for the parts. And we're supposed to have the sensor report by now. I want to know more about that huge ship docked at the station."

Dena popped the telescope output up on the screen with a legend. "Well, since I know how big the station is, from Centurion's war book, I can tell that ship is five hundred fifty-three meters long, including that pushing thing on the front, and seventy-five meters in diameter at those big tanks there. Which, again, according to Centurion's war book, would make it a T3-Class Imperial Auxiliary Logistics Ship. By its pennant number, stenciled on the bow, it's the Hydrogen Queen herself, lead ship of the class."

Lee brought up a picture of the tanker in question on her screen and set it side-by-side with the telescope view. "Wow. Totally correct. Well done, Dena."

"Thank you, thank you," Dena said. "Not just another tight shirt."

"Excellent identification, Nature Girl," Ana said. "Good presentation as well."

"Thanks, old man."

"Well," Dirk said, "I'm impressed, too, both with your newfound skills as a sensor tech and the size of that ship. As far as fleet tankers go, I've never seen one that big."

"I'll bet that's the missing fleet supply ship the tribune was looking for," Lee said. "We should tell him about it.

The fueling and tow capabilities would be super useful."

"Tell him after we get Scruggs," Ana said. "We don't owe him any more favors."

"True enough," Dirk said. "But it wouldn't hurt to have him owing us some. Lee, we're on course. I'm going to take a shower."

"Not enough water," Dena said.

"Fine. I'll spray myself with ship perfume, then."

"About time."

"How long till we hit the station?"

"Half shift or less."

"Call me if you need me."

Dirk unbuckled and left the control room. Ana smiled at Dena.

She shivered. "Centurion, please. It's nearly lunch time. You know how that makes me feel."

"Five hundred fifty meters? You measured that ship?"

"Five hundred fifty-three."

"You're lying."

"That's how long it is."

"But you didn't measure it."

"Nope." Dena grinned. "They've got their beacon on. All the data is there."

Ana snorted. "Well done, Nature Girl. Navigator, can we request a dock next to them? I might be able to... acquire some parts for us from the crew of the ship."

"Don't dock next to them," Dena said. "Or not right next to them. Dock here." She highlighted a spot several bays away.

"And why be that far away?" Lee asked.

"Because," Dena said, "then we're closer to the shuttle dock. The dock where the shuttles from this ship..." She highlighted another large ship in orbit. "Where this ship sends its shuttle. And, according to the beacon, this ship is the Artemis Star."

Ana grinned wider. "Scruggs's ship?"

Dena smiled. "Scruggs's ship. She's in town. Let's

rescue her and skedaddle."

CHAPTER THIRTY-FIVE

Weeks's eyes widened when the grenade armed. "Fire in the hole." He grabbed Scruggs, shoved her out the door, and dove right. Hernandez was a second behind him, diving and rolling to the left.

She smacked into the sitting guard Scruggs had pounded with the can of beans. He yelped and sat up, shaking his head.

"Go and, what—"

BOOM.

The shock wave knocked them down and shattered the apple sculptures on the dinner table. Green apple-shaped shrapnel blasted out of the room and hammered directly in the guard's forehead, smashing him down. Smoke billowed, and alarms bonged.

Weeks lay on top of Scruggs, chest to chest, pinning her to the ground. "You okay, kiddo?"

"I'm fine. How's your head?"

"About that. Why did you hit me?"

"It was the only way to escape."

"That was mean."

"So, sue me," Scruggs said. "How are the others?"

Hernandez loomed through the smoke. She rolled the guard over, checked his head, and rolled him back. "Dead. Skull's smashed. Those sculptures of yours are lethal."

"Your shoulder," Scruggs said. "You're hurt."

"It hurts, but they didn't break anything. Frangibles in the gun."

Weeks pushed Scruggs down. "Check the others. I'll keep her here for now. Then I'll take her—"

Scruggs slapped his chest with her hands. "Take me nowhere. I'll take you two out of here."

"You almost got killed," Hernandez said.

Scruggs shrugged. "So did you. Speaking of, how are

301

our friends inside?"

"Unless they're made of stainless steel, shredded, with those grenades." Hernandez crawled to the door, cursing as her arm dragged, and peeked around the corner. "Come out of there now, or I shoot."

Nothing answered, so she wormed inside.

Scruggs looked at Weeks, sitting above her. "Sorry I had to club you."

"That hurt a lot, kiddo."

"I'll bet. But that was your own fault. That was my plan B."

"That was plan B?"

"Should have taken the wine and what else was on offer."

"Then you wouldn't have bashed my head with random objects?"

"It wasn't random, it was designed to be a safe club. I read up on them. Besides, if we'd—well, if you'd been more... accommodating, I could have snuck out later while you were sleeping?"

"Your plan was to make love to me, and I'd be so overwhelmed by the experience I'd swoon? Was that it." Weeks grinned.

"No," Scruggs said, "the person who taught me well advised me. She said it wouldn't work that way."

"No, it doesn't."

"She told me we had to do it five or six times. After all that, you'd be so exhausted that you'd sleep through anything, and I could run out."

"Oh." Weeks bit his lip. "That might have worked."

Hernandez reappeared. "Shrapnel everywhere, three dead bodies. That girl, Alex, has a crushed chest from two frangible bullets. The other guard is peppered. He's gone, too, Michel bled out. Oh, and the furniture and walls are on fire."

Weeks gestured at the dead guard. "Four dead bodies including our friend here."

Hernandez grimaced. "Right, I'll stay here. You take Scruggs here to—"

"To where?" Weeks asked.

"Yes, to where?" Scruggs asked.

"Just... away. I'll wait here for the authorities, and I'll explain things."

"Like how you're such a good shot it took only two bullets from the gun you're holding, the one with all your fingerprints on it, to make the first corpse in the room, but the other two aren't your fault?"

"I'll take responsibility."

"For all of them?" Scruggs cocked her head. "How you going to explain the can shaped dent on the guy out here?"

"Can?"

"Beans. All I could get in a hurry."

"We have to keep you safe."

"Nope. That's already failed. I escaped. I came back to warn you about these hijackers. We need to get out while the getting's good."

Weeks peered into the smoke. "Where's the emergency response crew? They should be here by now."

"Two of the fabulous four are unaccounted for. I'll guess causing problems in engineering or somewhere else. Let's go." Scruggs looked up at Weeks, who was still holding her down. "You going to move?"

"What if I don't?"

Scruggs grabbed his head, pulled him down, and gave him a long sloppy kiss. She kept hold of his head for a dozen seconds, pushed him away, then slapped the bump on the side of his head.

Weeks yowled and rolled off.

Scruggs jumped up. "Let's go. To the shuttle."

"Why the shuttle?"

"If I remember all the discussions I overheard when you figured I was too stupid or too young to understand, your orders are to get me somewhere safe and then bring some private emergency messages to somebody important

303

in the core. Do you still have the messages?"

Hernandez's face darkened. She patted her pants and pulled out two message chips. She whooshed an exhale. "Right here."

"Fine. If you are still on the 'keep Scruggs safe' thing, then you need to go where I go."

The fire inside reached spilled whiskey. The alcohol caught with a whoosh and blew burning debris out the door.

"We can't stay here," Scruggs said. "Come with me. We'll grab a shuttle while things are confused. I've got my own things to do. You can come along if you want or head into the core to deliver your messages. But I'm not your prisoner anymore."

"You can pilot a shuttle?"

"Nope. I can bribe my way on board or steal one. Coming?"

"You're not in charge of us."

"I escaped. You're not in charge of me anymore. Now, to do your job you have to follow me."

Hernandez cocked her head. "You were faking the injury?"

"Yes."

"The clothes, all that stuff."

"Had you fooled, didn't I?"

"You did. Can you find this shuttle quickly?"

"Sure. You coming or not?"

Hernandez weighed the chip in her hands and coughed from the smoke. "Why not? We can't possibly screw this up any more than we have."

Scruggs patted a groaning Weeks on the shoulder. "Let's go, big guy."

"Could you stop hitting me, please?"

"Your options were fight me, or something else that starts with F. You chose poorly."

Hernandez furrowed her brow. "That's right. You two didn't..."

"Didn't have time," Scruggs said. "Let's go."

Scruggs found the maintenance door and led them through it.

Hernandez read out the stenciled legend, 3-17-4-L. "Deck 3 below main deck, frame 17, second compartment on the port side, living quarters. What's the shuttle bay number?"

"Don't know," Scruggs said. "You can read those numbers?"

"Universal ship numbering scheme. Teach you that first week in the navy."

"Huh, maybe the navy isn't as useless as Centurion says?"

"What?"

"Nothing. I don't know the number, but I know the way. Let's go."

They clambered down the service corridors to the shuttle bay. Other alarms went off as they passed different levels. Crew members ran in confusion, trying to figure out which ones were real and which weren't.

In the shuttle bay, the two pilots swapped stories.

"Howdy, Ms. Scruggs," the pilot said as they arrived. "Some sort of flap on. Sorry, but our next departure is canceled till the captain tells us. What happened to your shoulder, miss? And you need some pants, pal."

Hernandez had fashioned a bloody splint, and Weeks was still half naked.

"We can't wait," Scruggs said. "We're hijacking you and your shuttle and fleeing to the surface. Do you want bribes or violence?"

"Bribes or violence?" the copilot said. "Sounds like that time on Vidoco-four. Well, we can't take any more money. I mean, you've paid well before, but this is serious. The captain will have our hides if we do anything right now."

"I understand," Scruggs said. "Right-handed or left-handed?"

"What?"

"He's a lefty," the pilot said. "Very annoying. Bumps me in the cockpit all the time."

Scruggs pulled Hernandez's revolver from where she had it hidden in the small of her back. She stepped clear and aimed carefully.

BAM.

Everyone covered their ears, and the copilot grabbed his right arm. "Holy Mother of Empresses, that hurt. Are you crazy?"

"No," Scruggs said. "You said no bribes, which means violence. And I didn't hurt your working arm. And they're frangibles." She pointed the revolver at the pilot. "The camera will show we threatened you. Can we go, please?"

"You going to shoot me?"

"Probably not. But why not help us? We have money."

The pilot raised her hands. "I can't go anywhere without a copilot."

"Hernandez here is certified as a shuttle pilot. She'll be your copilot. Let's go."

"What's going on?"

"Let's say some people want to harm us," Hernandez said. "Bad people."

"Not buying it."

"Fine. We're career criminals who have just killed four people in cold blood, and we're running ahead of the authorities. Do we need to shoot you, too?"

The pilot raised her eyebrows, then laughed.

"Please," Scruggs said. "I need to get away."

"You." The pilot looked at Hernandez. "You're the one they said was one of her guards, protecting her."

"More or less."

"Ms. Scruggs. You're not a prisoner, are you? Not being held against your will?"

Scruggs held up the revolver. "What do you think?"

The pilot dropped her arms. "Departure in five minutes, then. Shall we?"

Weeks hauled the copilot upright. "Can't have you

giving the alarm, sorry. I'll strap you in."

The pilot glanced at the overhead camera. "I don't think you're going to shoot me but keep waving that gun at me so that the vids will show it."

"Sorry about shooting your friend. But it will make a nice story for him. Being he was a big, tough pilot in the navy, right?"

"He flew mail to fleet tankers. But it will make a good story to tell the passengers. Especially the younger, more impressionable women. I might use that story myself." Weeks pushed past the pilot, bundling the copilot on the shuttle. "Nice-looking boy. Is that who you were meeting? The married one?"

"No," Scruggs said. "Weeks isn't married. He's not the married one."

"Aha," the pilot said. "Not the married one. Busy night for you. Two men. Sneak on planet, sneak back. A hijacking." She smiled. "Reminds me of my early navy days with my girlfriends." She climbed into the hatch. "Did I ever tell you about that time on Sirius four. I was very young, not much older than you..."

The "Bye Bye-jacking," as Hernandez called it, went smoothly. The pilot treated it as a joke and pronounced Hernandez's copiloting "marginal but acceptable" and seemed to enjoy offering advice.

The real copilot, once he got feeling in his arm back, swapped old war stories with Hernandez about getting shot. Both pilots seemed to regard it as an interesting interlude in an otherwise boring job.

"There I was," the copilot said from the rear seat, cradling his arm, "on an urgent top secret mission—"

The pilot pushed the control stick. "To carry replacement parts for the soda machines on the fleet flagship's snack bar."

"I didn't know that at the time. Anyways, there I was, alone in the cockpit—"

"Except for some cheap tramp that you met in a sleazy

spacers bar."

"A very nice young lady—"

"Who you met in a sleazy spacer bar."

"Some very nice young ladies hang out in spacer bars."

"Of course they do."

"Where did you meet your husband again? Wasn't it at—"

"In a restaurant, a very nice restaurant."

"I thought it was waiting at the bar in a nice restaurant that neither of you could get into, so you decided to go somewhere—shall we say 'down level'—and he got in a fight?"

The pilot pulled the control rod slightly. "He did not get in a fight."

"My mistake. But there was a fight, wasn't there. Who started it?"

"I did. That girl shouldn't have hit on my man. She hit on him, so I hit her."

Scruggs came up front with Weeks, from the crew compartment. "You started a fight with a woman over your boyfriend."

"Yep. Hit her hard. If you see a woman messin' with your man, you need to go up and hit her, Ms. Scruggs."

"I don't think I'd do that," Scruggs said.

"You should stand up for yourself, Ms. Scruggs. Not let some woman push you around." The pilot tapped her controls. "Then again, you don't seem like the retiring type, being as you hijacked us and all. And smoothly done."

"Oh, I've hijacked ships before. You get better with practice."

"Wait," Hernandez said, "you've hijacked ships before?"

"This will be my fourth," Scruggs said. "I get better every time. Centurion says practice makes perfect."

The pilot and Hernandez exchanged glances.

"Well, keep up the good work, then," Hernandez said.

"Thank you," Scruggs said.

"What's your plan now?"

"My plan?"

"Sure," Hernandez said, grinning. "I figure we'll put you in charge, since you escaped custody, came back, fought off the kidnappers with a can of beans, seized a shuttle, and now we're on our way to become wanted interplanetary fugitives."

"Okay." Scruggs scrunched up her face. "When we land, we'll tie the two pilots up so they don't get into trouble, remove the video and audio records from the cockpit so the authorities have no idea where we're going next, seize any weapons we can find here in the shuttle, deplane, and flee the docking bay. Normally to flee I'd take a liner, but since the only liner in dock we kind of blew up, set on fire, and left dead people on, there would be too many questions. We need another way off-planet. Checking the ships in dock..." Scruggs leaned past Hernandez and tapped through a menu. "Some in-system freighters, no jump drives on those, a bulk freighter loading up. Anybody can catch that, a courier, that's too small, not enough life support for three. But there's an Imperial fleet tanker in port."

"You're going to steal a fleet tanker?" the pilot asked. "By yourself?"

"Hijack it," Scruggs said. "Not sure. We'll check it out though, get more information. That enough planning for you, Ms. Hernandez?"

"Well, yes."

"Outstanding. Carry on, then. But we need a pilot and an engineer. Unless, Ms. Hernandez, you or Weeks are ship certified."

"Shuttles only for me," Hernandez said. "Weeks?"

"Not even shuttles," he said.

"So, we need a ship with a crew that we can convince to take us somewhere. That Imperial tanker in port. How big is the crew on one of those."

"Seventeen," the pilot said. "Normally."

"Too big to control with only three people," Scruggs said. "But I met some of them on station. They said they were going for R&R. Let me check the roster of incoming ships."

Weeks grinned. "Kiddo has a plan. She appears to be in charge."

"You should probably stop calling her kiddo," Hernandez said.

"That seems like a big step."

"She'll brain you with a statue again. Are you going to get any clothes?"

"None here. Buddy is too small for me."

"Not that I'm complaining about the view," the pilot said, "But walking around in your underwear, you will draw notice."

"He likes it that way," Hernandez said.

"Oh, awesome!" Scruggs looked up from the console. "Heavyweight Items is inbound! They came after me!"

"What's a Heavyweight Items?" the pilot asked.

"Criminals, deserters, mercenaries, runaways, spies, failed revolutionaries, and disgraced Imperial officials."

"Perfect fit for you, then, right?"

"They're all my friends," Scruggs said. "Wow! They're here. It will be great to see them."

"Which ones? The mercenaries or the criminals?" Hernandez asked.

"Some are both," Scruggs laughed. "All of them." She tapped through a screen and highlighted a docking bay. "Can we dock there? That's next to them."

"Normally, no," the pilot said. "But why not? We're hijacked after all."

"Outstanding, thank you," Scruggs said.

"Ms. Scruggs," the copilot said, "You're hijacking this shuttle, and if the radio is correct, you started a war on board the Artemis Star, and you're holding a gun on me and all."

"So?"

"Now you want to meet this ship of disreputables and steal another ship. Right?"

"Could you maybe not share that with the authorities right away?" Scruggs asked.

"But you said you wouldn't hit a woman who was messing with your boyfriends."

"No," Scruggs said. "I wouldn't hit her."

"Because that's too much? Hitting a woman."

"Not too much, no." Scruggs shrugged. "I have no problem hitting a girl. But hitting her isn't effective. If I just hit her, she'd get up and keep fighting. Better to shoot her in the head or stab her in the stomach." Scruggs leaned back and stretched. "Or both."

CHAPTER THIRTY-SIX

"Docking in five," Dirk said. "Engineer?"

"Clamps are ready, Skipper," Gavin said over the intercom.

Dirk maneuvered Heart's Desire, which was operating as Heavyweight Items, into the docking bay. The station was moderately sized, moderately busy, and moderately bureaucratic in its requirements for docking. So unremarkable that, if the inhabitants ever voted on an official color, the winner would be beige.

CLUNK.

The intercom flashed.

"And docked. Give me a moment on the air lock seal."

Dirk and Lee unbuckled and pulled back to the air lock. Ana and Dena were already dressed to rescue Scruggs.

"I heard a docking."

Ana wore a starched outfit of pants and a jacket that couldn't be anything but military surplus over a reinforced skinsuit. Blackened combat boots, black utility belt, full helmet, and gloves completed the look. A revolver peeked out from under his jacket.

Dirk dumped his ship slippers and pulled on polished brown shoes. "Wait for the light and the engineer to confirm."

Dena's boots were also black but heeled and calf-high, matching her belt and long black leather jacket. Her pants were tight but had a side pocket where her slingshot sat and also had a holster for a revolver strapped to her thigh. Her hair was up in a bun, and she had an emergency air loss kit on her belt.

Lee slid a regular comm and a nav computer into her leg pockets and pushed by them to medical locker. She grabbed a medical kit, flipped the top, scanned the contents, then nodded and snapped it shut.

Gavin pulled up from below. He had his usual greasy coveralls, crowded tool belt, magnetic boots, and hard shell connections on wrist and neck.

"We ready?"

"Soon as you confirm safe docking," Ana said.

"I don't see any long guns."

"Station won't allow them. Hand guns only. We're trying to keep a low profile."

Gavin dug in the locker and removed a revolver and slid it into a slot on his tool belt, placing ammunition in the pouch next to it.

"Don't you have your own?" Ana asked.

"Of course. But extra never hurts." Gavin pulled a heavy wrench from the tool rack and slid that onto his belt. "And Mr. Wrench is always a good persuader."

Dirk finished putting on his shoes, stood, ran his hands through his hair, and checked his reflection in the viewport. "Everybody ready?"

He got muttered affirmative grunts.

Dirk nodded at Gavin, who checked the lock, then swung the internal door open. "Atmo on the other side. Let me override the interlocks, and we can all go through." He busied himself with a panel on the side.

"What's our plan?" Ana asked.

"Save Scruggs," Dirk said.

"That's it? Any details?"

"Whatever is necessary," Dena said. "That's the details."

Ana nodded. "Outstanding."

Gavin opened the outer door. Air lock doors always opened in, so any issues with air rushing out or pressure differences would end up slamming the air lock shut. The crowd had to reshuffle as he maneuvered them around, then they surged out.

Lee was first. She cleared the door and marched forward through the extended docking pier. Heavyweight Items had locked directly with the passenger lock on the left side of the bay, on the lower level. The station was the usual spinning wheel. As the cargo ring spun, out was down, so there were paired locks across from each other at equal separation across the whole wheel. To spinward was an oversized cargo container lock, unused at this time. Coreward lights on the ceiling made cones of brightness. The area between the two facing locks with their corresponding cargo and personnel air locks was clear to allow carts and come-alongs to move containers and packages. Overhead, cranes could scoop containers shoved through the cargo lock on to an electric railway that circled the level. Metal grills formed a walkway above the dock, with steps on the spinward wall.

Four figures approached Lee from the spinward shadows.

She peered at them as they approached. "Heads up. Visitors."

Ana pulled up to her left and drew two revolvers and pointed them at the dark figures. "Hold there!"

Dena stepped to the right and pulled out her slingshot.

Dirk and Gavin stopped next to her. Gavin produced a light from his belt and shone it forward.

To their left was a chubby woman in a flight suit with her hands raised. Next to her was a shorter slimmer figure pointing a revolver at her head. Two other shaded figures stopped behind them.

"Take this." The slim figure stuffed the revolver into the hand of the woman next to her and raised it to point at the chubby woman.

She ducked under the outstretched arm.

Ana cocked his revolvers. "I said hold there!"

A black furry bolt streaked by, barking. Rocky had followed them out of the lock. He cleared the group and jumped into Scruggs's waiting hands.

"Rocky!" Scruggs hugged him as he licked her face.

"Baby Marine!" Dena said. She surged forward and hugged her as well. "You're okay!"

"You're okay!"

"We're both okay."

Everyone else lowered their weapons.

"I'm so glad you're here," Dena said. "You're okay. Who are your friends. Who's the handsome one? Where did that big bump on his head come from." Her gaze dropped. "And why isn't he wearing pants?"

Scruggs insisted they all move out of the bay, back into the Heart's Desire. She carried a wagging, licking Rocky, and they all moved inside out of range of the cameras. Everyone hugged her, and she hugged back. Once inside, they gathered into the lounge.

"First," Dirk said, "introductions."

The pilot had lowered her hands. "Hello, I'm Lise. I'll be your hijackee for today. Would you be the criminals and mercenaries?"

"I'm the deserter," Dirk said. "That's my main function. But I can fill in as a criminal if one of the others gets sick and can't make it. You shuttled Scruggs down here?"

"Not quite. She hijacked the shuttle at gunpoint."

"She does that," Dirk said. "Why did you have your hands up?"

"Have to make everyone believe it was against our will. So, point guns at us for the cameras. She shot the copilot to make it seem more real."

"She does that, too," Dirk said. "Scruggs, they let you leave?"

"I kind of escaped," Scruggs said. "Ran away and got on-planet."

Dirk pointed at Weeks and Hernandez. "These two were supposed to keep an eye on you two."

"I was." Hernandez pointed at Weeks. "This one turned his back on her and got smacked on the head."

"Why'd you smack him."

"He wouldn't do what I wanted," Scruggs said.

"Why doesn't he have pants?" Dena asked.

"We were in bed when I clubbed him. Well, almost. I mean, we were supposed to be getting in bed, but he wasn't. I mean, he wouldn't. So, I hit him."

"Baby Marine," Dena said, "you're supposed to hit them after, not before."

"I got confused, sorry," Scruggs said.

"Lots of alarms coming in over the channels," Lee said. "What did you do to the Artemis Star?"

"Just hung out, shopped."

Dirk raised his eyebrows. Lee crossed her arms.

Ana grimaced. "You just shopped, Private? That's all."

"I got some clothes."

"Anything else?"

"I played some poker."

"And that was all, Private?"

Scruggs sighed. "We may have set the Artemis Star on fire."

"We?"

"Me. I. I did it."

"How?"

"With grenades."

"With grenades? Where did you get grenades?"

"We took them off some people. Confeds possibly. They were trying to kidnap me. Or Weeks. Or seize the ship."

"You don't know?"

"I didn't have time to ask, Centurion. I only had the three cans of beans."

"Beans?"

"I didn't have any weapons, so I grabbed what I could. I charged in and hit them."

"With a can?"

"Of beans, yes."

Ana switched his gaze to Hernandez. "Where were you while this was going on?"

"Cradling my arm that had been shot, while talking to the psycho that was trying to kill us."

"And pretty boy here?"

"He was a bit groggy from being hit, so he stood there with his hands up."

"Being hit?"

"Scruggs went to his room, seduced him, then hit him over the head and tied him up."

"And his lack of pants?"

"I assume she got him to undress first," Hernandez said. "It's kind of a natural progression."

Dena clapped. "Scruggs beaned you and tied you up? After she slept with you?"

"Before," Weeks said. "She surprised me."

"What was the surprise? Wanting to sleep with you or hitting you with a stick?"

Scruggs shook her head. "It wasn't a stick. It was a sculpture. One I made myself. Comet's passing. Ceramic, wood and plastic. I think I have real talent."

"Perhaps you should explain yourself in more detail, Private," Ana said.

It took Scruggs ten minutes to explain the trip, the dinner, the fantastic four, Michel and Alexandra, the guns, the grenades, the fire, the poker, and Confeds.

Ana rubbed his eyes. "So, you escaped your... minders, snuck off the Artemis Star, bribed your way out I assume?"

Scruggs nodded.

"Then, after bribing your way out, you found that some nefarious types were boarding with weapons and that they intended to kill Weeks and Hernandez here, so acquired what weapons you could, you reboarded, resnuck—whatever—attacked the Confed squad without warning, saved Hernandez and Weeks, fled, rode the shuttle down—"

"Hijacked," Lise, the pilot said, "Remember, I was hijacked. Keep to that story."

"Sorry. Hijacked a shuttle, and got back here to meet up with us?"

"And," Dena said, "this after seducing Weeks here, braining him and tying him up. Did you steal his money, too?"

"No. Was I supposed to?" Scruggs asked.

"We'll talk about that later," Dena said. She looked at Ana. "I'm so proud of her!"

"Me too," Ana said. "Outstanding job."

Dena sniffed. "You know, my little girl is all grown up now."

Scruggs finished explaining the whole thing, including her wanderings throughout the ship, much to the surprise of Weeks and Hernandez, focusing on the possible Confed linkage of her almost-kidnappers.

Lise asked to be excused, so they tied her hands behind her back, gave her a big bonus, and fake chased her out the air lock after exchanging comm codes.

"Hijack me any time! Free Trades!"

The alarms were getting shriller, and there had been a general call for off-duty police to report for a search.

"We're right here," Weeks said. "Why aren't they coming for us."

"They still don't know we left yet, I'll bet. In the confusion, they're not looking for the shuttles."

"That won't last forever," Scruggs said. "It's great to see you all, and it's so amazing that you came back for me, but, um, I kinda wouldn't like to be here when they figure out that the shuttle is gone. They'll probably hold all the shipping here. Can we go now?"

"That's all the thanks for rescuing you?" Dirk grimaced. "Or trying to rescue you. Guess you didn't need it after all."

"But I could have. That's the important thing," Scruggs said.

"And why are your friends"—Dena pointed at Weeks and Hernandez—"still here. Shouldn't they be going on their merry way?"

"We helped with the fires," Hernandez said.

"And the explosions," Weeks said.

"And the deaths."

"We'd rather not be found, either."

"We're all agreed, then," Scruggs said. "Staying on the station is bad. Can we go now?"

"We can't," Gavin said. "We don't have any fuel."

"But I thought—"

Gavin explained the whole fuel pump valve issue, the spare tanks, the fuel conversion issue, the problems with the fittings, and what had to be done.

"We'll get out of here as soon as we get enough fuel to get out of the system," Gavin said.

"How long will that take?"

"A full shift," Gavin said. "Could be longer."

"They'll come looking for me before then," Scruggs said.

"And us," Hernandez said.

"Some rescue this is," Weeks said.

"We did better than you, pants boy," Dena said. "We were ready to rescue Baby Marine here, not be rescued by her."

"We would have been fine without her. We had the situation under control."

"Was that before or after you were half naked and at gunpoint? What was your next move, then? Take off more clothes?" Dena laughed. "That's not a bad idea. Why don't you demonstrate for me?"

Scruggs looked at Ana. "Centurion, we need to get out of here, or we'll be stuck. Even if they decide to let me go, they'll want to run full scans on everybody, find out who they are."

"We're Imperial officers," Hernandez said. "We'll be fine."

Dirk leaned against the lounge wall. "The tribune is an Imperial officer, an Imperial noble, in fact. And he's not fine. He's got an arrest warrant out for him. Something strange is going on. Scruggs, from what we've learned, you're from an important family. They want you to come back, but why not send you a comm or a letter or send a friend out? Why this hundred-thousand-credit Imperial warrant?"

"I don't know," Scruggs said. "But I don't want to find out. That's why I ran away, so that I wouldn't have to deal with this."

"Several mysteries here," Dirk said. "Why the big warrant for Scruggs? What's happening with the tribune's arrest? Why did the Confeds invade and capture that system?"

"The Confeds have invaded? When?" Scruggs asked.

Dirk explained the war situation, the tribune, the arrest, the marines, and the upcoming battle.

"We have to go back and help," Weeks said. "We're Imperial navy. They need us."

"I don't know that they need you," Dirk said, "given your performance with Scruggs, perhaps not reporting for duty might be the most patriotic thing."

"And you're navy, too," Weeks said. "How come you're not back there fighting?"

"The navy put me in prison. The navy took my rank away. I'm not up on the navy right now."

"You're turning your back on the navy?"

"No, I'm not," Dirk said. "The tribune said that rescuing Scruggs before her death warrant was exercised was a matter of honor. That's why he sent me and Lee."

Lee nodded. "But now that Scruggs is back, that obligation is finished. We can go back and fight now."

"I'm not going back and fighting," Ana said. "I don't owe the Empire."

"Me neither," Gavin said.

"We came for Scruggs, to save her from the death warrant thing. Let's get out of here."

Scruggs paled. "Death warrant? What death warrant?"

"Did we forget that?" Dena said. "I think we did. Sorry Baby Marine, but the Emperor has condemned you to death."

"Her?" Hernandez said. "To death? Why?"

"Yes, why?" Scruggs asked.

Dena shrugged. "Don't know. Old man? Dirk? Lee? Any ideas?" All three shook their heads. "What are you guilty of, anyway, Baby Marine? What did you do?"

"Nothing, I ran away with you guys. To you guys? With you. I left home before I was an adult. I couldn't have done anything."

"Maybe they're after your money," Dena said. "Sandra Caroline Ruger-Gascoigne, you are charged with being rich. How do you plead?"

"Well, the family, my uncle, they all—"

"Guilty. I knew it," Dena said. "Off with her head. But let's have a drink first. Centurion, can you break out your Amiens Brandy, give us all a shot?"

"Do you have any idea how expensive that stuff is?" Ana asked.

"Oh, I do. I looked it up. That's the priciest booze I've ever tasted. It's good stuff. Can I have a double shot this time, maybe?"

"I think we should undock," Lee said. "Get away from the station. We can refine the fuel as we head out. That will keep Scruggs and these two safe. We'll head back out to Papillon and find the tribune. Scruggs can come with us."

"I already told you I'm not fighting for the Empire," Gavin said. "Besides, if we can't jump they can come out and catch us in anything—an orbital rowboat, we won't be able to get away."

"You won't have to," Lee said. "Somebody will have to stay with the ship while Pilot and Hernandez and Weeks go with the tribune."

"He'll be gone by the time we get back," Gavin said.

"Maybe not," Lee said. "He was having all those fuel issues. He might still be there working on them."

"Well, tell him we found his missing tanker," Dena

said. "That's that ship in the next bay over, right?"

"That's a fleet supply ship," Hernandez said. "Finishing up some repairs, according to the station listings."

"He'll be happy to know where it is," Dirk agreed. "Probably send somebody back to get it."

"The tribune wants that tanker?" Scruggs asked.

"Sure," Dirk said. "We explained the fuel issue."

"And we need fuel to get out of the system before we get caught."

"Right."

"And some of you want to go back and see the tribune, regardless. But you're worried you won't get there in time."

"Right," Dirk said. "Not to belabor the obvious, but we need a faster ship, more fuel, and a way out of here."

"Can we run a tanker? The Heart's Desire crew?"

"Sure," Gavin said. "It's not a real warship, just a big freighter, big tanker. Same systems as this ship, just everything's bigger."

Scruggs climbed up to the air lock level. They heard her rummaging around, then she came back down carrying the centurion's submachine gun.

"No long arms allowed on the station, private," Ana said.

"Got it, Centurion. But you've been telling me to break rules when I need to."

"If there is a good reason."

"Well, how about this—you're all dressed for a fight, why not give you one?"

***

Dena leaned on the air lock call button. "You look fine."

"I look like a low-rent gigolo," Weeks said.

"You do not. Well, perhaps an affordable, value-priced gigolo."

"We could have bought me different pants."

"No time. Dirk's almost fit you."

"Not well. I can barely move."

Dena leaned to look at his butt. "It is pretty tight. Don't bend over. Say, do you have any underwear on under that?"

Weeks shook his head. "No space."

"In that case, bend all you want." Dena faced the air lock, unzipped her skinsuit a few inches, and fluffed her hair.

The air lock door swung open, and a crew man stepped through. "Who are you?"

"We're the entertainment," Dena said.

"Entertainment?"

"This is the Imperial Auxiliary Logistics Ship Hydrogen Queen, right?"

"Sure."

"Your friends down station. They felt bad for you, so they took up a collection. Weeks and I, we're here. For fun."

"Fun?"

"For your fun. How many of you are there?"

A woman's head poked out from inside the air lock. "What's going on?"

"The kids sent these... people out."

The woman tracked Weeks's pants. "Those are the tightest pants I've ever seen."

Weeks grinned at her. "They take forever to put on, but they're pretty easy to get off."

"I don't know..."

Dena unzipped her skinsuit lower, grabbed the man's hand, stepped back and twirled. "If you don't know, we'll show you."

Weeks grasped the woman's hand and dragged her out as well. "It'll be fun."

The man grinned. "Thanks, but I'm not sure that I want this type of fun."

A gun cocked behind the air lock door, and Ana pushed it back with the barrel of his submachine gun.

Hernandez stood next to him with a revolver.

"That's okay," Ana said. "We've got all different kinds of fun on the schedule tonight."

CHAPTER THIRTY-SEVEN

"I told you I am Subcommander Friedel of the Imperial navy," Dirk said on the radio. "And by order of the tribune and sector governor, the Lord Lyon, my ship and I will be riding on the tanker as she leaves. That is why we are docking there now."

The radio warbled in his ear, and he tapped it and waved like it was a buzzing bee. "I have more than sufficient fuel to attempt this maneuver," Dirk said. He leaned over to Lee. "Do we have sufficient fuel to land there?"

"Doubt it." Lee pointed at the warning lights on her board. "We burned most of it, getting clear of the station."

Dirk cursed and switched screens to view the fuel display. He cursed again and hit the intercom. "Engineer?"

"No."

"No what?"

"No, I can't give you any more fuel. I'm pumping it over as fast as I can. You'll have to get in with what you have."

"What I have will not do." Dirk pivoted the ship, pulsed the main drive, and watched his display. "How strong are the docking clamps?"

"Not strong enough," Gavin said.

The "no fuel" bong sounded. Dirk quieted it. "Fine. Strap in and hold on."

Lee tightened her straps and closed her eyes. "I don't want to watch."

"Me neither," Dirk said. But he turned up the front cameras.

The tanker's number three landing pad filled the display. In addition to all the onboard fuel tankage, supplies, passenger, and cargo air locks, there were four landing pads where smaller shuttle tankers could land, suck up fuel, then launch again.

For all intents and purposes, they mimicked station fueling docks—hoses, valves, with magnetic grapples and chains to lock on.

Dirk was aimed directly for the big 'I' in the middle of dock number three. He pivoted the ship and changed his aim to the closest edge. He tapped a few quick calculations, then fired the thrusters.

Down.

"Pilot," Lee yelled, "slow our forward momentum, not vertical rise—we'll slide right off. Not down."

"Thought you weren't watching," Dirk said.

"We're going to crash."

"We're going to impact. Impact in three, two, one."

SCREECH.

Heart's Desire slammed into the leading edge of the landing dock. The landing legs flexed as the thrusters pushed down, but the ship kept skidding across the dock. Dirk had slammed them down at the front of the pad, and they hit hard.

The different vectors of tanker, station, and landing ship smacked them together. Metal flexed and screamed inside the ship as they scraped along.

"Warning lights on the landing legs," Lee said.

"They'll hold," Dirk said. "The friction will stop us."

"Fuel exhaustion," Lee said.

"They'll hold."

Heart's Desire kept skidding.

The complex of fueling pumps appeared on the bow camera. "Pilot, we'll hit the far side."

"Nothing to do—"

CLUNK. SCREECH.

The port landing leg failed. The ship tipped on its side and screeched across the pad. Whorls of black dust spat up as the ship shredded steel fragments.

"Pilot, we're going to hit the fuel lines," Lee said.

"No, we won't," Dirk said. "Inertia will stop us."

Heart's Desire slowed. The friction of steel-on-steel was low, but the opposed vectors shoved into the surface. The ship slewed sideways and stopped with the air lock inches from the fueling connection port.

Dirk flicked through the cameras and put the mag plate up on the screen.

The intercom lit. "What in the name of the Emperor's armpits was that?" Gavin said.

"Have you deployed the mag locks, Engineer?"

"You broke the landing leg. How did you pull that off?"

"The mag locks, please," Dirk said.

Gavin cursed.

The camera showed the starboard magnetic lever extending, then clicking into the plate next to the fuel lines.

Dirk switched cameras to the portside and got a closeup of the tanker's hull. Heart's Desire's tilt had the camera focused down.

"That's good for horizontal," Dirk said. "Vertical?"

Gavin cursed some more, and the camera showed the port mag lever extending. It twirled and scissored as Gavin manipulated the bend of the lever until it clanked onto the tanker's hull, stabilizing the Heart's Desire.

"Outstanding." Dirk unbuckled his harness. "Thank you, Engineer. Let us proceed to the bridge." Dirk rose.

"That was—" Lee said.

"What? You should be used to these by now. I'll have to say, I think that was one of my better landings."

Lee shook her head and unbuckled herself. "Sad thing is, I believe you're right, Pilot."

***

It took ten minutes to get from Heart's Desire to the Hydrogen Queen's bridge. Fully skinsuited, Gavin led off, Dirk and Lee trailing. After the third set of stairs, Dirk figured out Gavin was lost.

"We're going to deck number one," Dirk said.

"But how do you know where the bridge is?" Gavin asked.

"Bridge is always on deck one. That's where the numbers start."

Gavin nodded a small nod, but he didn't move.

Dirk shook his head. "Follow me"

After a long walk down the corridor, Dirk tapped the entry button next to the label 1-1-1 and entered the control room. Ten times the size of the Heart's Desire. The floor shone, and the walls gleamed. The lights glinted off shiny metal.

"Wow, brand new." Dirk sniffed. "New spaceship smell, too."

"Makes our control room seem tiny."

"Makes our control room seem like somewhere you'd store old clothes." Dirk ran his finger over a console and examined it. No dust. "Old clothes you were getting ready to burn."

Two rows of four stations faced an entire wall of view screens. Dena and Hernandez already filled two of the front row seats. In the Heart's Desire, a crewman at one seat could lean over and tap the screens in front of their neighbor. Here, the padded arms and wide chairs made that impossible.

There were even footrests.

"This is the biggest control room I've ever been in," Gavin said. He shaded his eyes. "And the brightest."

"And the nicest smelling," Lee said. "Doesn't smell like burning plastic or scorched oil?"

"Join the Imperial navy, see the stars." Dirk raised his voice. "Captain on deck."

The two in front glanced over their shoulders, then returned to their screens.

"I said captain on deck."

"We heard you," Dena said. "We just didn't care. Everything go ok with the docking?"

Lee sat next to Dena and adjusted her chair. "We had some minor issues. Wow, is this comfy."

"Isn't it though? Check this out. Watch." Dena leaned down, pulled a lever, released the chair, and slid it back a foot. Then she spun in a full circle. "Pretty cool, huh."

Lee did the same. "Whee. That's neat. These chairs are comfy." She slid back in. "Gotta get navigation up. Are we undocked?"

"Not yet. I can't figure out the controls for that." Dena coughed and waved. "What's all that dust on your skinsuit? Where did that come from?"

"That's the antiskid coating from the landing pad," Lee said. "Special steel-carbon matrix. The pilot was unhappy with it being on the pad, so he had it scraped off."

"Why'd he do that?"

"Ask him."

Dirk slid into the remaining chair in the first row. "Not important. Where's Ana?"

"He's conducting a security sweep of the ship to make sure no other crew members on board that need to be restrained. Scruggs is with him."

"He doesn't need Scruggs."

"She said she wasn't much use in getting a starship undocked, and she wanted to learn about how to handle searches and prisoners, so she went along with him to learn."

Dirk nodded at Hernandez. "Where's your friend Weeks?"

"He went with them to make sure that Scruggs didn't learn that 'handling prisoners' is a synonym for shooting them and throwing them out air locks."

"Didn't take you long to figure out our centurion. But I don't think you need worry about Scruggs. She's not like that. He doesn't need to keep an eye on her actions."

Dena giggled. "I think he's keeping an eye on her other body parts," Dena said. "He may be regretting what he missed."

"I'm sure he'll get another chance," Hernandez said.

"Don't count on it," Dena said. "Scruggs is pretty shy. She has to work up to these things."

"Shy? She lied to us for weeks, snuck around the ship, bribed people, came back, seized weapons, beat someone up with a can of beans, got us shot, blown up and set on fire."

"And I'll bet she feels really guilty, too," Dena said. "Aha. Finally, here's the commo screen. Messages in the queue. Queries asking for help with a search for 'escaped terrorists who may have reached the station.'"

"Acknowledge the signal and then ignore it," Dirk said. "The station will expect an Imperial warship to follow comm procedure, but not offer any help."

"What do I do if they call directly?"

"Don't worry. We'll be out of there by then. These controls are amazing. This ship is brand new."

"Big jump drive, too," Lee said. "Long range. We can get back to the tribune in two jumps."

"It took, what, six—no, seven—to get here?" Dena said.

"We can jump so much farther at one go," Lee said. "And we've got so much internal fuel storage we can jump again right away without refueling. I'm setting up courses now."

The doors swished open in the back, and Ana came back in. "The navy's here, I see. Late as usual but at least present. When do we leave?"

"Where's the others?"

"Weeks is digging through cabins for somebody with the same size clothes. He's looking for a skinsuit as well. Scruggs stopped to feed Rocky and strap him in. Whoever made that harness for him, good job." Ana slumped into a chair in the second row. "Finally, a seat I can fit in without pain. Are we leaving now?"

Dena pulled the lever and spun her chair again. "Whee. Your chairs always hurt you?"

"Always. I'm too big on the shoulders and hips," Ana said.

"You never complained about the pain."

"Pain makes you stronger."

"Or grumpier and angrier."

"That, too, I prefer it. And I take the anger out on my enemies. The hate keeps me warm."

"You are some weird, twisted strangeness," Dena said.

Ana smiled. "Why, thank you, Nature Girl. That's very kind."

"Please don't smile. Pilot, more calls coming in asking for assistance."

Dirk leaned back, stretched his fingers, and started tapping his board. "I'll undock us as soon as the engineering interlocks are released. Lee, I see a course here already, thank you. Engineer, they've got us manually locked on. You need to go to engineering and override from there."

"Got it," Gavin said. "Um, I've never been on a ship this big. I don't know where engineering is."

Dirk paged through his screens. "6-53-0"

Gavin didn't move. "Um, I..."

"You don't know what that means do you?" Ana asked.

"No."

"I'll take you. I'm not doing anything important right now." Ana headed off the bridge Gavin following.

They exchanged words with Scruggs as she reentered the control room.

"Pilot. Navigator. Dena. Ms. Hernandez."

"Welcome back, Scruggs," Dirk said. "Grab a seat, do what you can with the sensors. We're dropping in five, soon as Engineer uncouples us."

"Super-duper." Scruggs belted into the second row. "The gangs all back together." She beamed a smile around the bridge. "Adventure awaits!"

CHAPTER THIRTY-EIGHT

Devin's office door was sitting open when Lionel dashed through. "Refueling complete, Tribune."

"Finally. Ours or everyone's?"

"Everyone's."

"Thank the spirits of dead Emperors." Devin shut off his terminal and stood. "How soon can we get moving?"

The acceleration alarm bonged. "Warning. Warning. High acceleration in five minutes. Stand by for dangerous maneuvering."

"I already gave the order. We need to get strapped in."

The two officers reached the Pollux's control room and dashed for their chairs.

The navigation officer was so absorbed he didn't even notice their arrival. He was arguing on the radio.

"I understand, sir, but Kamloops has to match our course exactly, otherwise the jump path won't work. We all need to arrive together." He listened intently for another ten seconds, nodding. "Yes, sir, I understand you want to keep reserve fuel, but we can't take drive efficiency into account. We need exact separations for this to work. You can't lag behind, not even a hundred meters."

Devin closed his straps and punched the all ships channel. "All Imperial units, this is Devin, the—no, strike that. This is the Mad Dog of the Verge. All units conform to flagship instructions exactly. Weapons, get positions off the navigation plan, target any ship that falls one hundred meters behind necessary position, and fire a warning shot. Second shot, fire for effect. Anyone who's not willing to die for the Empire in the next system will die in this one. God save the Empire!"

Devin snapped his fingers at the weapons section, and the officers there busied themselves calling out vectors and targets to each other.

Lionel called up a private channel. "Nobody will believe that."

Devin raised his eyebrows. "Who knows what the Mad Dog of the Verge might do? Navigation? What's the status of the fleet?"

"Four corvettes and one assault carrier in formation, sir, and responding to commands."

"Outstanding. Take us out on your plan. Jump when ready. You have full control." Devin relaxed in his chair.

"Can I call you Mad Dog rather than Tribune from now on?" Lionel asked.

"It suits me, don't you think?" Devin said. "Kind of rakish, swashbuckling."

"Kind of idiotic, insane," Lionel said. "But sure. Don't you want to give the orders to bring us out-system?"

"I wouldn't remember them," Devin said. "Too complicated. The navigation people spent days working this out."

"Are you comfortable giving orders you don't understand?"

Devin waved. "I don't understand most of the technology on this ship. I have to trust the people who set it up. I told the nav people what I wanted, and they did it."

"It will get us as close to the Sand Harbor Station as possible."

"True."

"The marines will be exposed for the least amount of time possible."

"So little time. We'll barely have time to do an analysis of the tactical situation."

"Nor will the enemy. The sudden appearance of a flotilla at the jump limit screaming in-system will frighten them."

"I don't know about the enemy, but it certainly frightens me. And speaking of the tactical situation, get Santana and the Captain of the Valhalla on screen, and stay online."

It took a minute for Lionel to get the other two officers online. Devin had met the captain of the Valhalla before only a few times and liked her, but the orders he was going to give weren't going to be popular.

"Tribune, good to see you," Santana said. "And good to finally getting moving."

"I'm happy to be moving as well. Subprefect, I'm amending the Valhalla's orders, confirm we are recording this. Captain, you as well." Devin waited till both officers nodded. "Very well. The Pollux and her escorts will, with you in company, arrive outside of the Sand Harbor jump limit at speed. What ever happens, the warships will make a single pass by Sand Harbor Station. If it appears that we can achieve substantial local superiority, or defeat all enemy units, you will continue your deceleration and board the station. If that does not appear to be the case, you will immediately prepare to crash-jump, and will not return to the Sand Harbor system without my direct orders. You have too many marines on board your ship to risk in a naval battle."

The captain nodded, as did Santana.

"Furthermore, my own bridge staff will make that assessment and so advise you. And, because, frankly, I don't trust you not to follow me in regardless of the odds, and I might be busy at the time, you will take any order to jump from this ship, from the subprefect, from the navigation officer, anybody, my steward's assistant even, as from me."

The captain and Santana started to speak, but Devin held up his hand. "No. There will be no 'misunderstandings,' no 'please-repeats.' No games. If I think you have a fighting chance to recapture the station, you'll get it. Any sort of reasonable opportunity, you'll get it. But if we're going to be overwhelmed, you're getting out right away. Do you understand your orders?"

Both nodded.

"Excellent. I have things to do. The Empire!"

The officers answered and Devin cut the connection. He looked around the bridge. "Navigation, what's our status?"

"Jump limit in twenty-seven minutes, forty-three seconds, sir. Fleet is on course. Jump laid in. All according to plan, sir."

"Excellent! What do I have to do?"

The navigation officer looked at the weapons officer. She shrugged. "Well, sir, we... I mean... we've got it all planned out. Perhaps..." She shrugged again.

"I get it." Devin slumped in his chair. "Execute. Execute. Execute."

***

Devin brought the ship to battle stations with an hour to go before jump emergence. Long enough for all the stations to double-check everything and enough time to make every minor check that was worth making but not so long that people would get bored.

"Emergence in two minutes, sir," Navigation reported. "All systems nominal."

"Thank you," Devin said. "Everyone, carry on with the plan until countermanded." He picked up a private channel with Lionel. "Any last-minute suggestions?"

"One."

"What?"

"Don't take any last-minute suggestions. Just confuses things."

"Ever jumped directly into a battle."

"On purpose? Nope. By accident, twice."

"Anything worth discussing?"

"Well, if two ships collide seconds after jump, nobody on either one survives. Not important how I know that."

"Thanks for sharing. You thought that would cheer me up?"

"Who knows what cheers up the Mad Dog of the Verge?"

A timer flashed on the main board, and the navigator counted down. Then blue lights flashed everywhere, and they were in normal space.

Devin watched the display boards in front of him. An excellent jump. All the ships remained in near-perfect formation. The Sand Harbor system opened in front of him, displays updating as light, heat, and radio sensors updated.

"Multiple targets," the tactical officer said. "Target-1. Under steady thrust. Multiple drive plumes visible. Looks like a convoy moving away from the station on the far side. Computer says six freighters and a frigate."

"Ignore the freighters. We can take a frigate, especially a Confed frigate," Devin said. "Will we be able to close?"

"Computers checking, sir. That convoy is far away, but highly visible. Under max thrust for the freighters. Target-2, a frigate and a corvette, also leaving the station but in our direction. They can certainly intercept us."

"We can take them," Devin said. "Even with the other frigate."

"And Target-3, docked at the station."

"Another freighter?"

"Not sure, sir. Sensors can't discriminate with the station in the background."

"How's all this compare to what was here before?"

"Valhalla had reported Confed forces as eight ships: two frigates, a destroyer, and five merchant ships, including two configured as auxiliary cruisers. Now, we have ten ships. Two frigates, a corvette, six merchant ships, and one unknown."

Lionel highlighted the corvette on the display. "It escorted a merchant convoy in, and it's staying. That frigate that was damaged is the outbound escort. Unknown ship could be the destroyer that was here before."

"Keep watch," Devin said. "How far to the jump limit?"

"Planetary jump limit in two minutes, sir."

Pollux sped on, the dusty brown-blue tapestry of the planet filling the display screens. Six drive plumes flashed in the far distance as the convoy departed. Two others fired to the side as Target-2—the frigate and the corvette—changed vector to meet them.

"Heat plume from the station. Target-3 is starting up. Starting an undock sequence, possibly."

"ID?"

"Uncertain. Not even tonnage right now."

"Subprefect," Devin said, "your analysis?"

Lionel had been working his displays. "We can theoretically catch the convoy, but only if Target-2 doesn't get in our way, and we miss the station. And even if we did, that escorting frigate will slow us down and force us to deploy. Most of those freighters will get away. Probably all of them."

Devin shook his head. "We're not here to attack freighters, we're here to liberate a station."

"Agreed. We can engage Target-2 unless they split up and run. Doesn't look like they're doing that. They're maneuvering to intercept us."

"Glad to find somebody who wants to fight today. Helm, maneuver to pass just within maximum effective range of Target-2. Weapons, set up to fire the positron beams on the frigate, and keep firing as it passes."

"They have missiles," Lionel warned.

"Which have to catch us. Suggestions? Devote some of the beam weapons to antimissile defense."

"Waste of time. Increase speed. The faster we blow by, the harder it is for the missiles to correct. As soon as we see a launch, one rapid down or up maneuver, and they'll skip by. Engage them with the beam weapons."

"We have missiles, too.

"We do. What we don't have is re-supply. We're moving fast, which messes up our targeting as well as theirs, but we'll be able to get close enough to use beams and take advantage of our superior sensors. Save the missiles for long range encounters "

"Agreed. Tactical. What say you?"

"As soon as we're within range, I'll do a box barrage around the frigate. No matter which way they go, one beam will get 'em."

With a box barrage, you assumed that your target would be maneuvering as you fired. Beam weapons are fast but not instantaneous. Light can travel three hundred thousand kilometers in a second, but a spaceship can move hundreds of meters in a second, and even a ten-meter miss is a miss. Half of a box barrage is aimed, assuming no change in vector of the target. Half is aimed where the target might be given what is known of the targets maneuvering capabilities. Since all military ships employed random walk courses in combat, always shifting the ship slightly, the dispersed beams had an excellent chance of at least one hitting.

"Sequence it, then. Helm, preprogram two major course corrections. Tactics, tie those into your targeting. Start firing when in range. Compensate for the course changes. Keep firing as we pass that frigate."

"Aye, sir."

"And make it harder for them. Increase speed to three G. Missiles have to burn more fuel. Send the course change to the corvettes."

Hands typed on screens. A warning bonged.

"Algoma slowing. Algoma reports drive issues. Maximum speed is dropping, one point-two-five G's."

"Did the drive fall off?" Lionel asked. "We can't slow to that."

"Tell her to maneuver independently and target any enemy she can reach. Tell the other three to target the enemy corvette. Or try to."

Corvette's weapon systems were designed to engage missile boats and were notoriously unreliable firing at ships that could maneuver.

"Jump limit in sixty seconds."

"Very well. Carry on."

Lionel bonged on a private channel. "That's your tactics? Charge in as fast as possible, close, start firing, and keep firing. Not much of a plan."

"No captain can do very wrong if he places his ship alongside that of the enemy."

"You going all historical again? Old Empire?"

"Age of sail on Old Earth."

"You know we're not on an ocean, don't you? No water. Stars, planets, that sort of thing?"

"This battle will be three seconds long, at most. The computers will do most of the fighting."

"As your tactical deputy, I feel it necessary to remind you that they have lasers as well."

"Defensive. Not as powerful, not as long ranged, and our computers and sensors are better. We'll be in the optimal range envelope."

The range envelope was the point where the sensitivity of Pollux's sensors, speed of her computers, and the range and power of the beam weapons maximized the chances of a hit and maximized damage to the target, while not giving the enemy as effective a chance to reply in kind. Effects were not linear. Doubling the range might drop Pollux's chance of a hit by ninety percent. Halving it might only increase the chance of a hit by ten percent and add minimally to damage, while doubling the enemy's chances of striking back. Everything was a trade off.

"Yay for technical advantage," Lionel said.

"Besides, this way they won't get a good feel for how effective our positron beams are on damage."

Laser damage fell off on a power law. All other things being equal, double the distance, one-quarter the damage of your laser. Half the distance, four times the damage. Positron beams had flat curves. As long as you hit, damage was almost the same at a one-hundred-meter range as at one hundred thousand.

"Passing the jump limit," Tactical said. "Target-2 has

stabilized on a reciprocal course."

"They want a fight." Lionel frowned. "Why do they want a fight?"

"To protect the convoy."

"They don't have to actually fight to protect the convoy. They just have to threaten."

"So, they threaten long enough for the convoy to get away from us. Tactical, give us a constantly run plot to intercept that convoy."

"Understood, sir." The tactical officer tapped his screen for thirty seconds. "Unable, sir."

"Unable?"

"Corvettes slow us down too much." He looked up. "I'm recalculating sending Pollux alone at max accel, sir."

Lionel grimaced. "This bothers me."

"The corvettes don't add much to our fighting strength here. We brought them along for missile boats and armed freighters, not real warships."

"Computer says they'll be out of range of any intercept by any ship in six minutes."

"We could get the convoy by ourselves?"

"Intercept, sir?"

Lionel shook his head. "Not worth it. They'll scatter, and we'd only be able to catch one ship, and we'd still have to deal with that frigate. The convoy is safe. Why are these chowderheads in front still closing?"

"They think they can take us."

"This is the newest class of frigate in the Imperial navy. We're nearly as big as an old style destroyer, and they can see that, even if they don't have weapons reports. The old Comet class, say, facing two enemies, we might know they were in a fight, but we'd still win. The Pollux? We're going to blast them to particles. Why aren't they running? At least one of them would get away, and if they were clever, we'd have to maneuver to protect the Valhalla, and both would escape. They've got to have identified her as a troop carrier by now."

"I don't see—" Devin said.

"Tactical, what's the update on Target-3?"

The tactical officer typed on his screen. "No update, sir. It's stayed on a dead line between us and the station. We can't even see the drive plume. Computer can't distinguish details with the station behind it. Strange."

"What's strange?"

"The stations putting out, not jamming, sir, but a lot of heat, light, and radar. It's not jamming, per se, but more like they turned on every light and radio in the station."

Lionel nodded. "Backscatter camouflage. But why. Unless..."

Devin's eyes widened. "Helm, maximum accel, ninety degrees up to the ecliptic. Hold that till I say stop. Sensors, tactics, soon as you get a clear view, tell me what Target-3 is."

Alarm bells bonged, and acceleration warnings flooded the speakers. Talking was difficult, and Devin could barely make out the tactical officer saying Target-3 wasn't able to match their maneuvering.

Devin's vision darkened. He'd have to ease back soon. His comm flashed for a channel, then dropped, flashed, then dropped. What the Emperor?

"Cut thrust," Devin gasped.

Nothing happened.

He tapped the thrust override code, one finger at a time.

The thrust dropped to zero, and Devin pulled in a deep breath, then another. The rest of the bridge did the same.

"Tribune," the tactical officer gasped. "Tribune." He huffed and took a few breaths before going on.

Devin didn't blame him. He wasn't sure he could talk right now, either.

"Tribune. Computer confirms. Target-3 is a cruiser. Four times our size."

CHAPTER THIRTY-NINE

"This is getting to be a habit." Lionel raised his eyebrows. "Bad habit."

"Tactics, confirm that Target-3 is a cruiser?"

"Computer confidence is rising as we speak, Tribune."

"Subprefect, your assessment."

Lionel fiddled with his board. "Tactically speaking, we should withdraw at speed."

"You want to withdraw?"

"No, I do not. But that's the recommended tactical solution. It's what the computer will say, and it's what I learned at staff college."

"You went to staff college?"

"Correspondence. And unlike you, I didn't sleep through the lectures. Devin, we have to get the marines out of here."

Devin hit his intercom. "Communications, get me—"

The Valhalla's bridge flashed up on his screen.

"Thank you. Captain, run for the jump limit, fast as you can, now. Get those marines out." Devin cut the connection and brought his own tactical screen up. "Can we get to the cruiser before he gets to the Valhalla?"

"Working," Lionel said. "Could be tight. He might not be able to make it. We're on course for Target-2—take them first, and quick."

"Do it. Helm, what's max sustainable acceleration? Fast as we can, but we have to be able to control weapons and drives."

"Four G's, sir, then drop to three short of combat range."

"Do it."

The ship surged forward, and Devin snapped back into his chair.

The comm officer's priority channel warning bonged.

"Brigadier Santana with an urgent call."

"Ignore it. Order the corvettes to scatter and run for the jump limit."

"They don't have any fuel," Lionel said.

"Confeds don't know that. It will confuse them."

The comm officer worked his board again, then waved.

"What now?"

"The corvette captains are... declining the order, sir."

"Declining it? What does that even mean?"

"Not acknowledging it. Their comms are working, we're getting telemetry, but they're not sending the acknowledgment. They are remaining on course for Target-2, sir."

"I'll have them shot for disobeying orders. Send them that."

Lionel laughed. "No, you won't."

"I won't? Because I'll suddenly suffer an attack of a forgiving natureness?"

"Because it is highly unlikely that you'll be here after you fight a confederation cruiser single-handedly."

"Computer confirms Target-3 is a Confed Cruiser, sir. Province class. Probably the Kazan."

Lionel ran up the specs on his screen. "Old but not decrepit. Lasers and missiles. We're faster and more agile."

"Do we range them?"

Lionel typed some more. "Maybe."

"We're facing superior enemy forces, and you 'maybe' me?"

"Probably maybe, then. How's that for an answer?"

Devin glared at him, then glared around the bridge. Most kept their heads down, but the comm officer waved at him. "What now, comm?"

"Sir, the commander of the Bouctouche asks for the date of his execution, so he can put it on his calendar. And he asks what's the dress for that type of event." The comm officer giggled. "He's sending his measurements, sir, asking if you can have Imin run him up a new uniform."

"You think that's funny, comm?"

The comm officer sat up straight and smiled. "Sir, under the circumstances, I do. Yes, I do."

Devin growled, then laughed. "It is, isn't it?" He chuckled again. "Comm, release the corvettes. Tell them to operate at their discretion. For the record, specify that permits retreat, running for the jump limit and surrendering if they so desire. Helm, prepare for that maximum acceleration for as long as we can take it. Give Tactical a few times in the middle to adjust things. Lionel, get engineering on the line—the chief engineer. Everybody ready?" He waited till everybody agreed. "Execute."

The distance decreased as Pollux raced into the planet's gravity well, easily outdistancing the escorting corvettes. Valhalla ran for the jump limit—or, rather, generated enough side vector that their course curved toward it.

The corvettes were all over the place, falling behind, trying to either intercept Target-2 or screen the Valhalla. Target-2 continued to close the Pollux. Target-3 abandoned trying to hide, and maneuvered to be in the most advantageous position to engage Pollux after her engagement with Target-2.

The helm dropped their thrust to one G for fifteen minutes to allow movement. The crew recalibrated the sensors, made minor repairs, took bathroom breaks, and scarfed down ration bars.

Lionel put the relative vectors up on the main screen. "Interesting tactical problem for Target-3. Slow down to keep us in energy weapon range longer or speed up to give his missiles more velocity advantage."

Devin cleared from his call to engineering. "What do you think he'll do?"

"Speed up. Try to hit us with the missiles."

"Even if that ruins his laser firing solution?"

"His lasers are low power and short ranged. Not worth anything. They think it will ruin ours as well, and we don't have any missiles."

"He'll be surprised," Devin said. "What is it tactical?"

"Terminal maneuvers in three minutes, Tribune."

"Sound maneuvering alarm."

Alarm bells bonged.

Devin played with his comm. He brought up the all-ships-hailing channel. "Confederation warships. This is Devin, the Lord Lyon. Imperial Tribune and the Mad Dog of the Verge. You have invaded Imperial territory. Surrender immediately or be destroyed." He cut the connection and rested his chin on his hand.

Lionel shook his head. "That's a suitably heroic pose. Want me to call in a sculptor?"

"Nope." Devin sat up straight and keyed the intercom. "The Empire."

The cheers could be heard even on the bridge.

"Time, Tactical?"

"Less than a minute, Tribune."

"Execute," Devin said. "Execute, execute, execute."

Devin had modified the plan after talking to the engineers.

First, as the Pollux came screaming into range, it closed on the lead corvette and fired a full salvo. That was an unusual tactic because the corvette wasn't a threat, and hurting it wouldn't reduce the threat from the other larger ships.

The abnormally strong salvo impacted the corvette in several places, and it broke apart. Atmosphere vented and burned. Fuel exploded. Secondary explosions blew pieces in all directions. Pollux slapped through the debris cloud and faced the frigate next.

The frigate launched missiles at the last second, and they used their own radar to home in on their enemy. They had considerable forward velocity generated by their host ship, but the Pollux thrusted full sideways, which pushed the Imperial frigate out of their path, and the missiles struggled to compensate.

The Pollux and the enemy frigate rolled, spun, and

pushed engines to maneuver out of each other's beam weapon's fire. The enemy frigate had fewer and less powerful beam weapons. One of them hit and raked across the Pollux's quarter, but it flashed over so fast and from so far all it did was melt hull plating.

Damage in a battle is all about the speed of energy transfer. A laser can burn through a hull plate with enough time, but a glancing blow is just that. Pollux escaped the enemy's lasers unscathed.

Pollux fired her own broadside of eight. Three of them impacted. Positrons produce beams of antielectrons. When these antiparticles meet electrons, they annihilate each other in an energetic explosion. Even a brief touch causes damages and explosions, and Pollux raked one beam down the length of the frigate, blowing major parts of the structure off. The other glancing hits blew smaller chunks apart.

As this finished, engineering fired a preprogrammed series of thrusters that sent the Pollux tumbling through space. She bounced clear of the debris and the battle, getting in two more positron hits before she passed out of range.

As the range was opening, the electronic brain of one of the frigate's missiles decided it couldn't catch the Pollux, and a near miss was the best it could hope for, so it blew itself up at closest approach, sending a shower of metal particles in all directions in a last gasp attempt to hit Pollux.

Two pieces of metal hit one of the main drive nozzles.

"Damage report?" Devin asked.

"Engineering shut down half of the drive system," Lionel said. "Broken nozzle will unbalance the flows. We won't have control."

"Can they fix it?"

"By putting crews out on the hull..."

Devin gripped his seat's arms. The Pollux had a counterclockwise yaw, about two minutes for a revolution, and a slightly faster reverse pitch. "Can the crews stay on the hull with this tumble?"

"Might be able to. But then Target-3 would know we weren't nearly as shot up as we look."

"We'll wait."

The destruction of the first corvette had created a cloud of debris and radiation that obscured the battle, and the raking of the accompanying frigate had added to it.

The Kazan's sensors were unable to get a good view of the battle's results. The Pollux's tumble was faked to simulate battle damage. One of the remaining low-power antimissile lasers fired off at regular intervals, simulating an uncontrolled discharge and obscuring the fact that they had positron beams rather than lasers.

"Very little other damage," Lionel said. "Just the drive nozzles and some docking cameras. But we are venting fuel."

"Always fuel. What about our friends?"

Lionel put a picture of the system up. "There's not much left to track of that corvette. It's all small pieces. The frigate's fusion reactor blew or was ejected. The back half is gone. The front half will hit the sun in about eighty years."

"Does it have any working weapons?"

"Theoretically it could. Do we care?"

"No. Carry on."

"Target-1, the convoy has started past the jump limit. Four of the freighters have jumped already. The last two are the biggest and probably the slowest and probably have the worse jump computers. The frigate hasn't jumped yet."

"Will he come after us?"

"Not vectoring in right now, that's for sure. He's waiting to see what happened. He can't catch Valhalla if she wants to jump—she's near the jump limit but not out yet. Algoma is heading there. Might as well. It doesn't have the speed to do anything else. The other three corvettes are, surprisingly, in formation. Moose Jaw got a hit on the frigate after we blew it up."

"That's good shooting!"

"They were firing at the corvette, and missed so bad they hit a different ship, but we won't tell them that."

"And our friend?"

"Our soon to be close friend." Lionel rotated his display and zoomed in. "CS Kazan. Light Cruiser. Eight missile tube and eight lasers. On course to intercept us in seventeen minutes. You owe me a hundred credits."

"Why?"

"As I wagered, he sped up, to give his missiles a better chance. Pay up."

"We never bet. You never bet."

"I meant to. And you're rich, pay up."

"That's not how it works. Can we take him?"

"He's already started firing missiles, assuming we're too damaged to maneuver. They're inbound, but we should normally be able to dodge them."

"So, dodge them."

"To do it properly, we'd have to cancel the tumble and generate a side vector, which means they'd know our thrusters weren't damaged and that our engines were."

Devin stared at the display. "Helm, pulse our engines at maximum but random intervals. Run no longer than five seconds at a time."

Lionel nodded. "They'll burn up fuel trying to correct for each course change."

"Hope so. And they won't get a complete read on our engines."

"Unless they wait till they're at terminal distance from us and then expend all of their fuel in one go."

"Let's hope that their computers aren't programmed that way."

"Let's hope."

The timer ticked down. The Kazan stopped wasting salvos of missiles when they figured out that the Pollux had enough maneuvering left to generate a vector change.

The missiles ran dry before they could close. Clearly, the Kazan's captain would wait till they were nearer so that the possible separation was less.

Pollux's helm cobbled together a program that fired the main engines only when they could generate a vector mostly vertical to the ecliptic, which brought them out of powered range again.

Lionel had to remind the chasing corvettes to mix their headlong approach with some random course changes, in case some of those shots were aimed at them. They ran the numbers and hurriedly complied.

A crafty Kazan weapons officer had hidden two shots per salvo that would have intercepted them ballistically after the fuel ran out, if they had stayed on their straight in courses.

The clock ticked down to closest approach. Devin planned to wait till the last possible few seconds, cancel their tumble, fire the mains at full thrust to dodge the missiles, and use the positron beams to fry the cruiser.

Timing was everything.

The tactical officer punched his screen. "Target-1 convoy has jumped. Confed frigate was the last one out."

"Corvettes?"

"The corvettes are nowhere useful, Tribune."

"Very well."

"Valhalla is past the jump limit," the comm officer announced. "Her captain says she has her jump set up, but there are no threats that can reach him before you engage the Kazan, so he's staying to provide a report."

"Tell her permission granted," Devin said.

Lionel raised his eyebrows. "She wasn't asking."

"I know."

"Brigadier Santana—"

"Continue ignoring him. Helm, tactical, are you ready?"

Both chorused assent.

"Put the clock on the board," Devin said. "Execute maneuvering and firing sequence on time zero."

They chorused assent again.

The clock ticked down. Forty-five seconds left. Devin to Lionel.

"Read any good books lately."

"I have."

"Really? What one?"

"It's called ten stupid questions to ask before you go into battle."

The clock kept ticking. It was down to thirty seconds.

"Tell them to me fast."

CHAPTER FORTY

Blue-white light from the primary glinted from the Kazan's bow. The Pollux's twist brought the reflection into view every minute, the primary's blaze climbing to a crescendo as it centered on the screen, then dimming as the forward camera's passed out of view. The display of the constant bright-dark cycle gave echoes of spring, of mortality, and might make one think of their place in a cold, uncaring universe.

Which not a single person in the control room of the Pollux paid attention to but instead watched the countdown to the upcoming maneuvers. The six-digit display dropped below the minute mark, and all conversation stilled.

Accel warnings bonged for a final time.

Devin had sent out a shipwide notice to strap in five minutes ago. The threat board was clear, the Kazan having abandoned half measures some time ago, saving its shots for closest approach.

"Missile salvo," Tactical announced. "Full load. Targeted on us. Intercept in thirty-six seconds."

The counter passed through thirty-four. Devin flexed his fingers. Lionel rubbed his ears. The watch standers tapped displays, then rested their hands.

"Missile's locked on us. Electronic counter measures unsuccessful."

Radar could be blocked or saturated, but the blazing heat and visual signature of the Pollux couldn't be missed by even the cheapest telescopes or infrared detectors.

The counter passed through twenty.

"We cannot escape missile envelope with current power. Suggest more thrust."

Devin pushed against the G forces and brought his private channel with Lionel up. "Well?"

"Board's green. Nothing to do but wait."

"I hate waiting."

"Honor to serve, Tribune."

"You serve the Empire, not me," Devin.

"What if they were the same, I wonder?"

Devin's eyes widened, and he turned his head to look at Lionel. "Treason? Now?"

"Why not now?"

"Five, four," the tactical officer counted.

At zero, the thrust died. The crew floated up against the straps but held snug. Long dormant thrusters fired, spinning the ship. The inertia of thousands of tons of metal, plastic, and meat resisted, but burning hydrogen pivoted the ship up, canceled the yaw and pitch, and pushed the roll to max. Once seventy degrees at the vertical to the ecliptic, the main engines fired at max strength, temporarily ignoring the safety limits.

The Pollux lifted away from the approaching light cruiser, and its missile barrage. The missiles fired their own thrusters, but they couldn't react as fast. They had only one chance. If they could pivot up fast enough to hit the Pollux, they would score a devastating blow. If not, they would scream under so fast they would never return.

Radar frequencies were saturated by counter measures. Visual sensors were minor components. But they all had infrared, and the biggest, brightest, warmest source in the neighborhood was the Pollux's drives. They all focused on that.

The Pollux raised up and over. The Kazan didn't waver, except for a random walk to confuse lasers. The Pollux had no lasers, but the positrons were light speed weapons. They stabbed out, the computer calculating the limits of possible maneuverability—this far to the left yaw, this far up pitch, this far if they combined. Beams filled predicted locations, and Pollux's spin caused them to rake across the potential area.

The Kazan almost escaped. Pollux had assumed they

were showing only a percentage of their available maneuvering capability and had predicted more violent moves. In fact, the Kazan's old and worn-out systems had been operating at maximum capacity for the entire engagement. Kazan's captain wasn't familiar with the range and power of the new positron weapons, and had put himself at the outer envelope of laser disruption. He expected to take hits, just not strong ones.

Pollux wasted the entire first salvo but one. The lone beam that hit sheared off most of the port side communication suite and damaged the Kazan's hull. An important hit but not critical or fatal.

The two ships closed. The light speed delay dropped, and Pollux's computer didn't see the expected violent maneuvers. It pointed more beams in closer to the expected course of the Kazan and, this time, raked it with four. The crisscrossing beams caused major damage to control lines, sensors, electrical power. Anything near the hull got sliced open. Backups of power and control deep in the core continued to function, but whatever they controlled on the hull got fried. Including the maneuvering jets.

The Kazan and the Pollux flashed physically by each other, but the Pollux was still climbing, spinning, and dodging. The Kazan lost all thrusters as they were fused or blown off. It settled on a straight course.

The Pollux's computer adjusted, pushing the beams back onto the now easily computable course. The Kazan ran through the entire battery of positron shots from bow to stern and back again as the Pollux raked it, passing below, until it pulled away.

The explosions started at the surface, and they were numerous. When it sped away, the Kazan looked like a carrot that had been sliced several layers deep. Core elements remained, but all surface located parts were stripped away, including sensors, thrusters, weapons, and any compartments on the hull.

The hulk of the Kazan droned on. Not tumbling, not rolling, just sailing serenely away into deep space.

But the Pollux had left it too late. Most of the Kazan's missiles slid underneath, passing by as the Pollux lifted. But the last two fired had more time to climb higher. Detecting the superhot gasses produced by Pollux's thrusters, the first missile decided that was a good place to explode. And explode, it did. Destroying itself, the following missile, and the rear assembly of the Pollux's drives.

The Pollux heaved up, spewed burned fuel in all directions, and automatic shut-offs cut the main drives. She slid sideways into the system.

Cheers filled the control room, even after the sudden shock of the upward push.

Devin grinned and looked at Lionel, who grinned back.

"All right, people, good job. Now, tell me about all those red lights I see. Our main drive is off line. I want to know why."

Everyone floated in their seats.

"All weapons reporting ready," Tactical said. "No active enemies in weapons range."

The sensor operator reported only minor damage and backed up the tactical officer. All Confed forces in the system were destroyed or combat ineffective.

Lionel pushed through his screens. "Hull integrity is good. No compartments open to space. Engineering reports wounded." He looked up. "And dead. They got bounced back there. They're working on a better report."

"Very well," Devin said. "Helm, stabilize this tumble and put us on course for the station."

The helm officer tapped his screen. Once, twice, and again.

Devin grunted. "Now would be good helm."

"Sir, I have no helm control, no thrusters, no main drive."

"You're offline?"

"Not the controls, sir, the engines themselves."

The private channel from Lionel flashed. Devin ignored it and called across the control room. "Subprefect."

Lionel nodded down at the intercom.

"Just report."

Lionel shook his head.

Devin grimaced and picked up the private channel. "What?"

"Thrusters back in a few minutes, engineering says. But that last missile blew the Imperial hells out of the main nozzles. We can't put the main drive back on, or we'll spew burned hydrogen in all directions, including into the ship."

"We can't maneuver?"

"If you call maneuvering blowing the back third of our own ship off, then, yes, we can maneuver, but for now, no, they have to rebuild everything."

"ETA?"

"Don't have one. Long, long, time, is what they said."

Another cheer filled the control room. The Kazan had blown up—some delayed damage.

Devin nodded to the bridge door. "Get down there and find out what's going on and report back."

Lionel nodded and climbed out under cover of the cheers.

Devin gazed at the main screen, and the white-and-brown planet, slowly growing in size, centered on the camera's view.

It was worse than expected.

Lionel came back and reported, "The nozzles are bashed in all the way to the combustion chambers. It's a wonder those weren't blasted, too, but the engineers say all they need is to replace the thrust vectors and associated nozzles."

"How long?"

"Two days in a shipyard."

"And here."

"No reliable estimate is what I was told."

"Which means, they don't know if they can do it."

"Nope."

"Did you talk to the chief and tell him how important this is?" Devin checked himself. "Never mind. He knows better than we do, and probably knew immediately when he saw the damage. I assume that my going back there—"

"Would be a horribly bad idea. You'd slow things down."

"Right." Devin regarded the planet looming on his screen. "Suggestions?"

"Call in the corvettes and the Valhalla. Have them tow us up or away."

"Tow? Tie Lines?"

Lionel shrugged. "We'll try something"

"Fine. I'm going to my cabin to write my report. Meet me there when you have news."

Spaceships are not usually towed but grappled with magnets or pushed by reinforced tugs. Magnetic plates and push points are standard pieces of warships. Places where a tug could push the Pollux ranged along the sides and stern of the ship. A good tug could clamp on, secure the attachments, then shove away.

Unfortunately, the push points were for the ones pushed, not the pushers. The first two corvettes arrived and commenced operations.

In four hours, the Moose Jaw managed to rip its starboard air lock apart by trying to use an attached cable to tow the Pollux, and the Bouctouche crushed its main sensor suite trying to push.

The Bouctouche's captain was apologetic when he called Devin's cabin. "Sorry, sir," she said. "They weren't great sensors. We won't miss them that much, but the ship structure—well, we felt her flex the last time we pushed. And the leading petty officer in engineering said—"

"Said that corvettes aren't supposed to 'flex.'

Discontinue your operations, Captain. We'll need your ship intact."

"Yes, sir. You're just too big. We have to go to max thrust to give you any sort of vector change, and our hull isn't built for that."

"Very well. Subprefect?"

Lionel had been fiddling with the wall display. "Sir?"

"Coordinate evacuation of nonessential personnel to the Valhalla when she closes. Leave the engineering people as long as we can but get everyone else off. Will Valhalla have enough life support for the whole crew?"

"They'll have to."

BONG.

An alarm sounded.

"What now?" Devin wondered. "Yes, Tactical?"

"Jump signature, no beacon, at the limit," Tactical announced over the channel. "Big ship. Bigger even than that cruiser, sir. Ten times our size. Still no beacon."

Devin grimaced at Lionel. "Reinforcements?"

Lionel brought up a course plot. "Direction's not quite right for the confederation."

"But not right for empire, either."

"Nope. Kind of… mid-way. But if they were ours, we'd have known they were coming. I'm thinking confed with poor navigating.

"I thought they fought well, the Confeds. They must have been expecting this. Very well."

"Battle stations?"

"Not yet. Let's go up."

The walk to the bridge was almost leisurely. The crew was bustling. They hadn't given up hope, but they knew they were in trouble.

"Any updates, Tactical?" Devin asked, settling into his seat.

"No, sir. I'm running a weapons plot."

"Ship that big is probably a battleship," Devin said. "Didn't know there were any out here. Think we can take her, tactical?"

"Nope," Tactical said. "I mean, we'll try, Tribune."

"I liked your first answer better," Devin said. "Had the virtue of being true. Well, whatever happens next, we can be proud of what we did here. Subprefect?"

"Tribune?"

"Inform the corvettes that they are free to operate independently. Again. Suggest they scatter and run. That battleship will come straight to us."

"They have no fuel..."

"I forgot. Tell them to do what they can. And order the Valhalla to run and jump."

"Again?"

"Again."

"And prepare to abandon ship. We won't give them this ship. Too new."

"Set up for auto self-destruct?"

"No, it will be fired manually. To make sure."

Lionel raised his eyebrows. "By who, pray tell?"

"You know who. Make sure everybody else gets off."

"Tribune, don't be so anxious to kill yourself."

"I'm not anxious. I'm resigned." Devin surveyed the bridge. "A fine ship and a fine crew. Pity. But I knew I'd die in the Emperor's service. I've known that ever since they yanked me out of the seminary to take my brother's place in the navy. It's too bad. I would have made a good priest."

"A great priest," Lionel said. "An amazing priest."

"Let's not push it. I would have liked to have met my nephew. I hear he looks like his mother. Tactical, any update?"

"No, sir. Wait. Beacon coming up."

Devin laughed. "That's insulting. Not even bothering to hide their capabilities."

"Coming up now, sir." The tactical officer frowned, then gestured the comm officer over.

The com officer unbuckled, walked across the bridge,

tapped the screen, nodded at tactical, then returned to his seat. His expression was blank.

"Well?" Devin said.

"Incoming call from the new ship, sir," the comm officer said. "From its commander."

"Put it on the screen," Devin said. "What's the commander's name?"

"The commander is." The comm officer grinned. "The commander's name is Friedel. The Duke Durriken Friedel."

Devin sputtered, and the screen lit, Dirk's face filled the display. "Tribune, greetings from the Imperial fleet Tanker Hydrogen Queen, myself commanding. Do you require assistance?"

CHAPTER FORTY-ONE

With the right tools, any job is easy. Fleet tankers had big drives, spare parts, and most importantly, reinforced push points, push bars, and cages built into their design. The Hydrogen Queen pulled up alongside the Pollux, extended a dozen magnetic clamps, and shoved it out of the collision course with the planet. The hull stress broke two sensor mounts and an ice cream machine in the process. The Pollux's crew fixed the sensors but complained about the lack of ice cream.

The fleet, or "Task Force Towboat," as Ana called it once—he figured out it irritated every navy officer in the system—regrouped, fixed battle damage, and refueled.

"You can't keep the tanker," Devin said over the comm. "I need it. And not enough of you to man three shifts for one thing, and I've got plenty of surplus crew to put on it."

"We manned it well enough on the way here." Dirk said. "We're doing fine."

"Is that why every time I call whoever answers the comm has just woken up?"

Dirk finger-combed his hair. Luckily, Devin couldn't see that he wasn't wearing pants, having just woke himself. "But what happens now?"

"I'm taking the fight to the Confeds," Devin said. "I've got warships, logistics, marines, and a grumpy disposition. All a good commander needs."

"And your crew is okay with your one-man crusade?"

"Why would I ask my crew?"

"Never mind. Tribune, what's going on in the Empire? The warrants? The arrests? What are you doing about that."

"First, I will thrash these impudent Confeds."

"Impudent? Thrash? Are you reading historical novels

again?"

Devin turned his comm to face the screen, displaying a book. "Your centurion fellow sent me some. He knows a surprising amount of history. Quite rousing stuff, these Old Earth writers."

"For uneducated primitives."

"Human nature doesn't change."

"Learn from the barbarians, then. Devin, somebody is out to get you. And your friends. And I know you haven't heard from your sister. Aren't you worried?"

"Very worried. But that's personal, not work."

"Your sister is the Empress..."

"And when the Empress contacts me, I'll deal with that. Right now, I have a clear enemy, a suitable fleet, and a tactical advantage. I'll deal with the Confeds with some judicious raiding, and that will solve the issue."

"What if they declare war and bring in major fleet elements?" Dirk asked.

"If that was the intent of their central committee, they would have done so already. This is local maneuvering for advantage. I'll smash up the local idiots, and by the time somebody senior with more ships shows up, I'll apologize, retreat, and we'll return to the status quo."

"And, in the meantime, your sister may be in trouble. And something strange is happening with the Empire, and you're not doing anything?"

"I'm investigating to find out what's happening in the core. While I'm dealing with this minor war, I'm sending a crack team to spy out the issues, collect intelligence, and report back to me. Even better, this team is commanded by a seasoned veteran, a decorated officer who leads a group of uniquely skilled individuals, capable of dealing with any and all situations."

"You mean you've found somebody stupid enough to go back into the core and nose around among your enemies, hoping they'll find out who wants you dead before they get zapped with a shock stick and dumped out an air lock?"

"I like my explanation better but sure."

"This commander sounds like an idiot, a complete moron, with no sense of self preservation. Where will you get such a totally clueless twit like this?"

Devin smiled into his comm.

"Oh, no," Dirk said. "No, no, and a third time. No-o."

Devin grinned and gave the cross-chest salute. "The Empire!"

***

"So, after we're fueled up," Dirk said, "and the last of the supplies are loaded, we'll jump with the fleet to meet the freighters Devin left behind. We'll be refueled first, and we can beat them back to Imperial space and get ahead of any news. Devin is going to 'discomfort the enemy,' in his words, with his ships, and we're tasked with investigating what's happening to the Empire, the warrants, the arrests, and all that."

The crew was all gathered in the lounge.

"As excited as I am to get away from ISS tugboat," Ana said. "After all this I don't owe the Empire anything."

Lee nodded. "We only went back that last time to help Scruggs. I'm happier out here on the verge."

"We need to eat," Dena said.

"And those parts will run out quickly enough," Gavin said. "And anyway, Skipper, you blow hot and cold on this. Why are you helping?"

"The tribune has recalled me to active duty," Dirk said. "I'm back in the navy now."

"Good for you, Pilot," Lee said. "But the rest of us might be, well, a little hesitant."

"I have here"—Dirk held up his hand—"an encrypted message chip from Devin to his sister, the Empress. Who better to deliver it than one of her own Praetorians, someone she trusts implicitly?"

Lee sighed, then gave an Imperial salute. "I serve the Empress."

"I don't," Ana said. "I serve me. What's in it for me?"

"And me," Dena said. "What do I get?"

"This chip"—Dirk held up another—"is a substantial credit line backed by the tribune to hire us at regular mercenary day-contract rates, with substantial bonuses."

"Day rates?" Ana asked. "As in not long term-contract rates?"

"Day rates," Dirk confirmed. "Till mission accomplished."

"The more expensive day rates?"

"Top of the hiring schedule."

"Hmm. What about expenses? What type of expenses are we authorized?"

"Everything," Dirk said. "Food, supplies, weapons, ammunition, parts, repairs, lodging. And clothes."

"What type of clothes?" Dena asked.

"Any type we need, for the circumstances. Combat gear if we need to fight. Heavy weather gear if we're in an austere environment. And any necessary disguises, depending on what type of research we need to do."

"Shoes?"

"Whatever we want. New shoes for everybody. As often as needed."

"You've got an unlimited credit line to buy shoes?" Dena said.

"Yes."

"God save the Empire," Dena said. "Get settled in, old man. We're going spying!"

"Not sure," Ana grumbled. "Seems too easy. I'm suspicious."

"Look, old man. Buy yourself some nuclear-powered rifle ammunition or suchlike, and we're set."

Ana grunted. "I have always wanted a crew served rocket assisted automatic mortar."

"We'll get two," Dena said. She frowned. "Automatic mortar?"

"Multiple tubes."

"Why do you need multiple tubes?"

"To fire the rocket assisted projectiles two at a time, of course. All right, I'm in."

"Gavin?" Dirk asked.

Gavin shrugged. "As long as I get paid."

"You will." Dirk looked around. "Where's Scruggs?"

"Down here." Scruggs popped up from under the table. "I was playing with Rocky. I don't think this is a good idea."

"The tribune has asked us," Dirk said.

"Don't like him," Scruggs said.

"The Empress needs our help," Lee said.

"Never met her."

"Rocket propelled mortar rounds, Private?" Ana said.

"We have lots of mortars."

"Shoes, Baby Marine. New shoes."

"I have plenty of shoes." Scruggs put her hands on her hips. "Not good enough."

A warning bonged.

Lee checked her comm. "We've cleared the jump limit, Pilot."

Dirk put the chips in his pockets and dusted his hands. "I'm going up front to put Lee's jump in. Scruggs, you don't have to come. We've got enough help here. We can put you off at a planet you want." Dirk climbed forward, then stopped and looked over his shoulder. "Of course. It could be fun."

The remaining four crew stared at Scruggs. She looked down at Rocky, who wagged his tail. "What do you think, Rocky?"

Dena grabbed her shoulder. "It'll be fun, Scruggs. New planets, new people, new fights, new shoes."

Scruggs bit her lip.

"You know what they say," Dena said.

"What do they say?" Scruggs asked.

"Adventure awaits," all four chorused.

Scruggs laughed, then leaned out of her chair and yelled up to the control room. "Pilot?"

"What?"

"Everything laid in?"

"Yes? Why?"

Scruggs wrestled with Rocky. He barked, grabbed her hand, and wrestled with it till she laughed.

"Jump."

GET A FREE EBOOK

Thanks for reading. I hope you enjoyed it. Word-of-mouth reviews are critical to independent authors. Please consider leaving a review on Amazon or Goodreads or wherever you purchased this book.

If you'd like to be notified of future releases, please join my mailing list. I send a few updates a year, and if you subscribe you get a free ebook copy of Sigma Draconis IV, a short novella in the Jake Stewart universe. You can also follow me on Amazon, or follow me on BookBub.

Join my mailing list here:
https://BookHip.com/JTHTJK

Andrew Moriarty

ABOUT THE AUTHOR

Andrew Moriarty has been reading science fiction his whole life, and he always wondered about the stories he read. How did they ever pay the mortgage for that spaceship? Why doesn't it ever need to be refueled? What would happen if it broke, but the parts were backordered for weeks? And why doesn't anybody ever have to charge sales tax? Despairing on finding the answers to these questions, he decided to write a book about how spaceships would function in the real world. Ships need fuel, fuel costs money, and the accountants run everything.

He was born in Canada, and has lived in Toronto, Vancouver, Los Angeles, Germany, Park City, and Maastricht. Previously he worked as a telephone newspaper subscriptions salesman, a pizza delivery driver, a wedding disc jockey, and a technology trainer. Unfortunately, he also spent a great deal of time in the IT industry, designing networks and configuring routers and switches. Along the way, he picked up an ex-spy with a predilection for French Champagne, and a whippet with a murderous possessiveness for tennis balls. They live together in Brooklyn.

Please buy his books. Tennis balls are expensive.

BOOKS BY ANDREW MORIARTY

Adventures of a Jump Space Accountant

1. Trans Galactic Insurance

2. Orbital Claims Adjustor

3. Third Moon Chemicals

4. A Corporate Coup

5. The Jump Ship.

6   The Military Advisor

7   Revolt in the Palace (Forthcoming)

Decline and Fall of the Galactic Empire

1. Imperial Deserter

2. Imperial Smuggler

3. Imperial Mercenary.

4. Imperial Hijacker